Praise for Amanda Cabot's Writing

"*Summer of Promise* is an engrossing story of love and adventure that is sure to capture your heart!"

Kathleen Morgan, author, *A Heart Divided* and *A Love Forbidden*

"Amanda Cabot's characters and storytelling are extraordinary. I'm in love with her books."

Laurie Alice Eakes, author, *Lady in the Mist*

"Cabot weaves a powerful story of healing."

RT Book Reviews on *Scattered Petals*

"Crafting characters rich with emotion, Amanda Cabot pens a compelling story of transcending faith."

Tamera Alexander, bestselling author, *From a Distance*, on *Scattered Petals*

"Amanda Cabot does such a great job describing the setting of the Wild West that you almost feel you are there with the characters, sharing their life."

Book Bargains & Previews

"Amanda Cabot has a tender skill for writing a novel that includes not only amazing characters and some bits of humor and love, but also the wonderful messages of God's redeeming love and grace."

www.ReviewsbyMolly.com

SUMMER
of PROMISE

Books by Amanda Cabot

TEXAS DREAMS SERIES
Paper Roses
Scattered Petals
Tomorrow's Garden

WESTWARD WINDS SERIES
Summer of Promise

WESTWARD WINDS • BOOK 1

SUMMER
of PROMISE

A NOVEL

AMANDA
CABOT

a division of Baker Publishing Group
Grand Rapids, Michigan

Published by Revell
a division of Baker Publishing Group
P.O. Box 6287, Grand Rapids, MI 49516-6287
www.revellbooks.com

Printed in the United States of America

Library of Congress Cataloging-in-Publication Data
Cabot, Amanda, 1948–
       Summer of promise : a novel / Amanda Cabot.
           p.   cm. — (Westward winds)
       ISBN 978-0-8007-3459-6 (pbk.)
       I. Title.
    PS3603.A35S86 2012
    813′.6—dc23   2011027833

This book is a work of fiction. Names, characters, places, and incidents are the product of the author's imagination or are used fictitiously. Any resemblance to actual events, locales, or persons, living or dead, is coincidental.

12 13 14 15 16 17 18   7 6 5 4 3 2 1

For Jane McBride Choate, a wonderful friend, a talented author, and a woman whose love for her sister helped define my heroine. Thank you, Jane, for your friendship, support, and inspiration.

❧ 1 ❧

There were times when Abigail Harding wished she were an only child. This was one of them. If it hadn't been for Charlotte, she would not be cooped up in a stagecoach, crossing land so barren that not even coyotes favored it, all the while accompanied by a woman who had never heard that silence was golden.

"It's a mighty pretty day, ain't it?"

Abigail winced as the coach swayed, tossing her against the side for what seemed like the hundredth time. Though Concord coaches were reputed to be the most comfortable ever made, nothing could smooth a rutted road. Ruts, she had been informed by her talkative companion, were preferable to mud, which could bog down the wheels, leaving passengers no alternative but to disembark into the muck.

Thankful for small mercies, Abigail nodded. "The sky is beautiful," she admitted. That was the only positive thing she could say about this desolate countryside. She certainly wasn't going to claim that she found Wyoming Territory beautiful when she most definitely did not, but she also saw no need to insult Mrs. Dunn, even if she wished the woman would stop talking. Abigail was no stranger to loneliness, and, judging from the stories she'd told, neither was the widow. That was probably why she had taken Abigail under her wing when she saw her waiting for the stagecoach in Cheyenne, ignoring Abigail's protests that she could manage on her own and had in fact come all the way from Wesley, Vermont, without a companion. It would be most unseemly, Mrs. Dunn had claimed, for Abigail to continue to travel unaccompanied, particularly when one of the other passengers on the coach bound for Deadwood was a single man.

"He's a soldier," her self-appointed protector had hissed, as if Abigail was unable to recognize a uniform. "That oughta mean he's honorable, but you cain't be too careful." Even the sight of a married couple purchasing tickets wasn't enough to dissuade Mrs. Dunn. She kept a firm grip on Abigail's arm. "They're rich folks," she declared, pointing to the pile of finely tooled luggage that accompanied them. "They won't want nothin' to do with us."

And so Abigail found herself on the backseat next to the woman who passed the hours knotting and unknotting her reticule strings, while the lieutenant lounged on the front seat next to the wealthy couple, one of his feet propped on the empty bench that formed the middle row of indoor seating, his cap tipped over his eyes. Propriety was clearly observed, for he and Abigail were separated by the entire length of the coach, and they spoke only when the stagecoach stopped and he helped Abigail and Mrs. Dunn descend the steep steps.

As Mrs. Dunn had predicted, the couple, who'd introduced themselves as Mr. and Mrs. Fitzgerald of New York City, had said little beyond complaining that they were forced to ride facing backwards. When Abigail had offered them her spot and the unoccupied one between her and Mrs. Dunn, the widow had protested. "You cain't sit with the man. It ain't done." She'd clutched Abigail's arm and kept her pinned to the seat. The obviously disgruntled Fitzgeralds had resorted to talking quietly to each other and completely ignored Mrs. Dunn. Though Abigail couldn't blame them, that had left her as the sole object of the overly proper widow's conversation.

"So, you like our sky." Mrs. Dunn nodded at Abigail in approval. Her brown eyes, which had filled with tears when she spoke of her beloved husband's death and the difficulty of maintaining their ranch without him, sparkled once more. Though her husband had been deceased for more than a year, Mrs. Dunn still wore full mourning, claiming that she would never cease to love him. Her decidedly unfashionable dress bore a heavy coat of gray-brown dirt, and even the veil that covered the top half of her face had dust motes caught in the mesh, compliments of the constant wind that stirred up dirt and propelled it eastward at what seemed like little less than tornado speed.

Though she felt no desire to continue the conversation, good manners forced Abigail to say, "I've never seen a sky so clear or such a deep blue." All that was true. What was also true was that this part of the journey was the worst yet. The train had been reasonably comfortable, and Cheyenne had proved to be less primitive than she'd expected, even though it appeared that the entire male population believed that at least one weapon was a necessary part of a man's wardrobe. Unfortunately, now Abigail was in the middle of nowhere, and nothing Mrs. Dunn could say would change that. There was no sign of life, unless you counted the brush that blanketed the rolling hills where trees should have been.

That brush was alive, all right. Alive and ready to attack. The cactuses were bad enough, but the real villains were the yuccas. Why had God created a plant with spiky leaves edged with razor-sharp points? Surely it wasn't to rip holes in an unsuspecting woman's skirt. Mrs. Dunn claimed that the yuccas would be blessed with beautiful white blossoms later this month. Be that as it may, Abigail considered their existence proof that this was not a place where civilized persons should live. Yuccas and wind that howled incessantly were not Abigail's idea of paradise on Earth.

"I don't reckon Wyoming Territory looks much like home to you."

Had Mrs. Dunn read her thoughts? This place that had been Charlotte's home for a year appeared decidedly unsuitable. Abigail frowned as she stared out the window. Try though she might, she could not picture her older sister enjoying life in such a wilderness. Elizabeth, the youngest of the three Harding children, might consider it an adventure, but Charlotte favored fancy gowns, meals served on fine china, and the company of sociable women. Even though she had assured Abigail that Fort Laramie was far more appealing than one might imagine an Army fort to be, it was still surrounded by desolate countryside.

Perhaps that was why Charlotte's letters had seemed so strained. Perhaps that was why Abigail had been unable to dismiss her concerns. Perhaps that was why she'd felt compelled to board a train and leave her carefully planned life behind. When she had left Vermont, she had been certain it was God's will that she come here. Now she wasn't certain of anything.

Fixing a smile on her face, Abigail turned back to her traveling companion. The Fitzgeralds, probably as bored as she, appeared to be dozing. "You're right. Wyoming is quite different from Vermont," she said, trying not to sigh as she thought of her home. "Most of the state is very green. In fact, that's how it got its name. The word *Vermont* is derived from the French words for 'green' and 'mountains.' Its nickname is the green mountain state." Abigail bit her lip as she realized that she'd fallen into schoolmarm mode. Mrs. Dunn didn't want a lesson in etymology any more than Abigail wanted to be here. If it hadn't been for her worries about Charlotte, Abigail would have been home, enjoying fresh air while she played tennis with Woodrow and made plans for their life together. Instead, she was stuck in a hot, dusty stagecoach with Mrs. Dunn, the Fitzgeralds, and the soldier who was pretending to be asleep.

Mrs. Dunn eyed their companions before giving Abigail an appraising look. "So, your sister married a soldier." Abigail had admitted as much when she'd purchased passage only as far as Fort Laramie. Mrs. Dunn was going a few miles farther, and the Fitzgeralds were headed for the end of the line, the gold mine town of Deadwood.

"That's good." Mrs. Dunn's nod dislodged some of the face powder she'd applied with a liberal hand. Mama would not have approved of the way Mrs. Dunn had painted her face. She had maintained that only actresses and fallen women felt the need to enhance their God-given beauty, but Mama had not experienced the Wyoming sun and wind. Perhaps paint and powder were the only ways to maintain a woman's complexion.

"Soldiering's a mighty fine profession," Mrs. Dunn announced. "A woman could do a lot worse."

And a lot better. Charlotte could have married a man whose profession was something—anything—other than killing. Abigail bit back the retort. There was nothing to be gained by starting an argument. Instead, she kept a smile fixed on her face and let the older woman continue her monologue. Perhaps she'd tire eventually. Though Abigail estimated that the widow was only in her midforties, she moved like a much older woman, the result, she said, of stepping into a gopher hole. "I done broke my ankle, and it ain't never healed right. I reckon I'm gonna limp for the rest of my days." Her story had done nothing to convince Abigail that Wyoming was a desirable place to live. Wind, dust, gopher holes. Each mile revealed a new unpleasant aspect to Charlotte's home.

Mrs. Dunn leaned over and patted Abigail's hand. "It wouldn't surprise me none if you found yourself a husband while you was at the fort. Soldiers are mighty lonely, always lookin' for a wife. You just gotta be careful, cuz they ain't all honorable."

"I'm not looking for a husband." Even if she weren't almost promised to Woodrow, the last place Abigail would seek a spouse was at an Army fort. The life of a soldier's wife was not for her. No indeed. God might have sent her here, but he didn't intend for her to stay. Abigail was as certain of that as she was that something was seriously wrong in her sister's life.

Knotting her reticule strings again, Mrs. Dunn shook her head. "Nonsense. Every woman is lookin' for a man of her own. Look at this here lieutenant."

Abigail had done exactly that when they'd entered the coach. The man, who'd introduced himself as Lieutenant Bowles, was at least half a foot taller than her own five and a half feet, with blond hair and eyes almost as deep a blue as the Wyoming sky. His uniform was the same design as the one Jeffrey had worn for his wedding to Charlotte: a dark blue double-breasted wool frock coat with seven brass buttons marching down each side, lighter blue wool trousers with a white stripe indicating membership in the infantry. The difference was that while Jeffrey had seemed a bit ill at ease, this man wore his uniform as comfortably as he did his skin.

It was true that Abigail had noted how Lieutenant Bowles's uniform highlighted broad shoulders and long legs, but what caught her attention time and again were his lips. Though no fuller than normal, they were surprisingly expressive, curving and twitching in response to Mrs. Dunn's more outrageous comments, even though the rest of his face remained as impassive as if he were truly sleeping.

"He'd be a good husband for you," Mrs. Dunn declared.

Abigail darted a glance at the man in question. Though he appeared to be fighting a smile, she was not amused by Mrs. Dunn's tendency to make pronouncements with no foundation. Look at the way she tried to enforce her decidedly old-fashioned views of propriety. There would have been nothing wrong with Abigail's sitting on the opposite seat.

"Most likely he ain't married. 'Course, you cain't be sure. He might have a sweetheart somewhere. I'm fixin' to ask him when he wakes up."

Abigail sighed. The lieutenant had the right idea. She should have pretended to be asleep.

Ethan Bowles struggled to keep his lips from frowning. If the old biddy knew he was awake, he'd have no peace. She'd continue the relentless questioning—little less than an inquisition—that had convinced him to feign sleep in the first place. And this time she'd focus on his marital status. Once she learned that he was unattached, it would be far worse. Ethan gritted his teeth. Why was it that people felt the need to match make? First his grandfather, then virtually every married woman he'd met. You'd think they would realize that some men were meant to be bachelors, with him first on that list. But, no, they seemed to believe that every single man was a candidate for the state of wedded bliss. Wrong, wrong, wrong.

He shifted his weight slightly, wishing he could open his eyes. The trip went more quickly when a man could enjoy the scenery. And this trip had more than the territory's natural beauty to enjoy. The young woman, Miss Harding she'd said her name was, was downright easy on the eyes, even if she was wearing clothing that had to be uncomfortable. The high neckline and long sleeves were practical, as was the dark blue color—not too different from his uniform. But the skirt made no sense. Those pleats barely cleared the ground, which meant that they served as dust magnets, and then there was that silly bump in the back. Oliver, his friend who claimed to know everything there was to know about women, had informed him that ladies called them bustles. Ethan called them ridiculous. Why would a woman saddle herself with something that had to get in the way when she sat? The only good thing he could say about the widow was that she didn't have any such impediments. Her dress might not be fashionable, but it was more practical than what Miss Harding and Mrs. Fitzgerald were wearing.

Despite the preposterous clothing, Miss Harding was worth a second look. Underneath that fancy hat, her hair was pulled back in one of those knots that women seemed to like, but even that couldn't hide the fact that it was a pretty shade of brown. What intrigued Ethan most were her eyes. It was a shame he was pretending to be asleep, because he was still trying to figure out what color they were. Not quite brown, not quite green, but downright pretty, especially when she smiled. That was when he was sure he'd seen hints of gold in them.

The widow was right. Soldiers out here didn't get to see too many women, and women as beautiful as Miss Harding were as rare as gold nuggets in the North Platte River. Even though he had no interest—no matrimonial interest, that is—in Miss Harding, Ethan couldn't deny that he would have enjoyed looking at her, but he sure as shooting didn't want to get trapped into another conversation involving the widow, and so he kept his eyes closed. Years of ignoring his grandfather's barbs had taught him the value of feigning indifference.

"Did you live on a farm in Vermont?" The widow was talking again, and since Ethan wasn't available, she was questioning Miss Harding. The poor woman. By the time the lady with those intriguing eyes reached Fort Laramie, her every secret would be revealed.

"No." It was only one word, but Ethan heard the reluctance in Miss Harding's voice. It appeared she wasn't enjoying the interrogation any more than he had the volley of questions the widow had fired at him when they'd first entered the stagecoach. "I teach at a girls' academy." His lips twitched as he realized that was the reason she sounded so prim and why she'd given the little lesson on the origin of Vermont's name. Schoolmarms, at least schoolmarms in Ethan's experience, were prim and proper. They had to be.

He heard the intake of breath before Mrs. Dunn spoke. "In my day," she said, her voice leaving no doubt of her disapproval, "girls stayed home and cared for their parents until they married. They didn't take jobs away from able-bodied men."

Of course, in the aftermath of the war there were fewer able-bodied men than there had been before Antietam and Gettysburg and the other battles that had destroyed hopes along with lives. Ethan wondered whether Miss Harding would mention that. Instead she said simply, "It was my parents' wish that I become a teacher. Fortunately, I find it rewarding."

And he found soldiering rewarding. Most days, that is. Today all he felt was frustration. Frustration with the men who cared nothing for their oaths and obligations and who deserted the Army, and even greater frustration with himself for being unable to find them. He'd gone to Cheyenne expecting to locate the pocket of deserters who were reported to be living there. Instead, he'd found nothing but dead ends. That was why he was heading back to the fort a day earlier than planned. He would have only wasted time if he stayed in Cheyenne, and if there was one thing Ethan hated, it was wasting time. If he was going to earn his commanding officer's respect, he could not afford to spend a whole day doing nothing more than strolling city streets.

While Mrs. Dunn continued to speak, enumerating the advantages of living in Wyoming Territory, Ethan did his best to ignore her words.

"One thing you gotta say about livin' here," the widow said, her voice reverberating against the sides of the stagecoach, "it's mighty peaceful."

Despite his resolve to pay no attention to the women's conversation, Ethan found himself listening for Miss Harding's response. When it came, it was little more than a mutter. "Some might call it boring."

It was boring. Abigail gazed out the window, trying not to frown at the endless miles of unchanging scenery. Since they'd left the road ranch where they'd eaten a surprisingly tasty dinner and where her skirts had had the unfortunate encounter with yucca leaves, there had been nothing but rolling hills under the biggest sky she'd ever seen. As she'd told Mrs. Dunn, the sky was beautiful, but Abigail needed more. Even a cloud would have helped break the monotony. Unfortunately, not a single one dotted the sky. There was only sun and wind and scrubby hills.

How could Charlotte bear it? Perhaps she couldn't. Perhaps that was the reason her letters had sounded so melancholy. Though her sister denied it, Abigail knew that something was dreadfully amiss.

If only she had a book. It would be several hours before they reached Fort Laramie, and now that Mrs. Dunn had fallen asleep, Abigail could read. Unfortunately, all her books were safely packed in her trunk, leaving her with nothing to do but stare out the window. Hills and brush, brush and hills. Nothing more. Boring.

Abigail wasn't sure how long she'd had her eyes focused on the distance when she saw the cloud of dust. For a moment, she stared at it, wondering if it was a mirage. She'd heard that travelers in the desert conjured images of oases with life-giving water, only to discover that the shimmering pools of water were nothing more than a trick of light. Abigail did not seek water; she craved signs of human habitation, but the dust must be a mirage, for Mrs. Dunn had said there were few settlers in this area. Abigail was simply imagining that the brown cloud was caused by horses. Still, the swirling dust grew nearer, and as it did, she saw that the cloud was caused by two riders, one on a dark horse, the other a palomino.

Abigail swallowed deeply, unsure whether the shiver that made its way down her spine was caused by anticipation or apprehension. "Someone's coming." Though she hadn't intended to, she spoke the words aloud. The response was instantaneous.

"Where?" Lieutenant Bowles moved quickly, confirming Abigail's assumption that he had not been asleep. One second he was lounging on the seat, the next he was staring out the window, watching the approaching riders, those expressive lips thinning, then turning into a frown.

"It's trouble," he said shortly. "Probably road agents." In one fluid movement, he unholstered his revolver and balanced it on the window ledge.

Abigail cringed as unwelcome images crowded her brain. *No!* she wanted to shout. *Stop!* She bit the inside of her cheek as she forced the memories away. *Think of something else. Anything.* Seizing on the unfamiliar term the lieutenant had used, she asked, "Road agents?"

"Bandits."

Abigail's heart began to pound. Though she had read several of the penny dreadful novels she had confiscated from students, she had thought the stories of bandits holding up stagecoaches were exaggerations. Now it was apparent that she was going to experience a holdup, and—if the stories had any validity—that meant . . .

She bit her cheek again, the metallic taste telling her she'd drawn blood. Blood, just like . . . She focused on Lieutenant Bowles, trying to banish the memories.

Without taking his eyes off the horsemen, the lieutenant motioned toward the opposite side of the coach. "Stay back," he ordered, "and keep the others quiet." Though Mrs. Dunn was still so deeply asleep that she had released her grip on her reticule and Mrs. Fitzgerald was snoring lightly, Abigail did not doubt that the women would scream if they realized what was happening. She had no idea what Mr. Fitzgerald might do, but she knew that any distraction could be dangerous.

Abigail took a deep breath, trying to calm herself, then darted another look at the approaching men. She wouldn't— she absolutely would not—look at the lieutenant's revolver. "They're soldiers." She whispered the words, not wanting to waken the others. The approaching riders' uniforms were the same shade of blue as Lieutenant Bowles's. The difference was, these men wore bandannas over their faces. It could be to protect them from the dust, but the lieutenant's intake of breath said otherwise.

"Probably deserters, up to no good." He leaned out the window, twisting to face the front of the coach, and yelled at the driver. "Don't stop. No matter what happens, don't stop unless I tell you to."

"But, sir . . . ." Fear colored the coachman's words.

"Trust me. Keep going."

The driver cracked the whip, and the horses began to run, setting the coach to lurching. As her reticule tumbled from her lap, Mrs. Dunn's eyes flew open.

"What's going on?" she screeched, her eyes focusing on the lieutenant's drawn weapon. The scream wakened the Fitzgeralds, and the woman clung to her husband, fright darkening her eyes.

"Quiet, everyone." Abigail used her best schoolmarm tone, the one that never failed to silence unruly children. "It's bandits." She wrapped her arm around Mrs. Dunn's shoulders and pressed the widow into the seat. If Lieutenant Bowles was going to save the gold or whatever it was the outlaws sought, he needed no interference.

"No!" Mrs. Dunn struggled against Abigail, her eyes darting from the lieutenant to her lap. "My reticule. I need my reticule."

The heavy bag had slid to the other side of the coach, where it lay near the lieutenant's feet. Though Mr. Fitzgerald looked as if he would retrieve the reticule, Abigail shook her head. "Not now." From the corner of her eye, she saw the bandits approach. In seconds they would reach the coach. And then . . . *Dear Lord, keep us safe.*

"Smelling salts! I need my smelling salts." Mrs. Dunn's imperious tone only worsened Mrs. Fitzgerald's whimpering.

As the widow stretched her arms toward her reticule, Abigail dug inside her own bag and pulled out a small vial. Mama had been insistent that a lady always carry smelling salts, claiming one never knew when there might be an emergency. Even Mama, who had been blessed with an active imagination, had probably never envisioned a time like this. "Here." Abigail uncapped the bottle and thrust it under Mrs. Dunn's nose. When the widow snorted with what sounded like indignation, Mrs. Fitzgerald buried her face in her husband's coat, sobbing softly while he murmured reassurances.

Outside, the palomino's rider said something to his companion, and the other man raised his rifle to aim at the stagecoach driver. Abigail shuddered as dread surged through her veins. *Please, no.* The driver was an innocent man, only doing his job. He did not deserve to die. No one did. Not like this. As the coach continued to lurch, Abigail heard the sounds of a whip cracking and a desperate shout. She tightened her grip on Mrs. Dunn. Though she might not be able to help the driver, she could keep the friendly widow away from the window and danger.

"Gif me the *Gelt*," the bandit shouted, his heavy accent telling Abigail that German was his native language. As the lieutenant muttered something under his breath, his tone left no doubt that that something was uncomplimentary. "Gif me the *Gelt*," the man repeated.

It was the lieutenant who responded, never taking his eyes off the would-be robber. "There is no money, and you won't get anything else."

"Don't pay him no mind," the man on the palomino told his companion. "He's only one, and we're two." Though unschooled, this man's voice bore no accent.

"Halt, I say," the German ordered. "Halt or I vill shoot." He punctuated his threat with a shot into the air. "That vas a varning. The next one vill not be."

When Mrs. Dunn started to speak, Abigail clasped a hand over her mouth. Nothing she could say, nothing any of them could say, would help. Everything depended on Lieutenant Bowles. *Help him.* Abigail sent a silent prayer heavenward.

Though she had followed the lieutenant's instruction and moved away from the window, she had a clear view of the two outlaws. The one with the heavy accent lowered his rifle until it was once again pointed at the driver. He was closer now, the sight of his rifle causing her stomach to roil.

"Halt!" the bandit yelled. "I vant the *Gelt*," he shouted, his voice so filled with malevolence that Abigail knew he would not hesitate to kill.

"Help!" Panic colored the driver's voice as he pleaded, "Help me."

There was only one possible recourse. Abigail knew that, even as the prospect sickened her. If the lieutenant didn't act now, the driver would be dead. It was a clear choice: kill or watch a man—perhaps more than one—be killed.

As the lieutenant squeezed the trigger, the deafening sound of the revolver filled the coach. "Oh no!" Mrs. Fitzgerald slumped forward in a swoon.

"Stop!" Mrs. Dunn shrieked as she fought to escape from Abigail's grip. "The Lord says 'thou shalt not kill.'"

But the lieutenant had not killed, Abigail realized with a sense of incredulity. Somehow, though she had not thought it possible, he had only wounded the bandit enough that the man dropped his rifle and was clutching his hand.

"Let's go." The other bandit reined his horse and spun around, racing away from the stagecoach, not even glancing back to see whether his wounded companion was behind him. The German, doubled over in pain, followed more slowly.

The danger was past. The Lord had answered her prayers. There had been no killing. Not today. Abigail felt the tension drain from her, leaving her as limp as a wilted stalk of celery. As Mr. Fitzgerald waved Abigail's smelling salts under his wife's nose, Abigail released her grip on Mrs. Dunn and turned toward the lieutenant, who was now looking at the other passengers as if assessing their condition. "Thank you," she said softly. "I don't know what we would have done without you."

"Just doing my job, miss." His voice was as calm as if he foiled robberies every day of the week. Perhaps he did. The lieutenant leaned out the window again and addressed the driver. "You can stop now. I doubt they'll be back, but I'll ride next to you, just in case."

"What about us?" Mrs. Dunn demanded. She had retrieved her reticule and clutched it as if it held her most prized possessions, not simply a handkerchief and a vial of smelling salts. "I reckon we need protection too."

Though the lieutenant's lips twitched, his voice was serious as he said, "You'll be safe, ma'am, but you might feel better if you pulled down the shades and sat in the middle of the coach."

Now that the danger was past, Abigail could not stop her limbs from trembling. This land was worse, much worse, than she had thought. Dust and wind and relentless sun were nothing compared to murderous outlaws. If it hadn't been for the lieutenant, who knew what might have happened?

She looked out the window at the desolate landscape, no longer searching for signs of life. Barren countryside, even yuccas, were better than the alternative. When her gaze met Lieutenant Bowles's, Abigail said firmly, "Wyoming is no place to live."

She might have imagined it before, but this time there was no question about it. He was trying to control his amusement. "Could be you're right." His lips curved upward as he added, "But you have to admit it's not boring."

25

2

Fort Laramie wasn't as bleak as she'd expected. In fact, it was surprisingly civilized. With no stockade fence surrounding it and no gates, it looked more like a village than a military establishment. In fact, were it not for the men in uniform marching around the center square, Abigail might have thought this was an ordinary town. But nothing about Wyoming was ordinary.

Once the bandits had ridden away, the lieutenant had climbed on top of the coach to sit next to the driver, leaving Abigail with an uncharacteristically silent Mrs. Dunn and the obviously distressed Fitzgeralds. The couple clung to each other, speaking softly, while Mrs. Dunn huddled on the opposite end of the backseat, twisting her reticule strings and muttering what sounded like "all wrong." Though Abigail suspected the widow was referring to the aborted robbery, the same words could be applied to her own journey. What had seemed like such a good idea back in Vermont now seemed all wrong. Perhaps she'd been mistaken. Perhaps Charlotte did not need her. Perhaps God had not meant for her to come to Wyoming.

Brushing aside her doubts, Abigail looked around as she tried to keep pace with the lieutenant. After he'd arranged for another officer to guard the stagecoach until it reached Deadwood, he had insisted on accompanying Abigail to her sister's house, promising that her trunk would be delivered later.

"You'll be safe here," he assured her.

Though Abigail was not certain she would feel safe until she was back in Vermont, she was relieved that Charlotte's home was not on the stark, treeless prairie she had just crossed. While no one would call Fort Laramie a forest, there were trees. A cluster of cottonwoods grew next to the river; others lined three sides of the central area that the lieutenant told her was the parade ground; still others dotted front yards of houses whose porches and gables, not to mention their neat picket fences, made them unexpectedly attractive. And though the parade ground was clearly meant for military exercises, someone had created what the lieutenant explained were birdbaths in the corners. Perhaps four feet across, the shallow cement-lined ponds were edged with bricks, and judging from the number of birds that were drinking from them, they served an important purpose.

Who would have thought that an Army fort would boast such amenities? Whitewashed buildings, sidewalks, street lamps, even grass. It was more than Abigail had believed possible.

She took a shallow breath. Lieutenant Bowles. Ethan, she corrected herself. He'd insisted she call him Ethan, and she'd agreed that he could use her given name. Ethan set a brisk pace, perhaps forgetting that she had yet to become accustomed to the unfamiliar climate. Between the sun, the dry wind, and the altitude, Abigail found herself unable to walk at her normal speed without panting or, even worse, feeling as if she were going to faint. Unlike Mrs. Dunn and Mrs. Fitzgerald, Abigail never fainted.

"Jeffrey didn't mention that he and Charlotte were expecting visitors," Ethan said as they rounded a corner. Though he'd raised an eyebrow in apparent surprise when she'd told him her sister's married name, his voice bore no hint of the breathlessness that plagued Abigail.

He stamped his foot on the wooden walkway, frightening away the small pack of dogs that had begun to follow them. The dogs were yet another difference from Vermont. While Abigail had seen an occasional dog running loose at home, she had never encountered packs of apparently wild dogs. But the lieutenant didn't want to talk about the fort's canine population. He'd asked about Jeffrey and Charlotte.

"They didn't know I was coming," Abigail admitted. "Charlotte might have tried to dissuade me if I'd told her." And Abigail had had no intention of being advised to stay home. As dearly as she loved Charlotte, her older sister was overly cautious. When Charlotte heard about the would-be bandits, she would undoubtedly tell Abigail she had acted foolishly. But what else was a sister to do when her questions remained unanswered and her worries multiplied?

Ethan's arms swung rhythmically as they walked toward Charlotte's new home. It was, he'd explained, at the far end of the parade ground, the southeast corner. Officers' housing and public buildings like the store lined the southern and western sides of the parade ground, while barracks stood along the other sides.

"So you just climbed on a train and came all the way from Vermont, almost getting yourself robbed or possibly kidnapped in the process." There was no mistaking the surprise in the lieutenant's voice. "Are you always that impulsive?"

Impulsive? Perhaps. Papa had claimed that Abigail listened to her heart and disregarded her head, but she wouldn't admit that to this man. Even though it might have been true once, a schoolteacher needed to set a good example, and so she had spent years ensuring that she thought before she acted. "I prefer to think of myself as the sensible sister." That was the term Woodrow used, and it was, he maintained, one of Abigail's most attractive characteristics. Woodrow had never accused her of being impulsive.

The tall lieutenant who was so different from Woodrow grinned. "And so that sensible sister suddenly got the notion of coming to boring Wyoming Territory."

Though he phrased it as a statement, Abigail sensed that he sought an explanation. Instead, she countered with a question. "Do you have any siblings?" When Ethan shook his head, Abigail nodded slowly. "Then you may not understand how much I miss my sister. The last time I saw her was over a year ago at her wedding." There was no need to tell him that since their parents' deaths, her sisters were Abigail's whole family.

Ethan shooed another group of dogs away before he turned back to face her. "Jeffrey mentioned that they were newlyweds when they arrived. His company was transferred here a couple months before mine."

Abigail looked around. Though the fort was more pleasant than she had pictured, it was still a far cry from Vermont's pastoral scenery. The surrounding hills were a lighter green than at home, and the trees lacked the variety that characterized Wesley and the other small towns where Abigail and Charlotte had lived. And even though there was an undeniable charm to some of the mansard-roofed houses, Abigail doubted they contained the luxuries Charlotte had always craved. "I can't imagine honeymooning here."

The lieutenant slowed his pace a mite and looked down at Abigail, his blue eyes sparkling with barely controlled mirth. "Believe it or not, Abigail, some of us consider Wyoming beautiful." He gestured into the distance. "You can see almost forever. Out here, you're not closed in by trees."

"That may be true, but who wants to see miles of grasslands? They're . . ."

"Boring." As they had on the stagecoach, his lips twitched as if he were trying to restrain a smile. "You're wrong about that. The prairies aren't boring. When you look closer, there's more variety than you might think."

"I'll take your word for that." No matter what Ethan Bowles said, Abigail had no intention of being here long enough to explore the surroundings. Once she satisfied herself that Charlotte was all right, she was heading back East. Vermont—and more important, Woodrow—were waiting for her.

"We're almost there." They had walked the distance of what Ethan had called Officers' Row and were approaching the next corner of the parade ground. Just around the bend was a large building under construction, the noise of hammers and workmen's shouts carrying clearly on the wind. "The new administration building," Ethan said when Abigail glanced in that direction. "When it's done, it'll house the school and library as well as the commanding officer's and adjutant's offices."

Abigail's ears perked up at the mention of a school. It was silly to care about that when she wouldn't be here long—two weeks at the maximum. Still, she stared at the cement walls taking shape and wondered what the classroom would be like.

"This is it." The lieutenant stopped at the gate to a large house with a wraparound verandah. Although a single set of steps led to the porch, a wall divided the porch, and a door on each side indicated that the structure served as two residences. "Your sister's is the one on the left," Ethan said. Touching his hand to his cap in a brief salute, he added, "I'll leave you now."

Abigail swallowed. There was no reason to feel apprehensive, and yet she did. Perhaps it was the aftermath of the aborted robbery, but what had seemed like a good idea now seemed . . . impulsive. She held out her hand to the lieutenant. "Thank you again for what you did on the stagecoach."

He touched his hand to hers briefly, then shook his head. "I'd prefer if you didn't mention the incident to your sister. News travels quickly here. I'd like my commanding officer to hear it from me."

Abigail smiled. If gossip was common, it appeared that Fort Laramie resembled a small town in yet another way. "Certainly." She could delay no longer. She placed her hand on the gate. "Good-bye, Lieutenant . . . er . . . Ethan."

As his brisk footsteps receded, Abigail climbed the three steps and knocked firmly on the door. In a moment she would know whether coming to Wyoming had been a mistake. Her heart pounded at the thought of being reunited with Charlotte. How she'd missed her sister! In the space of two months, both Charlotte and Elizabeth had moved away, leaving Abigail the only Harding sister in Vermont. But now she was here, and she and Charlotte would be together, even if only for a short time.

But Charlotte wasn't home. Abigail was about to rap on the door again when it cracked open. For a moment, Abigail simply stared. Then she pushed the door open and stepped inside, closing it behind her. "Charlotte." The woman standing before her looked like her sister, and yet she did not. Though it was late afternoon, Abigail's normally fashionable sister was dressed in a loose wrapper and house slippers, her dark brown hair undone as if she'd only just arisen from bed. More concerning, though, were Charlotte's pallor and the fact that her face was thinner than Abigail had ever seen it.

If she was shocked, so was Charlotte. Her sister pressed her hand to her heart and her face lost even more color. "Abigail." The word was little more than a whisper. "What on earth are you doing here?" She looked around. "Is Woodrow with you?"

It wasn't the welcome Abigail had hoped for, but ever since she'd arrived in Wyoming, nothing had been what she'd expected.

Why would Charlotte think that Woodrow would have accompanied her? "I came because I missed you, Charlotte." *And I was worried.* Though she did not voice the words, Abigail knew her worries had been well-grounded. Something was desperately wrong. She took a step forward and wrapped her arms around her sister, trying not to wince at the realization that Charlotte's body was little more than skin over bones.

Charlotte drew back slightly and looked at Abigail, her

eyes studying her face, almost as if she wanted to reassure herself that the woman who hugged her was not an illusion.

"Oh, Abigail, I missed you too, but I never imagined you'd go anywhere without Woodrow. When I saw you standing here, I thought perhaps you'd eloped and were spending the summer traveling."

Abigail shook her head at the notion. Ethan Bowles might find her impulsive, but that was one adjective no one would apply to Woodrow Morgan. Woodrow was sturdy and stable, a man who planned his life as carefully as he did his lessons. "Woodrow believes we need to wait another year before we marry, but I couldn't wait that long to see you."

"I'm so glad you've come." Color returned to Charlotte's face. "What am I doing, leaving you standing in the hall-way?" She gestured toward the first of two doorways leading off this section of the narrow corridor. "Let's go into the parlor." Though the hallway with its highly polished dark wood floor extended the length of the house, if closed, a second door would keep visitors from viewing the less formal rooms. That door was now open, allowing Abigail to see that there were two more doors on the left side of the hall, and that a staircase led from the back entrance to the second floor.

The parlor was a surprise, this time a pleasant one. With two windows on the front and bright white paint, it was light and airy, filled with furniture that would not have been out of place in one of the finest homes in Vermont. It even boasted a piano.

"Tell me all about your journey," Charlotte encouraged once she and Abigail were seated. Though she had gestured Abigail toward the settee, Charlotte took the chair opposite her, keeping her eyes fixed on her sister, as if she feared she would disappear. "How long can you stay?" Without waiting for an answer, Charlotte shook her head again, setting her uncombed hair to bouncing. "Let me get you some tea." Her expression was apologetic as she said, "Truly, I have not forgotten all those lessons Mama gave us on being a good hostess. I'm simply surprised to see you here. It's such a long way from Vermont to Fort Laramie."

Abigail smiled at the realization that, though she might be pale and thin, this was the sister she remembered. Charlotte's brain moved so quickly that it was sometimes difficult to keep up with her. Conversations could be tiring, simply because of the number of changes of subject.

"Tea would be wonderful. The air is so dry that my throat feels parched most of the time."

"You must be careful. The sun is stronger here. At these high altitudes, you need to protect your skin." That was vintage Charlotte, taking advantage of being the oldest sister to advise her younger siblings. But perhaps there was more to the warning than simple sisterly concern. Perhaps it explained why Charlotte was so pale. Perhaps she'd been afraid to expose her skin to sunlight. Still, while that was a possible reason, it wouldn't explain why her eyes had lost their sparkle and why she was so thin. A more likely reason, although one Abigail wished she could dismiss, was that Charlotte's childhood illness had recurred.

"Let me help you." Abigail followed her sister into the kitchen. Like the parlor, it was well furnished.

Charlotte shook her head. "Nonsense. Mrs. Channing—she's the woman who cooks and cleans for us—will be back shortly. She's only gone to the commissary to buy some beef. In the meantime, I think I can boil water for a pot of tea."

34

Though her words were brave, Abigail noticed that Charlotte's hands trembled as she lifted the heavy iron teakettle to place it on the stove, and she sank onto the long bench, as if the effort had exhausted her.

"Are you all right?" The words slipped out before Abigail realized what she was saying.

"Of course I am." Charlotte looked down at her casual dress and frowned. "I was a bit fatigued this afternoon, and so I took a nap." She raised her eyebrows in the imperious expression Abigail remembered from their childhood. "You remember that Mama used to take naps, don't you?" When Abigail nodded, Charlotte added, "I'm perfectly fine."

Though Abigail did not believe her sister, Charlotte would only become more intractable if she said anything more. That childhood bout of pneumonia had left Charlotte with more than a lingering weakness. It had made her overly sensitive to questions about her health.

As they waited for the water to boil, Charlotte leaned forward, resting her hands on her knees. "Now tell me what Elizabeth said when you announced you were coming. I thought you were planning to visit her this summer."

"I was, but I changed my mind. Elizabeth's so busy with her studies that Christmas will be a better time for a visit." It was rationalization, Abigail knew, but she had believed that Charlotte needed her more than their younger sister, whose medical school classes kept her almost too busy to sleep. Though Abigail missed both sisters dreadfully, it was Charlotte who worried her.

A smile crossed Charlotte's face as she rose to measure out tea. "Oh, Abigail, you're so impulsive."

There was that word again. "That's what Ethan said."

"Ethan? Ethan who?"

Though there was no reason, Abigail felt her face flush. "Lieutenant Bowles," she said as calmly as she could. "He was one of the passengers on the stagecoach from Cheyenne."

"Ah, that Ethan." Charlotte nodded with approval. "Jeffrey says he's a good man. He's another West Pointer, you know."

Once again, Charlotte was seizing on any subject other than her health. Knowing there was nothing to be gained by pursuing that now, Abigail picked up the tea tray and carried it back to the parlor. "Your house is lovely," she said when they were once more seated. "I'm surprised you have a pianoforte." And not simply a piano, but a Steinway. That was a far cry from the battered instrument their parents had taken from one parsonage to the next, its case seeming to acquire at least one more nick with each move.

Charlotte stirred sugar into her cup of tea before she replied. "Jeffrey insists on buying the best of everything. He's very good to me."

Surely it was Abigail's imagination that her sister seemed as if she was reciting lines she had delivered many times. "Then you're happy here." She made it a statement rather than a question.

"Of course. Who wouldn't be?"

Once again, Charlotte's words rang hollow.

"Bowles."

Ethan turned at the sound of the familiar voice. Though Jeffrey Crowley used his first name in private, he was formal in public, declaring that West Pointers had an obligation to maintain standards of dignity. Jeffrey's boots were always perfectly shined, the creases in his uniform impeccable. Though that was nothing more than they'd been taught, Ethan suspected that Jeffrey's insistence on dignity came from years of being taunted for his carrot-colored hair and freckled face rather than any protocol he'd learned at the Point.

"What are you doing here?" Jeffrey continued, his green eyes narrowing as he strode next to Ethan, appearing content to accompany him wherever he was going, which in this case was to their superior officer. "I thought you weren't due back until tomorrow."

Because he had not yet briefed Captain Westland, Ethan did not mention the attempted robbery. "There was nothing to be gained by staying in Cheyenne." And, as it turned out, much to be gained by being on that particular coach.

Keeping his voice even, Ethan said, "I hit one dead end after another in Cheyenne, so I decided to come back. As luck would have it, I wound up accompanying your sister-in-law."

Jeffrey's blink was the only sign he was surprised. A couple inches shorter than Ethan, Jeffrey was a good twenty pounds heavier, with what Ethan's grandfather used to call a boxer's physique. "Why on earth did Elizabeth come? I thought she was still in school."

"Not Elizabeth, Abigail. I gather she missed Charlotte's company."

To Ethan's surprise, Jeffrey muttered a curse that had nothing to do with the four dogs that scampered beside him, barking, yipping, and trying to jump on him. "Abigail's trouble. According to Charlotte, she's always acted without thinking, and here's the proof. She's in my home. What did I do to deserve her?"

The answer was simple. "You married her sister. Didn't I tell you that marriage is more trouble than it's worth?"

"Wait until you meet the right woman. You'll change your tune then." Jeffrey stared into the distance, as if searching for a solution to what he obviously considered an unpleasant situation. "Come home with me and stay for supper."

Ethan shook his head. Though a home-cooked meal was enticing, he had things to do. "I need to see the captain. Besides, I know better than to intrude on a family gathering."

But Jeffrey would not be dissuaded. "Charlotte's my family," he insisted. "Abigail's an unfortunate appendage. C'mon, Ethan, do me a favor. I don't want to beard the lion alone."

A lion? Abigail Harding was more like a swan with that long, graceful neck. "Oh, all right." It was less than a gracious acceptance, but the invitation had been less than gracious. "That'll give me a chance to tell you what happened on the trip back."

Frances Colfax let out a string of curses that would have blistered the paint, had there been any paint to blister. Paint was the last thing she needed on the shanty walls. This place was fine the way it was—a tumbledown building so weathered by the wind and sun that no one would spare it a second glance, even if they happened to spot it. And few did, for it was a dugout, set deep into the hillside, miles away from the closest ranch. This was the perfect spot to stash her clothing and an even better one for stashing the takings. When there were takings.

Carefully folding the last of the seven petticoats that had made her look like a refugee from the War Between the States,

Frances cursed again. Her words were nothing compared to what the baron would say when he heard about today's fiasco. It couldn't have been much worse. That lieutenant wasn't supposed to be on the coach. Frances had been assured that no one from the fort was scheduled to travel then, much less an officer. The passengers were supposed to be a bunch of rich folks who deserved nothing more than to contribute their jewelry and cash to Frances's fund. It was bad enough that there was only one couple instead of the four or five she had expected. It was even worse that the attack took place earlier than it was supposed to and that she had somehow fallen asleep. That was a fact she had no intention of mentioning to the baron. She would focus on that cursed Lieutenant Bowles's interference.

Frances brushed the gray powder from her hair. By the time she was done, no one would find any connection between Frances Colfax, who had once dazzled audiences with her portrayals of Juliet, Desdemona, and her personal favorite, Lady Macbeth, and Mrs. Dunn, a helpless widow.

Helpless, hah! If it hadn't been for that schoolmarm, Frances would have stopped the lieutenant's sharpshooting, knocking that Colt out of his hand before he had a chance to aim. But the schoolmarm was stronger than she'd appeared, and she'd kept Frances from retrieving her reticule. The chit didn't know that what Frances wanted from it wasn't smelling salts but her derringer. Frances wasn't only one of the finest actresses ever to tread the boards, she was also a crack shot, and—unlike the baron—she wouldn't hesitate to kill a woman. No one stood between Frances Colfax and success.

Fastening the last button on her riding clothes and preparing to head for the ranch, she frowned as she pictured the baron's reaction. Instead of money and jewels, they had a wounded man to deal with. Not good. Not good at all. If his hand was as badly injured as she thought, Schiller would be useless for at least a month. The baron would not be happy.

"Your stagecoach was robbed? Oh, Abigail, how dreadful!" Blood drained from Charlotte Crowley's face, and she looked as if she were about to swoon. For the life of him, Ethan didn't understand why women trussed themselves up so tight that they could hardly breathe. Look at the way Mrs. Fitzgerald had fainted at the first sign of danger. Even the widow had sought her smelling salts. And now Jeffrey's wife appeared faint.

Only Abigail seemed immune to the swooning disease. She might be impulsive, but at least she didn't swoon, even when she was terrified. Ethan had seen the signs—the wide eyes, the rapid breathing, the pale face—but he'd also seen her control her fear. Thanks to her actions, his job had been easier. Abigail was a sensible woman.

"Why didn't you say something earlier?" Charlotte demanded, her eyes filling with tears as she looked at her sister.

Though there was a distinct resemblance between the two women, Abigail's eyes seemed to change their hue with her moods, while no one would question the color of Charlotte's eyes. They were brown, almost as dark brown as her hair. Her features were as patrician as Abigail's, and some might claim she was the more beautiful of the two. Ethan would not have been one of them. While he would not deny her beauty, Charlotte Crowley had always struck him as a cold woman. Cold, however, was not an adjective he would use to describe her sister.

"We weren't robbed. It was an *attempted* robbery," Abigail said before Ethan could explain that she had remained silent at his request. Though he had planned to tell Jeffrey privately, as soon as they were seated in the dining room, Jeffrey had asked what had happened, and Ethan found himself giving an abbreviated explanation of what had occurred on the stagecoach.

Abigail laid a hand on her sister's arm as if to comfort her. Charlotte might be the elder, but today it appeared that Abigail had assumed that role. "Lieutenant Bowles—Ethan, that is—kept the bandits from doing anything more than threaten us."

"But, still, you could have been hurt." Charlotte shook her head in dismay.

"I wasn't. The worst thing that happened was that Mrs. Dunn kept my smelling salts. She was one of the other passengers on the coach," Abigail added. "The poor woman was so upset she was afraid she might faint." Ethan's admiration for Abigail grew. Though he knew she'd been frightened, she was making light of it to keep her sister from worrying.

Jeffrey sawed at his roast, though the meat was tender enough to be cut with a fork. "So, what happened?" He addressed his question to Ethan.

"Abigail's story is accurate. Two road agents, at least one a deserter, threatened the driver. It was clear they were going to shoot him if he didn't stop the coach, so I shot first."

While Charlotte gasped, her husband pursed his lips. "I hope you killed the miscreant."

Ethan raised his eyebrow at the vehemence in Jeffrey's voice. It wasn't like him to care so passionately about anything other than his wife. Everyone in the garrison knew the man was besotted with Charlotte, but why did he care how Ethan had resolved the robbery attempt?

"There was no need for killing. With his shooting arm wounded, Schiller won't be robbing coaches anytime soon."

"Schiller?" Jeffrey sputtered the name. "You recognized the men?"

"Only one. Even with a bandanna covering half his face, there was no mistaking Schiller's accent. At one point, he got close enough that I could see his green eyes, so I know for certain that's who it was." Ethan speared a piece of meat. "If I'd been mounted, I would have gone after him. As it was, I made certain he and his partner didn't threaten this coach any longer."

Abigail, who'd been silent, laid down her fork. "What did the bandits hope to get? Mrs. Dunn and I had no valuables, and I wouldn't have thought that even Mrs. Fitzgerald's jewelry was worth facing a hangman's noose."

It was a valid question. Ethan accepted the bread Charlotte offered him and began to butter it. "The dime novels make it appear that stagecoach robberies are an almost daily occurrence out here. That used to be true, especially when gold was being transferred from Deadwood to Cheyenne. But then the stage companies developed an armor-plated coach that some call the Monitor."

The sparkle in her eyes told Ethan Abigail recognized the reference. "Like the ship from the Civil War."

"Exactly. That and the presence of armed guards effectively halted theft of the gold shipments. Now road agents hope to find wealthy passengers."

42

Abigail nodded slowly. "The Fitzgeralds seemed to have money, but I still wonder if it would have been enough."

"They probably assumed the coach would be full. It usually is. Most days the inside seats are all taken, and there are at least a couple men on top, but even if the bandits had known how few people were on board, deserters can be mighty desperate and mighty foolish. In my book, you'd have to be both to leave the Army like that." Only cowards ran away.

"Do many men desert?" The expression on Abigail's face said this was more than idle curiosity. Perhaps her schoolteacher roots were showing, and she was gathering information for a class.

"All too many. The rate has been up to 30 percent. Isn't that right, Jeffrey?"

His fellow officer nodded.

Abigail let out a small gasp. "Almost a third of the men? That's terrible. Why do they leave?"

Trying not to frown as he thought of the men who'd simply disappeared, Ethan admitted that he wasn't certain. "Some claim they're bored with Army life, others that they're discouraged by the low pay, but those don't seem like good reasons to abandon your sense of honor. And if you're going to ask why they targeted this particular coach rather than any other, I don't know that either."

Jeffrey pointed his fork at Ethan. "Did you ever consider that they were looking for you?" The man had to be joking.

"Me? What would anyone hope to get from a first lieutenant? Everyone knows about Army pay."

"Don't forget that Schiller was a private. Compared to him, you're wealthy. But there's another possibility. Perhaps they were planning to hold you for ransom. After all, your grandfather is as rich as Croesus."

If there was one subject Ethan did not want to discuss, it was Curtis Wilson, the nemesis of his childhood. Unfortunately, once Jeffrey got started, he was like a terrier with a bone. If Ethan said nothing, Jeffrey would continue asking questions until he received a response. "My grandfather may be wealthy," Ethan said, choosing his words carefully, "but I assure you that he would not spend one silver dollar to ransom me."

And that was fine with Ethan. When he had left Curtis Wilson's house, he had sworn he would never again be beholden to him.

"Jeffrey won't be back until late," Charlotte said an hour later after the men had left and Charlotte and Abigail had retired to the parlor, leaving Mrs. Channing to wash the dishes. It had been a delicious meal, and yet Abigail could not ignore the undercurrents. Though Jeffrey had said nothing more, she sensed his disapproval of Ethan's actions and his conviction that the bandit should have been killed. He was wrong. Human life was precious. That was why God had commanded his people not to kill.

Though Papa had tried to comfort her the day she'd found Luke, explaining that it had been an accident and that Luke was at peace now, Abigail had been unable to forget the horror of sudden death. Killing was wrong. How could Jeffrey claim otherwise? Ethan had done what had to be done. He had stopped the outlaws from killing the driver, and he'd done it without taking another's life. That was heroic. No matter what Jeffrey thought, Ethan had done the right thing.

Abigail looked at her sister, who sat on the chair opposite her, her feet propped on an exquisite needlepoint stool. If she was bothered by Ethan's actions, it wasn't obvious.

"Jeffrey and the other officers spend most evenings at their club." Charlotte continued her explanation. The sparkle that had lit her eyes when Jeffrey was present faded.

"That must be lonely for you." Perhaps that was the reason her sister's letters had sounded so unhappy. Even if other men deserted their wives each evening, Charlotte and Jeffrey had been married little more than a year. Surely they still craved each other's company. When Charlotte did not respond, Abigail hesitated. She was hardly an expert on marriage, and yet she could not ignore her sister's distress.

"Something's wrong," Abigail said slowly. "You can deny it all you want, but I can see that you're ill. Is it your lungs again?" Even when he'd declared Charlotte cured of pneumonia, the physician had cautioned that her lungs would remain weak and that she must take precautions to avoid overtaxing them.

"I'm not ill." Charlotte shifted so that she was no longer facing Abigail and stared out the window for a long moment. At last, seemingly reluctantly, she turned back and met Abigail's gaze. "I'm not ill. I'm *enceinte*."

Her sister was going to have a child!

"Oh, Charlotte." Abigail rose to draw her into her arms. "That's wonderful news. You're going to be a mother, and Elizabeth and I will be aunts. But you'd best be forewarned. I have every intention of spoiling that baby of yours."

Though Abigail smiled, her sister's expression remained

somber, and she stood stiffly, as if merely tolerating Abigail's hug. "It would be wonderful news if I felt better. Look at me." Charlotte gestured toward her midsection. "The baby's due in late October, but I can still wear my normal clothes. I've been so sick that I haven't gained the weight I should have."

Her eyes filled with tears. "Oh, Abigail, I'm afraid I'm going to lose this baby, and I don't know what I'll do then." Before Abigail could murmur comforting words, Charlotte continued, "Jeffrey wants a son so badly. Sometimes I think that's the only reason he married me."

❧ 3 ❧

The rain had stopped. Abigail gave a silent prayer of thanks as she raised the shade to look outside. Though fatigue had overcome her by the time she climbed the stairs to Charlotte's spare room, the expected deep sleep had eluded her. Instead, she had lain awake, trying to reconcile her sister's fears that Jeffrey did not love her with the memory of their wedding. While the day had been gloomy and a light drizzle had begun to fall as Charlotte and Jeffrey emerged from the chapel at West Point, Jeffrey had been the picture of a happy groom, so smitten with his bride that he did not notice the less than perfect weather, and Charlotte's smile had been radiant.

"I've found the perfect man," she'd whispered to Abigail later that day, causing Jeffrey, who had somehow overheard, to laugh.

47

"You're wrong, Charlotte," he'd said. "I'm far from perfect, but you're the answer to all my dreams. You've made me the happiest man alive."

Surely love like that did not fade. Surely Jeffrey did not love Charlotte only because she would bear his children. But Charlotte didn't seem convinced. The instant she'd pronounced the disturbing words, she had clapped her hand over her mouth. "I didn't mean that," she had said, tears welling in her eyes. Though her lips formed the words, her eyes told a different story. Charlotte still harbored fears, and that worried Abigail as much as her sister's letters had.

There had to be something she could do to help her, and yet though she tossed so much that she tangled the sheets, Abigail had been unable to find a solution. When she'd finally slept, her dreams had been troubled, and she had wakened twice, startled by the rumbling of thunder and the sound of rain beating on the roof. Although Vermont had its share of thunderstorms, none had been as fierce as last night's storm. It seemed that everything in this territory was bigger and wilder than at home. Was that part of the reason for Charlotte's worries? Marriage and impending motherhood required adjustments. So, too, would living in environs like these. Perhaps the combination was more than Charlotte could bear.

There had to be a way to help. *Show me, Lord,* Abigail prayed. *Show me the way.*

"So, tell me about her. Is she as pretty as they say?"

Ethan frowned as he stared into the mirror. Living with the other bachelor officers had convinced him that one of the few advantages of being married was the greater privacy it afforded. No one would burst into Jeffrey's house to ask about Abigail, but here a man couldn't even shave in peace. The sight of Oliver Seton's face reflected next to his own was proof of that. He could, he supposed, feign ignorance, pretending he didn't know who the "she" was who had captured his best friend's fancy, but that would accomplish little. Where women were concerned, Oliver was as difficult to discourage as a hungry badger at a prairie dog burrow.

Taller than Ethan by a couple inches, Oliver befuddled the cooks. Though he ate twice as much as the others, he remained the thinnest man on the post, and it was not uncommon to see the tall man with the light brown hair trying to wheedle another loaf of bread from the bakers. To Ethan's amusement, the second lieutenant who'd been transferred to Fort Laramie along with Ethan frequently applied the same enterprising skills to the pursuit of women.

"Miss Harding is quite attractive," Ethan admitted as he brushed shaving lather onto his cheeks. The truth was, Abigail was beautiful, though he wouldn't tell Oliver that. The man needed no encouragement. Even if she were as homely as a mule, Oliver would soon be chasing after her. "She looks a bit like her sister, but . . ." Ethan searched for a word to describe the differences. "Softer," he said at last.

Oliver leaned his lanky frame against the door frame and grinned. "That's the best news I've heard all year. I know a man shouldn't be fussy, but some of those laundresses are downright dog-faced."

"So long as they get the sheets clean, why do you care?" It was a rhetorical question. Oliver, like many of the single men on the post, sought the company of any unattached female, ignoring even a total lack of pulchritude. And, when he wasn't pursuing an eligible woman at the fort, Oliver spent his evenings with the soiled doves at Peg's.

"I don't understand you, Ethan. Haven't you read your Bible? Man is not meant to live alone. That's why God made Eve."

"And why Noah took the animals two-by-two." Ethan paused as he ran the razor down one cheek. He had no intention of shedding blood just because Oliver Seton chose to dispute Ethan's lack of interest in the fort's single women. "You've already given me that sermon."

"Maybe so, but I still don't understand why you're not concerned about finding a wife. Life would be a lot less lonely with one." And, as odd as it might seem to some, loneliness was a definite factor, even on a post with hundreds of men.

"Not every man is cut out for marriage," Ethan said as mildly as he could. He'd spent more than half his life listening to his grandfather expound on the reasons for marriage, insisting that when Ethan wed it would be to solidify an important business relationship, something that could help expand the railroad or bring it new customers. When Ethan had turned twelve, Grandfather had announced that he had selected four girls, any one of whom would make Ethan a fine wife once he was old enough to marry. He'd further admonished Ethan to be particularly courteous to those girls' fathers when they visited, for they were valued suppliers. Ethan had heard enough to know that that was not for him. He wouldn't marry for business reasons any more than he'd consider sharing the rest of his life with a woman who was more interested in his uniform than in the man inside. He'd met enough of those to last him a lifetime when he'd been at West Point. There was, however, no reason to tell Oliver that. Ethan ought to simply order him to leave, but despite Oliver's annoying tendency to harangue him on the subject of marriage, the man was normally good company.

"I suppose I ought to be grateful." Oliver tapped the end of his unusually long nose. "If you're not sparking her, perhaps Miss Harding will take pity on me, even with this nose."

"Perhaps." There was no reason why the thought should rankle, and yet it did.

"Morning, Bowles."

Ethan turned, hoping the day would improve, if only briefly. Even before he'd finished shaving, he'd received a summons to the captain's office. Though he wanted to ask permission to search for the deserters, the fact that he'd been summoned was not good news. He'd finished his ablutions in record time and was on his way to learn what his superior officer had in store for him when Jeffrey joined him. Perhaps Jeffrey knew something he did not, something that would explain the huge grin on his face.

"You seem happy," Ethan told his colleague, "and I don't imagine it's over the prospect of drilling soldiers in the mud." The previous night's rain had turned the parade ground into a soggy mess.

"Nope," Jeffrey agreed, "I hate that as much as the next man." He glanced down at his freshly polished boots, his grimace saying he knew what they'd look like in a couple hours. When he faced Ethan again, his smile restored, he said, "Before you ask, my good mood has nothing to do with that pickle-faced sister-in-law of mine. I still don't like

51

the fact that she's invaded my home. Life was fine with just Charlotte and me."

Though he kept walking, recognizing the folly of keeping the captain waiting, Ethan couldn't help reacting to Jeffrey's terminology. Pickle-faced? What could Abigail have said or done to deserve that description? Though he considered her trip impulsive, it seemed a pity that Abigail had come all this way for such a grudging welcome.

"On second thought," Jeffrey continued, "maybe Abigail is part of the cause. With her here, Charlotte and I figured it would be difficult to keep our news a secret, so we're telling folks—and you're the first to hear."

"I'm honored. Now, tell me, what's the big announcement?" Although Ethan had strong suspicions, he knew Jeffrey would not appreciate speculation. He wanted fanfare or at least exuberant congratulations.

Jeffrey's somewhat homely face glowed as he pronounced the words Ethan had expected. "I'm going to be a father. Isn't that grand?"

"It is indeed." Ethan clapped his friend on the back. "Congratulations, old man."

"This is what every man wants, isn't it—a son?"

Ethan nodded, knowing it was the expected reaction. He wouldn't point out that the child might be a daughter, any more than he'd say that a man didn't always get what he wanted.

"Now all I need is my captaincy. The extra pay sure would be handy." Jeffrey frowned. "I tell you, Bowles, one thing I don't like about the Regular Army is how slow promotions are. It wasn't like that when my grandfather served. I feel like a ghoul, waiting for some captain to die so I can have his rank. Awful, isn't it?" He frowned again. "You're lucky. I wish I had a grandfather like yours to pull wires for me. Who knows? Maybe he'll get you transferred somewhere good."

"You don't know my grandfather if you think he'd do that. He hates the fact that I'm in the Army." As he mounted the steps to the captain's office, Ethan didn't bother to hide the anger that often accompanied thoughts of Grandfather. "I joined the Army despite him." More precisely, because following in his father's footsteps was the best way Ethan knew to spite his grandfather.

"Attention!" The company lined up in front of him thrust their shoulders back, their heads up. Ethan's gaze moved down the row, noting that, despite the constant grousing over ill-fitting uniforms of dubious quality, most of the men would pass even a West Point inspection. Unfortunately, that was not the reason he'd summoned the men. An inspection would have been far easier than today's duty. Though Ethan had hoped to be leading a search party for Johann Schiller and his accomplice, the captain had informed him that Lieutenant Montgomery would be doing that, while Ethan dealt with another problem. The captain's idea of priorities didn't mesh with Ethan's, but an order was an order.

"We've got ourselves a problem, men." As if on cue, a pack of snarling dogs bounded toward them, teeth bared, tails announcing that each member of the pack wanted to be the top dog. "Captain Westland is displeased with the number of unleashed canines at the fort. Each and every one of them must be captured." Although how that would occur, Ethan could only guess. There were at least a hundred dogs, and when they sensed that they were being hunted, they could be as wily as coyotes.

"If they're registered," he continued, "you will return them to their owners and inform said owners that it's time to register again. Furthermore, you will advise said owners that once their canines are registered, the dogs must be kept under control, either restrained by a leash or kept in a fenced area. Beginning tomorrow, any canines found running loose will be killed."

A corporal requested permission to speak. "What happens to the unregistered dogs, sir?"

"Either you find someone who wants to register them and pay the tax, or . . ." Ethan gestured toward the river. "They meet their fate. Understood?"

"Ve haf to bathe the dogs?" a private asked.

"No!" Ethan glared at the men whose faces broke into grins at the absurd question. "No baths. You will drown them."

"Down?"

Swallowing his annoyance, Ethan tried not to be dismayed by the realization that the soldier wasn't attempting to be amusing. He simply didn't understand.

"Hold them *down* in the river until they *drown*."

The way the soldier shook his head told Ethan it wasn't because he disagreed with the dogs' fate but because he still didn't comprehend the command.

"Begging your pardon, sir." Corporal Keller stepped out of formation. "Request permission to translate." Though his accent was heavy, he always understood Ethan.

"Permission granted." What a sorry state the Army had come to, when enlisted men needed an interpreter. They were amateurs, rank amateurs, like Schiller and the other deserter.

The would-be bandits hadn't realized that their chances of success would have been far greater if they'd approached the stagecoach from opposite sides. Amateurs!

The corporal spoke rapidly, and as he did, Ethan saw comprehension dawning in several of the men's eyes.

"Good work, Corporal Keller." Maybe now Ethan's day would improve.

It was good that Fort Laramie had boardwalks. Thanks to the rain, the road that circled the parade ground was muddy and dotted with puddles, and the parade ground itself appeared soggy. Abigail would have taken Charlotte's advice to wait until the sun had had a chance to dry the mud if the only item she had sought was a replacement for her smelling salts. But witnessing her sister's continuing morning sickness had made her determined to waste no time trying to relieve it.

Elizabeth had advised both peppermint and ginger teas when Abigail had suffered an upset stomach, and they'd been as therapeutic as her sister had claimed. Surely the post trader—the sutler, to use the term Charlotte had told her was more common—would have mint, even if he didn't carry ginger. That was the reason Abigail was headed for the one-story stone building at the northwest end of the parade ground.

The sun was bright, the sky that faultless blue that seemed characteristic of Wyoming in the summer. Even the wind had subsided, leaving a day that promised to be beautiful, assuming, of course, that one found anything about Wyoming beautiful. Abigail doubted that the soldiers marching in the center of the parade ground had any reason to rejoice as mud spattered their pant legs and clung to their boots.

And then there were the other men who raced after a pack of dogs, twirling ropes as if they planned to lasso the unfortunate animals.

"Kommen sie hier!" a man shouted. Abigail laughed as the dogs refused to come. *"Kommen sie hier,"* the soldier repeated. Didn't he realize that the dogs had no intention of obeying, even if they could understand German? The only sign that they heard the command was that two turned their heads, perhaps judging their pursuers' distance, before they yipped and shouldered their way into the center of the pack.

Where had they come from? It was true that she'd seen a number of dogs yesterday and had heard some howling last night, but Abigail hadn't realized there were so many. The pack she'd been watching raced by, yelping and snarling at the soldiers who were attempting to catch them. Though close to twenty dogs had run past her, that was only one group. On the other side of the houses, she heard another pack, and the barks at the far end of the parade ground told her that still more were circling the bakery. Abigail stared into the distance, trying to gauge the total number.

Wham! She collided with a large object. There was no mistaking the uniform or the firmness of the body beneath it. Thanks to her inattention, she had run into a soldier. Abigail raised her eyes and felt blood rush to her face at the realization that the man she had hit was Lieutenant Bowles. Ethan. How embarrassing.

"I'm sorry." It must have been the impact that was making her breathless. Surely it wasn't the amusement she saw in those deep blue eyes. Surely it wasn't the fact that she was close to a man, close enough to smell soap and something else, something she couldn't identify. If she was going to be breathless about a man, surely it should have been Woodrow who caused her heart to pound and her breath to catch. But Abigail had never felt like this around Woodrow.

"I'm sorry." She repeated the apology in a desperate attempt to regain her sense of normalcy. "I'm afraid I wasn't watching where I was going."

Ethan's lips curved. "Neither, it would appear, was I. I'm the one who must beg your pardon."

As she took a step backward, hoping the distance would slow the racing of her heart, Abigail gestured toward the men chasing dogs. "What's happening? I've never seen so many dogs."

"Neither had Captain Westland. Three of them jumped on him this morning."

"With muddy paws." Abigail tried not to smile at the picture her words conjured.

"Exactly. He was exceedingly displeased."

"And so he ordered them corralled?" That would explain the soldiers' lassos.

Ethan nodded. "That's part of it. The dogs have become such a nuisance that the last commanding officer increased the tax on them. Some owners believed the amount exorbitant and chose not to register their dogs, so they let them run wild."

"And now you have even more." Though most of the animals she'd seen were adults, five black and tan puppies had trailed behind the last pack and had apparently just discovered the delight of chasing their own tails. Abigail watched, amused that the runt of the litter, whose tail was longer than his siblings', was the only one to catch it. One sharp nip convinced him of the folly of that particular game, and he wandered off to nurse his aching tail.

"Precisely. This morning's decree was that any dogs that are not registered must be gotten rid of."

"You mean . . . ?" Abigail bit her lip, not wanting to think of the fate awaiting the unfortunate animals.

Ethan nodded again. "They'll be drowned in the river."

"Even the puppies?" Tiring of chasing their own tails, two of the larger ones had begun to chase their smaller littermates. As they ran, their ears flapped and their oversized paws spattered mud.

"Puppies are not puppies forever." Ethan's voice held a hint of mirth. "They may be cute now, but soon they turn into a nuisance."

"With muddy paws." As his littermates scampered away, the smallest one, realizing he'd been abandoned, tried to catch up with them. But his legs were too short, and all he managed to do was stumble into a puddle, turning his once tan chest and legs brown. Abigail smiled as the puppy, apparently enjoying the sensation of muddy water on his legs, flopped onto his back and began to roll in the mud.

"Muddy paws?" Ethan chuckled. "This one looks like he has muddy everything."

The pup rose and shook his fur, sending droplets of mud toward Abigail before he plopped down in front of her and looked up with the biggest brown eyes she'd ever seen on a dog. Right now those eyes were beseeching Abigail, tugging at her heart. "Oh, Ethan, he's so cute. You can't drown him."

"What do you propose?"

As she started to shrug, a memory surfaced. It had been the Christmas Charlotte was eight and Abigail six. Though Abigail had made many wishes, Charlotte had longed for only one gift: a puppy. At night when they were supposed to be fast asleep, Charlotte had confided that she was certain their parents would grant her wish. But when Christmas morning arrived, though their stockings had been stuffed with fruits and nuts, there had been no dog. "A puppy is too much trouble," Papa had explained. Only Abigail knew the number of tears Charlotte had shed and how deeply hurt she had been five Christmases later when Elizabeth had begged for and received a dog.

There was no undoing that, but maybe—just maybe—this woebegone puppy could fill an empty spot in Charlotte's life. Abigail bent down and gathered the muddy creature into her arms. "I know the perfect home for him." He was wet and squirmy and smelled worse than almost anything Abigail could recall, and yet she smiled as the puppy attempted to lick her face.

"Don't laugh, Ethan, but he's going to be a very belated Christmas gift. My sister needs this little ball of fur."

4

"Are you certain? A puppy is not . . ."

"A puppy forever." Abigail couldn't help smiling. Not only was the puppy wriggling in her arms as if he thought he'd been suddenly transported to paradise, but Ethan's quizzical expression inspired laughter. His lips twitched, and he raised his eyebrows so high they nearly touched his cap. Abigail looked at the subject of Ethan's amusement and smiled again. "I know that, and in this case, it's good that he'll outgrow puppyhood . . . if there is such a word. His antics will entertain Charlotte now, but he should be settled down a bit by the time . . ." Abigail paused, realizing she had ventured into a forbidden topic. Charlotte hadn't indicated whether anyone other than Jeffrey and the midwife knew she was *enceinte*, and, in any case, it was unseemly for a woman to mention such a personal event to a man who was not part of the family.

Ethan's lips curved in another smile. "You mean by the time the child arrives?"

"Yes." A wave of relief washed over Abigail at the realization that she would not have to explain her sentence fragment. As a teacher, she insisted that her pupils speak in complete sentences, and normally she followed her own advice, but Charlotte's delicate condition was not a normal occurrence. "I wasn't certain whether anyone knew about Charlotte," she said, once again choosing not to be more explicit. "At home, no one would have discussed the upcoming event, but everything is so different here." She gestured toward the parade ground where the soldiers were still trying to capture the dogs and where the wind blew the flag straight out from the pole.

"So you've told me, more than once. As far as the child goes, Jeffrey practically shouted the news from the rooftops this morning. I've never seen him so excited." Ethan gave Abigail a crooked smile. "Almost as excited as you looked when you picked up that muddy ball of fur."

Abigail pretended to bristle. "I'll have you know that this muddy ball of fur, as you so rudely refer to him, is an adorable puppy."

Ethan held up his hands in mock surrender. "Is that adorable puppy . . ." He grinned as he pronounced the words. "I can't say it with a straight face, so let's start again. Is this little fellow your cure for boredom? You seem to think that everyone who lives in Wyoming must be bored."

Abigail hadn't thought of the puppy in those terms. If anything, she would have called him an answer to prayer, for she did not doubt that he'd been put in her path for a reason. "Perhaps he will be. What I do know is that everyone, regardless of their age, needs to play." Mama and Papa had set the example at each of the churches where Papa had been called to serve, organizing skating parties in the winter, croquet games in the summer, and long hikes during spring and fall. Even mud season, that unpleasant time when the snow was melting but flowers had yet to bloom, had been brightened by charades. Abigail would remind Charlotte of that when she gave her the dog.

She patted the top of the puppy's head, wondering whether the short fur would be soft once the mud was removed. "Charlotte—and maybe even Jeffrey—can play with him."

Ethan's eyebrows, which had settled down, rose again. "Somehow, I can't picture Jeffrey playing with a puppy."

Abigail couldn't either, but that mattered little. What was important was that Charlotte would have a companion when Abigail returned to Vermont. What was important right now was getting him to his new home and getting him cleaned up before Jeffrey arrived for dinner.

As Abigail turned and headed back, Ethan fell into step beside her. "You'll need to register him and, of course, make sure you keep him under control."

"Fortunately, the yard is fenced."

"But dogs have been known to dig under fences."

"True." Abigail looked down at the puppy, who had fallen asleep in her arms. Though he looked angelic now, she wouldn't vouch for his behavior once he wakened. "I'll buy a rope. I assume the sutler carries roping."

"Along with almost everything else you could want." Ethan nodded when they reached Charlotte's house. "Good day, Abigail, and good luck."

"Now, why would I need luck? I'd say both he and I are already lucky." Abigail nodded at the dog in her arms.

"Let's wait a week and see whether you still feel that way. Puppies can get into a lot of mischief."

"Not this one." Still laughing at Ethan's comical look, Abigail walked around the house to the back door. If she was fortunate, Mrs. Channing would not have arrived yet. Charlotte had said that the cook was a bit of a martinet and did not like having her routine disturbed. A puppy would be a disturbance to anyone's routine.

"Charlotte," Abigail called as she entered the rear hall, "come here. I have something to show you." Fortunately, there was no sign of the cook. At the sound of footsteps, the puppy wakened and began to wriggle in Abigail's arms, then gave out a sharp yip, as if greeting Charlotte.

Abigail felt her pulse accelerate as she waited for her sister's reaction. Would Charlotte think she was crazy, bringing a bedraggled puppy to her? After all, it had been many years since she had begged for one.

Charlotte's response was everything Abigail had hoped for. "A dog." She clasped her hands with childlike wonder, and a smile lit her face. "What on earth are you doing with a dog?" The hesitation in her voice told Abigail she was afraid to raise her expectations only to have them dashed.

"I couldn't bear to think of him being drowned," Abigail said when she'd explained what the soldiers were doing. "Besides, I hoped you'd enjoy his company. I told Ethan he was a belated Christmas gift." When tears filled Charlotte's eyes, Abigail wrinkled her nose and added, "A smelly gift." Carefully, she transferred the puppy to her sister, smiling at the way Charlotte held him at arm's length, then relented and let the little creature lick her face.

"Oh, Abigail, he's darling. Of course I'll keep him."

Charlotte stroked the puppy's head, grimacing when she noticed that her fingers were covered with dried mud. "But why does he smell so awful?"

"I found him rolling in a mud puddle."

"Oh, my. Well, a bit of soap and water will take care of that." Charlotte carried the puppy into the kitchen and nodded when Abigail reached for a kettle of water. "Even though it's summer, we should probably heat it a bit." Smiling at the wriggling ball of fur, she crooned, "First a bath, then we'll get you something to eat."

Abigail set the kettle on the flame and looked around for a pan to use as a bathtub. While it was larger than she would have liked, the washtub would have to do. No matter how cute he was, the dog was not going into a cooking pot.

She glanced at her sister as she dragged the tub into the center of the room. Charlotte beamed with happiness, validating Abigail's decision to save the puppy.

Charlotte looked down at her new pet. He'd started to squirm, and the contented yips turned to whimpers. "This little one needs a name. What do you think, Abigail? What shall I call him?"

Another whimper was followed by the sound of liquid hitting the floor. "Oh no!" Charlotte's pleasure turned to a cry of dismay and she held the dog away from her, trying to keep her previously immaculate cashmere skirt from being spattered.

"Puppies." Abigail grabbed a rag. "I'll clean up the puddle."

When the floor was once more dry, Charlotte studied the dog. "Mud puddles. Other kinds of puddles." She tipped her head to one side, considering. "That's it," she said, a smile of satisfaction lighting her face. "His name is Puddles."

"Perfect." If Abigail knew anything about dogs, this wouldn't be the last puddle the pup would leave in the house. She poured the now warm water into the tub and beckoned to Charlotte to give Puddles to her. "You might want to stand back," she cautioned. Unlike yesterday when Charlotte had been wearing a washable morning dress, today she had donned an elaborately trimmed gown. Though similar to the fashions Abigail had seen in *Godey's Lady's Book*, the lace trim and handmade buttons told her this was one of her sister's designs. Charlotte was a talented dressmaker. No question of that. The problem was, this particular gown was not suitable for bathing a dog.

As Abigail had expected, the puppy protested. Muddy water was fine. After all, that was his idea, but a bath was something else. As Abigail soaped his fur, Puddles barked and yipped, then began to howl, all the while struggling to escape from her grip.

"Won't Mrs. Channing be surprised when she sees him?" Charlotte asked from her perch on the bench, safely out of range of the now sodden puppy who looked as if he wanted nothing more than to shake every last drop from his coat. "Of course, she won't want him here in the kitchen. She'll probably threaten to quit, and then I'll be in trouble." Charlotte sighed. "Servants are almost impossible to find. No sooner does a woman get settled here than she's courted by every single man at the fort. This is definitely the place to be if you're looking for a husband."

"But I'm not." Abigail kept one hand firmly on Puddles's back as she started to soap his belly. Though he was a small animal, he wiggled so vigorously that she wished she could ask Charlotte for assistance, but she wouldn't risk ruining her sister's gown.

"Of course you're not looking for a husband." Charlotte nodded briskly. "Woodrow is a fine man, very sensible and down-to-earth. He'll make a good husband."

And he'd give Abigail what she'd longed for all her life, a permanent home. Woodrow shared not just Abigail's love of teaching but also her belief that the perfect life, the one God intended for them both, was to settle in one of the charming cottages within easy walking distance of the academy and raise their children there. But Woodrow was thousands of miles away. What was important now was getting Puddles clean.

Abigail pulled the puppy out of the water, holding him suspended over the tub while she rinsed him with water from a pitcher. "He'll have to be trained if you plan to keep him indoors." She wrapped Puddles in an old towel before handing him to Charlotte.

"I don't know anything about training dogs."

Abigail tried not to frown at the evidence that once again she'd been impulsive. She should have considered everything a dog needed before she rescued one. "I don't know much, either, so I guess we'll have to learn together."

"It'll be like old times." The smile on Charlotte's face told Abigail that any problems they encountered would be surmounted with laughter. That was good. That was very good.

"I thought I'd better warn you." Ethan found Jeffrey on his way to the hospital. Though Ethan had been less than pleased by the order to ensure that the canine problem was resolved, it was an easier task than his friend's. Today was Jeffrey's day to listen to the surgeon's complaints. It was the same each week. The doctor claimed that the enlisted men currently serving as nurses were negligent in their duties and required discipline. The men groused that the extra twenty cents a day pay they received was insufficient for the indignity of cleaning bedpans, not to mention the increased likelihood of contracting a communicable disease. Working in the bakeries, though unspeakably hot during the summer, was preferable to hospital duty, or so the men insisted. There was no way to resolve the problem other than to rotate men out of the hospital, but that had the predictable effect of causing the surgeon to complain that he had to train a fresh group.

"Is Dr. Pratt on the rampage again?" Jeffrey slowed his pace, as if grateful for an excuse to delay his meeting.

"Not that I heard. I just thought you should know that it appears you're going to have a new addition to your household."

Jeffrey grinned. "That's not news. If you recall, I told you that. Late October's when the child is expected."

Ethan suspected Jeffrey's grin would fade when he heard about the morning's events. "I wasn't referring to that addition. There's a four-footed one, and he came today."

As three dogs rounded the corner of the sutler's store and began to bark, Jeffrey frowned. "Not a dog. Say it isn't so."

"'Fraid I can't. Abigail decided to rescue a puppy. For some reason, she seemed to think your wife needed a pet."

"What Charlotte needs is one fewer sister." Jeffrey's frown turned into a scowl. "I can't explain it, but the first time I met Abigail, I knew I didn't like her. Have you ever felt that way?"

Ethan had. One of the other plebes had gotten under his skin the first year at the Point. He'd never been able to identify the reasons, but he'd gone out of his way to avoid the man. Still, it was hard to understand how Abigail could have affected Jeffrey that way.

"No matter what I do," Jeffrey continued, "I suspect we're stuck with Abigail for the rest of the summer. She told Charlotte she'd only be here for a couple weeks, but I don't believe her. Heaven only knows how much trouble she'll cause before she leaves." Jeffrey shook his head again. "A dog."

"It might not be so bad." Abigail's assertion that everyone needed to play continued to reverberate through Ethan's brain. Was that part of the men's discontent? Unlike the officers, enlisted men had little free time for play. Their days were filled with drilling and the much-hated fatigue duties. Though he didn't claim to be an expert, it seemed to Ethan that the officers' wives had the opposite problem—too much idle time. "I imagine life here is lonely for the women."

Jeffrey did not agree. "How can that be? It seems there's always something going on. If it isn't a tea party, they're organizing a sewing circle. You're wrong, Ethan." It was a measure of Jeffrey's distress that he used Ethan's given name in public. "Charlotte's not lonely. She does not need a dog, and she most definitely does not need Abigail. Everything was fine until she arrived." Jeffrey frowned. "There's got to be a way to stop Abigail from meddling."

He stared into the distance, as if the answer would come down the hill from the hospital, but all that came was a warm breeze. After a few seconds, Jeffrey snapped his fingers. "I've got an idea. You should start taking your meals with us, and maybe you could escort Abigail on a walk a couple times a week. That might keep her too busy to concoct a new scheme."

68

It might, but it sounded dangerously like courting. "I'm not interested in your matchmaking."

Jeffrey's eyes widened in what appeared to be genuine surprise. "It's not that. Heavens, no. The last thing I want is for you to marry Abigail. I'd never get rid of her if you did. Besides, you're safe. Charlotte says she's practically engaged to one of the other teachers at that girls' academy in Vermont."

Casual as they were, Jeffrey's words hit Ethan with the force of a mule's kick. It stood to reason that a woman as beautiful as Abigail would be spoken for. He shouldn't care—he didn't care—that Abigail had a sweetheart. After all, it wasn't as if he were searching for a wife. Oliver was the one who chased everything in a skirt. And yet there was no denying that Abigail was different from the other women Ethan had met.

Jeffrey was still talking, oblivious to the odd sensation in the pit of Ethan's stomach. "All I need is for you to occupy a bit of her time. Any time Abigail's with you is time she can't be making mischief." Jeffrey rolled his eyes and grimaced. "A dog. I won't even ask what could be next for fear it will happen."

"Think of it this way. Maybe a dog will keep both your wife and Abigail busy."

"C'mon, Ethan. I need your help. We West Pointers have to stick together. Besides, Mrs. Channing makes a fine roast."

That she did. And the truth was, spending time with Abigail would be no hardship. Unlike the women his grandfather had chosen for him, Abigail appeared capable of discussing matters other than ladies' fashions. She'd demonstrated strength on the stagecoach, and this morning had proven that underneath that cool exterior was a tenderhearted woman, one who cared for a little puppy and, unlike most of the females he had met, one who didn't mind a little mud on her clothing. No doubt about it. Abigail Harding was an intriguing woman.

"All right," Ethan agreed, "as long as you understand there's nothing romantic about it."

"Of course not." Jeffrey flashed him a triumphant grin. "Your heart is safe."

"You are the luckiest man alive." Without waiting for an invitation, Oliver settled himself in one of the chairs in Ethan's room and stretched his legs out before him.

Ethan stopped polishing his boots long enough to frown. "A lucky man wouldn't have to worry about his men deserting." Though the men had completed what he referred to as the canine detail without too much complaining, he couldn't forget how disgruntled they'd been at the thought of chasing packs of dogs, nor could he forget that two of his men had deserted last week. They were the reason he'd gone to Cheyenne.

"You need to stop worrying about them. If Captain Westland wanted you to worry about them, he wouldn't have assigned you to take care of the stray dogs."

And wasn't that a sorry state of affairs—rounding up dogs rather than deserters? While the captain's assertion that the desertion rate was far lower than it had been a year ago was accurate, Ethan couldn't stop thinking about Johann Schiller and the other man and wondering whether some of the soldiers under his command would be joining them. Schiller had deserted only a week after Ethan had arrived at Fort Laramie, but during that time he'd observed that the man was well-regarded by the others. Had his discontent poisoned them? Perhaps he had been in contact with Wessen and Kelly, the men who'd left last week, and that was the reason they had gone over the hill. If so, it was possible that others were getting ready to leave. It would be bad enough if there were more deserters, even worse if they started robbing stagecoaches.

Oliver rubbed his nose, a sure sign that he was excited. "Forget the deserters. What's important is that you're going to see Miss Harding twice a day, every day. I'd give anything to be in your boots."

Giving the boots in question a final buff, Ethan managed a grin. "The food will be better than our usual fare," he conceded.

"Food? Who cares about food? As long as it's not mushrooms, I'll eat anything. What I want is a wife."

"I hate to disappoint you, but if you're considering Miss Harding for that position, I hear she's practically engaged to some professor back home."

Oliver grimaced. "You just found something that turns my stomach more than mushrooms." Oliver clutched his midriff, feigning gastric distress. Then a smile split his face. "You said 'practically,' didn't you?" When Ethan nodded, Oliver's smile widened. "That means there's hope. If the man was foolish enough to let Miss Harding come all this way without him, he can't love her as much as I do."

"You haven't even met her."

Oliver would not be discouraged. "The moment I saw her, I knew she was the woman for me. Now all I need to do is figure out a way to afford a wife. Miss Harding deserves more than a second lieutenant's pay." Oliver leaned back and closed his eyes, as if the lack of visual distractions would improve his cogitation. "There's got to be a way."

And there had to be a way to improve morale enough that men wouldn't want to desert.

Ethan placed his soup spoon carefully on the plate and smiled at his hostess. There was no doubt about it. The food at the Crowley residence was far superior to that served to bachelor officers. As for the enlisted men's fare—the best that could be said about their rations was that a soldier didn't starve. But here a man didn't simply eat; he dined. Since the day was cooler than normal for June, Mrs. Channing had prepared a thick, creamy soup and served it with freshly baked bread. Delicious. The only thing that marred the meal was Mrs. Channing's frequent frowns, all of which seemed to be attributable to the puppy, whose barks made it clear he was not pleased with being relegated to a box in the hallway when the two-legged members of the household were elsewhere.

Ethan turned to his hostess. "It doesn't sound as if your dog is too happy."

"Didn't you hear?" Charlotte's smile was brighter than Ethan had ever seen it, confirming the wisdom of Abigail's seemingly impulsive action. "Whenever Puddles misbehaves, he's Abigail's dog."

As Abigail chuckled, Ethan gave her a smile. It wasn't his imagination. The chilly atmosphere that had filled this room yesterday was gone, replaced by what appeared to be genuine happiness. "Then I guess he's yours most of the time. Including right now."

Abigail shrugged. "He just wants someone to play with him. Think about it. We took him away from his littermates and the rest of the pack. Now he wants to join this pack."

Though Jeffrey appeared appalled by the description of his family as a pack, Ethan couldn't disagree with Abigail's assessment, especially since it dovetailed with the idea that had obsessed him since this morning.

"Do you agree, Jeffrey?" he asked. "Do you think everyone needs to play?" Though Jeffrey had no way of knowing it, his answer was critical to Ethan's plans.

Jeffrey took a sip of cool tea before he replied. "I hadn't really thought about it, but yes, I do believe everyone needs *some* play." His lips tightened as the puppy's barks turned to whimpers. "Not necessarily with a dog, though. So, Ethan, what did you have in mind? And don't pretend you haven't concocted some scheme. I can see it in your eyes."

Ethan had no intention of denying it. "I was thinking of a bat and ball, not a dog." Abigail's comments about boredom had haunted him, and when she'd spoken of the need for play, the idea had sprung into his mind. "I know some of the other forts have baseball teams," he continued. "From what I've heard, they're popular, probably because they give the men something to do with their free time."

Abigail's eyes sparkled almost as much as they had when she'd rescued Puddles. "That might lessen your desertion rate."

Exactly. "I have to admit that was part of my motive. I wouldn't want anyone at Fort Laramie to be bored." Ethan stressed the final word and was pleased when Abigail laughed. She might have found the stagecoach ride and the countryside boring, but she showed no sign of ennui now.

"Then Charlotte and I will have to watch the games, won't

we?" Abigail gave her sister a fond smile as she added, "Can't you picture Puddles's excitement?"

When Charlotte nodded, Ethan's spirits rose another notch. There was only one more person to convince. "What about you, Jeffrey? Would you be willing to be the captain of a team?" Though Ethan was confident his company would like the idea, they needed an opponent.

Jeffrey's grin was almost as wide as it had been this morning when he had announced his son's impending arrival. "And have the opportunity to trounce you? You bet!"

"Oh, my dear, you must tell us all about your ordeal." Mrs. Montgomery, the taller of the two women who'd come to visit Charlotte, peered over the top of her spectacles. If she minded that her hostess had disappeared into the kitchen to order tea for them, she gave no signal, but addressed her conversation to Abigail. "I was simply appalled when I heard you'd ridden that stagecoach all alone."

"Now, Adele, she wasn't alone," the second woman, who'd been introduced as Mrs. Alcott, said. "Lieutenant Bowles was on the coach." She gave Abigail a sly smile. "You couldn't have asked for a better traveling companion. Why, Lieutenant Bowles is the most eligible bachelor at the fort."

Abigail nodded slowly as she chose her words. Whatever she said, she did not want to give these women, who appeared to devour gossip as Puddles had the dried ends of the roast, any misconceptions. It was true that Ethan's company was pleasant and that she enjoyed his ready sense of humor as well as his obvious concern for his men, but that didn't mean Abigail cared about him romantically. She did not. It was Woodrow she loved, not a man who'd never have a permanent home, not a man who wore a gun and was trained to kill.

"I was thankful Lieutenant Bowles was there," Abigail told her sister's guests. "I don't know what would have happened to the other passengers and me otherwise." When she closed her eyes, she could still picture the German-speaking deserter's malevolence.

"Who else was on the coach?" Mrs. Alcott asked.

As Abigail named the other passengers, Mrs. Montgomery raised an eyebrow. Tall and what Mama would call statuesque, though Abigail would have applied the adjective "plump," Mrs. Montgomery appeared to believe that her carrot-red hair and green eyes were best complemented by flamboyant clothing. That was the only reason Abigail could imagine that she had chosen a peacock blue dress. In contrast, her companion's demure cream-colored muslin appeared almost mousy. "Mrs. Hiram Dunn?" Mrs. Montgomery asked.

"I don't believe she mentioned her husband's name. All I know is that they owned a ranch north of here and that she's been widowed for a few years."

"Then that's not Mrs. Hiram Dunn. He was a miner who struck it rich at Deadwood and settled in Cheyenne. It's odd, though." Furrows appeared between Mrs. Montgomery's brows. "I thought I knew all the ranchers in this part of the territory. You see, my husband is considering settling here once his commitment is over, so he's taken it on himself to learn who's who among the ranchers. I don't recall any Dunns, though."

Mrs. Alcott intervened. "It's of no importance, Adele. What matters is that Abigail is here, and we need to welcome her to Fort Laramie properly. I think we should hold a dance in her honor. That will give all the men a chance to meet her."

Where was Charlotte when she needed her? Abigail smiled as sweetly as she could, addressing her reply to both women, though she sensed that Mrs. Montgomery was the dominant one. "It's very kind of you to offer, but it would be unfair to give anyone the impression that I'm . . ." She paused, once again searching for the right word. At last she settled on *available*. "When I return to Vermont, I expect to be betrothed to one of my colleagues."

Mrs. Montgomery gave a small harrumph. "My dear, it's only a dance." As Charlotte entered the parlor carrying the tea tray, Mrs. Montgomery smiled. "Isn't that right, Charlotte?"

Charlotte nodded. "The enlisted men will have their baseball games, and we'll have a dance. It's perfect." Lifting the teapot, Charlotte filled a cup and handed it to Mrs. Montgomery. "Now, ladies, what do you think would be the best date?"

5

Abigail smiled. What else could she do, when Puddles sat at her sister's feet, gnawing on a bone and occasionally giving her adoring looks, looks that Charlotte returned? In the three days since the puppy had become part of the family, Charlotte had regained much of her sparkle. She laughed at Puddles's antics, did not complain when the puppy chewed one of her favorite slippers, and had somehow placated Mrs. Channing when Puddles refused to remain in the wooden crate that was supposed to be his bed. Charlotte had even managed to eat a normal breakfast this morning, and though it would take weeks for the hollows in her cheeks to disappear, at least today her face had a rosy hue.

As if she sensed her sister's scrutiny, Charlotte looked up. As soon as they'd finished breakfast, she and Abigail had repaired to the parlor, planning to finish their sewing before the day's heat made having extra yards of fabric draped over one's lap unpleasant. "Do you think Elizabeth would like living here?"

Abigail blinked, surprised by the question. She had written their sister a letter yesterday, trying to make Wyoming sound appealing but feared she had failed. "I don't know. She seems to like New York. Even though her studies keep her busy, I think she enjoys city life."

"Cheyenne's a city."

"That's true." Abigail stared at her sister. "Why are you asking this?"

"Because it's wonderful having you here, and I was trying to figure out a way to get all three of us together." A wistful smile crossed Charlotte's face.

Abigail couldn't let her sister continue. "You don't honestly think I'd stay here permanently, do you?"

Shaking her head, Charlotte said, "I know it's just a dream and that your place is back in Vermont with Woodrow, but it would be nice."

Abigail fingered the petticoat she was hemming while Charlotte put the finishing touches on Abigail's dress for the dance. "I'm not like you, Charlotte. I don't want to live somewhere where the wind howls every day. I don't want to move every year or two. I want a home of my own."

Charlotte nodded shortly. "I understand." She clipped a thread, then rose, holding the dress she'd been sewing in front of her. "What do you think?"

"It's beautiful." Abigail fingered the dark green muslin that had been nothing more than an ordinary summer frock two days ago. Now, thanks to her sister's talented needle and the judicious application of lace, it was a ball gown. "It's truly amazing how different it looks." Charlotte had lowered the neckline, declaring the original one frumpy, but had acceded to Abigail's desire for modesty by adding a lace insertion to the bodice. Then, in what Abigail considered sheer genius, her sister had appliquéd medallions from the remaining lace onto the skirt. The result was the loveliest gown Abigail had ever owned. "You have a real gift," she told her sister. "I would never have thought that a bit of lace would turn a plain dress into something so pretty."

Though Charlotte's eyes sparkled at the praise, she said only, "Mama used to claim I had an eye for fashion."

"She was right. It's a wonderful talent." Puddles barked, as if agreeing.

Charlotte draped the dress over a chair. "Let's go to the sutler's store and see if we can find a gift for Elizabeth. If she can't be with us, at least she'll know we're thinking about her."

With Puddles firmly attached to his leash and jumping with apparent glee as the women led him out the front door, Abigail and Charlotte descended the steps. "Let's take the long way," Charlotte said, gesturing to the right. "It's such a nice day."

It was a pretty day. The wind was gentle, at least by Wyoming standards, and did not threaten to blow Abigail's hat away, and several puffy cumulus clouds drifted across a sky that was almost as deep a blue as Ethan's eyes. Abigail nodded. Though she'd accompanied Charlotte on several walks, they had always gone the opposite direction, retracing the route Abigail had taken when she arrived.

As they rounded the corner, Puddles strained at the leash,

trying to reach the wagon loaded with freshly cut lumber and six disgruntled-looking soldiers that was making its way toward the site where the administration building was taking shape. "No, Puddles. The men can't play."

That elicited a chuckle from the men. "Well, ma'am," one said with a grin, "that would be a sight better than cutting trees. I shore didn't think this was what I'd be doin' when I signed up for the Army."

When they were out of earshot, Abigail turned to her sister. "I didn't want to hurt the men's feelings, but I think Puddles was more interested in the wood than in them. He seems to be attracted by smells." Abigail had noticed that when she opened a jar of pickles and again when she dabbed toilet water on her wrists. In both cases, Puddles had bounded to her side, his nose twitching.

"There are even more smells here," Charlotte said as they passed a long adobe building. "This is one of the infantry barracks. The other ones are on the far side of the parade ground."

Abigail had seen the buildings from Charlotte's house, but a closer look revealed the gap between officers' and enlisted men's housing. There was no doubt the Army had a caste system. While Charlotte's home boasted many amenities, these edifices were almost spartan. No wonder the enlisted men were resentful enough to desert.

Ethan and Jeffrey had reported that the men had been excited by the prospect of playing baseball and had exhibited friendly rivalry as they'd decided who would play each position. At the time Abigail had wondered whether part of the reason for the men's enthusiasm was that the rules about fraternization were relaxed for sports, with officers and enlisted men playing together. Now she wondered if they looked forward to an opportunity to demonstrate their superiority, if only on the ball field.

"I wouldn't want to live there," she said as she looked at the barracks.

Charlotte laughed. "It's not just the barracks or even Wyoming. You never wanted anything to do with soldiers. I remember that you'd run away when the boys played war games at recess. The rest of the girls used to watch."

But the rest of the girls had not seen what could happen when boys played soldier with their fathers' rifles.

Abigail tried not to shudder as the memories washed over her. Instead, she did what Papa had always advised: she tried to think of something more pleasant. "What kind of gift did you have in mind for Elizabeth?"

Charlotte shrugged. "I'm not sure. We'll have to see what the sutler has."

When Puddles plopped himself in front of her and refused to move, Charlotte bent down and scratched his head. Apparently mollified, the puppy began to scamper again. "Silly dog. Now, what was I saying? Gifts. Jeffrey and I gave his siblings canned oysters for Christmas, and they seemed to enjoy them." Charlotte's brow furrowed. "From the little he's said, I've gathered that the family had a difficult time when Jeffrey was a child. There was rarely enough food for all of them—Jeffrey has eight brothers and sisters—and he told me he'd never received a gift at Christmas. I think that's why he was so happy to be able to buy something for all of them."

And that would explain why he insisted on Charlotte having the best of everything.

They'd reached the corner of the parade ground. If they continued straight, the road led toward the bakery, the commissary, and what everyone called Suds Row, the laundresses' homes. Charlotte started to turn left to continue circling the parade ground, but Abigail's attention was caught by two women approaching from the other direction. Their hair was the brightest blonde she had ever seen, and the flamboyant colors of their dresses would have made Mama wince.

"Come on." Frowning, Charlotte grabbed Abigail's arm and pivoted on her heel, heading back toward her house.

"What about the sutler?"

"We'll go when *they* aren't there." Charlotte's frown deepened. "No decent woman would be in the same room with them, but just you watch. Some of the men will follow them." Charlotte glanced at the company of soldiers drilling on the parade ground, as if she expected them to break formation and run after the women. "I don't understand why the Army lets them onto the fort. It's bad enough that they work at Peg's Place, selling whiskey and . . ."

Charlotte's face reddened, perhaps with anger, perhaps embarrassment. Though she clamped her lips together and refused to pronounce the final word, Abigail knew exactly how the women earned their living.

Frances uncorked the bottle and splashed some of the amber liquid into a glass. The whiskey might not be as good as some she'd drunk when the troupe had been on tour, but it was decidedly better than the stuff served on the opposite side of the building. This back room where she waited for her visitor was off-limits to all but the high rollers. Not that this one would be rolling any dice today. Today was all business—their other business.

"You told me there weren't going to be any Army personnel on that coach." Frances almost laughed at the man's confusion. He'd probably expected some sort of greeting, but she'd learned it was best to open with a sally, letting your opponent see that you held the upper hand. You'd have thought the Army would have taught him that, but he appeared unprepared for her attack.

"Bowles wasn't supposed to come back for another day. How was I supposed to know he'd be bored in Cheyenne?"

The beads of perspiration dotting the man's forehead bore witness to his discomfort. Good. He deserved to be uncomfortable. The baron had certainly made her uncomfortable when he'd heard about the stagecoach fiasco.

"You're paid to know." Frances took another sip of whiskey, watching the man's unease grow. Enough. She needed him almost as much as he needed her. "Want a drink?" She poured a generous quantity into a second glass and pushed it toward him. As he drank greedily, she adopted a friendly tone. "We need a replacement for Schiller. He's useless until his hand heals, and I don't want to wait that long. The baron's getting anxious. We need another soldier to go over the hill."

"I don't know. I haven't heard of anyone planning to desert."

Frances let out a sigh. "It's not likely they'll tell you, is it? You'd be honor bound to report them, and then where would they be? Locked up in that guardhouse. But you've got to know who's unhappy. It's mighty hard to hide that. Just give me a couple names. I'll take care of the rest."

The man shook his head, and for a moment Frances

thought he would refuse, but then he downed the rest of his whiskey. When he'd wiped his lips, he muttered two names, keeping his eyes on the table as he pronounced them. "Is that all?" he asked.

"Yes." For now.

The man shoved his chair back and bolted from the room, his gait revealing his anger. Frances waited until the door closed behind him before she laughed. He might not like it, but he was caught as surely as a trout with a hook in its mouth. Perfect.

To Abigail's relief, Saturday was sunny and warm, windier than she would have liked, but not oppressively hot. The worst heat, Charlotte warned her, would come during July. Since June in Wyoming had already proven to be considerably hotter than Vermont, Abigail was glad that she would be leaving right after Independence Day.

When they reached their destination, Abigail discovered that the house where the dance would be held was similar to Charlotte and Jeffrey's, a large building divided into two residences. Located on the west side of the parade ground close to the bachelor officers' quarters, the post surgeon's house, and the sutler's store, it appeared to be a few years older than Charlotte's house, but the rooms were larger. The majority of the furniture had been removed from the parlor to provide space for dancing, leaving only a few chairs around the perimeter for those who tired of the exercise.

"Come see what we have in store for you." Mrs. Montgomery, who'd been waiting inside the house, gestured toward the dining room, where the table was laden with silver platters covered with what appeared to be a variety of cakes and cookies and a large punch bowl. An epergne filled with fresh flowers formed the centerpiece, flanked by heavy cut-glass candlesticks. It was a surprisingly elegant setting, and, though she was almost two thousand miles away, Abigail could have imagined herself back in Vermont, were it not for the wind howling outside. Her two hostesses wore heavy satin dresses that would not have been out of place in Boston, complemented by two of the elaborate hairstyles depicted in Frank Leslie's *Gazette of Fashion*. "It's beautiful. I feel honored to be here."

"We're pleased to have you with us." Mrs. Alcott smoothed her light blue skirts. "Tonight is, after all, special."

And it was. Mrs. Alcott's parlor was soon crowded with so many people that Abigail wondered how they would manage to dance. Though Charlotte had told her there were only seventeen officers at the fort, and at least one of them had not arrived, the room was filled. The wives, dressed in their finest, mingled with the bachelors, while Mrs. Montgomery and Mrs. Alcott stood at the entrance to the parlor, introducing Abigail to each newcomer. Though she knew she'd never recall their names, what she would remember was the genuinely warm welcome each one offered her. Young or middle-aged, male or female—it didn't seem to matter. They all made Abigail feel as if her visit would be one of the highlights of their summer. She spoke briefly with each one, forcing herself to keep her attention focused on the person she was greeting, and yet in the brief interval between conversations, she glanced around the room, searching for the one familiar face she had expected.

He was not here.

Abigail bit back her disappointment. Though she couldn't explain how it had happened, in the few days that she had been at Fort Laramie, Ethan had become an important part of her life. He had begun to take meals with the family, and while it might be disloyal, she found his conversation more stimulating than that of her sister or Jeffrey. They had all discussed the dance—indeed, it seemed to be Charlotte's primary topic of conversation, eclipsing even Puddles—but Abigail could not recall Ethan saying that he planned to attend. She had simply assumed that he would be here. And he was not.

"I think we're ready to start dancing." Mrs. Alcott looked at the small clock hanging on the wall. It was a quarter past eight, time for the evening's festivities to begin.

Abigail nodded and started to turn, but the sound of boot steps in the hallway made her pause. He had come after all.

"Good evening, Abigail." Ethan removed his cap and inclined his head toward his companion. A couple inches taller than Ethan, the man had brown hair, light blue eyes, and the longest nose Abigail had seen. "This young man would like to meet you," Ethan continued. "May I present Second Lieutenant Oliver Seton? Oliver, this is Miss Abigail Harding."

A rush of color flooded the man's face. "I'm pleased to meet you, Miss Harding. Will you do me the honor of sharing the first dance with me?"

Abigail looked down at the dance card Charlotte had insisted she carry. "I'm sorry, but that one is already spoken for." Jeffrey had insisted on accompanying her for the opening dance, claiming that Charlotte needed to rest. "I am, however, free for the third dance." As she inscribed his name on her card, the lieutenant grinned, his thin face still flushed with what appeared to be embarrassment.

"May I have the fourth?"

"Certainly." Abigail nodded at Ethan.

By the time the third dance ended, the room was over-crowded and overheated and the sounds of a dozen different conversations made it difficult to hear the musicians. Yet, despite the less-than-perfect conditions, the guests appeared to be having a good time, even those men who wore handker-chiefs tied around their upper arms to indicate that they were taking the women's role. That was, Charlotte had explained, common practice, since men outnumbered women at the post. "There'd be little dancing, otherwise," she had said.

"Would you prefer to spend this dance outdoors?" Ethan asked when he reached Abigail's side. Lieutenant Seton, who'd insisted he would be honored if she called him Oliver, though he would not be so presumptuous as to employ her given name, had tried to convince Ethan to give up his dance but had met with a stern rebuke.

"If you hadn't insisted on polishing your boots a second time, we would have been here on time," Ethan told the lieu-tenant as he placed Abigail's hand on his arm. "You could have asked Miss Harding for another dance then. Now her card is probably full."

It was, but that gave Abigail less pleasure than the knowl-edge that Ethan had not been reluctant to come this evening. And, though she'd been looking forward to dancing with him, some quiet time outside now held more appeal.

"I'd be glad to go outdoors, if you don't mind," she told him.

Ethan favored her with one of the grins she liked so much. "Not at all. Bumping into other people in a hot room is not my favorite pastime." Like her, he had had partners for the first three dances, and beads of perspiration dotted his forehead. "In fact, bumping into people whether the room is hot or cold is not something I particularly enjoy."

Abigail chuckled as he opened the door to usher her onto the porch. Though the wind continued to blow, the house protected this side of the porch, making it a pleasant spot.

"My grandfather insisted that I learn to dance," Ethan continued, "but I have to admit I've never enjoyed it. You and Charlotte, however, appear to relish it." Despite Jeffrey's claim that his wife needed to rest, Ethan had shared the first dance with Charlotte, whirling her around with such enthusiasm that Charlotte had laughed out loud. Now he leaned back against the railing, facing Abigail, looking as if nothing was more important than her response.

"Perhaps it's because dancing is still a novelty for us. Charlotte and I learned how less than two years ago." When Ethan raised an eyebrow, encouraging her to continue, Abigail did. "Our father believed that dancing was temptation sent by the devil. Mama didn't agree, but out of respect for him, none of us danced while he was alive."

"He sounds like some of the preachers I've met."

"He was a preacher." Though Ethan's eyes widened in apparent surprise, Abigail smiled, remembering her father. "Papa was a brilliant man. His faith in God was strong, and he knew how to share that faith with others. Mama used to tell us that many people claimed Papa's sermons were the best they'd ever heard and that he'd been blessed with the ability to make complex subjects seem simple."

Abigail stared into the distance for a moment, watching the wind chase clouds across the sky. Though the sun had set, the moon was large enough to light the sky. "All that was good, but Papa could also be dogmatic. When he was convinced he was right, he wouldn't listen to others' views. Although I was too young to realize it at the time, I suspect that's the reason we moved so often—that he antagonized congregations with his strong views. As it was, it seemed that we lived in a different town every year until I was sixteen."

"That must have been difficult." A hint of sympathy colored Ethan's voice, and Abigail wondered whether he understood how much a child—at least the child she had been—craved permanence.

"I hated it. We'd just get settled, and then we'd move. It felt as if I was always getting used to a new house and a new school. The worst was having to make new friends. If it hadn't been for my sisters, I don't know what I'd have done."

Ethan's eyes darkened with an emotion she hoped was not pity. She welcomed sympathy but didn't want pity. "As you know, I have no experience with siblings, but the part about frequent moves sounds a bit like the Army. It can be difficult until you get used to it."

"That's one of the reasons I was surprised when Charlotte married Jeffrey. I thought she hated the impermanence of our childhood as much as I did. It appears I was wrong." The change in Charlotte's mood since Abigail had arrived, coupled with her comments about wanting all three of them reunited, made Abigail suspect that the problems she had sensed from Charlotte's letters were caused by loneliness, and that was something Abigail understood. As much as she enjoyed teaching at Miss Drexel's, she missed her sisters.

Ethan raised his eyebrows slightly. "Perhaps Charlotte's feelings for Jeffrey were strong enough to overcome the obstacles. Or perhaps she's like many of us and considers seeing new places an adventure."

"Is that why you went to West Point, for an adventure?"

"Not really. As a child, I wanted to be like my father. He was a soldier, so I decided to be one too. I figured that the best way to do that was to attend the academy." Though his words were light, Ethan's expression told her there was more to the story, and—judging from the shadows Abigail saw in his eyes—it wasn't all happy.

"Your father must be very proud of you."

Ethan shook his head. "My father was killed in the war. I'm not sure he even knew I was born."

And yet, even knowing that he too might be killed, Ethan had volunteered. Abigail didn't pretend to understand that. What she did understand was that his father's death would have left a hole in Ethan's life. "I'm sorry." It was inadequate, but Abigail wasn't certain what else to say. Her family's frequent moves seemed trivial compared to the loss Ethan had sustained. "Did your mother marry again?"

Ethan's face turned to an impassive mask. "She died when I was less than one, leaving me to be raised by her father."

That must be why Jeffrey had spoken of Ethan's grandfather. He was the sole parent Ethan had known. Abigail could only hope that he'd been a loving one, and yet she doubted that, for Ethan had said his grandfather would not have ransomed him. At the time, she had been shocked by the statement, but she hadn't realized its full significance. Now she wondered if his relationship with his grandfather had contributed to Ethan's decision to become a soldier.

Her consternation must have been reflected on her face, for Ethan said brusquely, "Let's talk about something more pleasant. Why don't you tell me about the school where you teach."

Though her heart ached for Ethan, Abigail recognized the wisdom of his request. The dance would end soon. It would be best if they could return to the party with smiles on their faces, and so she said, "Miss Drexel's is a small girls' school in Wesley, Vermont. Normally we have no more than forty pupils. The founder had dreams of having a hundred girls, but forty is all the house can hold."

As the wind whistled, Ethan raised an eyebrow. "It must be a large house if it can accommodate that many children, plus the teachers and classrooms."

Abigail walked to the edge of the porch and gestured toward the large white building that had formerly served as bachelor officers' quarters. Nicknamed "Old Bedlam" because of the raucous parties the men had held, it was one of the oldest buildings on the fort. "It's smaller than Old Bedlam, but it is three stories high and made of marble."

"Marble?" Ethan's eyebrow rose another quarter of an inch. "That sounds ostentatious."

Abigail would hear no criticism of the place that had given her both a home and an occupation. "That's no more ostentatious than using lime grout here. There's a marble quarry only a few miles away from Wesley, making that one of the least expensive building materials."

"I stand corrected. I should never have challenged a schoolmarm." Ethan gave her a teasing look, his earlier sadness if not forgotten at least hidden. "So, what do you teach, besides building techniques?"

"English, German, and French, although I've had to handle other subjects when one of my colleagues was ill."

"How many colleagues are there?"

"We're five in total. Mr. Barnett is our headmaster. His

wife teaches art and music. Miss Thayer is our arithmetic teacher, and Woodrow is in charge of history and geography."

"Woodrow?"

Abigail felt the blood rise to her cheeks at the realization that she had referred to him so informally. "Mr. Morgan," she corrected.

Ethan's smile faded. Surely it wasn't the fact that she'd called Woodrow by his name. After all, she called him Ethan. "He must be the one Jeffrey mentioned, the one you'll probably marry."

Abigail tried not to frown. Though she had told the other women about her expected betrothal, somehow it didn't seem appropriate that Jeffrey had mentioned it to Ethan. But now that the subject had been introduced, there was no point in denying it.

"That's Woodrow," she said firmly.

What a fool he was! Why had he asked all those questions, practically forcing Abigail to speak of Woodrow? He'd been so anxious to avoid speaking of Grandfather that he'd thought any other subject would be preferable. He'd been wrong. Now he had the memories of the sparkle in Abigail's eyes when she pronounced the man's name and the certainty in her voice as she'd confirmed that Woodrow Morgan, professor of history and geography, was the man she intended to marry.

The thought shouldn't have rankled. It was only because he'd been out of sorts this evening, first because Oliver had made them late, then because the conversation had turned to Grandfather, that he was bothered about Woodrow Morgan, but he was, and so after he escorted Abigail back to the dancing, Ethan returned to the porch, hoping that the cool evening air would clear his head. It did not.

Swallowing deeply, Ethan stepped off the porch and made his way to the rear entrance. His throat was so dry that he needed something to drink, even if only the sweet punch the ladies seemed to think was the proper beverage for a dance.

"She's more beautiful than I imagined." Oliver's appearance at Ethan's side dashed his hope for solitude. Though the rest of the assembly remained in the parlor, awaiting their hostesses' signal to gather in the dining room for refreshments, Oliver must have spotted Ethan. For once, the young lieutenant appeared to have no interest in food and ignored Ethan's suggestion that he pour himself a cup of punch. Instead, Oliver continued to wax eloquent about the guest of honor. "She's beautiful. Polite too. Why, she never once said anything about my nose."

Ethan forbore suggesting that no well-bred woman would embarrass a man by alluding to a physical imperfection, just as he would tell neither Mrs. Montgomery nor Mrs. Alcott that the punch would have benefited from less sugar.

"She dances better than any partner I've ever had. While she was in my arms, I thought I'd died and gone to heaven." Oliver continued the litany of praise. "I tell you, Ethan, she's the perfect woman. You'll see what I mean when you fall in love."

Enough. Ethan had had enough of the sickeningly sweet punch and enough of Oliver's sermons. "Save your breath, Oliver. No matter how many times you tell me about Eve and the animals in the ark, it won't make any difference. As for love—that's for the poets." He spun on his heel, anxious to leave.

Oliver followed, talking all the while. "That's what they all say, just before they fall. I tell you, Ethan . . ."

"And I tell you, enough is enough."

But though he tried to dismiss Oliver's words, they continued to reverberate through his brain. Love. His grandfather had told him about love the day he'd discovered the cook's granddaughter was visiting. A few years younger than Ethan's ten years, she was in Ethan's estimation the most beautiful creature on Earth, with long blonde braids and eyes a deeper blue than the bluebells the gardener claimed had been Ethan's mother's favorite flower.

"Nonsense, my boy. You're not in love. Love is a delusion poor people indulge in," Grandfather had announced when Ethan had declared that he loved little Hilda. "It's their excuse for marriage. We know better. Marriage is designed to strengthen alliances."

"Is that why you married my grandmother?" Ethan had seen the daguerreotypes of his grandparents on their wedding day. They both looked so solemn that he had no trouble believing they had never felt the way he did about Hilda.

Grandfather took no offense at the question. "Of course. Her father owned the largest coal mine in Pennsylvania, and my railroad needed that coal."

Though he was old enough to have known the folly of asking Grandfather questions he didn't want to answer, Ethan had blurted out the one that had been on the tip of his tongue ever since he'd discovered there were no pictures of his father in the big old house that made Grandfather so proud. "Why did my father marry my mother?"

Grandfather had clenched his hands around his cane, and his face had turned such a deep red that Ethan wondered if he was ill. "Your father . . ." He spat the words, turning them into an epithet. "Your father wanted to get my money. He tricked Veronica into marrying him, using the oldest of traps." At the time, Ethan hadn't understood what Grandfather meant, but as he'd grown older and listened to servants' gossip more carefully, he'd learned that his mother had been expecting a child—him—when she and Father married.

"His scheme didn't work," Grandfather had sputtered. "That despicable cur never got a penny of mine. I saw to that, even before he ran off and joined the Army. He claimed he was going to make the world a better place. Hah! The world was a better place the day some Rebel had the good sense to put a musket ball through Stephen Bowles's heart."

When he'd left Grandfather's house for the last time, Ethan had decided that, in addition to his other sins, his grandfather was a hypocrite. How dare he condemn Ethan's father for marrying for money—if that was what he had done—when he himself had married for coal? How dare he try to expunge all memories of his daughter's marriage, as if Veronica Wilson had never become Veronica Bowles? And how dare he demand that Ethan bear his own name rather than be known as a Bowles?

Though he'd dreamed of confronting his grandfather, Ethan had known it would accomplish nothing. Grandfather would simply tell him he was mistaken or, even worse, he would ignore him. And so Ethan had bided his time, taking advantage of the fact that no one would connect his real name with Curtis Wilson, the railroad magnate whose reputation caused ordinary men to tremble. By the time Ethan had been accepted at the Military Academy, there was nothing Grandfather could do.

6

Abigail wakened to the sound of retching. Grabbing her wrapper, she hurried to Charlotte's room, heedless of her bare feet, and found her sister bent over the chamber pot.

"What can I do to help?" Either some of the refreshments at the party had not agreed with Charlotte, or she was having a relapse of her morning sickness. Abigail hoped it was the former. Since her sister had not been ill since she arrived, both she and Charlotte had believed that Charlotte had finally passed that stage of her pregnancy.

"Shall I brew some peppermint tea?" Abigail asked. There had to be something she could do to help, and Charlotte had agreed that the herbal infusion had steadied her stomach the first time she'd drunk it.

Charlotte looked up, her face so gaunt and lined with pain that anyone who didn't know her true age would have believed her ten years older. "Just the thought of anything in

97

my stomach makes me ill." She wiped her mouth and put the cover on the chamber pot. As she struggled to rise, Abigail slipped an arm around her shoulders and guided her back into bed. Though Jeffrey might have helped, he had left soon after the bugles announced reveille, his boots clattering on the stairs as he'd headed for the company's dress inspection. It was, Charlotte had told Abigail, a weekly event and the reason worship services were not held until afternoon.

"There is something you can do." Charlotte's voice was weak and thready as she leaned against her pillow. "Fetch Mrs. Grayson."

Abigail tried to hide her alarm. Though she had not seen Charlotte's previous bouts of morning sickness, today's must be much worse than usual if she wanted the midwife to visit. "Of course."

Within minutes, Abigail had gotten directions to Mrs. Grayson's home and had dressed. Though she hated leaving Charlotte, even for the time it would take to summon the midwife, there was no alternative. Descending the stairs, Abigail found Puddles sitting at the bottom, whining in obvious distress that his legs were still too short to climb the stairs. Impulsively, she gathered him into her arms and carried him to Charlotte. At least if Puddles was there, her sister would not be alone.

"He knows something is wrong," she told Charlotte, "and he wants to be with you."

"All right." But there was no enthusiasm in Charlotte's voice. That was not a good sign.

"I admit that I'm concerned," Mrs. Grayson told Abigail half an hour later. Her examination had taken less time than

Abigail had expected, and now the older woman sat in the parlor, drinking a cup of coffee. A few inches shorter than Abigail, the sergeant's wife who served as a midwife to the women at the fort was at least forty pounds heavier, and though her brown hair was not yet streaked with gray, her demeanor was that of an older woman. Perhaps her profession had aged her.

"It looks like morning sickness. I've never seen a case where it lasted this long, but I've heard it can happen." Mrs. Grayson drained the cup, then nodded when Abigail offered to refill it.

When Abigail returned with a fresh cup of the steaming beverage, she took a seat opposite the midwife and leaned forward. There was no reason to mask her worries, for Mrs. Grayson shared them. "I told Charlotte this wasn't normal, but she insisted it wasn't serious. What can we do?"

"I can't say for certain, but today's sickness may be the result of being overly excited last night. That wouldn't bother most women, but Charlotte cannot afford to take any chances." Mrs. Grayson laid the cup on the small table and looked directly at Abigail, her brown eyes radiating concern. "I wouldn't say this to your sister, but I'm afraid she may lose the baby if this continues. She keeps losing strength, and that's not good for her or the baby."

As she recalled Charlotte's animation the previous evening and the way she'd whirled around the dance floor, Abigail found it difficult to reconcile that image with the woman who could barely hold her head up this morning.

Mrs. Grayson took another sip of coffee. "I want your sister to remain in bed for a week. Give her bland food and ensure there are no disturbances."

"What about the puppy? He might cheer her." When

Abigail had returned, she had found Charlotte asleep, Puddles cradled in her arms. Though Mrs. Grayson had frowned at the sight of a dog on the bed, Abigail was encouraged by the fact that her sister slept.

The midwife tipped her head to one side, considering. "It probably won't hurt, but I'd advise you to limit the creature's time with her, especially since he's not yet trained. And if your sister appears to be tiring, take him away. It's vital that she regain her strength." Mrs. Grayson rose and headed toward the kitchen. "I'll speak to Mrs. Channing about suitable foods."

When the midwife had left and Mrs. Channing had promised to listen for any signs that Charlotte might have wakened, Abigail retrieved the now rambunctious puppy. She might as well take him with her while she told Jeffrey what had occurred. The walk would help wear off some of Puddles's energy.

"Abigail, what are you doing here?" Jeffrey looked up from the report he was reading, his nose wrinkling with displeasure at the sight of the puppy. "And why did you bring that mutt?"

"I'm sorry, but I didn't want to leave him with Mrs. Channing."

"Charlotte could have—"

"No, Charlotte could not." Care for the dog, or even descend the stairs. Abigail had tried to think of a gentle way to break the news to Jeffrey, but she found herself bristling at his peremptory tone, and so she did not mince her words. "Charlotte is very ill."

The blood drained from Jeffrey's face, leaving his freckles in stark relief against his pale skin. "But she was fine last night."

Her brother-in-law's obvious distress caused Abigail to soften her voice. "That was last night. This morning, she's so weak that she asked me to fetch Mrs. Grayson. She's ordered a week's bed rest for Charlotte."

"Bed rest. That hasn't happened before." The slight trembling in Jeffrey's voice told Abigail he appreciated the gravity of the situation. "Charlotte's got to get better. She has to." Furrows appeared between his eyes as another thought assailed him. "What about the baby?"

Abigail almost sighed with relief that Jeffrey's first thought had been for his wife. Charlotte's fears that Jeffrey loved her only because she would carry his children were unfounded.

"The baby's all right at this point," Abigail said, "but Mrs. Grayson doesn't want to take any chances. That's why she's insisting Charlotte have no disturbances." As she had walked around the parade ground and seen the men in formation, Abigail's thoughts had turned to the tall blond soldier who made mealtime so pleasant. "Would you explain to Ethan that our meals will be very simple and that it would be better if he not come to the house at this time?"

"Of course." Jeffrey was silent for a moment. "Charlotte should be Mrs. Channing's only concern. Ethan and I will eat with the other officers." He stared into the distance for a moment, his jaw clenched. When he spoke, Jeffrey's voice was fierce. "Nothing must hurt my wife or my child."

"I'll be all right." Though Charlotte's face was still pale and she continued to have bouts of morning sickness, she looked better than she had two days earlier. She stretched out her hand to clasp Abigail's and held it tightly. "Honestly,

Abigail. I'll be fine. After all, it's not as if you're deserting me. You'll only be gone for an hour or so, and I know you must be bored. It can't be any fun being cooped up here with me sleeping most of the time and Jeffrey gone."

To Abigail's surprise, Jeffrey had taken to heart Mrs. Grayson's advice that Charlotte should not be disturbed and was hardly ever at home. He ate with the bachelor officers, and when he returned late at night, he slept on a pallet in the parlor rather than climbing the stairs and risking the possibility of disturbing his wife. Jeffrey stopped in once or twice a day, spending no more than five minutes with Charlotte before leaving again. To Abigail's way of thinking, it was her sister who must be bored . . . and lonely. That was one of the reasons she hesitated when Charlotte suggested that she take her mare on a ride.

"You really need to be outside more," Charlotte continued. "It seems to me the only activity you get is chasing Puddles and brushing twigs out of his coat."

"For a little dog, he has a lot of energy," Abigail admitted. "There are times when I'm out of breath just trying to keep up with him." The puppy loved to run, and Abigail wouldn't deny him that pleasure, even though it meant running around the yard in what her mother would have called a most unseemly manner. It was almost as tiring trying to get Puddles to hold still long enough to be brushed. "I suspect I'll never figure out what he gets into." The twigs, as Charlotte called them, were not ordinary twigs. These stuck to Puddles's hair as if they had a hundred tiny hooks.

"Tumbleweeds." Charlotte's answer was succinct. "They have sharp edges everywhere—worse than a rose's thorns."

"Worse than a yucca?"

Charlotte tipped her head to one side, as if pondering the question. "Maybe not, but yuccas don't chase you. Tumbleweeds do."

"And Puddles catches every one." In doing so, he'd deepened Mrs. Channing's disapproval. Each day she delivered a litany of complaints about what she called "the despicable creature's despicable behavior," insisting that the only reason she remained was Charlotte's illness. "It wouldn't be fair to desert Mrs. Crowley now," she announced, "but when she's back on her feet . . ." The threat, though not voiced, was clear.

Charlotte looked down at the puppy with the outsized paws who was sleeping peacefully on the floor. "He may be rambunctious, but he's such a delight. I don't know what I'd do without him—and you, of course." Charlotte's mischievous smile told Abigail she had deliberately pretended that she was an afterthought. "Puddles and I will be fine while you're gone. So, go, enjoy yourself and don't rush back. I feel like taking a long nap."

It felt good to be on a horse again, Abigail admitted to herself as she emerged from the stables on Sally's back. The mare was as gentle as Charlotte had claimed, and since all three Harding sisters wore the same size clothing, Charlotte's green riding habit fit Abigail as if it had been made for her. The familiar-looking enlisted man who'd been cleaning out the stalls had started to call her Mrs. Crowley, then blushed when he realized his mistake.

"It's all right, Corporal," Abigail said. "I'm flattered that you think I look like my sister." Though Mama had claimed that all her daughters were lovely, Abigail knew that Charlotte was the beauty of the family. Even Woodrow had commented on Charlotte's good looks, while he'd never told Abigail she was beautiful. Woodrow was not a flatterer.

As the corporal saddled the mare, Abigail narrowed her eyes slightly, trying to remember where she had seen the man. "Oh," she said, smiling at the memory. "You're the soldier who was chasing the dogs and calling to them in German."

"*Ja,*" he admitted. "I did that, but it did no good. They paid me no mind, no matter vat language I spoke." Though the man's accent was heavy, his grammar was impeccable. Mrs. Barnett, who claimed that a slight accent was charming but that poor grammar was a mark of ignorance, would be impressed.

As thoughts of the headmaster's wife flitted through Abigail's head, she wondered what Woodrow was doing today. Was he too preparing for a ride? More likely, he had found someone for a tennis match, for tennis was his favorite summer pastime. Miss Thayer was a good tennis player. Perhaps she would challenge him. Or perhaps one of the students would ask for lessons. Henrietta Walsh's parents had paid Woodrow to teach her last summer, and the girl had spent the entire school year regaling anyone who would listen with stories of Woodrow's prowess. But Woodrow and tennis matches were almost two thousand miles away.

Abigail watched as the corporal tested the saddle cinches. "Do you vant me to go vith you, ma'am?" he asked. "I vill ask my sergeant for permission."

Abigail shook her head. "No, thank you, Corporal . . ." She let her voice trail off, hoping he would offer his name.

"Keller, ma'am. Dietrich Keller."

"Thank you, Corporal Keller, but my sister assures me I'll be safe riding alone so long as I stay close to the fort."

"*Ja*, you vill. Good day, ma'am."

Abigail rode slowly through the fort, giving herself a chance to get used to Sally. Despite Charlotte's admonition to take a long ride, she had decided she would do no more than circle the outside of the garrison. Fort Laramie was located on a deep bend of the Laramie River, with the river forming its southern and eastern boundaries. Though she knew that horses could easily ford the river, Abigail would not risk getting Charlotte's habit wet. That's why bridges had been invented. She'd cross the bridge at the east end of the garrison, then follow the river, retracing her steps when the fort was no longer in sight.

Abigail settled into the saddle, smiling at the puffy cumulus clouds scudding across the sky. Though Wyoming would never compare to Vermont's green beauty, there was no denying that the sky here was magnificent. The sounds were different too. At home, she heard dairy cows mooing. Now that she was outside the fort, Abigail realized that the noise of soldiers marching, the shouts and bugle calls that were part of daily life, and the seemingly incessant construction noise blocked the natural sounds. Out here, the wind was dominant, rustling through the long grasses, carrying bird calls and odd whistles on its breezes.

Abigail looked around as the whistling grew louder, accompanied by occasional squeaks. The source, she discovered, was a prairie dog sitting on top of his mound, apparently announcing her arrival to the rest of his colony. She reined in Sally and watched for a moment, recalling the stories Mrs. Dunn had recounted on the stagecoach. Prairie dogs, the widow had claimed, were social creatures whose favorite pastime appeared to be standing on their hind legs, exchanging gossip with their neighbors. That certainly seemed to be true. Seeing the number of animals standing on the mounds of dirt they'd excavated from their underground homes, all apparently chatting to each other, Abigail knew why the colonies were referred to as prairie dog towns.

The critters were as cute as squirrels, but Abigail knew that their burrows presented dangers to the unwary. Recalling Mrs. Dunn's story of breaking her ankle when she stumbled into a gopher hole, Abigail guided Sally away from the prairie dog town. She wouldn't risk injuring her sister's mare.

"How much farther shall we go?" she asked the horse. Predictably, Sally said nothing. Abigail spotted a large cottonwood a hundred or so yards farther. "That's where we'll turn around," she announced.

And she would have, had she not seen a figure sitting on the riverbank, shaded by the tree. The full sleeves and long skirts told Abigail this was a woman; the slumped shoulders and bent head telegraphed despair. Even from a distance, Abigail could see that the woman was sobbing.

"C'mon, Sally," she urged the mare. "Let's see if we can help."

Seconds later, Abigail was on the ground. Though it might be difficult to mount Sally again, she wouldn't approach the young woman on horseback. Something in the woman's posture told her that she was as wary as a wild animal. A stranger on horseback would be more intimidating than one on foot. But even walking was enough to alarm the woman. As soon as Abigail dismounted, she jumped to her feet. Though she straightened her shoulders and tossed her blonde hair over her shoulders in what could be viewed as a defiant gesture, her expression was one of desperation.

"Can I help you?" Abigail's heart turned over at the anguish she saw in the woman's eyes. A lighter blue than Ethan's, they bore more pain than Abigail had ever seen in such a young face. For, even through the heavy coating of powder that reminded Abigail of Mrs. Dunn and the paint that would have appalled Mama, Abigail could see that the woman was no older than she.

"How can I help you?" Abigail rephrased the question, for there was no doubt that this woman needed her help.

The woman shook her head, setting the blonde hair that was her greatest beauty to swinging and releasing a whiff of perfume. "I don't need no help. Nothing's wrong, Miss . . ."

"Harding." Abigail completed the sentence. "I'm Abigail Harding, but I won't believe that nothing's wrong."

The woman rubbed her eyes, brushing the tears aside. Her face might have been pretty were it not blotched with tears. "It's nothin' you can change. Anyhow, you shouldn't oughta be talkin' to me, Miss Harding."

"Why not?" This woman wasn't part of the Army with its rules about fraternization. Her painted face and the strong perfume made Abigail suspect she was one of the women Charlotte had scorned last week, but even if she were, that was no reason for Abigail not to try to help her. If anything, it was a reason she ought to.

Abigail gave the woman her brightest smile, the one that had won over many a bashful student. "Please tell me your name. I don't want to address you as just 'miss.'"

The woman wrapped her arms around her waist, as if to comfort herself, and Abigail noticed that her dress, though made of a simple cotton, was the same shade of blue as her eyes. Though Charlotte might cringe at the thought that she had anything in common with this woman, it appeared they both cared about fashion.

"My name's Leah," the woman said softly. "No one calls me 'miss' anything. I'm just Leah."

"If you tell me your surname, Leah, I'll use it."

She shook her head. "That wun't be proper. You shouldn't be talkin' to me at all."

"Why not?"

The woman's blue eyes reflected pain and something else, something Abigail thought might be shame. If she was what Mama would have called a fallen woman, Leah might be embarrassed to admit it.

The pretty blonde took a deep breath and blurted out, "I work at the hog ranch."

Abigail felt herself relax. She had jumped to a conclusion, and it was wrong. "There's nothing wrong with raising pigs, Leah."

Leah's laugh held no mirth. "You ain't from around here, are you? There ain't no pigs on a hog ranch. Peg's is a place where men go to drink whiskey and play poker and . . ." Leah stopped, clearly trying to choose her words. "To visit women," she said at last.

"I see." And Abigail did. It wasn't just the land that was different in Wyoming. People here spoke a different language. Bandits were called road agents, houses of ill repute hog ranches. But one thing remained the same: whether she was in Vermont or Wyoming, Abigail could not ignore a person in need.

"I reckon you oughta get on that horse and leave, Miss Harding. You shouldn't oughta be associatin' with folks like me. You shouldn't oughta have stopped."

Abigail glanced at Sally and saw that the mare was grazing contentedly. There was no reason for her to depart and every reason to stay. She shook her head, dismissing Leah's suggestion. "I saw a woman who looked lonely and sad, and I thought I might be able to help."

"I told you, ain't no one can help." Leah brushed aside the tears that welled in her eyes. "I hate what I do, but I ain't got no choice."

Abigail wouldn't believe that. "There must be something else. I heard that the officers' wives are always looking for servants."

A look of astonishment crossed Leah's face. "You think they'd hire me? That's a purty picture—me cookin' and cleanin' house for some lady when I used to entertain her man. It ain't gonna happen, Miss Harding. Oh, I can keep a house clean, and I cook better than most, but ain't no fancy lady gonna let me inside her house. They're afraid of me."

Was that why Charlotte had reacted so strongly? Abigail dismissed the thought as quickly as it flitted through her brain. Charlotte and Jeffrey were practically newlyweds; he loved her; there was no reason to believe he had strayed.

"Perhaps you could cook at Peg's instead of entertaining men."

Leah shook her head. "Peg wun't agree. The men don't care much about the food, but they sure don't mind plunking down their coins for some entertainment."

"You could leave." Even as Abigail pronounced the words, she knew how unlikely the prospect was. Where would Leah go, and how would she get there? In all likelihood, she had no money.

"I cain't." Leah's shoulders slumped. "Peg said she'd hunt

me down if'n I left. You see, the fellas like me better than the other girls, cuz I'm young and my hair is yellow. The other girls gotta wear wigs to have yellow hair."

"And they resent that."

"Yes, miss, they do. I ain't got no friends."

Abigail's heart ached for the young woman whose life had been so different from hers. As much as she wished it was otherwise, she doubted she could do anything to alter Leah's circumstances. There was, however, one thing she could do. "I'd like to be your friend," Abigail said softly as she extended her hand.

Leah shook her head, ignoring the outstretched hand. "That ain't proper."

"You did what?" Charlotte pushed herself into a sitting position and glared at her sister. Though she was awake when Abigail returned, she'd been lying down; now shock and anger propelled her upward.

Refusing to match her sister's raised voice, Abigail spoke softly yet firmly. "You heard me the first time, Charlotte. I told Leah I wanted to be her friend, and I do."

"Are you daft? She works at the hog ranch. You know decent women don't associate with soiled doves." Spots of color appeared on Charlotte's cheeks as she warmed to her lecture. "Whatever were you thinking, or weren't you thinking?"

"I thought that a woman needed my help. You'd have done the same thing if you'd seen her." Abigail wasn't certain of that. The Charlotte she'd known in Vermont would have sought to help a woman in distress, but the Wyoming Charlotte, Charlotte the wife, was different.

110

Charlotte shook her head. "You're wrong. I would never have gotten that close. You must have noticed that she wasn't dressed like us."

Abigail looked at her sister. Even her nightdress was more elegant than most women's, with delicate pin tucking and the finest of lace decorating the neckline. "No one dresses as well as you do. They don't have your skill with a needle or your eye for fashion, but Leah's dress was perfectly respectable."

Charlotte was not to be placated. "I don't care what the harlot was wearing. What I do care is that you spoke to her. Oh, Abigail, when will you outgrow your impulsiveness? One of these days, you need to realize that you can't help everyone." Charlotte shuddered. "A soiled dove! How could you?"

"How could I not?" Though Mrs. Grayson had admonished Abigail to keep her sister calm, she had to explain. "I remembered Mama and Papa talking about the Golden Rule. I thought Leah needed love, and maybe I could offer it."

As her words found their mark, Abigail watched Charlotte's face soften. "You're right," she said. "It's just that I hate the thought of that kind of temptation so close to the fort. And . . ." She hesitated for a second, as if choosing her words. "I worry about you, Abigail. I know you mean well and that you want to solve every problem you see, but you can't. I'm worried that you'll get hurt trying."

Abigail put her arms around Charlotte's shoulders and hugged her. "Don't worry, big sister. I'll be fine."

Ethan looked around, pleased with what he saw. The team was as ready as they could be, considering they'd had only a few days' practice. Fortunately, Jeffrey's team had had no more time. Both teams practiced each evening between supper and retreat, and the men who didn't have guard or fatigue duty took turns pitching, hitting, and catching during the day. Tonight was their first game, and though Jeffrey could—and did—brag all he wanted about his team, Ethan believed his was better. Dietrich Keller, the corporal who'd translated the canine detail orders, had proven to be a formidable pitcher, while Oliver had become a first-rate batter. The rest of the team approached the sport with enthusiasm, albeit not much skill. But their skills were improving and—even better—so were their moods. A win was just what they needed to give their morale a decided boost.

That was the primary reason Ethan wanted his team to win—for their sakes—but he couldn't deny the desire to prove Jeffrey wrong. The man had a tendency to boast, as proven by the name he'd chosen for his team, and it would be gratifying to see him get his comeuppance.

"You let your team choose the name?" Jeffrey hadn't bothered to hide his scorn when he'd learned that Ethan's team was to be called the Laramie Blues, in honor of both the fort and the color of their uniforms. "You're the captain. You should have made the decision."

Ethan forbore pointing out that he had made the decision, and that decision was to let the team determine its name.

"All right, men. You know what to do." Ethan addressed his team, hoping his pride in them would instill confidence. "Let's show Crowley's Champs who the real champions are."

Dietrich Keller grinned. "The Blues vill vin tonight. I feel it in my bones." As the rest of the team cheered, Ethan led them onto the field.

It was an hour and a half later, and Dietrich's prediction had yet to come true. Ethan realized that he'd been wrong in underestimating the other team's skill. Their pitcher might not be as good as Dietrich, but their catcher and shortstop were first rate, with the result that they had reached the final inning, and Ethan's team was ahead by only one run.

"We gotta win." Ethan heard his second baseman mutter the words. While there was a man on first base, the Champs had two outs, and the batter was two strikes down. All it would take was one more strike.

From his position in left field, Ethan looked at the crowd that had gathered to watch the game. It seemed as if every soldier who wasn't on duty and almost every civilian were standing on the sidelines, cheering on their favorite team, booing when they didn't like the umpire's call.

Ethan wasn't surprised that Abigail had come, even though her sister remained confined to her bed. After all, Abigail had attended practice each night, bringing Puddles with her. Though the catcher had joked that the dog was trying to take his place on the team, Puddles had proven to be more than a squirming, barking ball of fur. He'd served a useful purpose, retrieving runaway balls. The only problem was, he'd taken those balls back to Abigail. Despite her efforts to teach Puddles to return them to Dietrich, she'd had no success. Still, the team had enjoyed the dog's antics, and Ethan . . . well, anything that was good for the team was good for him.

And so, while he wasn't surprised that Abigail had come to the game tonight, he could not deny that he was pleased. It was true that she cheered both teams, but that didn't seem to bother the Blues. Ethan had overheard some of the men speculating which team she'd favor and had learned that most recognized that Abigail was duty bound to cheer the team her brother-in-law led. "Wish she'd brought the dog," one had groused. But tonight there was no mischievous puppy, only a beautiful woman with what appeared to be a genuine interest in baseball.

Ethan dragged his attention back to the game. Dietrich was winding his arm, preparing for the final pitch. The batter would miss. The inning would be over. His team would win.

Crack! It was the unmistakable sound of a bat connecting with a ball. Ethan blinked in astonishment as he saw the ball speeding past the infield. It was the best hit of the night. He ran, determined to catch it on the fly, but the ball bounced before he could reach it. Behind him, Ethan heard the crowd roar and knew the batter had reached first base. Judging from the shouts, the man on first had gotten to second and was heading for third, while the batter raced toward second. There was still hope, Ethan told himself as he ran for the ball. He'd get it to the catcher, the runner would be out, and the game would be over. But Ethan was too late. By the time he snagged the ball, the first runner had reached home and the batter was on his way to scoring a home run. The Blues had lost, and it was Ethan's fault.

"Congratulations," he said as he shook Jeffrey's hand a minute later. "Your team played a good game."

Jeffrey's smile was little less than a smirk. "I told you we were the best. Now you have proof."

Knowing that his team was listening, Ethan said only, "There's another game next week."

"And the results will be the same." Jeffrey turned toward his team. "You did a good job, men. I'm proud of you."

As Jeffrey's team left the field, Ethan turned toward his.

"The Champs were good, but you were great. If I hadn't been here, you would have won." Though Ethan kept his voice even, he hated even pronouncing the words and admitting that he'd failed his men.

Dietrich shook his head. "If you had not been here, ve vould not have had a team."

A murmur of assent greeted his words. "Dietrich's right," one of the other men said. "Next time will be different."

For their sake, Ethan hoped so.

7

Was she the only one who had noticed that he was upset? The slump of his shoulders and the downward twist of his lips had been momentary, but she had seen them. An instant later Ethan had looked as if nothing was amiss as he strode to Jeffrey's side to congratulate him. Was that something he'd learned at West Point, how to hide his emotions? Perhaps it was, but Abigail knew what she had seen: Ethan was bothered by his team's loss. That was why she lingered on the parade ground, waiting until the enlisted men headed for their barracks.

"It was a good game," she said as she approached Ethan. For once, Oliver, who usually offered to escort her home after practice, had left as soon as the game ended.

Ethan shook his head. "We should have won. The Blues are a stronger team than the Champs. If it hadn't been for me, we would have won."

So that was what bothered him. It wasn't the loss as much as his belief that he was responsible. Was that another thing he'd been taught at the Military Academy, that he was solely responsible for his men? That might be true in battle, but baseball was different.

"It's a team, Ethan. That means everyone plays a part. Winning or losing depends on the whole team, not one person."

He looked at her as if she were speaking a foreign language. "You don't understand."

"I think I do. You're afraid you've disappointed your men. But, Ethan, think about why you organized the team in the first place. You wanted to give them a new interest, something to do. You didn't want them to be bored."

Though his lips remained flattened, Abigail saw a spark of enthusiasm in his eyes. Hoping to fan that spark, she said, "I watched everyone on the field, and one thing I can assure you: no one was bored."

"You may be right."

"Of course I'm right." Abigail fisted her hands on her hips and feigned indignation. "Didn't you learn that schoolteachers are always right?"

For an instant she thought he might smile, but instead Ethan's frown deepened. "It's the strangest thing, but when I congratulated Jeffrey and watched him smirk, I could have sworn I was looking at my grandfather. I could almost hear him tell me that I had failed to live up to his standards."

Abigail wasn't certain whether she heard sorrow or bitterness in Ethan's voice, but neither was good. "I wonder if any of us meets our parents' expectations. I know I disappointed mine more than once."

The sun was beginning to set, and the breeze that teased Abigail's hair was cool, a reminder that while days might be warm, Wyoming evenings could be downright cold. Abigail knew she should return to Charlotte's home, and yet she did not want to leave Ethan.

He was silent for a moment, as if considering what she'd said, but when he spoke, his words surprised her. "It must have been difficult, being a minister's daughter. Living with my grandfather wasn't always easy, but at least the fire and brimstone were confined to Sundays."

What kind of church had Ethan attended? As quickly as the question entered her brain, Abigail knew the answer. Papa had been asked to leave several congregations when the parishioners had declared him too soft. They had wanted sermons that promised fire and brimstone to anyone whose opinion varied from their own. Instead, they'd discovered that Papa had opinions of his own and that those opinions didn't always match the church elders'.

"My father wasn't that kind of minister." Abigail nodded when Ethan started walking toward her house. They could continue their conversation on the verandah. "He preached that God is a God of love."

"No thunderbolts from on high? No threats of eternal damnation?"

"Not very often. Papa wanted us to strive for the reward Jesus promised. He said that if we accepted Jesus as our savior and spent our lives following his example, we wouldn't have to worry about fire and brimstone."

"Promises instead of threats. It's an intriguing approach."

"Not just toward faith. That's what you offered your men when you organized the baseball games. You gave them the promise of entertainment and a new challenge. You didn't threaten anything."

Ethan chuckled. "Next I suppose you're going to tell me it doesn't matter that we lost the game."

"Of course."

"And if I tell you I'm not convinced, you'll tell me you're always right."

"Of course."

Ethan's laughter was the sweetest sound Abigail had heard all night.

If it hadn't been for the reason, Ethan would have enjoyed the ride. Though he knew Abigail would disagree—vehemently, in fact—in his opinion, there was nothing quite as beautiful as the Wyoming prairie. Where else could you find sky so clear that a fanciful man could believe he was looking all the way to heaven? Where else was the ground carpeted with the smallest flowers imaginable, each an example of miniature perfection? Where else did the wind carry the scent of sagebrush for miles? Wyoming was beautiful. No doubt about that. Unfortunately, the gently rolling hills and the occasional ravine that added to its beauty also provided ideal terrain for men to hide. And hide they had.

Ethan frowned as he shaded his eyes and stared into the distance. They had to be close. Even though they had a twelve hour head start, they were on foot. By all rights, he should have found them by now, and yet those two miserable cowards continued to elude him. He'd lost the trail more times than he wanted to admit, and it was only his instincts that propelled him in this direction.

Chances were good that they were headed for the gold fields of Deadwood. That's where most of the deserters went, thinking they'd get rich overnight. It didn't happen, but there was no denying the allure of gold. That was the reason the official search party had gone northeast toward Deadwood. While he did not doubt the deserters sought gold, Ethan hadn't been convinced they had any desire to dig in the dirt. As a result, he'd saddled his horse and headed south, scouring the area parallel to the stagecoach route. His instincts told him that these men, like Private Schiller, craved instant riches.

"C'mon, Samson. We'll find 'em."

The horse needed no urging to gallop. Seconds after Ethan's command, he was flying across the prairie, his mane streaming behind him, his hoofs pounding the ground. And then it happened. One instant Samson was galloping; the next he missed a step and lunged forward, stopping abruptly. A prairie dog hole. It had to be. Though Ethan had spent hours being entertained by the social rodents' habits, there was nothing amusing about stepping into one of those holes. They were wide enough to trap a horse's hoof and deep enough to break his leg, particularly if he was galloping.

Ethan dismounted quickly and began to murmur words of encouragement to the stallion. "It'll be all right," he said as ran his hands up and down the horse's leg, checking for injuries. Samson was fortunate, Ethan realized as he ran his hand over the horse's fetlock. The leg was not broken, merely badly bruised. "C'mon, boy," he said, encouraging the horse to walk. As he'd hoped, though Samson favored that leg, he was able to put weight on it.

Pulling a bandage from his saddlebag, Ethan began to wrap his horse's leg. "You'll be fine in a few days," he told his mount, then grimaced. There would be no more riding today. Not only did that mean that he would have to walk back to the fort, but—even worse—he would not catch those miserable deserters.

Ethan tried not to frown as he trudged toward Fort Laramie. It wasn't Samson's fault that he'd caught his leg in the hole, any more than it was the stallion's fault that the men had chosen to go over the hill. And it most definitely was not his fault that Ethan was out of sorts now. He'd been confident that baseball would solve the desertion problem, and yet it obviously had not. One of the men who'd fled the post in the middle of the night had been part of his team. Though logic told Ethan that desertion was not a spur-of-the-moment decision, he could not dismiss the niggling fear that their team's loss had contributed to the man's disappearance.

That was absurd. As absurd as the fact that he missed taking meals with the Crowleys.

Samson snorted and tossed his head, almost as if he could read Ethan's thoughts and was taking exception to them. The horse wasn't a mind reader. Of course he wasn't. But if Ethan were being honest, he'd admit that what he had looked forward to was spending time with Abigail, not the rest of the family.

Abigail was not like any woman he'd met. It was no wonder Jeffrey considered his sister-in-law trouble. She had an opinion about everything and did not hesitate to share it. Look at the way she'd tried to convince Ethan that the team's loss wasn't his fault. She hadn't succeeded—not completely—but she had given him many things to think about, not the least of which was that Grandfather's view of God might be wrong. Unfortunately, thanks to Charlotte's indisposition, Ethan no longer enjoyed verbal sparring matches at meals. Instead, the most he could hope for was ordinary conversation with the other officers, conversations that all too often consisted of Oliver singing Abigail's praises.

Though it wasn't the first time Oliver had been smitten, this time seemed worse than normal. He turned a simple smile into a sign of undying love. Why, he was even convinced that Abigail attended baseball practice for the express purpose of watching him bat. As soon as practice ended, Oliver would rush to Abigail's side, pat the dog, and mutter inane comments. Ethan cringed each time he heard the senseless words pour forth. One night Oliver had spouted several verses of poetry. Surely it hadn't been Ethan's imagination that Abigail had appeared tempted to laugh.

A hawk soared lazily, its wingspan casting a welcome shade for the seconds it was overhead. Though beautiful, the Wyoming sky lost a bit of its appeal when a man was forced to walk beneath it for hours on end. Ethan uncapped his canteen and took a quick swig. He shouldn't let the sun bother him any more than he should be bothered by not sharing meals with Abigail. She'd be gone before the leaves fell unless Oliver convinced her otherwise.

Ethan's lip curled in distaste as he considered the possibility of Abigail remaining at Fort Laramie as Mrs. Oliver Seton. A preacher's daughter and a man who saw nothing wrong with spending his evenings at Peg's, drinking, gambling, and cavorting with the women. Ethan could not imagine them together. And then there was Woodrow.

Ethan pulled out his watch and frowned. It was time to let Samson rest again. Though the horse would not complain, Ethan would not risk further injuries to the leg. That was why he spent a quarter of each hour sitting on the ground while Samson gave his leg a rest. That was good for the horse. The only problem was that the inactivity gave Ethan more time to think, and today his thoughts were not happy ones.

Thanks to Samson's unfortunate encounter with a prairie dog hole, the deserters most likely would not be caught, at least not today. Or tomorrow. Though Ethan would have ridden all night had Samson not been injured, his horse was showing signs of fatigue, and he would not risk another stumble. He and Samson would spend tonight camping on the prairie. Tomorrow would be a better day. It had to be.

But when he entered the fort late the next morning, Ethan's relief at being home evaporated at the sight of two familiar figures emerging from the sutler's store. Why was Abigail walking with Oliver, and why, oh why, did he care?

She shouldn't be annoyed, Abigail told herself as she removed her gloves and untied her bonnet ribbons. She'd accomplished what she set out to do: buy the thread Charlotte had requested and a tin of mints she hoped would remind her sister of the afternoons they had spent as children, playing house with their dolls, serving imaginary tea, and pretending that mint lozenges were fancy cakes. That was what mattered, not the fact that Oliver Seton had entered the store while she was there and had insisted on accompanying her home. Short of being rude, there had been no way to refuse. She could hardly have said, "I'd prefer to walk alone," even though that would have been the truth. Oliver was a nice enough man. She'd grant him that. It was simply that she didn't enjoy his company the way she did Ethan's.

Even though it had been only a day and a half since she'd seen him, she missed Ethan. Abigail frowned as she climbed the stairs. It was silly to wish there had been a baseball practice last night. The men needed to rest occasionally, and she needed to stop thinking about Ethan. She'd soon be on her way back to Vermont and Woodrow. That was what mattered, not Oliver's unwelcome company or Ethan's absence.

Abigail frowned again when she entered Charlotte's room. She was certain she had not left the door ajar, but it was clearly unlatched. Charlotte was asleep, and Puddles's box was empty. That explained the half-open door, but it provided no clue to the puppy's whereabouts. Abigail closed the door quietly and descended the stairs. Puddles must be sleeping in the yard. That would explain why she hadn't heard the yips and barks that signaled he was playing with an invisible companion.

Though he slept in a crate at night, Mrs. Channing refused to have him in either the kitchen or the pantry during the day, and he grew bored when Charlotte fell asleep. Simply letting him run in the backyard hadn't worked, for the puppy would sit on the back step, scratching at the door and howling until Mrs. Channing paid him some attention. Even the swats on the rump that the cook delivered didn't discourage Puddles. In desperation, Abigail had taken to tying him to a tree in the side yard whenever he was not with her or Charlotte. Not being able to see the entrance to the house appeared to have done the trick, because the pup would play for hours, batting at butterflies and chasing ground squirrels as far as his rope allowed.

Mrs. Channing must have tied him in the side yard when she went to the commissary. Abigail rounded the corner of the house, frowning when she saw no black and tan dog under the tree. The only evidence that he'd been there was a piece of rope that had obviously been chewed. Puddles had learned a new trick, a bad one. If he'd left the yard, he could be in trouble, for the soldiers were still patrolling, trying to rid the fort of runaway dogs.

"Puddles! Puddles! Where are you?" There was no answer. Abigail walked around the yard, looking for the dog. "Come here, boy. We'll play catch." But even the magic word *catch* did not elicit a reply. When she saw the door to the privy ajar, Abigail sprinted the few yards and flung it open. Puddles had hidden there once, apparently attracted by the smells. But today the outhouse was empty.

The mischievous pup could be anywhere on the fort. Abigail retrieved her gloves and hat and set out, leash in hand. When she found him—for she would not consider the alternative—she'd ensure that the dog was tightly leashed. And there would be no bone for him tonight.

Abigail looked across the parade ground. Other than a few soldiers heading toward Suds Row, it was empty. Remembering how attracted Puddles was by strong odors, Abigail nodded and increased her pace, heading toward the stables. Most of the horses and mules were out at this time of the day, but their smells would remain. Rolling in the straw and muck could be enough to entertain the puppy for an hour or more. Abigail tried not to grimace at the thought of bathing him if he had indeed rolled in something less fragrant than hay.

Slightly out of breath, Abigail blinked several times when she entered the stables, letting her eyes adjust to the relative darkness. She heard the snuffle of a horse and the rustling of a smaller animal. Puddles?

"Not now, boy."

Abigail grinned. There was no mistaking that voice or the disappointed yip that followed it. Puddles was here, and so was Ethan. She hurried to the back of the stable and found Ethan crouched on the ground, unwrapping a horse's leg while Puddles, apparently believing that the bandage was a new toy, tried his best to grab it.

Abigail bent down and attempted to scoop Puddles into her arms, but he scampered away. "I'm sorry, Ethan. I don't know how he got away. Come here, Puddles."

The dog took another step backward.

"Go." Ethan accompanied his order with a gesture toward Abigail. The dog hunkered down and refused to move. "Go!" This time Ethan's voice held a note that Abigail suspected sent tremors of fear through grown men. Even recalcitrant puppies recognized the sound of a command, for Puddles moved slowly toward her.

When she'd slipped the leash onto the dog, Abigail turned toward Ethan. "He seems to think he's yours."

Ethan ran his hands over the horse's leg, then rose. To Abigail's surprise, he looked as annoyed as she had felt when Oliver had accompanied her from the store. "I suspect Puddles is more interested in Samson than me."

Now that her eyes had adjusted to the darkness, Abigail realized that Ethan's uniform was more wrinkled than she had ever seen it, and his normally well-shined boots were coated with dust.

"What happened?" The horse was moving slowly around the stall, clearly favoring his front right leg.

"The poor old fellow." Ethan put a reassuring hand on Samson's muzzle. "We were searching for deserters when he stepped into a prairie dog hole. Fortunately, his leg's only

126

bruised, but it took us a day and a half to get back." That explained the dusty clothing and the reason Abigail had not seen Ethan yesterday evening. It might even explain his uncharacteristically dour mood. Ethan had obviously walked and spent the night under the stars rather than put more strain on his horse's leg.

He patted Samson again, then nodded toward the stable's entrance. "I'm done here. May I escort you and Puddles to your house, or do you have someone else waiting?" The sharp note in his voice surprised Abigail. Ethan must be more tired than she'd realized.

"Thank you." Though there was no question of safety on the fort during daylight hours, Abigail would not turn down the opportunity to be with Ethan. Somehow when she was in his company, she felt more alive than usual, and each time they were together, she learned something new about him. Ethan was a far more complex man than she'd thought at first, and that intrigued her.

"Come, Puddles." Abigail tugged the leash, urging the puppy to leave the stall. Though initially reluctant, when he saw that Ethan was accompanying her, Puddles raced to her side, then whirled in front of her, tangling his leash in her skirts in his eagerness to be next to Ethan.

"See," Abigail said as she extricated her skirts from the rope and transferred the leash to her other hand, "he thinks he belongs to you."

Ethan shrugged. "More likely he's intrigued by the smells on my boots." The fact that the puppy was trying to lick them gave credence to his theory. "I walked a long way, so there's no telling what scents I may have picked up."

Puddles turned and looked back at the stable, causing

Ethan to raise an eyebrow. "Your dog is fickle. He'd rather be with the horses than either of us."

Abigail nodded, remembering the way Puddles had whined when she'd returned from her ride. "I'd take him with me the next time I go riding, if I could figure out a way to carry him. Those legs are much too short to keep up with a horse."

Ethan frowned. "I didn't realize you'd been out. Who went with you?" He seemed annoyed, but perhaps that was only fatigue.

"No one. Charlotte assured me I'd be safe as long as I stayed in sight of the fort."

"Perhaps," Ethan agreed, "but this is not Vermont. There are dangers here you never dreamt of. Prairie dogs, poisonous snakes, deserters." He seemed to be ticking items off a list. "You shouldn't leave the fort alone. If you want to ride again, I'll accompany you. Samson won't be ready tomorrow, but if you'd like to ride, we can go out the next day."

It was a generous offer, and yet the frown that accompanied it told Abigail that Ethan considered it a duty, not a pleasure, and that hurt more than a tumbleweed's thorns. She had thought she and Ethan had become friends, but friends didn't act this way. What had changed?

"I'm so proud of him." Abigail patted Puddles's head as she laid him on the floor next to Charlotte's bed the next morning. Though he'd proven adept at descending the stairs, he still needed help climbing, and so Abigail carried him rather than watch him struggle. Her sister was sitting up, propped against a pile of pillows, and her face had more color than it had the previous day. Even better, she had had no morning sickness today.

"Puddles used the paper I put beside his box," Abigail announced. "I didn't even have to coax him. When I went downstairs this morning, he was standing by it, proud as could be. I think he's going to be easy to train."

Charlotte smiled and held out her arms for the puppy. "I wish I had more energy," she said as she placed him on the quilt beside her, smiling again when he rolled on his back to have his belly scratched. "Playing with him wears me out."

"Mrs. Grayson said she thought you were stronger, and you look better this morning."

"I feel better but not good, if that makes any sense." Charlotte pulled Puddles into her lap and stroked his ears. "I keep remembering how Mama spent her last years in bed. Oh, Abigail, I don't want to wind up like that."

"You won't." Abigail infused her words with emphasis. Somehow, some way she had to convince her sister that she would not be an invalid like their mother. "This isn't like Mama's sickness. You're not ill; you're simply expecting a baby. Before you know it, the baby will be here, and you'll be back to normal."

"I pray that's so." A few minutes later, Charlotte handed Puddles to Abigail. "I'm so tired," she said. "This is what worries me—that I sleep all the time."

"Mrs. Grayson said that was the only cure she knew."

"I hope it works."

"It will." Abigail kissed her sister's forehead and descended the stairs, crooning to the now squirming puppy.

Half an hour later, leaving Puddles in the yard securely tied to his favorite tree with a length of chain, Abigail entered the parlor. If she couldn't do anything for Charlotte, at least she could put this room back to normal. Now that Jeffrey was sleeping here rather than upstairs, it needed daily cleaning. Though he stashed his bedroll in the pantry and tried to restore furniture to its appointed positions, he never managed to hide the evidence that he and his dusty boots had been here.

Abigail sniffed as she straightened one of the antimacassars. It wasn't her imagination. The room did hold the faint scent of perfume. How odd. Mrs. Channing did not wear scents, and the fragrance was not the rose water Abigail used nor the lily of the valley Charlotte favored. Still, there was something familiar about it. Abigail sniffed again as she tried to recall where she had smelled it before. It was somewhere in Wyoming. She thought back to the stagecoach. Mrs. Dunn had worn no toilet water. Perhaps Mrs. Fitzgerald's perfume had been similar.

Abigail hadn't heard Jeffrey return to the house last night, but that wasn't unusual. Since he'd started taking meals with the other officers and sleeping in the parlor, he'd been late coming home each night. Abigail rarely saw him and realized she had little idea of how he spent his time or with whom, but surely he hadn't been with another woman. Jeffrey loved Charlotte. He would not betray her.

As she opened the windows to air the room, Abigail saw a company of soldiers marching in formation across the parade ground. Lined up four abreast, they seemed to move as one. There was nothing like that in Wesley, Vermont. Abigail sighed. Today Vermont felt more than two thousand miles away. It seemed part of a totally different world. Her life there had been neatly ordered. Each day resembled the one before, and her future had seemed secure. There were no bandits, no deserters, no lieutenants with inexplicable moods. Most of all, there were no worries that her brother-in-law might have broken his marriage vows.

Oh, Lord, what should I do? If she confronted Jeffrey, he would deny any wrongdoing. If she told Charlotte, she would only worry more.

For once Abigail was thankful for the Wyoming winds, for within minutes, the room was freshened, the hint of perfume gone, replaced by the scents of grass and sagebrush. The wind swept away more than the perfume, for as the room returned to normal, a sense of peace settled over Abigail, and the small voice deep inside her told her this was where she was meant to be.

Filled with a rush of energy, she looked at the desk. Though she had meant to wait until tomorrow before writing to Woodrow, she plucked a piece of stationery from the desk drawer and uncapped the bottle of ink.

Half an hour later, Abigail inscribed her name at the bottom of the last page and began to reread her letter, checking for mistakes. When she reached the end, she was frowning. Four pages, thirteen paragraphs, and almost all of them mentioned Ethan. If she sent this to Woodrow, he'd believe her life revolved around Ethan Bowles. It did not. It most certainly did not. Woodrow was the man she planned to marry.

8

It wasn't the first time Abigail had dreamt of her wedding. Ever since she'd been a child, she had conjured images of the day she would marry. The details had changed over the years, but for the past year, they had remained constant. And so she dreamt that she was standing in the back of a small chapel, watching her sisters precede her down the aisle. She wore the same gown she always did; she carried the same flowers. When Elizabeth was halfway to the altar, Abigail began her processional, smiling as she approached her groom. It was always the same. Until last night. Last night, instead of facing her, her groom had his back turned, and he appeared taller than Woodrow. Instead of brown hair, the groom was blond. And when he turned, Abigail saw that he was not Woodrow at all. She had wakened, her heart pounding at the realization that she had dreamt of Ethan.

It meant nothing. A dream was only a dream. But, though she told herself that a hundred or more times, she had been unable to fall back to sleep. And now she would have to face the man who had starred in her dream, for today was the day she was supposed to ride with Ethan. Fortunately, he would have no way of knowing the images her traitorous mind had conjured.

As she stepped off the porch, Abigail smiled at the sight of two women battling to keep their parasols open. Today was not a day for parasols, at least not in Abigail's estimation. Were it not for the wide ribbons that secured her hat, the wind would have turned her bonnet into a tumbleweed.

Another smile crossed Abigail's face at the memory of the huge plants that danced in the wind, seeming to travel almost as quickly as a horse. She was not moving at that speed, but she walked briskly, not wanting to be late and give Ethan another reason to be annoyed. It was bad enough that his invitation had been so grudging.

When Abigail arrived at the stable, Ethan was already waiting, and Sally and a roan stallion were saddled. It appeared that Samson wasn't ready for riding, for Ethan stood next to him in his stall.

"Good morning, Abigail." Surely it wasn't her imagination that Ethan's greeting was hesitant. Was he remembering his curt words the last time they'd spoken, or was it simply that he would prefer to be alone? He patted Samson's rump, then turned back to Abigail. "Before we head out, I owe you an apology. I was in a sour mood the other day. It wasn't your fault, and I'm sorry to have subjected you to it."

A rush of pleasure swept through Abigail as she realized there had been no need to worry. "I accept your apology."

She extended a hand and smiled when he gripped it tightly. "It must have been difficult, walking so far."

Ethan shrugged as he helped Abigail mount Sally. "I'm part of the infantry, which means I'm used to walking. That wasn't what bothered me. It was a combination of Samson's injury and not catching the deserters. I wasn't happy about either one."

Though she knew there had been more deserters, Abigail had heard none of the details. "Were they from your company?"

Ethan nodded and swung into the roan's saddle. When they emerged from the stable, he said, "Private Dickinson was on my baseball team."

No wonder Ethan had been out of sorts. Abigail wasn't certain how she would have reacted if she'd been in the same situation, but she knew she would not have been happy. Though Ethan looked straight ahead, as if trying to decide which direction they should go, she saw his lips tighten and knew she had to say something. "I imagine it felt like a betrayal when he deserted."

"It did. You know I was hoping the team would help keep the men here, so to have someone leave the very next day. Well . . ." Ethan pulled on the reins as they approached the bridge. "I kept asking myself what else I could have done."

Abigail waited until they had reached the opposite side of the river before she spoke. "My father used to say that we should try to guide others, but we need to remember that the decisions are theirs. We can't blame ourselves for their actions, because we don't control anyone except ourselves."

"That's a strange thing for a preacher to say." Though furrows had appeared between Ethan's eyes, his voice remained even. "Wouldn't he remind you that God is in control of everything?"

Shaking her head, Abigail gave Ethan a small smile. "That's not what Papa believed. He taught that God has given us everything, including free will, and that it's up to us whether we accept his gifts."

"Your father sounds very different from the ministers I knew."

Ethan cleared his throat, as if signaling that he wanted to change the topic of conversation. "Which direction did you go last time?" When Abigail pointed to the right, he nodded. "Let's go the other way so you can see a different part of the countryside."

"It all looks the same to me."

Though Abigail dressed her words in a joking tone, Ethan responded as if she had been completely serious. "In that case, you haven't been looking carefully. My mission for today is to change your opinion."

They rode for a few minutes, and though Abigail did not want to admit it, she could discern no difference from the landscape she had seen riding the opposite direction. There were the same low hills, the same scrubby brush, the same occasional outcroppings of limestone. The ground was covered with the same mixture of short curly grasses and long straight blades, all interspersed with yellow flowers and flat white stones. It wasn't ugly, but it was a bit monotonous. Abigail much preferred talking about the upcoming Independence Day celebration, which Ethan claimed was one of the highlights of the year. "Mind you," he said, "I wasn't here for it last year, but the men all say that it's the biggest celebration of the summer with games, fireworks, and good food."

As a large bird soared overhead, Abigail smiled. Even she

had to admit that the sky was magnificent, especially with the hawk or eagle or whatever it was casting its shadow on the ground.

"Let me guess. Is food the main attraction?"

Though he shrugged, Ethan's grin confirmed her supposition. "Anything's better than dry bread and coffee—no milk or sugar, just coffee. That's what the men are served for supper most days."

Abigail wrinkled her nose. "That does not sound in the least appetizing." Even the bland meals Mrs. Channing had prepared for Charlotte were more appealing than that. "Have you considered the possibility that food might be the reason men desert?"

She had been half joking, but Ethan nodded. "Low pay, poor food, and harsh conditions. It's a tough life, but I still can't sympathize with men who don't live up to their commitments. They gave their word when they enlisted." He stared into the distance, the clenching of his jaw telling Abigail that his thoughts had strayed into unpleasant territory. "My grandfather and I don't agree on very many things, but I do agree with one thing he taught me, and that's that a man's honor is his most valuable possession."

Papa had said the same thing, telling his daughters that they must follow through on any promises they made. "I think my father would have liked your grandfather."

Ethan muttered something that sounded like a scoff. "I doubt that. Grandfather is not a likeable man."

His tone hinted at a conflict that was deeper than a few disagreements and confirmed her impression that Ethan's childhood had been a difficult one. How sad! Abigail could not imagine growing up in a household that wasn't filled with

love. While her parents had never had many material possessions, they'd lavished love on their daughters, but it seemed
that Ethan's life had been the opposite. He'd never known
poverty, but he also had never known love. Though Abigail
longed to learn more about Ethan and his grandfather, the
glint in his eyes told her that was a forbidden subject, and
so she simply nodded before she asked Ethan whether there
would be a baseball game as part of the Independence Day
celebration.

Though he shook his head, he was smiling, perhaps because he liked the idea, perhaps because he was relieved that
Abigail had not pursued the subject of his grandfather. A
moment later, he reined in his horse. "Aren't the flowers beautiful?" he asked when they had both stopped.

"Those are flowers? I thought they were stones."

Ethan laughed as he dismounted. "I assure you, they're
flowers. C'mon."

He was simply being a gentleman, helping her off her horse;
there was nothing untoward in his actions. Yet Abigail had
never been so aware of the warmth of a man's hands. It
was almost as if the outline of his fingers were imprinted
on her waist. She took a step backward, trying to regain her
equilibrium.

"You have to get close to appreciate them."

Grateful for the excuse to move, Abigail knelt next to
one of the white patches and discovered that what she had
believed to be stones were masses of the smallest flowers she
had ever seen. Though each was no more than a fraction
of an inch across, the blossoms clustered together to form
a beautiful mound of white. As she bent her head to study
them, Abigail discovered that each flower had five distinct

rounded petals and a yellow center so small that it was practically invisible.

"Oh, they're lovely," she said softly. Perhaps Ethan was right. Perhaps she needed to look more closely, and perhaps it wasn't only flowers that benefited from a closer look. Perhaps she needed to view people differently too. Unbidden, Leah's image filled her mind, making her wonder what she would discover if she spent more time with her.

Unaware of Abigail's internal turmoil, Ethan chuckled. "Be careful, Abigail. Before you know it, you'll find yourself liking Wyoming."

It wasn't a matter of liking or disliking, Abigail realized. It was simply that life here was very different from Vermont. At home she would have been too busy to spend a morning searching for wildflowers. "We don't have flowers like these in Vermont," she admitted. "Do you know what they're called?"

Ethan quirked an eyebrow. "I'll have you know they didn't teach horticulture at West Point, but . . ." He paused for dramatic effect. "Someone told me these are Rocky Mountain phlox."

Rising, Abigail looked around and spotted another white-flowering plant. This one was considerably larger than the stone-like clusters. "What is this?" she asked, moving closer to inspect it. "The flowers look like poppies, but I've never seen white ones."

"Be careful," Ethan cautioned as she bent to touch the paper-thin petals. "They're called prickly poppies. If you touch the leaves, you'll learn why."

From a distance, the bluish-gray leaves appeared innocuous, but as she looked more carefully, Abigail saw that they did indeed have sharp edges. "I venture to say they're not as dangerous as yuccas."

"Few things are as sharp as a yucca," Ethan agreed, "but the flowers are pretty enough."

"That's what Mrs. Dunn told me."

"Mrs. Dunn?"

It was Abigail's turn to laugh. "How could you forget our companion from the stagecoach?"

He groaned. "Ah yes, the widow with the wagging tongue."

Abigail hoped he didn't remember that one of the widow's wags of the tongue had concerned Ethan as a potential suitor. That was a dangerous subject to contemplate, particularly when the wind carried Ethan's scent, teasing Abigail with the memory of how she'd inhaled it when he'd helped her dismount. "Mrs. Dunn meant well, and she gave me some good advice. Thanks to her, I was careful to keep Sally away from prairie dog holes."

"How cruel of you to remind me that Samson was not so fortunate." The crook of his lips that accompanied Ethan's words told Abigail he was only joking. "Just for that, I may not help you back on your horse."

But he did, cupping his hands so she could step into them as she mounted Sally. It felt strange, using a man's hands that way, and yet there was something comforting about it. Perhaps it was the reminder that, while she might be in a seemingly wild place, she was not alone. They'd ridden farther than Abigail had dared on her solitary ride, leaving the fort far behind, yet she'd felt not a twinge of concern. Instead, she had enjoyed the countryside, Ethan's company, and their conversation. Strangely enough, she even enjoyed the silence, the times when their casual conversation faded and they rode side by side without speaking.

Woodrow could not tolerate silence. When he and Abigail were together, he was either telling her something or asking her a question. There were no long pauses and certainly never minutes without a spoken word. This was different. The silence was comfortable.

Abigail wasn't certain how long they'd ridden when she realized that they'd made a large circle and were now approaching familiar landmarks. The solitary cottonwood by the river was surely the one where she'd met Leah, and the outline of grayish white buildings told her they were close to the fort.

As they approached the tree, Abigail saw that Leah was there again. Though she wore the same dress, her shoulders were not slumped. Instead, her posture seemed almost jaunty. Abigail said a silent prayer of thanks as she tightened the reins and headed toward the young woman. She would not return to the fort without greeting Leah. Though she had no solution to Leah's dilemma, she could at least offer friendship. "Good morning, Leah," Abigail called out. "I'm glad to see you again."

Ethan said nothing, unless a snort could be considered a form of communication, but he remained at Abigail's side.

As she drew closer, Abigail saw that Leah's hair was damp as if she had washed it in the river. A pang of regret twisted Abigail's heart. When would she learn? Though she'd meant to encourage her, Abigail's impulsive action had put Leah in an embarrassing position. No lady would allow a strange man to see her hair unless it was properly coiffed. Leah gathered the long, thick tresses in her hands and held them behind her head, and as she did, the wind carried her scent toward Abigail.

For a second Abigail felt as if she would faint. Though she wanted to deny it, she could not. Leah's was the perfume Abigail had smelled in the parlor. That was why it had seemed familiar. Leah had been wearing it when Abigail had met her. *Oh, Jeffrey, how could you?* Abigail clenched her fists, trying to control her anger.

Perhaps her distress communicated itself to Leah, for she did not meet Abigail's gaze as she said, "Good morning, Miss Harding. Sir. I must be going now."

"And we'd best be getting back to the fort." Though he phrased it as a comment, there was steel in Ethan's voice, making his words tantamount to a command. His rigid posture told Abigail he disapproved of Leah as much as Charlotte did.

Ethan waited until they were out of earshot before he spoke again, and when he did, his words were harsh. "How do you know that woman?" he demanded.

Still reeling from the thought that Jeffrey spent his evenings with Leah, Abigail met Ethan's gaze, refusing to be cowed by his apparent anger. She was angry too, but her anger was directed at Jeffrey and all the other men who took advantage of Leah's helplessness. "If you're referring to Leah, I met her the first time I came out riding."

Ethan's lips tightened. "You know what she is, don't you?" It was as she had feared. Ethan judged Leah by the way she earned her living and refused to see that there was an ordinary woman beneath the painted face.

"I know *who* she is," Abigail countered. "Leah is a woman caught in unfortunate circumstances."

Ethan shook his head. "What do you know of her circumstances? Have you ever seen a hog ranch?" He stared

141

into the distance for a long moment before he said, "Maybe you should."

He turned away from the river, apparently ignoring the sight of Leah walking in the same direction. They rode for less than a mile, but for the first time Abigail found the silence uncomfortable. Ethan was seething, the severe line of his lips leaving no doubt that he was displeased. The only question was whether that displeasure was aimed at Abigail or Leah.

As they approached a dilapidated collection of buildings, Ethan gestured toward them. "This is it. This is Peg's Place."

Though Abigail had heard complaints about the condition of the frame buildings at the fort, they were well-built edifices compared to these. Peg's Place consisted of a cluster of flimsy wooden structures whose paint had long since faded and peeled. The center building was flanked by three smaller structures on either side, and what appeared to be a stable stood at the far end. If this was where Leah lived, it was no wonder she looked so . . . defeated. That was the only word Abigail could find to describe her.

A couple chickens scratched in the dirt, while two women leaned against one of the smaller buildings. Though the women were considerably older than Leah, their garish clothing left no doubt of their occupation. They looked up with interest at the sound of hoofbeats, but when they saw Abigail, they resumed their conversation. One swatted at a fly, and as she did, the scent of her perfume reached Abigail. It was the same as Leah's, the same one that had lingered in the parlor. While that might mean that Leah was not the woman Jeffrey visited, it did not exonerate him. The evidence seemed clear: Jeffrey had visited the hog ranch at least once.

"Good morning, Miss Harding." The postmaster greeted her with his customary grin as he approached Charlotte's house at the same time as Abigail. "The letter you've been waiting for arrived today."

As he handed her an envelope bearing Woodrow's distinctive script, Abigail murmured her gratitude. Woodrow's letter was just what she needed, an antidote to the realization that Jeffrey had frequented Peg's Place and Ethan's admonition that she stay away from Leah.

"I reckon that's from your beau," the postmaster said. "You better hurry and read it."

Abigail did, not even removing her bonnet before she slid the closely written pages from the envelope.

The academy is lonely without you, Woodrow had written. *I think about last summer, recalling the times we rowed across the lake and the picnics we shared under the willow trees.* The letter continued for several pages, detailing Woodrow's plans for a new history class, and Abigail found herself skimming his words, looking for something more personal. She found it on the last page. *I miss you. You must come home, Abigail. You've been with your sister long enough. I insist you take the next train. It's time to begin making plans.*

Though he said nothing more, Abigail knew those plans were for their future. She stared out the window, looking at the now deserted parade ground. A week ago she would have been thrilled that Woodrow missed her and wanted to discuss their life together. She ought to be happy, but all she heard was the peremptory tone to his words. *I insist you take the next train.* The words grated. It wasn't simply that Woodrow was ordering her around the way Ethan ordered his men. Though she couldn't explain the reason, Abigail was not ready to return to Vermont.

"So, what did the old man want?" Jeffrey asked.

Ethan frowned. The two men were seated at the end of the long table, enjoying what passed for dinner. The only good news of the day was that the midwife had declared Charlotte well enough to resume her normal activities. Jeffrey had been grinning as he'd announced that Ethan was invited to share meals with them beginning tomorrow. There was no doubt that Mrs. Channing's cooking was excellent. Ethan knew he'd enjoy that. What wasn't clear was how Abigail would feel about having him there. He could blame no one but himself for that.

He hadn't been wrong when he'd explained that decent women did not frequent the hog ranch or speak to its residents. The problem was, he'd sounded just like his grandfather, all stern and disapproving. Ethan had hated it when Grandfather had used that superior tone, trying to quell Ethan's enthusiasm with his scorn, so it was understandable that Abigail had been annoyed with him.

The truth was, Ethan should not have interfered, but he hadn't been able to help himself. He didn't want Abigail hurt, and nothing good could come from her association with Leah. No matter how innocent it might be, the officers' wives wouldn't approve, and their disapproval could make

Abigail's life here decidedly unpleasant, and so he'd spoken more harshly than he intended, with the result that he'd hurt her. Now he owed her an apology. Another one.

"The captain." Jeffrey stabbed a piece of meat with so much force that his fork chattered against the plate, bringing Ethan's thoughts back to the present. "What did he say?"

"He was not happy. It seems some firearms were stolen last night, and he ordered me to get to the bottom of it." Ethan frowned, remembering how he'd spent the remainder of the morning. "As you would expect, none of the men admitted knowing anything. I'm not sure whether they're telling the truth or protecting someone. All I know is that Captain Westland expects me to find the rifles and the thief, and he wants results now."

Jeffrey's smile was sympathetic. "Good luck with that. The rifles are probably already sold."

"To whom?" If Ethan could find out who bought them, he might be able to learn the thief's identity.

"Ranchers, Indians, travelers—although not so many of the last two anymore." Jeffrey took a swallow of coffee before adding, "If you're wondering how I know, the last time this happened, the old man put me in charge. I guess it's the duty they fob off on the newest lieutenant."

"Did you find the thief?"

Jeffrey's pursed lips made his answer redundant. "No. One rancher admitted he bought his rifles from a soldier. He claimed he couldn't recognize the man—said we all look alike."

Ethan had heard that before, and he supposed that if a man wasn't particularly observant, all men in uniforms did resemble each other. "Does this happen very often?"

"Not anymore. It used to be more common," Jeffrey admitted. "My theory is that the thief is an enlisted man who needs extra money. You might want to see who's been gambling and losing a lot lately."

Ethan nodded. "That makes sense." With the paymaster coming only every two months and sometimes being delayed, soldiers were almost always short of money. "Of course, I doubt anyone will tell me what I need to know." He couldn't simply walk into the enlisted men's club and ask who was down on his luck. Officers weren't welcome in the club under the best of circumstances, and searching for a thief did not qualify as the best of anything.

"Cheer up!" Jeffrey refilled Ethan's coffee cup along with his own. "By next week, the captain will have forgotten about the rifles, or if he hasn't, he'll have something else that's more important. That's what happened to me."

"That would be good news." Finding the deserters was more important, at least to Ethan.

Jeffrey reached into his pocket. "I almost forgot. I saw the postmaster this morning, and when he mentioned there was a letter for you, I offered to deliver it."

Ethan looked at the envelope, surprised by the sight of unfamiliar handwriting. "I wasn't expecting mail."

"Maybe it's good news."

But it wasn't. When he returned to his quarters and opened the envelope, Ethan discovered that the letter was from Mrs. Eberle, his grandfather's housekeeper. It was the first time she'd written, and, judging from the poor grammar, the scratched-out words, and the barely legible penmanship, Mrs. Eberle had had difficulty composing the letter. Ethan had difficulty with the contents.

The housekeeper claimed that Grandfather was failing. That was hardly a surprise. Curtis Wilson was seventy-two years old, and the doctors had started warning him that he had a bad heart back when Ethan had lived with him. What was a surprise was Mrs. Eberle's final paragraph. "Reckon you oughta come to New York right away. Your grandpa needs you." Hah! Grandfather didn't need anyone. Ethan crumpled the letter and discarded it.

Unfortunately, it was not so easy to dismiss the ideas Mrs. Eberle had planted. They haunted him through baseball practice, leaving Ethan so distracted that he turned practice over to Oliver, claiming it was important for the team to have a variety of leaders.

Retreat was over, and there were still a couple hours of daylight before he had to be back for tattoo. Ethan headed for the door. Even though the wind had died down and the mosquitoes would be biting, he had to get out of his quarters. If he stayed here, his thoughts would continue their endless circle, reminding him of the deserters, his grandfather, and the expression on Abigail's face when he'd practically commanded her to stay away from the hog ranch.

A brisk ride would clear his head. But as he walked toward the stables, he saw a familiar figure. Two familiar figures, Ethan amended, for Abigail was accompanied by Puddles. Admittedly, it was debatable which was accompanying the other. While Abigail might claim that she was taking Puddles for a walk, the puppy seemed to be leading the way and setting the pace.

Ethan considered an abrupt retreat. After all, it was possible Abigail would not welcome his company. But, though he told his feet to turn around, they did not, and he soon found himself only a yard away from the beautiful woman and her dog. The woman was smiling, as if she bore no grudges, while the dog jumped on him, leaving dusty footprints on Ethan's trousers. It was a warmer welcome than he deserved, and perhaps it meant there was no need to voice an apology.

"He's growing, isn't he?" Ethan bent to rub Puddles's head, then looked up at Abigail.

If she was unhappy about seeing him, she gave no sign. Instead, it seemed as if this morning's disagreement had not occurred. Perhaps she too wanted to forget it. "I thought he felt heavier when I bathed him." Abigail's smile was wry as she added, "That's not a favorite event for either one of us. The truth is, he eats so much that I'm surprised he isn't twice this size."

"Before you know it, he'll be full grown."

Abigail's smile faded, and as she gazed at the parade ground, her expression seemed almost melancholy. "I won't be here to see that."

Ethan swatted at a mosquito, reflecting that the insect's bite hurt far less than the prospect of Abigail's departure. It would accomplish nothing for him to admit that he would miss her, and so he forced a smile. "True, but you have something else to look forward to. You'll be back in Vermont." *With Woodrow.* Ethan would not pronounce those words. They were worse than the mosquitoes constantly buzzing at him.

"I'm not sure how long I'll be here. I had planned no more than a month. Now that Charlotte seems better, I could leave, but . . ." Abigail paused, and Ethan sensed that she was trying to choose her words carefully. "I received a disturbing letter today."

148

Though she said nothing more, Ethan suspected the letter had come from Woodrow. The man was a fool if he'd said something to upset Abigail. Ethan flinched at the realization that he had been the one to upset her this morning. He was hardly the one to cast stones. But that didn't mean he would introduce Woodrow's name. Instead, he said, "It must have been the day for unpleasant letters, because I got one of my own." He tightened his fists as he recalled the contents. "I hate it when people think they know what's best for me."

"I know what you mean. I guess I don't like being ordered around."

"Nor do I."

Abigail raised an eyebrow. "That's an odd statement, coming from a man who chose a career in the Army."

"It does sound strange, doesn't it?" They had rounded the corner of the parade ground and were approaching Abigail's house. Ethan slowed his steps, not wanting their conversation to end. "It's different, though, when the order comes from my commanding officer. It's his job to give orders and mine to obey. I knew that when I joined the Army. I might not always like the orders, but I know this is the life I'm meant to lead."

Abigail's smile faltered. "I wish I were so certain. I used to be, but now . . . now I'm not."

The admission surprised Ethan. The Abigail he knew—the Abigail he *thought* he knew—was the personification of confidence. What had happened to change that?

"What did you think you were meant to do?" he asked.

As Puddles whimpered, annoyed by his mistress's failure to walk as quickly as he wished, Abigail picked him up and cradled him in her arms. "I imagined that I would marry and raise a family." She gave Puddles a smile as she stroked the puppy's ears. "I pictured myself with six children—three girls and three boys—all of us living in a house near a lake."

Ethan tried not to frown. It shouldn't matter to him that there were no lakes in this part of Wyoming. She wasn't staying here. "It sounds as if you've got it all figured out." He shouldn't be continuing this discussion, for it was like picking the scab off a partially healed wound.

Abigail set Puddles back on the ground, waiting until she was once again upright before she answered. "It's what I thought I wanted," she said softly, "but I'm not certain it's God's plan. That's what worries me."

"I'm hardly the person to advise you about that, but you're a minister's daughter. If you asked your father, what would he have said?"

Abigail's eyes widened, and then she smiled. "That's easy. Papa would say there was only one way to find out, and that's to ask him. God, that is."

Her words echoed through her head as she entered her room. Ask God. She had been doing that. Or had she? Abigail stared at the floor. Had she really asked, or had she merely told God what she wanted and then waited for his approval of her plans? She feared she had done the latter. Perhaps that was why she hadn't received an answer.

Slowly, she sank to her knees and bowed her head in prayer. *Father in heaven, I'm sorry. I trust you. I know you have plans for me, and they're better than my plans. Show me your plan.* There were no answers, nothing but the feeling of peace that filled her heart. That was enough for now. The answers would come.

150

Half an hour later, Abigail heard Charlotte stirring in the room next door. Knowing Jeffrey wasn't home, Abigail opened the connecting door. Her sister was sitting up in bed, her color better than it had been that morning.

"Will you brush my hair?"

It was the first time Charlotte had asked Abigail to perform what had been a nightly ritual when they were children. Abigail smiled as she realized this was the answer she had sought. Charlotte needed her, if only to brush her hair.

When Abigail nodded, her sister climbed out of bed and took a seat on her dressing stool. "I want to look pretty for Jeffrey," she said as she handed the silver-backed brush to Abigail. "I've missed him so much."

"Of course you've missed him. He's your husband." Unbidden, the memory of the hog ranch women's perfume disturbed Abigail's thoughts. She would not upset Charlotte by speaking of that, and yet she could not forget.

In her distress, Abigail must have made a sound, for Charlotte's eyes narrowed as she studied Abigail's face in the mirror. "I know you miss Woodrow. That's why, as much as I love having you here, I think you should go home. You deserve your own life."

Abigail shook her head. "Not until I'm sure you don't need me anymore. You're the reason I came here."

"I know, and I appreciate it, but I have Jeffrey."

Could Charlotte depend on Jeffrey? Abigail wasn't certain. "I still worry about you, sister of mine." It was the term of endearment they'd used as children. Abigail employed it deliberately, hoping it would make Charlotte smile.

It did. "There's no need to worry," her sister insisted. Though she spoke firmly, her words did not convince

Abigail. "I'll be fine, and you need to go home. Woodrow is waiting."

Abigail drew the brush through Charlotte's hair, setting it to crackling. "I will go home, but only at the end of the summer." As Charlotte started to protest, Abigail raised a cautioning hand. "I've prayed about this, Charlotte, and I believe this is what God wants. If Woodrow and I are going to have a life together, he will wait for me. My place is here with you."

And with Leah and Ethan. She might fail, but she had to try to help Leah. As for Ethan, though he wouldn't admit it, he needed help too. Abigail wasn't sure what she could do. All she knew was that God wanted her to do something, and until she knew what it was, she was not leaving Wyoming.

9

The baron had arrived. Though he walked lightly for a man, the cloud of cigar smoke that surrounded him announced his presence before his footsteps were audible. Frances closed the door to her private residence and made her way into the back room where she and the baron conducted their business. No one—not even the baron—was allowed into her chambers. Unlike the girls she hired, she did not entertain men in her quarters. It was there that she kept mementos of her past, tangible proof that the woman everyone in this part of Wyoming knew as Peg was actually Frances Colfax, former star of the stage. Even the baron, who thought he knew everything about her, didn't know that.

"Want a whiskey?" Of course he did. The man who was no more a baron than she was named Peg always wanted one. She poured a generous serving into one glass before splashing a smaller quantity into another. No sense in muddling her wits. When the baron was here, she needed all of them.

"What have you got for me?" he asked when he'd downed the amber liquid and held out the glass for a refill. Other than his prominent nose, Frances found nothing distinctive about the man who'd been her business partner for six years. He was of medium height with steel gray hair and light blue eyes. Dressed as he was today in a finely cut suit, he looked the part of the cattle baron he claimed to be, but Frances knew that if he wore Levis, chaps, and a chambray shirt, he'd blend into a group of ranchers.

She also knew he wouldn't like her answer. "Mostly Colts." She opened the crate that she'd dragged into the room earlier this morning, revealing a dozen revolvers and two rifles.

The baron's lips tightened. "Springfields are worth more." He lifted one of the rifles from the crate and aimed it at her. Another woman might have flinched, but Frances knew it was an empty threat. Even if the rifle were loaded, which it was not, the baron wouldn't shoot her. One night when he'd had more whiskey than usual, he'd revealed that while he had few scruples, he would not kill women or children. When it was unavoidable, he assuaged his conscience by ordering someone else to pull the trigger.

"I'm not stupid, Baron. I know the value of rifles. The problem is, our friend"—Frances infused the word with scorn—"said this was all he could get. Things haven't been the same since the cavalry left the fort. Fewer men mean fewer weapons."

The baron returned the rifle to the crate. "This'll do for this week. Rumor has it some rich folks are headed for Deadwood next week. It would be a real shame to pass up the opportunity to get better acquainted with them, don't you think?"

Frances nodded as her mind began to whirl with possibilities. It was too soon for Mrs. Dunn to travel again. Who would she be this time? A wealthy widow? A spinster aunt? An aging schoolmistress? She'd find the right role, and then, just as she had on the stage, she would play it to perfection.

"One more thing," the baron said as he slid the crate toward the door. "I heard someone's been looking for Big Nose's stash. Could be it's our friend at the fort. If it is, he'd better be prepared to share."

Frances poured herself another glass of whiskey, wondering if there was any truth to the baron's story. She doubted there was anyone in Wyoming who hadn't heard of George Parrott, better known as Big Nose. One of the territory's most daring and successful outlaws, he'd met his fate at the end of a hangman's noose a few years earlier, leaving few mourners but plenty of people speculating on where he had hidden a large shipment of gold.

Rifles were good, stagecoach travelers' jewels even better, but nothing could compare to Big Nose's gold. It was time to discover just what the man at the fort knew.

Independence Day had finally arrived, and for once, the Wyoming winds were not howling. It was, in fact, almost calm—a rarity, and one that would enhance everyone's enjoyment of the holiday. Abigail was not surprised by the men's anticipation of the day. Even with the addition of baseball, their lives were monotonous, and the celebrations promised a welcome diversion. What did surprise her was Charlotte's enthusiasm. It seemed that no one was as excited as her sister. Ever since she'd recovered from her last bout of illness, she had been filled with energy. Not only did Charlotte have Mrs. Channing working extra hours to bake special desserts for the men, but—despite Abigail's protests—she had insisted on sewing a new gown for Abigail.

"You have nothing patriotic," Charlotte had declared when Abigail had suggested that she would wear one of the frocks she had brought from Vermont. "This is our nation's birthday. You need to be properly dressed, and that means red, white, and blue." And so she had chosen a deep red poplin for Abigail's tunic, accenting it with white lace. Wide bands of the lace trimmed the collar, cuffs, and lower edges, while narrower lace appliquéd on the front of the bodice gave the illusion of a jacket. Though Charlotte had promised to make a matching skirt, today the exquisitely trimmed tunic would be worn over a pleated navy blue skirt to complete the red, white, and blue color scheme. Charlotte had even trimmed Abigail's straw hat with wide blue ribbons and red rosettes and had attached red and blue ruffles and ribbons to her white parasol.

"It's beautiful." Abigail pirouetted in front of the cheval mirror. Though Charlotte's dress was far simpler than Abigail's, the design was nonetheless striking. Since Charlotte had finally begun to gain weight and could no longer lace her corset as tightly as before, she had created a one-piece semi-fitted dress with princess lines from the same navy blue fabric that she had used for Abigail's skirt. Dark red cuffs and collar set off the deep blue, and though the buttons that actually fastened the gown were hidden by a placket, the dress appeared to be closed by the most ornately braided frogs Abigail had ever seen. Marching from the high collar to the hem, the frogs added an elegant touch of white to Charlotte's costume.

"We're certain to be the best-dressed women on the post, thanks to you." Abigail smiled. Though everyone at Fort Laramie knew of their relationship, the use of the same materials in their gowns proclaimed their sisterhood, and that felt good.

The doubt Abigail had once had about the wisdom of coming to Wyoming had disappeared. This was where she was meant to be. She was certain of that, even if she did not yet know all she was meant to do. She had ridden to the large cottonwood three times, looking for Leah, but the woman had not been there. And though she saw Ethan each day at mealtimes and twice a week for baseball games, she was no closer to knowing how to help him. The bright spot was that Charlotte was happy.

Abigail gave her sister another smile. "I don't know how to thank you for this beautiful gown."

Charlotte shrugged, as if the hours she had spent designing and then creating the dress were of no account. "You know I love to sew, and I have plenty of time. Besides, it gives me pleasure to have someone wear what I've made."

Abigail had wondered if Charlotte's newfound happiness was in part because she had more things to occupy her days now that Abigail was here. If that was true, what would happen when Abigail returned to Vermont at the end of the summer? Charlotte's words gave her an idea.

"I heard some of the officers' wives complaining about how difficult it is to go to Cheyenne for fittings for their clothing. Have you considered becoming the post's seamstress?"

At first the only sign Charlotte gave that she heard the question was the almost imperceptible tightening of her lips. Then she shook her head. "I did think about it when we first arrived, but Jeffrey wouldn't approve. He believes it's his responsibility to provide for his family."

And once Jeffrey made up his mind, he was unlikely to change it. Abigail tucked an errant curl back into her sister's coiffure as she said, "It's fortunate Papa didn't feel that way." Abigail could not recall a time when sales of Mama's jellies and candies had not been an important source of income for the Harding family.

The shake of her head said Charlotte disagreed. "Papa didn't have much choice. Each time we moved, there were months without pay."

"I hadn't realized that." Abigail's heart clenched as she wondered what else she had missed.

"We weren't supposed to know, but I heard Mama and Papa talking once. They didn't realize I was in the next room when they were worrying about how they were going to clothe us. Apparently there was enough money for food, but all three of us girls had worn out our clothes." Charlotte rose and opened one of her bureau drawers. Though her back was to Abigail, Abigail could hear the distress in her sister's voice. "It was the only time I can remember hearing Mama cry. She had cut up her dresses to make clothes for us the year before, and there weren't any left. The next day, a box of used clothing appeared on our porch."

"I remember that. Mama said it was the answer to prayer."

Charlotte turned, a pair of gloves in her hands. "It wasn't the answer to my prayer. The only dress that fit me was a putrid green. It was the ugliest thing I'd ever seen, and I hated it, but I couldn't say anything, because I didn't want Mama to cry again."

Abigail looked at the beautiful gown Charlotte was wearing.

It was a far cry from the detested green frock. "I remember that dress," she said softly, "but I don't remember it being ugly. What I remember is that you crocheted the most beautiful collar and cuffs for it, and every girl in school wanted a set just like yours."

Charlotte shrugged. "I had to do something to make it a little less awful. I never forgot that dress, though, and I swore that when I grew up, I'd never have another ugly gown."

"And you don't." Abigail's heart ached for the girl her sister had been. Though they had shared secrets over the years, she had never realized how much Charlotte had been affected by hand-me-down clothing. No wonder she'd become such an accomplished seamstress. Clothing hadn't mattered to Abigail, but having a permanent home did. She wondered what Elizabeth would say if she were here. Was there something her younger sister had found lacking in her childhood?

When they descended the stairs, Charlotte took an obviously unhappy Puddles to the side yard and tied him to the tree. "Sorry, boy, but you can't go with us. Today is for people only."

The puppy whined. Abigail smiled. "He thinks he is people." Fierce barking appeared to confirm her impression.

Abigail and Charlotte walked along the east side of the parade ground, waiting for the first event of the day, the full dress parade. Scheduled for late morning, it would be followed by a thirty-five gun salute at noon and then what many enlisted men considered the highlight of the day, a special dinner. Not only had the company cooks been given extra rations of meat, but the officers' wives had sent desserts. There would even be butter for the bread today.

"Are you sure you feel all right?" Abigail asked as she and Charlotte waited for the parade to begin.

Her sister nodded. "I feel wonderful, but even if I didn't, I wouldn't miss this for anything."

As if on cue, a bugle announced the beginning of the parade. Abigail found herself standing taller, her eyes shining with pride as she watched the men march onto the parade ground. Though they were forbidden to smile, she saw the excitement reflected in their eyes and knew that it was more than anticipation of a special meal. At least for the moment, these men were enjoying being part of the Army. It was a longer parade than normal, an extra circuit of the parade ground, and yet when it ended, Abigail found herself wishing it would continue.

When the men had filed off the parade ground, heading for their mess halls, Abigail and Charlotte made their way to Mrs. Montgomery's home, where she and Mrs. Alcott had arranged a communal meal for the officers and their families. Each household brought at least one dish to share, while the hostesses provided beverages. Though Charlotte had volunteered to help arrange the food, both women refused, citing her delicate condition, and so Charlotte and Abigail simply stood on the porch, waiting for Jeffrey and Ethan to arrive.

As the men approached, Abigail found herself comparing them. When she'd been a child, she had thought that soldiers were like the gingerbread men her mother used to make for Christmas, all the same. But as she'd matured, she'd realized how wrong she was. These two men were the perfect example. Though Jeffrey was several inches shorter than Ethan, he appeared to be the larger man, with broader shoulders and a more solid build. And, unlike Ethan, whom any woman would call handsome, Jeffrey was not a man who would inspire a second glance . . . except from Charlotte. During their brief courtship, Charlotte had declared Jeffrey the most wonderful, most handsome, most distinguished man she had ever met. Charlotte, Abigail had realized the instant she had set eyes on Jeffrey, was a woman in love, for Jeffrey was neither handsome nor distinguished. Ethan, however, was the personification of both of those adjectives.

"Did you enjoy the morning?" the object of her thoughts asked as he climbed the steps at a normal pace. Jeffrey had bounded up them and drawn Charlotte to the side for a private conversation.

Abigail nodded. "All except the cannons. I don't know if I'll ever get used to them." In Abigail's mind a gun was a gun, and they were all dangerous. "The parade seemed even better than the ones on Sundays."

Ethan's smile told Abigail he understood. "I thought so too. The men are excited that today's our nation's birthday." His grin widened. "It reminds us of why we're proud to be Americans and why we joined the Army."

He opened the door and ushered Abigail into the house, where the other officers and their wives stood in line, waiting to help themselves to the bountiful buffet laid out on the table. The adults appeared pleased, and cries of delight filtering through the door confirmed that the children were enjoying their picnic in the backyard. It was meant to be a special day for everyone, and yet though he smiled, Abigail thought she detected sadness or perhaps worry in Ethan's eyes.

"I doubt you need to worry about deserters today." She spoke softly, not wanting the others to overhear.

"I wasn't." Ethan gestured at the table. "Jeffrey pointed

out that no one would be foolish enough to pass up a good meal. The men's dinner may not be this elaborate, but it's much better than normal."

If the prospect of desertion wasn't causing Ethan's barely concealed emotion, Abigail suspected it was the letter he'd received the same day that Woodrow's summons had arrived. Ethan had seemed more serious since then. Abigail made a silent resolution to ask him about it the next time they were alone.

The food was as delicious as the aromas promised; the conversation was pleasant; Charlotte was glowing with happiness, basking in Jeffrey's attention. It was a close to perfect meal, and yet Abigail wished it were over and that she could find an opportunity to speak with Ethan.

Jeffrey rose. "We'll join you later." The meal had ended, and the men needed to prepare for the afternoon's activities.

When Ethan and Jeffrey had departed, Abigail turned toward Charlotte, noticing that her sister looked peaked. "Why don't you rest here?" she suggested. "I can check on Puddles." They had agreed that the puppy could not be left alone for the entire day and had planned to take him for a walk between dinner and the first of the games.

When Charlotte nodded, Abigail picked up the parasol her sister had decorated to match her dress. As she walked briskly toward her sister's home, she hoped that Puddles had not gotten into more mischief. Yesterday he'd discovered the joy of digging, and the Crowleys' yard would never be the same. Jeffrey had not been pleased. When he'd seen the damage, he had declared in a tone that was reminiscent of Woodrow disciplining errant pupils that the dog could not be allowed to continue destroying the little amount of grass they had.

"You're taking our nation's birthday seriously, aren't you? Even your parasol is patriotic."

Abigail turned, startled by the sound of Ethan's voice. "I didn't hear you coming."

"You looked as if you were lost in your thoughts. Were you wishing you were back in Vermont?"

Something in Ethan's expression told her the question was more than a casual inquiry. For some reason, he cared about her response. "No," she answered honestly. "I'm happy to be here." It was the truth. "I was simply thinking that Jeffrey reminded me of someone."

Ethan nodded as if he understood. "Jeffrey's a fine soldier and a man of honor. If he reminds you of someone, that's good. Isn't it?"

"I suppose so." Fortunately, Woodrow wasn't a soldier. He would never carry a gun. He would never kill another human being. But Ethan was correct. Woodrow was honorable, and that was important. Even more important was the fact that he and she wanted the same things from life: a home, family, stability. If he lacked a sense of humor, well . . . no one was perfect.

They'd reached the Crowley home, and as Abigail had feared, Puddles was awake, furiously digging holes in the ground.

"No, Puddles!" Abigail gave the puppy a stern look before she sighed. "Jeffrey will not be happy about this." She studied the piles of dirt, wondering how she was going to restore the lawn. Even if she did, there was no guarantee that Puddles wouldn't try to dig another tunnel.

"Is there a shovel?" Ethan asked.

Abigail's gaze moved from the dirt to Ethan, clad in his dress uniform. That was hardly appropriate garb for digging in the dirt. "I thought everyone was changing uniforms for the games."

"Everyone who's participating is," Ethan agreed. "I'm not. My job is to announce the winners and award prizes. It seems to me it's more special for the men if I'm in full dress when I do that."

How thoughtful! "I cannot allow you to clean up after Puddles when you're dressed this way," Abigail said firmly. "Besides, Puddles will simply undo all the work, anyway. But I'll warn Charlotte. Maybe she can sweet-talk Jeffrey a bit."

As Ethan nodded, Abigail took a deep breath, knowing that if she let this opportunity pass, another might not present itself for days. "I hope you don't think I'm prying, but you look as if something's bothering you. I've found that talking often helps."

Ethan was silent for so long that Abigail feared he would refuse to answer. "You weren't supposed to notice. No one was."

"Because you're an officer, and officers solve their own problems?"

Ethan's eyes widened. "Yes," he admitted.

It was what Abigail had feared, masculine pride combined with his West Point training. "You're also a person, and people confide in their friends." She paused, giving him a small smile. "I'd like to think I'm your friend."

He nodded slowly. "You are. But, as you probably guessed, I'm not used to talking about myself."

She would have to probe if she were to learn anything. "You said you weren't worried about deserters."

When Puddles whined for attention, Ethan picked up a stick and tossed it across the yard. Yipping with delight, the puppy ran after it. Although she did not deny that Puddles needed the exercise, Abigail wondered whether Ethan had used the dog as a delaying tactic or whether he was simply ignoring her comment.

She looked at him, surprised when his lips curved again and she heard amusement in his voice. "I said I wasn't worried about that today." He emphasized the last word. "The truth is, I worry about deserters almost every day." His tone was once more serious. "I worry that they're connected to the theft of the revolvers; I worry that there'll be another stagecoach robbery; and I worry about . . ." His voice trailed off, but the tightening of his lips told Abigail that the last, unspoken worry was the most serious.

"About what?" she asked softly.

Ethan tossed the stick again. When Puddles scampered away, Ethan turned back to Abigail. "Did you resolve whatever was in the letter that disturbed you?"

His question, though unexpected, told Abigail two things: the mysterious letter had caused Ethan's greatest worry, and he was reluctant to share its contents with her. Perhaps if she told him about her letter, he would be willing to confide in her.

She nodded slowly. "My letter was from Woodrow." When Ethan inclined his head slightly, Abigail realized he'd surmised that. "He insisted that I return to Vermont immediately—practically commanded me to take the next train."

"But you didn't."

"No, I didn't. I realized that it wasn't time for me to leave. I still have things to do here."

The afternoon was so still that Abigail could hear the buzzing of insects in the neighbors' vegetable garden.

"I suppose you prayed about that." There was no scorn in Ethan's voice, only interest.

"And then I listened." Abigail gave him a rueful smile. "For me, that's always the hardest part—waiting for God's response. I'm too impatient. I want answers right away, but it doesn't always happen that way."

When Ethan said nothing, Abigail took another deep breath. "What was in your letter?"

He let out a chuckle that held no mirth. "Oddly enough, it was similar to yours. My grandfather's housekeeper wrote to say that he is failing and I should go back to New York to see him."

The bitterness in Ethan's voice told Abigail he had no intention of doing that. "Why won't you go?"

"Like you, I have things to do here."

It was an excuse. Abigail knew it. There were other officers at the fort, but he had only one grandfather. "Fort Laramie's problems aren't going away. It sounds as if your grandfather is."

"Maybe, but he and I have nothing to say to each other."

Abigail bit her lip, trying to find the correct words. She didn't claim to understand the relationship between Ethan and his grandfather, but Papa had given more than one sermon about the need to make peace before it was too late.

"Are you sure of that?" she asked.

Ethan shrugged, then shook his head. "Perhaps I should pray about it. But now . . ." He pulled out his watch. "It's time to return to the parade ground."

Though she knew nothing had been resolved, Abigail sensed a lightening of Ethan's mood and prayed that it would continue.

The afternoon was even more enjoyable than she had been led to expect, highlighted by races: foot, sack, and Abigail's favorite, the slow mule race. She and Charlotte stood on the sidelines, laughing as the men tried to keep their mules moving, but only barely. Though the goal was to be the last mule to cross the finish line, it was a delicate balancing act, for a mule was disqualified if he stopped for more than two seconds. And mules, being more cantankerous than a rooster and harder to train than a puppy, were inclined to move when and only when they chose to.

"Now I understand why dogs aren't allowed. Their barking might make the mules run."

"Or at least trot." Charlotte wrapped her arm around Abigail's waist and smiled. "I'm so glad you're here. It makes the day extra special." Charlotte gave Abigail a little squeeze. "Perhaps you and Woodrow will come next year."

Abigail looked around the parade ground, trying and failing to picture Woodrow there. "Perhaps."

The races continued until it was time for supper, and then after another better than normal meal for the men, the dancing began.

"I hope I won't step on your feet," Oliver said as he led Abigail to the center of the parade ground. Once again he'd been the first to ask for a dance, with Ethan second. Though Charlotte had wrinkled her nose at the thought of sitting on the sidelines, she had taken Mrs. Grayson's advice to refrain from any vigorous activity and was seated on one of the benches that lined the open area. Since Jeffrey was nowhere to be seen, Ethan had agreed to remain with Charlotte until it was his turn to dance.

"I'm certain you won't crush my toes," Abigail told Oliver. "You dance well." It was not flattery. Though he reminded her of a scarecrow when he walked, Oliver's dancing was flawless.

"That's because I'm with you," he said. "You're the best

partner I've ever had." But that was flattery, for it had been Abigail who missed a step. She wasn't normally clumsy, but she caught her heel on the edge of the oiled canvas that had been laid on the parade ground to form a dance floor and almost tumbled into Oliver's arms. It was only his quick reflexes that kept her upright.

"May I have another dance?" Oliver asked as the set came to a close.

"And risk your toes?" Abigail shook her head. "I'm afraid not. My sister told me that etiquette says a lady may not dance more than once with a man unless they're married or engaged to be married." Though she had apparently flouted convention by speaking to Leah, Abigail wasn't willing to break any rules tonight.

Oliver shrugged as if he'd expected her refusal. "Then there's no problem. All you need to do is agree to marry me." He took a step away from her and placed his hand on his heart. "Will you do me the honor of becoming my wife?"

He wasn't serious. He couldn't be. And yet instead of sparkling with mirth, Oliver's eyes appeared serious. Abigail took a deep breath and began to recite the words she'd tried to drum into her pupils' memory. "As greatly honored as I am by your proposal, I fear I must . . ."

A frown marred Oliver's face. "You don't have to continue. I can tell that your answer is no." He gave her an appraising look. "I know I took you by surprise. Next time will be different. You'll learn that I don't give up easily."

Before Abigail could reply, Ethan stood at her side, ready to claim his turn as her partner.

"She refused me," Oliver announced as he headed toward Charlotte.

Ethan fixed his eyes on Abigail, and she saw a hint of amusement in them. "What did he do, ask you for a second dance?"

"That was part of it. He also proposed marriage, although I doubt he was serious."

As the fiddler began to play, Ethan drew her into his arms. "He was serious. Oliver is always serious when he falls in love. The problem is, he falls in love every time an unmarried woman comes to the fort, and he falls out of love just as quickly."

"I thought so." Abigail smiled as she whirled across the makeshift dance floor in Ethan's arms. Though there had been moments of awkwardness with Oliver and she'd been conscious of the unevenness of the canvas beneath her feet, now Abigail felt as if she were floating an inch or so above the surface. Suddenly, the fact that she was dancing on canvas rather than polished wood and that mosquitoes buzzed nearby seemed like an adventure, not an accommodation to the realities of life on an Army post.

As the dance steps took them to the perimeter of the floor, Abigail saw Oliver smiling at Charlotte. "If I'm not mistaken," she told Ethan, "Lieutenant Seton has recovered from his disappointment."

"Fickle man." Ethan tightened his grip on her hand when they reached the edge of the canvas. "I would never be so callow."

"Don't tell me you've never fallen out of love." A man as handsome as Ethan Bowles had to have had at least one sweetheart.

"It's the truth," he insisted. "How could I fall out of love when I've never fallen in?"

Though his words were light, Abigail sensed there was

more to the story than he'd told, but now was not the time to ask. Instead, she matched his casual tone. "That is a definite problem."

"And one you don't share."

"Oh no." Abigail feigned a serious expression. "When I was eight years old, I was convinced that the grocer's delivery boy—he was all of ten years old and a grown man in my eyes—was my knight in shining armor."

The darkness had fled from Ethan's eyes, leaving them sparkling with mirth. "And then what happened?"

"He gave Charlotte a bouquet of dandelions." Abigail blinked her eyes as if trying to restrain her tears. "My heart was broken . . . for at least a day."

As she'd hoped, Ethan laughed.

Ethan stood at the side of the parade ground, watching the dancers take their places, looking at the sky and trying to judge how long it would be before the fireworks began. He had no other dances promised. Not only were there too many men, but he didn't enjoy dancing . . . except with Abigail. She was unlike any woman he'd met—smart, caring, and not afraid to laugh at herself. If he were a marrying man, which he most definitely was not, she would be the type of woman he'd want for a wife. And, even if he were a marrying man, there was Woodrow.

"Isn't she wonderful?" Oliver's voice held the same fatuous tone it had when he'd declared himself in love with Miss Smyth, the post's newest laundress.

Though he knew the answer to the question, Ethan couldn't help teasing Oliver. "Isn't who wonderful?"

Oliver's eyes widened, as if the answer should be apparent. "Miss Harding. Abigail. She's the most wonderful woman I've ever met."

Ethan wouldn't disagree with that assessment, even though he could not imagine Abigail as Mrs. Oliver Seton. "You think she's wonderful even though she refused you?"

"She'll change her mind. I know she will. I tell you, Ethan, she's the woman for me, even if she's not as beautiful as her sister."

Ethan blinked in surprise. "You think Charlotte's prettier than Abigail?"

Oliver nodded. "Any man with eyes can see that, but Jeffrey spotted her first. Lucky man. Abigail's next best."

The thought of Abigail as second best made Ethan clench his fists. Charlotte had a head filled with air. She would never have tried to help him out of the doldrums as Abigail had done, for she would not have even known he had sunk into the mire. Second best? Hah!

"You're crazy, Oliver. Anyone can see that Abigail's twice the woman Charlotte is. I'm not denying that Charlotte is pretty, but Abigail is in a class of her own."

Oliver's eyes narrowed as he regarded Ethan. "It sounds like you're interested in her yourself."

Ridiculous. The thought was absurd. "Of course I'm not. I'm only pointing out the facts."

"I'm warning you, Ethan. You may outrank me, but you'd better not be setting your sights on Miss Harding, because I aim to marry her." Without waiting for a reply, Oliver stalked away.

Ethan frowned. There was no reason Oliver's words should have left a sour taste in his mouth. After all, neither of them would be marrying Abigail Harding. So, why did Ethan care that Oliver seemed so determined to woo her? It was foolishness, plain and simple.

Ethan walked around the perimeter of the parade ground. He wasn't looking for Abigail. He simply needed something to do until the dancing ended. He didn't care if she was dancing. He didn't even care if she granted Oliver a second dance. It didn't matter. But, though he told himself he didn't care, Ethan's eyes searched the makeshift dance floor, looking for a beautiful woman in a red, white, and blue dress.

There she was. Ethan felt the blood drain from his face. What on earth was she doing now?

The man was unhappy. While the others who weren't dancing gathered in groups, talking, gesturing, and appearing to be having a good time, this one stood alone, his back to the crowd, his slumped shoulders betraying his feelings. Abigail frowned when he turned slightly and she recognized him as the soldier who had helped her in the stable. Corporal Keller. He'd been outgoing that day, and now something had made him morose. Unbidden, the thought of desertion planted itself in Abigail's mind. Surely the corporal wasn't planning to leave the Army, and yet . . . Ethan had said that several of the most recent deserters had been German-speaking. One of the would-be stagecoach robbers had been of German descent. Could it be that Corporal Keller planned to join them?

Fixing a smile on her face, Abigail approached the soldier. "I wonder if I could ask a favor of you." As he turned, a startled expression on his face, she continued. "It seems I have no partner for this dance. I know it's horribly forward of me, but would you keep me company?" She wouldn't dance with him, for that would cause Charlotte to frown, but surely there were no regulations forbidding an officer's sister-in-law from talking to an enlisted man.

Corporal Keller nodded. "*Ja*, I vould be honored."

As they walked a short distance away, Abigail smiled at the corporal. "Are you enjoying the celebration?" Since she'd spoken to him, he appeared to have dismissed whatever had been bothering him. Perhaps she had been wrong. Perhaps he had had only a moment of melancholy and hadn't been considering anything as drastic as desertion.

He wrinkled his nose in feigned annoyance. "It vould have been better if my mule had been slower." He had taken second place in the slow mule contest. "But it has been a good day."

Abigail thought about the day, trying to recall what she had seen the corporal doing. "You had to translate instructions for some of the men, didn't you?"

"*Ja*. I mean yes. They vant to learn to speak better, but it is hard."

"Why? I understood that the garrison has classes for the men as well as the children."

"*Ja*, but . . ." The corporal's expression sobered. "The teacher is not very patient. He makes a man feel like a *Dummkopf*."

Abigail's frown matched Corporate Keller's. "That's terrible. No teacher should do that."

"He is the best we have. Better than no one at all. That is vat I tell the others. Ve learn something."

"What does he teach you?"

"History and arithmetic."

"But not English?"

"No." Corporal Keller opened his mouth as if to add something, but as the music changed, so did his whole demeanor. The sparkle left his eyes, and his shoulders slumped ever so slightly. Abigail might not have noticed it, had she not seen him standing alone before.

"Is something wrong?" she asked softly.

For a moment she thought he might not respond, but at last he said, "It's the music. It reminds me of Marta." When Abigail raised an eyebrow, encouraging him to continue, he said, "She is my girl back home. The last time I danced vas vith her, and this vas the song the fiddler played."

"When was that?"

"Almost a year ago. Ve vanted to get married before I enlisted, but her father said ve had to vait. Now I save every penny to bring her out here as my bride. It is lonely vithout her."

Abigail suspected Corporal Keller's story was shared by others. Enlisted men's pay was barely enough to sustain a single man, much less a family, and unlike the officers, who had more freedom, enlisted men could not marry without permission. Loneliness was a fact of life.

"I understand. There's a man waiting for me back in Vermont." Abigail closed her eyes briefly, but the image she conjured was not Woodrow. Instead she pictured a tall blond man with blue eyes. Ethan.

He was waiting when the dance ended, his lips pressed in a tight line, his eyes filled with what appeared to be anger. "Did you have a nice time with Corporal Keller?"

Abigail felt her mouth gape with surprise. It sounded as

if he was jealous. She couldn't imagine Woodrow caring if she spoke to another man, yet Ethan did. As an unfamiliar warmth flowed through her veins, Abigail nodded. "Corporal Keller looked lonely to me, so I thought I'd talk to him." She wouldn't admit that she had thought him close to deserting. The man did not deserve to be questioned simply because he missed his sweetheart. "He told me about his girl back home and how he's saving money to bring her here."

"I see." Abigail heard Ethan's intake of breath. "It was kind of you to talk to him."

Smiling at Ethan's obvious relief, Abigail added, "I know you worry about men deserting. I thought that if I helped boost Corporal Keller's spirits, he might be happier. Happy men do not run away."

"You were right." Ethan's smile warmed Abigail's heart. He was her friend—only her friend, of course—but that was enough. Her friend glanced at the sky. "The fireworks are about to start. Will you join me for them?"

Abigail could think of nothing she'd enjoy more.

As Ethan led the way to seats on the perimeter of the canvas, Charlotte waved from the opposite side, her smile once more radiant, for Jeffrey sat beside her. Neither one seemed to care that Abigail was not with them. That was fortunate, for Abigail did not want to share the evening with anyone other than Ethan.

Who was this man seated so close that she could feel the warmth radiating from his arms? He was unlike any man she had ever met, complex and changeable and compelling. Like many men, he seemed reluctant to express his feelings, and yet Abigail did not doubt that he had deep emotions. He cared for his men, and though he might deny it, she sensed that he had strong feelings for his grandfather. Ethan was a passionate man, but there was more to him than passion. Though quick to anger, he was also quick to admit he was wrong. No one, not even Papa, had been so willing to confess his own faults. Only a strong man would do that. Ethan was strong, he was passionate, he was . . .

Boom! Abigail shuddered as the first of the fireworks exploded, and then she smiled. Ethan was like the fireworks. Though there was an almost deafening noise when shot into the air, it was followed by moments of breathtaking beauty. Unforgettable. The fireworks were unforgettable, and so was Ethan.

10

It was somethin' terrible." The woman shuddered as she pronounced the words, and if she hadn't been seated, Ethan was certain her legs would have crumpled beneath her. Though Mrs. Cassidy was taller than most women, with the sturdy build he associated with farm women, the day's events had clearly taken their toll, leaving her shaking with fear. "They stole our valuables, and then . . ." Unable to pronounce the words, the woman began to sob, burying her face in her husband's chest.

Mr. Cassidy looked directly at Ethan, his gray eyes sober. Ethan guessed him to be in his midthirties like his wife, his face weathered from too many years in the sun and wind. "What my wife was fixin' to say is that them bandits took a woman with 'em. There she was, on her way to visit her grandson, and they drug her off the coach and put her on a horse. It were downright awful, it were."

Ethan pulled his chair an inch closer to the couple, as if to reassure them that he meant no harm. The other occupants of the stagecoach had given basically the same story, but he needed to interview each one, for it was always possible that he'd learn something—some tiny detail—that would help him find the people who'd perpetrated the crime.

The bandits had been both clever and lucky—clever by choosing a new spot for the holdup, one so far from the previous ones that no one was patrolling in the area, and lucky that there were no soldiers on the coach. Two men had come in from Cheyenne yesterday, and three more were scheduled on tomorrow's coach, but there had been no military presence today. Had there been a soldier on board, Ethan knew the outcome would have been far different.

As Mrs. Cassidy raised her head to look at Ethan, he saw that sorrow had replaced fear in her expression. "She was the nicest folk you ever did want to meet. Why, she had some of the best-tasting lemonade. She made it specially for her grandson, but she weren't selfish. No, sir. She made sure all of us got a good taste of it." Mrs. Cassidy licked her lips, as if recalling the taste.

Her husband's frown deepened the lines in his cheeks. "If you ask me, Mavis, there was somethin' funny about that lemonade. I was downright sleepy after I drunk it, and you know I don't never sleep during the day."

"You're talkin' nonsense, Herb. That coach put a body to sleep. It weren't the lemonade. You're just riled that the widow wouldn't give you a second helpin'."

Though Ethan had little interest in the couple's spat, his ears perked at the word *widow*. Was this the information that would help him find the robbers? He shook himself mentally.

The chances that this was the same widow who'd ridden the stagecoach with him and Abigail were slim. After all, Wyoming was a big territory with plenty of widows. There was no reason to think that Mrs. Dunn had been kidnapped, and though she'd talked almost constantly on the trip from Cheyenne, she had said nothing of having a grandson in Deadwood. She wasn't from Pine Bluffs, like this widow. Instead, she had claimed to have a ranch near the fort. Moreover, Mrs. Dunn had not been as elderly as the passengers had indicated. They'd been consistent in that detail. The woman who had been in such a hurry to reach Deadwood had snowy white hair and more wrinkles than a prune. But he still had to ask.

"By any chance, did the widow tell you her name?"

Mrs. Cassidy nodded, her tears gone. "Why, naturally, she did. I told you she was right friendly like. Said her name was Mrs. Black."

Not Mrs. Dunn. It had been a long shot, but even if it had been the same woman, Ethan couldn't see how that would lead him to the bandits. All it would prove was that Mrs. Dunn traveled to Cheyenne occasionally and that she had neglected to mention her grandson on the previous trip.

"What did she look like?" Though he could see little value in asking, the captain was counting on Ethan to be thorough.

"Just like any other granny." The man muttered the words.

His wife jabbed him with her elbow. "You men don't notice anything." She turned to Ethan and said, "She had the prettiest red dress you ever did see. Said she was done mournin' and wanted somethin' to give her a bit of color, bein' as her hair was so white."

As he had expected, the woman who had been kidnapped was not Mrs. Dunn. Her hair, what Ethan had been able to see beneath her black veil, had been brown, mottled with a little gray. "Do you remember anything else? I want to find her, and every detail helps."

The woman looked thoughtful. "She wore spectacles—real thick ones—and she uses a cane."

There was nothing unusual in that. Many people of Mrs. Black's age relied on spectacles and a cane.

"Anything else?"

"Nope."

Ethan rose. There was nothing more to be learned here. All that remained was to report to Captain Westland. He made his way to the post headquarters, dreading the next quarter hour.

When Ethan completed his report, the captain removed his spectacles and wiped them with a cloth. It was not a good sign, Ethan knew, but rather a delaying tactic while his commanding officer decided what to do. "Less than a month." Captain Westland sighed. "Those bandits are getting bolder, or maybe they're more desperate. Taking the money is bad enough, but a woman? They've got to be stopped." He made a show of folding the cloth and putting it back in his pocket. "There's only one thing to do. You and Seton head up a couple search parties. We've got to find that lady."

But by nightfall they had found nothing. The trail was cold, almost as if the bandits and their prisoner had vanished. Ethan shouldn't have been surprised, for the road agents had been remarkably good at disappearing after earlier robberies, but he had hoped that this time would be different. It had to be more difficult to hide three people than two, especially when one of them was a woman being held against her will, but the result was the same: nothing.

Abigail closed her eyes, enjoying the sensation of Charlotte brushing her hair. For a moment, she was drawn back to their childhood, when they told secrets as they gave their locks the hundred strokes Mama had declared essential to good grooming.

"He's smitten." Charlotte's words destroyed the pleasant illusion as they wrenched Abigail into the present. This was no secret, simply a young man's misguided attention. Tonight had been the fourth consecutive night that the lieutenant had come to the house, asking for what he called the privilege of Abigail's company. She would have refused him, but the duets he and Charlotte sang brought her sister so much pleasure that she had not.

"He only thinks he's interested in me," Abigail said firmly. "Ethan told me Oliver makes a practice of falling in love with every single woman on the post. It seems he falls out of love as quickly."

Charlotte's hand stopped, and she stared into the mirror, meeting Abigail's glance. "Then you wouldn't consider Oliver as a husband?"

"No. I don't love him." Unbidden, Ethan's image danced through Abigail's mind. How silly! Ethan was an intriguing man. There was no doubt that he was the most interesting man she had ever met, but he was not the man she was meant to marry. His life was far different from the one she craved, and beside that, there was Woodrow. While they might not

181

be officially engaged, they had an understanding. "I'm going to marry Woodrow."

Charlotte raised her eyebrows as she began to plait Abigail's hair. "Are you sure?"

Though Abigail nodded, something in her sister's voice made her ask, "How did you know Jeffrey was the right man for you?"

A soft smile crossed Charlotte's face. "I was so lonely after Mama died. You and Elizabeth had your own lives, but I felt as if I were cast adrift. I didn't know what to do. I knew I didn't want to teach again, but I wasn't sure what else I could do, so I prayed for help, and Jeffrey came. You know how he practically swept me off my feet."

Abigail had heard the story of Charlotte's trip to West Point for a friend's wedding and how she'd met the dashing young first lieutenant there. Though they had not been introduced, Jeffrey had kept Charlotte from falling when she had started to slip on some wet steps. Declaring himself her knight in shining armor, he had refused to leave her side for the rest of the day, and—as Charlotte told the story—by evening they knew they were in love.

Another smile softened Charlotte's face. "I love Jeffrey dearly. You know I do." She laid down the brush and placed her hands on Abigail's shoulders, turning her so they were facing each other. "I know you don't want advice, but I'm going to give it anyway. Don't marry anyone unless you love him so much you can't imagine living without him."

The morning was not going well, in large part because Abigail had not slept well. She had lain awake for hours, thinking about her sister's advice. Surely Charlotte was wrong. It wasn't difficult to imagine living without Woodrow. Abigail had done that before she met him, and she was doing it now, but that didn't mean she shouldn't marry him. They shared the same values, the same interests. Those were reasons for marriage. Good reasons.

And then, just when she'd dozed off, Abigail had heard Jeffrey return to the house. Though she hadn't looked at the clock, she knew it was late. She had thought it was her imagination that the cloying scent of perfume wafted under the connecting door, but when the perfume had been followed by the sound of Jeffrey's snores and Charlotte's muted sobbing, Abigail knew she was not imagining it. Her sister might love Jeffrey, but all was not well in her marriage.

Abigail had fallen asleep praying that there was an innocent explanation for both the perfume and Jeffrey's frequent absences, but Jeffrey had departed early this morning, and now Charlotte was indisposed. Claiming that her stomach was once again upset, she had accepted a cup of peppermint tea and asked for time alone. There was nothing Abigail could do for her sister but continue to pray.

She'd been doing exactly that when she'd heard the explosion of fury in the kitchen.

"That's it!" Mrs. Channing punctuated her words with a slap. "Get out! Get out! Get out!" A yelp and a whimper confirmed the object of her anger. Abigail hurried down the stairs to rescue Puddles from the cook's ire. When she reached the kitchen, she discovered an overturned barrel of flour and one now-white puppy cowering in the corner.

"If I lay eyes on him again, I'm leaving," Mrs. Channing announced. "That dog's a demon."

He wasn't, but Abigail knew better than to argue with Mrs. Channing when she was in this mood. Instead, she brushed the flour from Puddles's fur and tied the leash to his collar. "C'mon, boy. We're going for a walk. A long walk."

Not certain how long she would be gone, Abigail placed a jar of water and a hard-boiled egg in a cloth bag, then tied on her sunbonnet. Though the wind had subsided enough that she could have used a parasol, she didn't want the challenge of trying to hold that, the bag, and Puddles's leash.

The puppy, convinced that he was being rewarded, scampered at her side, detouring to sniff at a squirrel's hole, then barking furiously when Abigail dragged him away from the rodent's home. Though he strained at the leash as they passed a horse, Abigail kept him moving. There would be no riding today. Instead, they would walk until Puddles's legs were so tired that he would gladly sleep for the rest of the day.

Abigail led the dog across the bridge, laughing as he vacillated between being frightened and fascinated by the sound of water beneath him. "It's a river," she told him. "Like a puddle, only bigger." And far more dangerous, but there was no need to tell the puppy that. He'd discover just how deep the water was when Abigail let him wade into it. Her plan was to walk for at least half an hour, then let Puddles play in the water before they turned around. If all went as planned, not only would Puddles learn about deep water, but the river would wash the remaining flour from his coat.

They were approaching the bend of the river where Abigail had planned to let Puddles have his first aquatic adventure when she saw a woman walking briskly from the opposite direction. There was no mistaking the bright blonde hair that fell luxuriantly over her shoulders or the way she sashayed, a motion Mama would have deplored, declaring that no good woman would move in such an enticing manner. But Mama was not here, and Abigail had been given the opportunity she sought to speak with Leah. She wouldn't ask whether she had seen Jeffrey last night. Leah probably wouldn't admit it, even if she had. But if Abigail could find a way to get her away from the hog ranch, that might help not just Leah but Charlotte and Jeffrey too. To do that, they had to talk.

Leah had other ideas. Abigail could tell the moment she recognized her, for Leah turned abruptly and increased her pace to little short of a run.

"Wait for us!" Abigail cried. Puddles, intrigued by the sight of an unfamiliar person, tugged at the leash.

Leah paused. "You shun't be seen with me," she said when Abigail and Puddles reached her side. "It ain't proper."

Abigail shook her head. "My friends are my choice, and I choose you."

A hint of moisture sparkled in Leah's eyes, making Abigail wonder if she had anyone she considered a friend. Perhaps to hide the tears, Leah bent down and petted Puddles. "Ain't he the cutest thing?"

Abigail chuckled. "His name is Puddles, and there's at least one person who does not consider him cute." As Abigail recounted his adventure with the flour bin and Mrs. Channing's anger, Leah smiled.

"That's what puppies do." She knelt next to Puddles and placed her hands on both sides of his snout. "You didn't mean to make the nice lady angry, did you?" As if he understood, Puddles gave a short bark, then licked Leah's face.

The dog still needed a bath, and seeing Leah's rapport

with him gave Abigail an idea. "It looks as if you've had experience with dogs."

Leah nodded. "There were lots of dogs on the farm. Pa used to let me play with them." A wistful note filled her voice.

"Do you have any now?"

She shook her head. "Peg won't let us. I don't reckon she likes animals too much. I heard tell she complained when the first cat took up residence, until one of the girls told her cats eat mice. Now we have two. Cats, not mice. That's all."

"It's time for Puddles to learn how to swim. Do you want to help me?"

Leah's eyes widened. "Are you sure?"

"I wouldn't have asked otherwise. You seem to know a lot more about dogs than I do. You'll be helping both Puddles and me."

With a quick nod, Leah took Puddles's leash. "Let's go visit the river." When they reached the bank, she sat on the ground, giving Puddles only enough rope to wade into the shallow water. The puppy, attracted by the sound of the current and the smell of wet grass, rushed in bravely, then fled when the cool water hit his belly.

"He sure is the cutest thing. I wish Peg would let me have a dog."

"Is Peg the owner of the hog ranch?" Abigail didn't want to make any assumptions.

Leah nodded. "I heard tell she's got a partner, some man none of us ever seen. He comes at night when we're busy, but we always know when he's been there, cuz we can smell his cigars. Phew!" Leah pinched her nose in apparent distaste. "I reckon we're lucky that he's the only one with cigars like that. We hate 'em, just like we hate what we do."

Though Mama had taught her not to pry, Abigail could not stop herself from asking, "Why do you work there?"

Leah turned to face her. "There ain't nothin' else I can do. When my folks died, it turned out they was behind on payments." Leah's lips tightened. "The bank done took the farm, and there weren't nowhere for me to go. I ain't got no schoolin', and there weren't no man askin' to marry me." Leah gave Abigail a fierce look. "Don't go feelin' sorry for me. I'm still alive, and it could be worse. Peg don't beat us or nothin', and when she goes off to visit that sister of hers, no one minds if I take a walk."

Despite Leah's admonition, Abigail pitied her. "Is Peg gone now?"

Leah nodded. "She left three days ago. I reckon her sister is poorly again. I heard tell she gets spells, and only Peg can help. It's lucky for her Peg is willin' to go."

Abigail thought of how she'd traveled more than halfway across the country to see her sister. "Do you have any sisters or brothers?"

"No, ma'am. I'm all alone."

Abigail shook her head. "Not anymore. I'm here, and I want to help you."

"How?"

Abigail had no answer.

11

"Are you certain you want me to attend?" Abigail looked up from the tiny sandwiches she was arranging on a silver platter. "I don't want to embarrass you, but you know I can't sew well." Unfortunately, this afternoon was the monthly meeting of the Fort Laramie Officers' Wives' Sewing Circle. Had the location been anywhere other than Charlotte's home, it would have been easy to simply not attend, but short of feigning illness, there was no way to avoid the gathering.

Charlotte's eyes widened, as if she were surprised by her sister's question. Perhaps she was surprised by the repetition, for this wasn't the first time Abigail had asked. "Of course I want you here." Charlotte opened a jar of pickles and began to arrange them on a small plate. "Nothing you could do would embarrass me."

Abigail wasn't certain about that. Her sister might find her friendship with Leah embarrassing, particularly if what Abigail feared was true and Jeffrey had been frequenting the hog ranch. That was why Abigail had not mentioned meeting Leah when she and Puddles had been out walking. By the time Abigail had returned, Charlotte had abandoned her bed and was downstairs, placating Mrs. Channing. It was not an easy task, and Abigail hadn't wanted to complicate the day, especially since it had begun so poorly.

Even now, two days later, she chose not to tell her sister about Leah, though she had spent hours trying to think of a way to help the young woman. It was frustrating that she'd been unable to suggest anything to aid Ethan in his search for the kidnapped widow, but surely there was something she could do for Leah. The poor woman had nothing—and no one. But today was a day for Charlotte, and so Abigail focused on the sewing bee.

"I hope your baby won't mind all the uneven stitches." Abigail had purchased a length of flannel at the sutler's store and was making a sacque and bonnet for her sister's child.

Charlotte's somber expression turned into a smile. "The baby won't know anything other than that the clothes are warm and clean and dry. I, on the other hand, will cherish them as a gift from the baby's aunt." Her smile broadened. "And don't worry about your stitching. I probably shouldn't say this, but yours will not be the most crooked stitches. Mrs. Montgomery is worse than you with a needle."

"The poor woman!"

An hour later, half a dozen women were gathered in Charlotte's parlor, their sewing bags still unopened as they discussed the latest happenings at the fort.

189

"I'm appalled, simply appalled, by the kidnapping," one woman said as she accepted a cup of tea from Charlotte. "Why, I told my Thomas, I wouldn't feel comfortable going to Cheyenne again unless he accompanies me. He tried to comfort me, but I could tell that he was just as worried. Ladies, I don't know about you, but I'm staying right here until the Army can guarantee me that it's safe to travel again."

The other women nodded and murmured their assent. "It's a downright shame," Mrs. Montgomery said as she polished her spectacles. "I wanted a new gown, but Lieutenant Montgomery and I agreed it wasn't worth the risk. What is this world coming to?" She turned to Abigail. "I trust you're not planning to return to Vermont until all this is settled."

"No, ma'am, I'm not. I don't plan to leave until the end of the summer."

Perhaps Charlotte noticed Abigail's uneasiness, and that was why she smiled at her guests and said, "Shall we discuss something more pleasant? I heard that the new administration building will be completed in October. I thought we should plan a celebration."

"Indeed." Mrs. Alcott nodded. "Perhaps we could have a reception."

"Another dance might be pleasant," Mrs. Montgomery offered.

As a spirited discussion of the merits of dances versus receptions ensued, Abigail settled back in her chair, noting that no one had begun to stitch. Perhaps the attraction of the sewing circle was not the sewing but the coffee, cake, and companionship. She couldn't fault the women for that when she herself found that many of the days dragged. Even talking to Charlotte and taking Puddles on long walks weren't enough to banish the boredom.

Two soldiers walked by the house, their heavily accented voices carrying through the open window. Mrs. Alcott frowned. "I don't understand why the Army accepted those men."

"Which ones?" Charlotte, who had returned to the kitchen for a fresh pot of tea, had not heard the soldiers' conversation.

"The illiterates." Her frown deepening, Mrs. Alcott continued. "Lieutenant Alcott told me some of them can't read a word of English. That's disgraceful."

"I agree." Mrs. Montgomery seconded her friend's assessment. "Why, Lieutenant Montgomery said the same thing. He orders regulations to be posted, and those men don't read them. It's a serious problem, and someone needs to fix it."

Abigail pressed her lips together to keep from smiling as ideas began to whirl through her brain. The men's problem just might be the answer to one of hers.

Two hours later, when the women had gathered their sewing bags and left, having sewn a few seams and devoured the tiny sandwiches and cakes Abigail and Charlotte had prepared, Abigail turned to her sister. "Do you think the Army would let me teach the men to read?"

Charlotte looked surprised, but she tipped her head to one side, considering. "You'll be here less than two more months."

"But two months are better than none."

A faint smile crossed Charlotte's face. "You sound as if you've thought it through, and all you want is my approval."

"It's true that I want your approval, but I hadn't formed any real plans. When the women started complaining about the illiteracy problem, it reminded me of Corporal Keller and his teacher." As she recounted her conversation with him,

Abigail's pulse began to race with anticipation. If she couldn't resolve Ethan's or Leah's problems, perhaps she could make a difference in some of the men's lives. And maybe, just maybe, that would somehow help Ethan.

Charlotte's eyes narrowed. "Mama was right when she said you're a lot like Papa."

This was the first time Abigail had heard that. "In what way?"

"You think you can solve everyone's problems." As Abigail started to protest, Charlotte held up a cautioning hand. "It's true. You came out here because you thought something was wrong and you could fix it. Then you met that unfortunate woman from the hog ranch, and you wanted to change her life. Now it's the immigrant soldiers. Mama said Papa was like that too. He wouldn't admit that there were some problems only God could fix. He kept trying to change everything, and all he did was get the parishioners so riled that they asked him to leave."

Abigail had not heard this story. "I thought it was because of his opinions."

"That was part of it. When he saw a problem, he'd decide what the solution should be, and he wouldn't rest until everyone agreed with him. But sometimes they didn't agree—like the time he tried to abolish child labor at the textile mill."

Abigail nodded. She'd been eleven at the time, old enough to have vivid memories of the church elders storming into the parsonage and demanding that they leave immediately. It had been Mama who'd convinced them to let the family stay until the end of the week.

Charlotte laid her hand on Abigail's. "Don't repeat Papa's mistakes. Make sure this is what God wants you to do."

Abigail nodded as she said, "I'll ask him."

192

Ethan looked at the woman who stood next to him at the edge of the river. Though she looked like a sailor in that navy dress with the white trim, and though the hat perched on her head had a jaunty angle to it, the concentration on her face reminded him of a child trying to learn a particularly difficult lesson. If he'd had any doubt that she was a novice, the way she held the pole would have quashed that. Perhaps he'd been wrong in suggesting they spend the morning doing this, but when she'd admitted that she was bored by morning calls and afternoon sewing circles, he'd thought this might be a way to alleviate her ennui.

"I find it difficult to believe you've never fished," he said lightly as he reached for the jar of bait. It was the perfect morning for fishing. Though the river was lower than it had been a month ago, it was still deep enough that fish lurked near the rocks. A light breeze stirred the cottonwood leaves, and a songbird warbled overhead. Best of all, since there were no other fishermen in sight, Abigail would not have to worry about displaying her lack of experience.

"Aren't there rivers in Vermont?" he asked.

She gave him a look that would have discouraged a man who didn't realize she was feigning indignation. "Of course there are. Ponds too. It's just that I never learned how to fish. Papa was more interested in books."

"Which is why you can speak French and German but can't bait a hook."

"Exactly." Abigail's mouth quirked into a teasing smile. "Besides, why would I admit that I know how to impale worms when ignorance means that you'll do the messy work?" She glanced at the open jar, then wrinkled her nose.

"Taking advantage of me, are you?"

"If I were, I'd never own up to it, would I?" Abigail handed him her fishing pole but averted her head when he reached for a worm.

Ethan chuckled at the realization that the woman who had stared down bandits was squeamish over baiting a hook. Perhaps it was simply her compassionate nature that made her pity the worm. Whatever the reason, Abigail's exaggerated expression of horror made him laugh, and that felt good.

Life at the fort, particularly since the most recent stagecoach robbery and kidnapping, had been a bit grim. Even the hotly contested baseball games had not managed to lift the pall that had fallen over the garrison, and so it was a welcome relief to laugh. Ethan would have enjoyed that under any circumstances, but sharing laughter with Abigail was particularly pleasant. Her smile made his pulse race, and when she laughed at something he said, Ethan felt as if he'd won an important battle.

"Does that mean you expect me to clean the fish too?" he demanded, matching her mocking tone.

She shook her head. "If we catch any, and I must admit I consider that an unlikely event, but if we do catch a fish, I imagine Mrs. Channing knows how to clean it."

"That sounds as if you don't."

"I don't."

Ethan handed her the pole, then baited his own hook. "So, Miss Harding," he teased, "what do you do if you don't fish or cook?"

She raised an eyebrow. "I never said I couldn't cook. And I simply have not had the opportunity"—she gave the word an ironic twist—"to learn how to clean a fish. That wasn't part of the classical education my father thought his daughters needed."

She was starting to sound serious, and that was something Ethan could not allow. Not this morning. This morning was for laughing.

"You didn't answer my question. How do you spend your time?"

"I teach."

She was missing the point. "It's summer. You don't teach during the summer."

"Most summers I don't actually teach, but I work on lesson plans. And some years when we have pupils spending the whole year at the academy, I teach them how to paddle a canoe or play tennis."

It sounded like his childhood in Grandfather's house, with every minute accounted for. "So you never play."

Abigail shrugged. "I didn't say that. I certainly played as a child. Papa used to say that summers were a time of promise. They were our chance to try something different and exciting. Then as we grew older, he told us we should use summers to explore possibilities for our lives."

Perhaps that was part of the reason she had come to Wyoming. Perhaps she had realized that her regimented life at the school wasn't as appealing as she thought. Perhaps Woodrow was not the paragon she claimed.

"Are summers at the school exciting?"

Ethan sensed that Abigail wanted to agree with his question but couldn't.

"Summers may not be exciting, but they're also not . . ."

"Boring?"

As he'd hoped, she laughed. "You're never going to let me forget that I said that, are you?"

Ethan shook his head. "I won't give up until you admit that Wyoming Territory is not boring. Did I neglect to tell you that I've made it my mission to convince you that this is the most beautiful place on Earth?" When Abigail rolled her eyes, Ethan simply grinned. "Look at that." He pointed to the animal nibbling grass on the opposite bank.

Abigail appeared unimpressed. "It's a rabbit. We have rabbits in Vermont."

"This is not an ordinary rabbit; it's a jackrabbit. Much larger, much faster, and its tail is black. Watch." The rabbit nibbled for a few seconds, its enormous ears swiveling as it ate, as if listening for an enemy's approach. Raising its head, it looked directly at Ethan and Abigail before bounding away.

"You're right." A hint of amusement colored Abigail's voice. "I've never seen one of those. It leapt almost like a deer."

"If you think that's leaping, you should see the pronghorns." Ethan made a mental note to show her a herd of the animals he'd been told were among the fastest in America. He looked at Abigail, noting how she seemed interested in everything around her. She wasn't bored; she was only pretending.

"Nature lesson's over," he announced. "It's time to learn that fishing is relaxing rather than boring." Ethan demonstrated casting, then stood on the riverbank next to Abigail as they waited for fish to take their bait.

Abigail stared at her fishing line, as if deep concentration would make the fish bite. After a few minutes, she began to relax and turned to face Ethan. "Will I scare them away if I talk?" When Ethan shook his head, she said, "I can't explain it, but I keep thinking about Mrs. Dunn. Remember her, the woman on the stagecoach?"

Ethan nodded. "The widow with the wagging tongue." That was how he thought of her, but unlike Abigail, thoughts of Mrs. Dunn rarely crossed his mind. "What makes you think about her?"

"I keep remembering that poor woman who was kidnapped, and I think about how Mrs. Dunn lives all alone, and I wonder if maybe the kidnappers knew about her and might be hiding out there. She could be in as much danger as Mrs. Black."

It sounded far-fetched to Ethan, but he wouldn't destroy the pleasant morning by saying that. "No one from the fort has been to her ranch." Ethan had spoken with each of the search parties and had a list of all the ranches they'd visited. Mrs. Dunn was not on the list.

"I want to find her and make sure she's all right."

Ethan figured it would be a quixotic mission. If there was anyone capable of taking care of herself, it was Mrs. Dunn, but Ethan had free time, and it would be far more pleasant to spend it with Abigail than polishing his buttons and buckles.

He felt a tug on his line. "Watch this," he said and pulled the fish out of the water. "That's the end of our first lesson." Ethan slid the fish into the creel and baited his hook again. "Now that you've seen how it's done, it's time to catch your own. If you do, I'll escort you to Mrs. Dunn's ranch."

"You will?" Abigail's smile turned radiant. If this was all it took to make her happy, he'd have to agree to more of her schemes.

"Once you catch a fish."

It was perhaps only ten minutes later, but he'd caught a second fish, and Abigail still had no nibbles. "I must be doing something wrong," she said with a hint of annoyance.

He'd taught her to recognize the light tug that signified a bite and had let her hold his pole when the second fish was firmly hooked. "It's all a matter of patience," he told her.

"That, unfortunately, is a virtue I have in short supply."

Ethan wasn't surprised by the admission. The Abigail he knew was always eager to complete a task. "That's one of the reasons I fish," he told her, "to learn patience."

She appeared intrigued and gazed at her pole as if it held a secret. "Does it work?"

"A bit."

"Where did you learn to fish? I don't imagine you fished in the Hudson River."

"Actually, I did. I learned while I was at West Point, but you're right. I never fished when I lived with my grandfather, even though we were only a few blocks from the river. The fish we ate came from the fish market. I imagine Grandfather would have had apoplexy if I'd done something so common as trying to catch our food." Ethan chuckled at the thought of his stern grandfather standing on the riverbank, a fishing pole in his hand. Perhaps if he had, he would have learned that life involved more than buying up smaller businesses and amassing vast sums of money.

"You know, I think my father would have enjoyed this, if he'd ever tried it," Abigail said a few minutes later. "Fishing *is* relaxing. It gives a person time to think." She stared at her pole for a moment, then pulled it out of the water. "I was right. I thought the worm was gone, and it was. Now, how did that happen?"

"A sneaky fish. It nibbled the worm instead of biting the whole thing."

"Unfair!"

"It's all right, Abigail. We can go to Mrs. Dunn's even if you don't catch a fish."

"Truly?"

"Truly."

"Oh, Ethan, thank you!" Abigail dropped her pole and flung her arms around him. "You're wonderful!"

He wasn't. Far from it, but Ethan had no intention of telling her that, not when her impulsive hug was the best thing he'd ever felt. What a perfect day!

12

"If I were a praying man, I'd say you were an answer to prayer."

Abigail stared at Captain Westland in astonishment. Behind his spectacles, his light blue eyes appeared sincere, and there was nothing in his expression to make her think he was being sarcastic, but this was far from the reaction she had expected after Jeffrey's grudging acquiescence.

"Then you agree?" She had to be certain she hadn't misunderstood. When she'd entered his office, the most she had hoped for was approval. Instead, she had discovered that the post headquarters was not what she had expected, and neither was Captain Westland's response to her suggestion.

Abigail had thought that the Orphanage, as Ethan had told her the building was called, would be spartan. It was not. Curtains softened the windows, and a woven rug covered the floor. Shelves laden with books hung on two walls, while a desk of highly polished wood stood along another. The biggest surprise was the tapestry cloth draped over the table where Abigail and Captain Westland now sat, for it made the room look almost homey rather than utilitarian.

Captain Westland's smile held a hint of amusement. "I not only agree that you should teach my men English, but I hope you'll consider taking on all the classes for adults. Sergeant Ransom—he's the man who's been teaching—is in the guardhouse for a month." The captain reached for the glass paperweight that adorned the table, though paperwork appeared to be confined to the desk, and tossed it from one hand to the other as he considered his next words. "One of my officers caught Ransom brawling last night. Can't have that, especially in a man who's supposed to be setting an example. So, what do you think? Will you take his place at least for a month?" He frowned as he added, "I'm sorry to say the pay isn't much."

Abigail felt almost giddy with relief. He hadn't dismissed her idea. To the contrary, he'd expanded it. Surely that was proof that God meant her to solve this problem. It couldn't be coincidence that Captain Westland needed a teacher the very same day that she'd decided to present her proposal. "The pay doesn't matter. I would be honored."

"Excellent. Lieutenant Bowles will get you anything you need." Captain Westland set the paperweight back on the desk and called, "Bowles!"

As Ethan entered the office, Abigail's smile broadened. When the family had discussed her idea at supper yesterday, he had been staunch in his support, countering Jeffrey's objections and Charlotte's concerns that teaching adults would be more difficult than young girls. Ethan had even offered to speak to the captain on her behalf, but Abigail had refused. It was important that the decision be made based on merit, not influence. But now that the captain agreed, she wanted Ethan to be the first to know.

"Bowles, this young lady has volunteered to take over classes while Ransom is in the guardhouse." He winked at Abigail as he said, "Maybe longer, if we can convince her to make Fort Laramie her home. You're in charge of that, Bowles. In the meantime, get her whatever she needs and make sure there's a sergeant in the classroom at all times. I don't anticipate any problems, but Mrs. Westland would have my hide if I let anything happen to Miss Harding."

"Yes, sir." Ethan saluted, then escorted Abigail outdoors. "You seem pleased," he said when they reached the road.

"I am, but I'm a little overwhelmed." She glanced around. The parade ground looked the way it did every morning, with men marching, others policing the perimeter for tumbleweeds and trash that the wind had carried across the prairie. At the opposite end of the street, workmen hammered and nailed, while others struggled to position windows in what would become the new post headquarters. Two birds splashed in a birdbath, and a cottontail rabbit scurried under a porch. It was a normal morning at Fort Laramie for everyone except Abigail. She'd gotten more than she'd wished for.

"I don't even know which classes I'm expected to teach. Do you suppose Sergeant Ransom would share his lesson plans with me?"

Ethan's laugh rang out over the parade ground. "Lesson plans? I doubt the man knows the meaning of the words."

Corporal Keller and another soldier approached, the lassos in their hands telling Abigail they were on canine patrol. She glanced in both directions, hoping Puddles had not escaped again.

"Corporal Keller," Ethan called. "Miss Harding would like a word with you." Once again Abigail was certain it was not a coincidence that the man who had alerted her to the need for better instruction happened to be walking by when she had a question about the classes.

The corporal's eyes lit with pleasure when Abigail explained that she would be teaching.

"*Sehr gut*," he said, then corrected himself. "Very good."

It would be good only if she knew what to teach. "Do you know whether Sergeant Ransom used lesson plans?"

Abigail's question was met with a blank stare. "Begging your pardon, ma'am, but vat vould lesson plans be?"

Though it would appear that Ethan was correct, it was possible the sergeant had them and that Corporal Keller did not recognize the term. "Normally it's a book with a list of everything he planned to teach that night along with questions for the students."

"*Nein.*" The corporal shook his head to emphasize his answer. "I never saw anything like that."

"Then can you tell me what Sergeant Ransom taught the last time?"

Corporal Keller wrinkled his nose as he considered the question. "It vas something about countries in Europe, ma'am. He had a map."

European geography. Abigail could think of few subjects less appropriate for soldiers in Wyoming Territory. "It looks as if I've got a lot of work to do."

"Yes, ma'am."

When the corporal left, Ethan turned back to Abigail. "Are you sure you still want to do this?"

"Of course. Now, do you know when classes are held?"

Ethan nodded. "Recently, it's been the same nights we practice baseball, Tuesday and Thursday. I suspect Sergeant

Ransom chose those evenings so he'd have the smallest classes possible. You heard the corporal. Who would look at a map of Europe when he could be playing baseball?"

The more Abigail heard, the further Sergeant Ransom fell in her esteem. "We can't have that. I'll hold classes Monday, Wednesday, and Friday. That way the other days will be free for your games."

"And your pupils will have an extra class each week."

Abigail nodded. "It sounds as if they need it."

"They do," Ethan agreed. "And since you need time to prepare your lessons, we can postpone our ride."

It made sense. Not only did Abigail need to create lesson plans, but Charlotte's words echoed through her head. *You can't solve every problem. Make sure this is what God wants you to do.* Abigail was confident that God meant her to teach the soldiers. This morning had been proof of that. She ought to concentrate on lessons, and yet she couldn't stop thinking about Mrs. Dunn and the kidnapped woman.

She shook her head. "It's only one day. I want to go." And, if she was being honest, she wanted to spend the time with Ethan.

The day was heavily overcast, the air so filled with moisture that Abigail was certain the clouds would leak, but they did not.

"It's a good day for a ride," Ethan said. "The horses won't tire as easily with the sun not blazing. But if you want to wait . . ."

She did not, and so soon after daybreak, Ethan and Abigail headed north. Though she admitted to Ethan that she hadn't always listened carefully to the widow, Abigail believed Mrs. Dunn had said her ranch was an hour or two north of the fort.

"And that means my men should have found it." Ethan's eyes seemed to move constantly, scanning the horizon, looking down at the ground they were passing. It was, Abigail supposed, what any good soldier would do, remaining alert to possible danger.

"Do you think the bandits are out here?"

Ethan appeared surprised. "Not here. Why do you ask?"

"Because you're obviously looking for something."

He shrugged. "I'm more concerned about wild predators. This is rattlesnake country, and these long grasses can hide them. I've also heard stories of wolf packs. Even though I've never seen one, I don't want to take any chances."

Abigail looked around. To her, the gently rolling hills with the occasional rock outcroppings did not appear threatening. "I thought you were trying to convince me that Wyoming is beautiful." And it was, in its own way. This wasn't Vermont with its pastoral countryside, its green hills dotted with dairy cattle, but the treeless prairies and the vast expanses had a beauty of their own. What Abigail had once called boring she now considered restful.

His expression remaining solemn, Ethan said, "Beauty doesn't mean there's no danger, but you don't need to worry." He touched the revolver on his hip and glanced at his rifle. "I'm a crack shot."

Abigail tried not to cringe. Guns were a fact of life here, and as much as she feared the devastation they could produce, she could not make them disappear. She took a deep breath, then stared at the horizon, relieved when she saw what appeared to be a cluster of buildings. "I think I see a ranch. Maybe it's Mrs. Dunn's."

Though small, the ranch house was well cared for, its windows sparkling clean, the front door freshly painted. A few flowers in cheerful yellows and reds brightened the corner of the porch, drawing the visitor's attention away from the sparse grass. As Abigail and Ethan approached, a woman stepped onto the porch.

"Welcome, strangers. What can I do for you?" Abigail guessed that the brown-haired woman whose loosely fitting dress could not hide the fact that she was great with child was around thirty years old, although her face was so weathered by the sun and wind that it was difficult to tell.

"We're looking for Mrs. Dunn," Abigail explained as she and Ethan dismounted. Even if they paused only briefly, it would feel good to stretch her legs. "She said she had a ranch in this part of the territory."

The woman shook her head. "I don't know any Dunns, but maybe Michael does." Cupping her hands around her mouth, she shouted, "Michael, we've got visitors."

A dark-haired man emerged from the barn, a boy of perhaps five or six at his side. The man walked more slowly than Abigail would have expected, matching his pace to his son's but showing no signs of impatience. As they drew closer, Abigail saw the reason for the boy's lurching gait. Though apparently healthy otherwise, he was afflicted with a clubfoot.

"I'm Michael Kennedy," the man said, extending his hand to Ethan. "You've already met my wife Hetty, and this is my son Paul. How can we help you?"

When Ethan explained, Mr. Kennedy shook his head. "I'm afraid I can't help you after all. There are no Dunns within a hundred miles of here, and the only stranger I've seen was a man. He came by about a week ago, offering to sell me a new rifle or maybe a gewgaw for Hetty. He had some mighty fancy jewelry with him."

Ethan's intake of breath told Abigail he suspected the visitor had been one of the bandits. "Was there a lady's brooch with red stones?" When Mr. Kennedy nodded, Ethan continued. "Do you remember what he looked like?"

"Mostly ordinary, but he had the greenest eyes I've ever seen."

That sounded like Private Schiller. Ethan had mentioned that the deserter's eyes were a deeper green than Jeffrey's. "Did he speak with an accent?" Abigail asked.

The rancher nodded again. "Think he might have been German. I could hardly understand him." It was indeed Schiller.

The boy looked up at his father. "He was a mean man. I didn't like him."

Mr. Kennedy tousled his son's hair. "I didn't, either. That's why I wouldn't buy anything, even though he offered a good price."

"They were probably stolen goods," Ethan said quietly, perhaps to keep from alarming the Kennedy family. Though his words were ordinary, his hands were clenched, as if in anger. It made no sense to Abigail. Why would Ethan be angry when Mr. Kennedy had refused to buy from Private Schiller?

Ethan continued his explanation. "There've been some stagecoach robberies, and some weapons were stolen from the fort."

"I kinda figured that." Mrs. Kennedy nodded as her husband spoke. "Even though the man claimed he was a rancher, something just didn't seem right."

"He wasn't wearing a uniform?" It was Ethan who posed the question.

"No, sir." The boy shook his head. "Except his boots. They were like yours."

The rancher laid a hand on his son's shoulder. "Good work, Paul. I didn't notice that."

As the boy beamed with pleasure, Ethan nodded, but once again Abigail noticed that he seemed uncomfortable. When Mrs. Kennedy invited them to stay for dinner, though Abigail would have welcomed the opportunity to get to know the family better, she declined the invitation.

"It doesn't make sense," Ethan said as they left the ranch. "It appears that the rifle thefts and the stagecoach robberies are connected and that Schiller is involved in both, but I can't figure out how. Schiller never struck me as a leader, and he sure didn't impress me as being smart enough to plan the robberies."

"I wonder where he got his civilian clothes."

Ethan shrugged. "He could have gone to Cheyenne. I imagine he got a good price for the Colts when he sold them. What puzzles me is how he got the guns. He must have snuck back onto the post, but that was taking a big risk. The guards are supposed to be on the lookout for deserters."

"They're probably looking for people leaving the fort, not entering."

Ethan's lips twisted into a rueful smile. "True. It seems we need to improve our security."

Though the sun had not emerged from behind the clouds, Abigail could feel beads of perspiration trickling down her neck. July in Wyoming was hot, even on an overcast day.

"I know you're worried about Private Schiller," she said a few minutes later, "but I keep thinking about Mrs. Dunn. Maybe I shouldn't—my sister keeps reminding me that I can't solve every problem—but I can't forget her. It's clear she lied to me, but what I don't know is which part was the lie, her name or the location of her ranch."

Ethan nodded. "And then there's the other question: why did she lie in the first place?"

Ethan fell silent, and for perhaps half an hour he said nothing. Though the silence was not uncomfortable, Abigail sensed that he was bothered by what they had learned this morning. There was probably nothing she could do, and yet she had to try. She waited until they stopped for their midday meal. Then, as she unpacked the lunch she'd brought, she said, "You've been deep in thought. Is it about Mrs. Dunn or Private Schiller?"

Ethan accepted the sandwich she offered but said nothing until he'd eaten a bite. "You're much too perceptive, Abigail. The truth is, I wasn't thinking about either our lying widow or the larcenous private. I keep remembering the way Michael Kennedy treated his son. He didn't seem to care that he was lame."

"I'm sure he cares. I imagine he wishes there were something he could do to help him and hates the fact that he's powerless." Abigail knew that if Paul had been her son, she would be praying for his healing every day, for a clubfoot was something only God could change.

"But he treats him as if it didn't matter."

Hearing the pain in Ethan's voice, Abigail tried to understand the cause. "It doesn't matter. Whether he's lame or whole, Paul is his son. He loves him." That had been obvious from the affectionate gestures. The gestures. As Abigail thought back, she realized that Ethan's uneasiness had been greatest when Mr. Kennedy had touched his son. "I think that's part of being a parent, loving a child whether or not he's perfect."

Ethan swallowed hastily, then washed the bread down with a swig from his canteen. "That's easy for you to say. You had parents who loved you. I had Grandfather."

There was no mistaking the bitterness in Ethan's voice, and once again Abigail wished she knew more about his childhood. It was difficult to offer comfort when she didn't know what had transpired.

"He loved you. He must have."

Ethan stared into the distance, his jaw clenched. "Did he, or did he simply want an heir to run his railroad?"

"You look happy." Charlotte laid down her sewing and smiled at Abigail. This was the second time they'd returned home as soon as baseball practice ended rather than spending the rest of the evening with the other officers' wives. Charlotte was putting the finishing touches on a new gown, while Abigail worked on her lesson plans and Puddles dozed at their feet. As happened most nights, Jeffrey had remained with the men.

"I am happy," Abigail agreed. It was true that she still worried about Ethan and wished there were something she could do for Leah, but she had taken Charlotte's advice and had left those problems for God to solve . . . at least until she started teaching. "The post school has proven to be a blessing." Abigail had investigated it the previous day and had been encouraged by the supplies she'd found there. Though she had been skeptical when she learned that the building had previously been a bakery, she had been pleased to discover that it no longer smelled of bread. The last thing she needed was to have her students distracted by thoughts of food. "Some of the children's books will be perfect for teaching the men to read."

"McGuffey's Readers?" Charlotte wrinkled her nose. "I used to hate them." As Puddles stirred, Charlotte bent over to pat his head, then winced as she straightened. "Moving isn't so easy anymore." When she looked down at her stomach, Charlotte's smile turned sweet. "The little one is active now."

Before Abigail could reply, there was a knock on the door. Puddles jumped to his feet and began to bark, a bark of excitement rather than alarm, telling Abigail that the visitor was someone they knew. "I'll go," she said, not wanting Charlotte to have to rise. Her sister's ankles had begun to swell, and walking was no longer a pleasure for her.

As Abigail opened the front door, she smiled. His hair was still damp, making it obvious that Lieutenant Seton had attempted to wash off the dirt and sweat of baseball practice. The one evening when he had not bathed, Puddles had spent the entire time sniffing his boots and trying to chew on his pant legs.

"Good evening, Mrs. Crowley and Miss Harding." Oliver accompanied his greetings with a warm smile. "I was hoping I could have the pleasure of your company this evening, but if I'm interrupting . . ."

Charlotte laid her sewing aside. "We're happy for the distraction. Come in." She gestured toward one of the comfortable chairs.

Though Abigail would have preferred to finish her lesson plans, she knew Charlotte enjoyed Oliver's visits, for he alone of the fort's officers seemed to share Charlotte's love of song. Remembering her manners, Abigail smiled at their guest. "May we offer you some refreshments?"

Oliver shook his head and addressed his words to Charlotte. "I must admit that I was hoping we'd sing another duet."

"Not 'Old Folks at Home' again." Charlotte feigned pleading. "I was singing 'way down upon the Swanee River' the whole next day, and Puddles hates it." As she crooned the first line from Stephen Foster's popular song, the dog began to whine. "See what I mean?"

"What about 'The Girl I Left Behind'?" Abigail suggested. "I found the music in the piano bench." She had heard that when soldiers used to leave the post, heading for battle, the company band would play that song.

Oliver shook his head. "I don't want to leave my girl behind. I want her by my side." He gave Abigail a look so filled with longing that a lump formed in her stomach. *Oh no, Oliver. You don't mean it. You know I'm not your girl, and I won't ever be.*

Oblivious to the thoughts that set Abigail's insides churning, Charlotte nodded vigorously. "That shouldn't stop us from singing it," she insisted. "It's a pretty song."

And it was. Were it not for her concerns that Oliver wanted something she could not give, Abigail could have spent hours listening to him and her sister, for their voices blended beautifully.

At the end of the evening, Abigail accompanied Oliver to the door. Though she hoped he would simply say good night as he had before, the way he cleared his throat and the uneasiness she saw on his face made Abigail fear that her hopes would not be realized. Perhaps if she kept everything casual, he would take the cue. "Thank you for coming," she said as they walked onto the front porch. "Charlotte always enjoys your duets."

"And you?" They were only two words, but Oliver's voice cracked with emotion as he pronounced them.

Please, Oliver, go home. Don't say something you'll regret. Though the plea was on the tip of her tongue, Abigail chose a neutral response. "I enjoy listening to both of you."

Oliver stroked his nose in a gesture Abigail had learned was a sign of nervousness. "That's not what I meant. I hope you enjoy my company as much as I do yours. I look forward to these visits all day."

His voice had deepened, the tone telling Abigail he was close to making a declaration. If only she could spare him the inevitable pain of rejection. "It's good to have friends," she said evenly.

Oliver shook his head. "You know I want to be more than your friend. I want to marry you."

"I'm sorry." And she was. Though Ethan claimed Oliver bounced back from rejection, she hated being the one to deliver it. "You know marriage is not possible. Woodrow . . ." Abigail hesitated as she tried and failed to conjure his image.

"Woodrow isn't here." Oliver completed the sentence. "I am. I lo—"

She would not allow him to continue. While it was true that Oliver's visits helped lift Charlotte's spirits and filled the empty space left by Jeffrey's absence, Abigail could not let him harbor any false hopes. "Good night, Lieutenant Seton." Perhaps the use of his title would tell him she regarded him as a friend, nothing more.

What appeared to be sadness filled Oliver's eyes as his smile faded. "Is there no hope for me?"

Abigail shook her head slowly. "I'm afraid not."

He stood for a moment, his lips flattened, his breathing ragged. At last, he reached out and captured her hand in his. Raising it to his lips, Oliver pressed a kiss to the back. "Good night, Miss Harding," he said as he released her hand and walked away.

There was absolutely no reason to be walking in this direction. Ethan stared at the moonless sky. Normally, this was not a time he enjoyed being outdoors, and yet here he was. Just because Abigail lived here and normally took Puddles for a walk at this time. Just because they had talked when he had joined her for that walk the last couple nights. Just because it was more fun talking to Abigail than anyone on the post. None of those were reasons to be here, and yet here he was, only a few yards from the house Abigail shared with her sister and Jeffrey. Though he had imagined her indoors, she was outside. The light from the parlor shone onto the porch, revealing Abigail.

Ethan's eyes narrowed. She was not alone. A man was at her side, standing closer than he ought to be. Oliver. Of course. The man had less sense than a grasshopper. Somehow, he couldn't see that Abigail was all wrong for him. Even if she weren't almost promised to Woodrow, she was too serious for him. They were mismatched, unsuited . . . Ethan searched for another adjective, but the only one that reverberated through his head was *wrong*. Abigail and Oliver were wrong for each other. All wrong.

As Ethan took another step forward, determined to inform Oliver of his folly, he saw him raise Abigail's hand to his lips. What was he thinking? The man *wasn't* thinking. That was clear. Ethan's hands fisted, and he longed to wrap them around Oliver's shoulders and shake some sense into him. Instead, he spun around and headed the other direction.

There was no reason to be so annoyed, no reason to care. Of course there wasn't.

It was dark, darker than it had ever been. The moon that had guided them was gone, and even the stars were hidden beneath a blanket of clouds. Though he knew there was a town over the next rise, no lights were visible. Or perhaps it was only that he could not see. Perhaps that was a blessing. Unfortunately, he could still feel, he could hear, and he could smell. It would have been better if he could not.

He lay on the ground in the shadow of the Dunker Church, one leg bent at an unnatural angle, the other crushed beneath the horse's body. All around him, men moaned. The roar of cannons had ceased, leaving only the stench of gunfire mingled with two other unmistakable odors: fear and dying men.

He was one of them. He knew it. No man could survive for long when he'd lost this much blood. That was why they'd left him. The orderlies were trained to pick up those with the greatest chance of survival. Later, they would return for the rest. But he would not be here. All that would be left was his body.

He clenched his teeth against the pain. Time was short. He could feel himself slipping away. This was not the way he had imagined it. The generals had been wrong. There was no glory in dying. As the agony of broken bones and a crushed body subsided, he was left with nothing but the deepest of regrets.

It was unbearable, knowing he would never see Veronica again, knowing he would never hold their child, knowing they would never hear his words of love. And yet, there was nothing he could do. The end was near.

"My son!" he cried as his last breath escaped.

Ethan bolted out of bed, his limbs trembling, his breath ragged. *It was only a dream*, he told himself as he stared out the window. Only a dream. But he had never had such a vivid dream. Tonight he felt as if he were there, seeing and feeling the aftermath of that horrible battle. He was no mere onlooker, seeing the bodies scattered on the fields outside Sharpsburg. No, indeed. He was there, inside his father's mind.

His father! Ethan clutched the windowsill, trying to still the shivers that raced up his spine. If his dream could be believed, his father had died in what was now called the Battle of Antietam. Though he hadn't thought of it in years, Ethan had heard about the Dunker Church and all the fighting near it. Now that church held a special meaning for him.

Was the dream the story of what had happened, or was he simply dreaming about fathers? Ever since the day he and Abigail had visited the Kennedy ranch, Ethan had been unable to forget the sight of Michael Kennedy ruffling his son's hair and putting his hand on the boy's shoulder. A longing had lodged itself deep inside Ethan, the wish that he had known such love and—even stranger—the desire to have a son of his own, a child he could love the way Michael Kennedy did his.

Ethan shook his head, trying to clear his brain. It was only a dream, and yet the details had been so real. No one had ever told him how his father had died, simply that he had been killed during the war. He hadn't known that his father had fallen at Antietam and that his horse had died with him, but now he had no doubts. The man Ethan had seen in his dream was Stephen Bowles, his father, the man Grandfather had reviled all his life.

Ethan had lost count of the number of times he'd heard the story of how his father had trapped Veronica. He'd pretended he loved her, using the oldest trick of all to ensure that she would have to marry him. He hadn't loved Veronica, or so Grandfather had claimed, and he most certainly had not loved the child he'd never seen. Stephen Bowles had loved nothing other than the prospect of Grandfather's money. According to Grandfather, Stephen Bowles was a despicable fortune hunter who had died before he realized that Grandfather had ensured he would never touch a penny of it.

That was the father Ethan had known. He had envisioned him as a younger version of Grandfather—cold, aloof, and demanding—not a man who would tousle a boy's hair. But the dream had felt so real. Had Grandfather lied?

13

It's a McGuffey's Reader." Abigail handed the book to Leah, hoping the young woman would accept it. If she could learn to read and write well, perhaps Leah could break free from the hog ranch. Surely with such basic skills she would be able to find a respectable position in Cheyenne. She could certainly be hired as a cook or housekeeper, and with more skills she might be able to work in one of the shops or a hotel. But first she had to gain confidence.

Leah's eyes widened. "For me?"

"It's a loan." Abigail nodded. "When you finish this one, I'll bring you the next." She pulled a slate and a piece of chalk from her bag. "I start teaching the soldiers tomorrow, and I hoped you'd let me practice on you." Abigail hadn't been certain Leah would come to the riverbank today, but she had brought an extra jar of water and two hard-boiled eggs in case the young woman was there and could stay for a lesson. It was the perfect time for Abigail, for Charlotte was occupied with morning calls and had agreed that it would be better for her sister to exercise Sally than to accompany her on what even Charlotte referred to as boring visits.

"You'd be doing me a favor," Abigail told Leah.

The pretty blonde's eyes widened again. "Really?"

"Really. Shall we begin?"

An hour later, Abigail smiled. "You're the best student I've ever had."

A flush colored Leah's cheeks. "You don't mean that."

"I do." Though the lesson had been a short one, it had shown Abigail that Leah's poor grammar was caused by a lack of education, not intelligence. And though a blanket spread on the ground beneath the old cottonwood was an unusual classroom, it had not deterred Leah.

"Where's your puppy?" she asked as Abigail closed the book.

"Probably getting into mischief at home. He would have been a distraction if I'd brought him."

Leah wrinkled her nose. "But a good one." She looked at the sun, as if gauging the time. "Reckon I oughta be goin'. Peg'll be madder than all get out if'n I'm late fer dinner. She don't like us girls to miss none."

"Any."

A puzzled expression crossed Leah's face. "Any what?"

"She doesn't like us to miss any."

As Abigail emphasized the correct words, Leah grinned. "I see." She repeated the sentence. "Thank you . . ." She hesitated for a moment before saying, "Abigail."

It was the first time Leah had called her by her given name, and though it might seem trivial to others, the gesture filled Abigail's heart with warmth.

"Can you come tomorrow?" she asked. As a teacher,

Abigail knew the importance of regular instruction. As a friend, she looked forward to spending more time with Leah.

Leah's nod was tentative. "I reckon so. But you better keep this. Peg don't . . ." She shook her head, then corrected herself. "Peg *doesn't* like us to have personal things."

As she handed the book to Abigail, Leah's sleeve rode up her arm, revealing deep purple bruises above her wrist. Abigail tried not to gasp, but the fact that the bruises were shaped like fingers told her this was no accident. The sooner she could get Leah away from the hog ranch, the better.

"So, what did you learn, Bowles?" Captain Westland asked when Ethan entered his office. The captain had been gone when Ethan returned from his ride with Abigail, and this was the first opportunity he'd had to report. It couldn't have come at a better time. Surely focusing his attention on the robberies would keep him from dwelling on his dream and the memory of Oliver kissing Abigail's hand.

"I'm puzzled." Ethan wasn't ashamed to admit that. "I didn't find the widow, but I did learn that Private Schiller seems to be involved with everything else. He and Forge were the ones who tried to hold up the coach I was on."

"I thought you said Schiller wasn't one of the men who kidnapped the woman."

"No, sir, he wasn't. But he had some of the jewelry that was taken then, plus some of our Springfields and Colts. It appears that the theft of firearms and the stagecoach robberies are connected."

A satisfied grin settled on the captain's face. "Good work,

Bowles. I hadn't dared hope we were dealing with the same group, but this is good news. Good news indeed."

"It could be. Everything points to Schiller. The reason I'm puzzled is, I don't believe he's smart enough to have planned those robberies."

The captain raised a quizzical eyebrow. "How smart do you have to be to point a rifle at a stagecoach and demand money?"

"There's more to it than that, sir. You need to figure out the right place for an ambush. One of the things I find interesting is that it's been a different location each time. Most people are creatures of habit. If something works once, they'll try it again. That hasn't been the case with these bandits." And that was frustrating. "I would not have thought Schiller was smart enough to realize that changing the holdup spot would make it more difficult for us to catch them. And how did he get back on the post to steal those guns?"

As he polished his spectacles, Captain Westland nodded. "You could be right about that. I met him a couple times, and he didn't impress me with his intelligence."

"I also don't understand why all the robberies take place so close to the garrison. If I were a bandit, I wouldn't want to be near soldiers. Everyone in this part of Wyoming knows we send patrols out occasionally. That increases the risk of being caught. If I were planning to rob a coach, I'd pick a location farther from civilization. There are miles of deserted country between Cheyenne and here."

"Good points, Bowles. What you've said makes sense, so, tell me, why do you think they strike so close to us?"

"I don't know, sir. I wish I did, but in the meantime I've got an idea for stopping them."

"Are you anxious about tonight?" Ethan asked as he took a slice of freshly baked bread. Today Mrs. Channing had served them a thick beef stew, accompanied by bread and butter.

Abigail nodded. Even though her lessons with Leah had gone well, she felt the same combination of anticipation and apprehension that always gripped her before the first day of school. "I am a bit concerned," she admitted. "I'm not sure . . ." Before Abigail could complete her sentence, a loud crash and the sound of breaking glass filled the air.

"That's it! Out, you fiend, out!" The thwack and yip that accompanied Mrs. Channing's shouts were followed by a slamming door. A moment later, the cook stormed into the dining room, her hands fisted on her hips, her face suffused with anger. "I've had enough. I told you to keep that mutt out of my kitchen. I don't know how he got in, but that monster tipped over a crock of pickled beets. That floor will never get clean," Mrs. Channing continued, "but that's no longer my concern. I've had enough. I quit."

Though the cook had threatened to leave before, this was the first time she had started to untie her apron. It was possible she meant only to replace it with one that was not stained with beet juice, but Abigail did not believe that. Nor did Charlotte. She laid a hand on the cook's arm, and her voice was clearly meant to placate the irate woman. "I'm sorry, Mrs. Channing. It was my fault. I couldn't bear to hear him whining when he was tied up outside, so I brought Puddles in while I was sewing. He fell asleep, and I forgot he was in the house."

Mrs. Channing shook her head. "You can apologize all you want, but the damage is done. I can't take any more of this. I'm leaving." Brushing off Charlotte's hand, she stalked back into the kitchen.

Charlotte stood for a moment, her indecision apparent.

"I'm sorry, Charlotte," Jeffrey said, "but I see only one solution."

"What is that?" As if she feared the answer, Charlotte sank into her chair and stared at her husband.

He laid his hand on hers. "You know what has to be done. Tell Mrs. Channing you'll get rid of the dog."

Abigail kept her eyes fixed on her plate, wishing she were anywhere but here. Puddles had been her idea. If she hadn't felt so sorry for the puppy, Charlotte wouldn't be in this predicament. And yet, Abigail couldn't regret the decision to save the dog, for Puddles had brought her sister many hours of pleasure. There had to be a way to save him again.

"Oh, Jeffrey, I can't." Charlotte's cry was so plaintive that Abigail looked up. As she had feared, tears filled her sister's eyes. "I like Puddles."

"And I like well-cooked meals," her husband responded. Though he still held Charlotte's hand, his tone left no doubt that he had made a decision.

"I can cook." Charlotte's eyes brightened. "I'm a good cook, and I can keep the house clean."

Jeffrey shook his head slowly. "It's not fitting for an officer's wife to cook and clean. Besides, you won't have time after the baby arrives. No, Charlotte, there's only one answer. The dog must go. I'll drown him myself."

"You can't!" As tears rolled down her cheeks, Charlotte fled from the dining room. Though Abigail had thought she would go to Puddles, instead her sister climbed the stairs, apparently seeking the solace of her room.

His face set in a firm frown, Jeffrey stalked to the kitchen. "It will be all right, Mrs. Channing," he said, raising his voice so it would carry throughout the house. "The dog will be gone by tomorrow."

Her appetite gone, Abigail laid down her spoon and looked at Ethan. "There has to be a way to save him."

"Maybe we can find another family to take Puddles. That way Charlotte could still see him occasionally."

Abigail's spirits rose, first at the fact that Ethan had said "we" rather than "you," and then again at the solution he'd proposed. It was Ethan's use of the plural pronoun that made her realize that while giving Puddles to another family was a good idea, there was a better one.

"You're right," she said, giving Ethan her warmest smile. "A new home is a wonderful idea. It wouldn't be forever—only until we could convince Mrs. Channing that he's not so bad." Abigail leaned forward, trying to lessen the distance between her and Ethan. Mama had always said that proximity aided in persuasion, and today she needed every ounce of persuasion she could muster. "Will you do it, Ethan? Will you take Puddles?"

"Me?" Ethan's look of incredulity left no doubt that he had had no intention of volunteering to be Puddles's savior. "I live in one room. I'm hardly ever there, and I know nothing about caring for dogs. Taking him would be a bad idea."

"No, it wouldn't." The more Abigail thought about it, the better the idea seemed. "Puddles knows you, and he likes you. If he stayed with you, he wouldn't be frightened. Oh, Ethan, this would be good for him."

"What about me?"

It wasn't an outright refusal, and that was good. Surely it

224

meant that he was considering the possibility. "This would be good for you too. Please, Ethan. He's such a sweet dog, and I promise it will only be for a month or so. If we don't find another solution, I'll take him back to Vermont with me." Abigail started to rise. As she had intended, Ethan hurried to her side of the table to pull out her chair. She turned and gave him her most persuasive smile. "Please."

"It's against my better judgment, but . . ." Though he tried to frown, Abigail saw amusement in Ethan's eyes.

"You'll do it?" she asked, hoping she'd understood his change of heart. While not perfect, this would be a good solution for Charlotte, and Abigail couldn't help but believe that Ethan would enjoy having a pet.

"Yes. I'll probably regret it, but . . ."

"You won't. I know you won't. Oh, Ethan, thank you!" Impulsively, Abigail leaned forward and pressed a kiss on his cheek. An instant later, she drew back in shock. What had she done? First she had hugged him. Now a kiss. What was happening to her?

Mama would have been horrified, for Abigail's behavior was outside the range of decorum. Abigail was horrified too, but for different reasons. She had never kissed Woodrow, for she knew the rules and had always followed them. Why, then, had she kissed Ethan? And why, oh why, had it felt so right?

"That's a cute little mutt." Oliver bent down to scratch Puddles's head before he settled himself onto a chair.

Ethan frowned as much at the interruption as the description of Puddles as cute. He'd had the dog in his room for less than an hour, and the puppy had already chewed a sock and dragged two towels onto the floor, worrying them into a pile, then flopped on top of his makeshift bed and looked up at Ethan with those mournful eyes, as if seeking approval. He hadn't received it, for all the while he'd been tearing around Ethan's room, he'd barked and yipped enough to attract the attention of everyone else in the building. Ethan didn't want that kind of attention. What he wanted was some peace and quiet.

The other men had merely laughed and continued on their way, but Oliver had entered Ethan's room and appeared to be prepared for a long visit. Puddles didn't need the distraction, nor did Ethan. He had other things to think about—things like his new pet and Abigail's kiss.

The dog was temporary, or so she had promised, but the kiss . . . Ethan sighed. It had meant nothing. It was simply the result of Abigail—impulsive Abigail—expressing her gratitude. It meant no more than the hug she'd given him the day they had fished. Ethan knew that, and yet he couldn't forget how soft her lips had felt against his cheek and how sweet she had smelled. He wanted time to think. Time alone to replace the memory with the reminder that she was promised—almost promised—to Woodrow. But it appeared he would not have that time soon, for there was no easy way to discourage Oliver.

"The problem is, Puddles won't be little for long," Ethan said as calmly as he could. "It seems he's already twice as big as he was a month ago." He shook his head. "I should never have agreed to take him, but I didn't want to disappoint Charlotte." Or Abigail. It had been Abigail's plea that had convinced him to assume responsibility for Puddles.

Oliver continued to stroke Puddles's head, then when the puppy rolled onto his back, he scratched his stomach, setting the dog to wiggling with delight as he said, "He's a good companion."

Abigail had said that too. "I don't need a companion."

"Everyone does. That's why most of us look for wives." Oliver was back to his favorite topic. Pretty soon, he'd talk about Adam and Eve, then Noah and the ark. Ethan only hoped he wouldn't propose a canine companion for Puddles. But Oliver did not recount any Bible tales. Instead, he pursed his lips as if he'd eaten something sour. "I wish I could find the right woman." Puddles, who seemed keenly attuned to human moods, began to whine.

"I thought you had."

Oliver stroked his nose. "Abigail? That's over."

Ethan looked at his friend. Had he been mistaken? Had the kiss Oliver had pressed on Abigail's hand been not a gesture of undying love but rather one of farewell?

"She refused me." Oliver's lips twisted into a caricature of a smile. "I don't mind saying, it's not a pleasant experience. It makes me think I ought to stick to the girls at the hog ranch."

"You know the dangers."

"You're not my father, Ethan, so don't preach at me. At least the girls there pretend they love me. Abigail never did."

"That's because she wasn't the right woman for you."

Unfortunately, the woman with the heart as big as Wyoming wasn't the right one for Ethan, either.

Abigail stared down at the blank piece of paper, the same piece of paper she'd pulled from the desk drawer fifteen minutes ago. She was supposed to be writing a letter to Woodrow. When she'd sat down, she had planned to tell him about the incident with Puddles, turning the spilled beets into an amusing story, but each time she picked up her pen, the only thought that whirled through her brain was the memory of how she'd kissed Ethan. It had been nothing more than a peck on the cheek, not enough to have given Mama the vapors, though she would have delivered a stern lecture over the possible consequences of Abigail's being so forward.

One second. Less than a second. That's all the longer the kiss had lasted. A reasonable person would have been able to dismiss the memory, relegating it to the scrap heap the way she did other insignificant events. Abigail had always considered herself a reasonable person, but try though she might, she could not forget what she'd done. Instead, she kept remembering how firm Ethan's cheek had been, how the faint hint of whiskers had seemed somehow intriguing, how his skin had smelled of soap and fresh air and an underlying scent that was unique to him. Instead of being sensible, she was acting like a lovesick schoolgirl.

14

Frances pulled out a deck of cards and began shuffling them. Though the man probably expected her to offer him whiskey, there would be none today. Whiskey was a reward for a job well done. The man she had summoned for a reprimand hadn't done his job at all, much less well. That was why Frances held the cards. She knew the sound reminded her visitor of the times he'd sat in this room, watching his stack of chips dwindle and with it his hopes for instant riches. It would grate on his nerves. Good. Excellent. Success depended on keeping the others off balance, and if there was one thing Frances knew, it was that she would not let success slip through her fingers. The man who now had beads of perspiration popping out on his forehead could be replaced. No one was indispensable, no one except Frances herself.

"I heard a nasty rumor," she said, watching his expression

229

while her fingers continued to play with the cards. "I heard that Lieutenant Bowles recommended that the captain put at least one soldier on every stagecoach between here and Cheyenne."

The man's eyes widened, confirming what she feared. He'd known nothing of the new plan. What a fool! He should have known, and even if he didn't, he should have pretended that he did. It was little wonder he was such a poor poker player. A man who couldn't master the art of concealing his emotions didn't deserve to win at poker or anything else.

"Seems to me you should have known, seeing as how he's your friend." Frances gave the cards another quick shuffle, just to watch her visitor squirm. "I've got two questions for you: why didn't I hear about it from you, and what are you going to do to stop it?"

As she'd expected, the man had no answers.

Ethan was not happy. He'd spent the day thinking about Private Schiller and the robberies and had begun to feel as if he were acting like Puddles. Ethan had given the puppy a bone, expecting him to devour it. Instead Puddles had moved his treat around, looking at it from every angle, taking a quick gnaw on one corner, then another, all the while regarding it with a combination of curiosity and concern. Did he fear that Ethan would snatch it away, or was he simply wondering how to consume such a huge object? Ethan didn't know. All he knew was that the problem of the firearm and stagecoach robberies loomed as large to him as the bone did to Puddles, and there was much less anticipation involved.

While he wanted to resolve the mystery, Ethan disliked the

direction his thoughts had taken. Like Puddles, he'd circled the question, gnawing at it from different directions, but no matter what he did, no matter how he looked at it, he kept coming to the same conclusion. It made sense to him. The question was, would it make sense to anyone else?

"Jeffrey, I need to talk to you for a minute," he said when supper was finished. It had been an odd meal. Ethan had been preoccupied, and that had made even casual conversation difficult. Add to that the fact that, while Abigail was visibly excited about her impending class, Charlotte had been almost totally silent, perhaps because of the absence of her dog. And although Jeffrey had eaten with gusto, apparently unaffected by the others' moods, he had said little.

"I'm in a bit of a hurry." As they walked onto the porch, Jeffrey gestured toward the left. "I'm headed to the Officers' Club. Tonight's poker night, and I don't want to be late."

Ethan had forgotten. "I can wait until morning."

Jeffrey shook his head. "No. Go ahead now. Otherwise, I'll just keep wondering what the problem is."

"I didn't say there was a problem."

"But there is, isn't there?" When Ethan nodded, Jeffrey grinned. "I could tell by the tone of your voice that whatever it was, it was troubling you. I hope it has nothing to do with my sister-in-law or that dog."

"It doesn't." Ethan took a deep breath, then said, "I think someone at the fort is involved in the robberies."

The blood drained from Jeffrey's face, leaving his freckles in sharp relief against his pale skin. "That's ridiculous! Where did you come up with a crazy idea like that? We know Schiller is responsible."

That was the reaction Ethan had feared. "I don't think

he's working alone. He's not smart enough, and he wouldn't know the guards' schedule. Whoever took the firearms had to know when they wouldn't be guarded, and that changes every week." Ethan continued to outline his reasoning, watching his friend's face. As the color returned, Jeffrey nodded slowly, keeping his eyes fixed on the distance. "It sounds pretty far-fetched to me, but I'll be on the lookout." Abruptly, he descended the steps and turned to the right.

Ethan blinked in surprise. "The Officers' Club is that way."

Jeffrey pivoted on his heel. "Oh . . . right." He let out a brittle laugh. "See what distraction does?"

"Good evening, gentlemen." To Abigail's relief, her voice sounded normal as she greeted her class. She looked around the former bakery that now served as the post's school. Fourteen of the fifteen students she had expected were seated at tables, their expressions ranging from cautious to eager. Though some of the soldiers were conversing among themselves, most sat stiffly, their tension palpable.

"We will begin our lesson with reading." Picking up a McGuffey's Reader from the table that served as her desk, she said, "This is the same book I used when I learned to read. Fortunately for me, you're more advanced than I was, because you already know the alphabet." As several men grinned, Abigail sensed that the tension was dissipating. Apparently they had been as apprehensive as she was. Abigail smiled at the realization that the first day of school was always a strain for pupils, regardless of their age.

"Let's get started. We're going to go around the room, and each one of you will read a sentence." It was a technique she had used with her youngest pupils when she'd discovered their attention wandering. "We'll spell out the unfamiliar words, and everyone will pronounce them. My father made me do that when he taught me German. He told me it wasn't enough to be able to read the words; I had to know how to pronounce them correctly." Abigail flashed a rueful smile. "You should have heard me say '*willkommen*' the first time." She gave the German greeting an exaggerated American accent, hoping for and receiving a big laugh from the class in response. "Now, let's begin."

By the end of an hour, Abigail saw signs of fatigue on her students' faces and knew that they'd reached their limits for the day. It must be difficult, she thought, to spend the entire day working at Army business, especially when that business included heavy labor like cutting timber or helping construct a new building, and still have any energy left for learning. It was one thing for the men to practice baseball in the evenings. That was a welcome change from the day's routine, and the physical exertion was nothing more than a continuation of the drills they'd performed during the day. But school demanded mental acuity while sitting almost motionless, a difficult task at any time but much more so at the end of the day.

Abigail closed her book and smiled at the soldiers. "You did exceptionally well, and now I'm going to say those words you've been waiting for: class dismissed."

Before anyone could move, Corporal Keller rose. "This vas good, very good. Thank you, Miss Harding."

As the sound of applause filled the room, Abigail felt her spirits rise. She might not have been able to help Leah today; she might be confused about Woodrow; she might still be worried about her sister; but at least she had been able to start the men on the path to learning. There was no doubt that this was part of the reason God had led her to Wyoming.

"Oh, Charlotte, it was wonderful," Abigail told her sister a few minutes later. "I would not have thought it possible, but this was much more fun than teaching children." The pleasure she had felt working with Leah had not been a fluke. Tonight had been even more rewarding.

Abigail pirouetted, letting her skirts swirl around her high-buttoned shoes. "And it's all due to you. Every time I looked at this beautiful new frock, I smiled, and that helped the soldiers relax."

As she had hoped, Charlotte smiled, but the smile appeared forced.

"Is something wrong?" Though there was no evidence of tears, her sister was visibly upset.

"No, it's just that I wish . . ."

"What do you wish?"

Charlotte's face crumpled. "I wish Puddles were here."

"Let's go see him. Ethan won't mind. In fact, he'll be grateful if we take him for a walk." Puddles was probably already driving him slightly crazy. As Ethan had said, he lived in one room, and the puppy was accustomed to a much larger space.

But although Abigail thought it was a good idea, Charlotte did not. "I can't. It'll only make it worse. I won't want to leave him there." Charlotte rose, her movements that of a far older woman. "Why don't you go? I'm going to try to sleep."

"Are you sure there's nothing I can do for you?"

"I'm sure." Charlotte closed the distance between them and hugged Abigail. "I'm glad your class went well. I'm happy for you. Truly I am."

But that did not disguise the fact that Charlotte was not

happy for herself. Though it was probably a combination of what Mama would have called Charlotte's "delicate condition" and the loss of Puddles, knowing that didn't mean Abigail could change it.

Since there was nothing more she could do for her sister tonight, she tied her bonnet ribbons, pulled on her gloves, and set out for the Bachelor Officers' Quarters. Though it would not be seemly for her to go inside, the BOQ was close enough to the sutler's store and the Officers' Club that there were bound to be men walking by who could tell Ethan of her arrival.

As she rounded the corner past the commanding officer's quarters, Abigail smiled. She wouldn't have to send a messenger, for there they were. The tall lieutenant was unmistakable, as was the black and tan puppy straining against the leash. Both were headed in her direction.

"You must have read my mind," Abigail said when they met in front of Old Bedlam. Two families who were sitting on the second story verandah waved at Abigail, the women's faces radiating sympathy. It seemed that the story of Puddles's banishment had spread quickly. Abigail shouldn't have been surprised, and she tried not to mind that her family had become grist for the rumor mill. Instead, she smiled at Ethan, grateful for the answering smile he gave her.

"I missed the scamp and wondered whether you'd let me take him for a walk."

Ethan looked at Puddles, who was jumping up and down, his excitement obvious. "I'd say Puddles has the same idea. He practically tore my arm off when he saw you." Ethan handed her the leash and waited while Abigail patted the dog and murmured reassuring words.

"How is it, being a dog owner?" she asked as they started to walk. Rather than continue the way Ethan had begun, which would have meant passing Puddles's former home, Abigail headed toward the former cavalry barracks and stables.

Ethan chuckled when Puddles spotted a bunny and jerked on the leash. "I didn't realize just how much energy a puppy has."

"But a puppy is not a puppy forever." Abigail tossed Ethan's words back at him, hoping he'd continue to smile.

He did. "Thank goodness. I'm not sure I could handle a whirlwind like him for too long."

Abigail bent down to ruffle Puddles's ears. His coat was smoother than many dogs', his ears almost as soft as silk. "You're not a whirlwind, are you, Puddles?" As if in response, the dog shook his head, then scampered away, once again tugging on the leash, as if suddenly bored by the adults.

"I heard your class went well," Ethan said as they began to walk. "From all accounts, you're a born teacher."

Abigail found herself flushing at the praise. "I enjoy it. The truth is, when I finished class tonight, I had more energy than I can recall. Usually I'm tired by nightfall, but not tonight. That's why I decided to take a walk."

"I'm surprised your sister didn't come with you. I thought she'd miss the dog."

"She does miss him. Too much. She got used to having Puddles around, but now he's gone, and if Charlotte is right, Jeffrey won't relent. I don't know what to do." Abigail bit her lip. She hadn't meant to confide her concerns to Ethan. The words had simply slipped out, perhaps because she felt more at ease with him than she had with anyone other than Charlotte herself.

Ethan tipped his head to one side, as if pondering Abigail's statement. "It sounds as if she needs something to take her mind off the dog and the fact that you'll be leaving when summer ends."

Abigail stopped and stared at Ethan. "I hadn't thought of that." She had made a concerted effort not to think about the fact that she and Charlotte would be separated again. When she thought of autumn, and that had happened less frequently over the past few weeks, she focused on her students and the beauty of sugar maples decked out in their fall finery rather than the fact that the season's change would mean leaving her sister.

"A lot of things are changing in Charlotte's life." Though Ethan did not voice the words, Abigail knew that one of those changes would be the baby's arrival. "My grandfather used to say that the best way to deal with a problem was to keep busy doing something else." Ethan chuckled. "That advice hasn't helped me figure out who's behind the stagecoach robberies, but it might help your sister. What does she enjoy doing?"

Abigail thought for a moment. "She's a wonderful seamstress, but Jeffrey won't let her sew for others. He says that would reflect poorly on him."

Ethan stared into the distance for a moment. "I can't imagine Jeffrey would object if she didn't charge for her services. All the officers try to make Christmas special for the enlisted men and their families. What if Charlotte sewed something for them?"

Abigail nodded, remembering how Charlotte and their mother had organized Christmas baskets for the less fortunate parishioners. "She could enlist the other women's help. They already have a sewing circle, but this would give them a goal."

And Charlotte would be the perfect person to coordinate

everything. Knowing Charlotte, she would find a theme and would design garments to fit it, all the while ensuring that the other wives knew their contributions to the effort were essential. It was something Charlotte could do now and even after the baby arrived. Perfect.

Abigail looked up. Though night was falling, they were close enough to one of the street lamps that Abigail could see the question in Ethan's eyes. He was still waiting for her to confirm that she liked his suggestion.

"It's the perfect answer. I love the idea, and I'm sure Charlotte will too. How can I possibly thank you?"

Ethan tilted his head to one side as a mischievous smile curved his lips. "How about another kiss?"

15

"A kiss?" Abigail's eyes widened with something that might have been shock.

How stupid could a man be? Ethan could have kicked himself for the words that had come from his mouth, seemingly of their own volition. Abigail was obviously appalled by the idea of another kiss. Justifiably so. Now that he thought about it, *he* was appalled. Of course she wouldn't want to kiss him, especially since the kiss he'd envisioned had been far different from the gentle buss on the cheek she'd given him when he agreed to rescue Puddles. The only excuse Ethan could find for suggesting such a ridiculous thing was that his brain must have taken a leave of absence. That was no excuse at all, especially since his foolishness had upset Abigail. What he needed to do was find a way to ease her discomfort.

"It was a joke, Abigail," he said, hoping she'd accept the implied apology. "I was teasing."

"Oh." Her expression changed. Surely it wasn't disappointment that he saw reflected from her eyes. It couldn't be, for he knew she hadn't wanted to kiss him. As if to prove that, the furrows between her eyes vanished as she said, "A joke. Of course. I understand."

The awkward moment was past. There was no reason to dwell on it, no reason to even remember how silly he'd been to propose a kiss. And yet that night when Ethan dreamed, it was of a woman kissing him, a woman with Abigail's hazel eyes and a smile that could light the evening sky.

Unfortunately, there was no way to arrange her hair without peering into the mirror. Abigail tried not to frown when the looking glass reflected dark circles under her eyes. What else had she expected when she'd hardly slept? She could blame it on Charlotte, pretending that if her sister had been awake when she returned, Abigail would not have spent the night tossing and turning. But the truth was, Abigail wasn't certain that would have helped. She'd lain in bed, reliving the evening. Class had been exhilarating, she'd enjoyed her time with Puddles, but what had kept her from sleep were Ethan's suggestions. Suggestion, singular, she corrected herself. The Christmas baskets had been a genuine suggestion, the kiss only a joke. That's what Ethan had said, and yet there had been a gleam in his eyes that had made her believe he was serious, that he had wanted her to kiss him.

Abigail frowned as she twisted her hair into a knot, securing it with half a dozen pins. Had Ethan really wanted to kiss her? The thought was like a haunting refrain that kept repeating itself inside her head. No matter how often she shook her head, it would not go away. She kept remembering his smile and the way his eyes had crinkled when he'd said, "Another kiss." He hadn't looked like someone who was teasing, and she . . . Abigail sighed.

There was no point in denying it. She had wanted to kiss him, really kiss him, not simply give him another peck on the cheek. She had wanted to feel his lips pressed to hers. The longing had been so strong that she could almost taste it, and that was wrong. Horribly, horribly wrong. A woman who was practically engaged to another man did not entertain such thoughts.

It was pure temptation, put in her path so that she would stray. But she wouldn't. She would not stray. She would not succumb to something she knew was wrong. She would not think about kisses. Whenever those errant thoughts appeared, she would turn them away, keeping her mind firmly fixed on Charlotte. Charlotte was the reason she had come to Wyoming.

A few minutes later, Abigail descended the stairs and followed her sister to the kitchen, waiting until they'd served themselves bowls of porridge before she introduced Ethan's suggestion. Though she hoped Charlotte would be enthusiastic, after last night, Abigail wasn't certain of anything regarding her sister. But then Charlotte smiled, and Abigail's doubts vanished. The malaise she'd seen the previous evening was gone, replaced by a brilliant smile and eyes that glowed with happiness.

"It's a wonderful idea!" Charlotte practically crowed. Laying down her spoon, she started planning. "I can sew caps and gloves. You know how I love gloves." She extended her hand and feigned smoothing a glove over her fingers. "Mrs. Alcott is a wonderful knitter. She can make scarves, and we can tuck some of Mrs. Montgomery's pretty handkerchiefs into the corners."

This was the Charlotte Abigail remembered from her childhood, filled with enthusiasm and energy.

When her sister frowned as she picked up her coffee cup, Abigail knew a new thought had assailed her. "What will I do if the others don't want to participate? I can't do it all alone," Charlotte said.

Abigail gave her sister a reassuring smile. "Leave it to me. All you have to do is invite them for tea."

That afternoon when Mrs. Alcott and Mrs. Montgomery were seated in the parlor, their little fingers properly crooked as they lifted their teacups, Abigail began. "Ladies, I need your help." Mama had taught her daughters that a sure way to gain people's approval was to ask for their assistance. "My sister is thinking about a new project, and—as worthy as it is—I don't believe it would be successful without your expertise."

The women nodded, and Abigail took heart from the fact that neither of them interrupted her as she explained the plan. Mrs. Montgomery seemed almost as interested in the molasses cookies Charlotte had offered as in Abigail's story.

"Charlotte is skilled with a needle, but there's nothing better than a warm knitted scarf or a handkerchief with a delicate tatted edging." Charlotte had confided that Mrs. Montgomery fancied herself the resident expert at tatting.

"Naturally we'd help you," Mrs. Alcott said.

Mrs. Montgomery nodded. "Just tell us what you need." She took another cookie from the platter and bit into it, obviously savoring the sweet. "What I need is someone who can bake like Mrs. Channing. Mrs. Nelson makes delicious roasts, and her bread is light as air, but she can't seem to master desserts." Mrs. Montgomery broke off another piece of cookie. "I must admit that I enjoy a good dessert." When she'd swallowed the bite, she wagged her index finger at Charlotte. "Be careful. I may steal your cook away from you."

Though she was certain the other women noticed nothing, Abigail heard her sister's soft intake of breath and suspected that Charlotte's thoughts had taken the same direction as hers. Was it possible they'd discovered a way to get Puddles back? A second later, Charlotte looked as poised as ever. "Perhaps we could arrange a trade," she said casually, as if the thought wasn't making her heart beat at twice its normal speed. But it was, for Abigail saw the telltale vein on her sister's hand. "Mrs. Channing isn't completely happy here, even though we sent Puddles away."

Mrs. Montgomery nodded. "I heard about the pickled beets."

Charlotte managed a little laugh. "I imagine everyone on the post heard about that. It took a lot of bleach to get the floor clean again."

"Well, I have no dogs, so that wouldn't be a problem." Mrs. Montgomery took another cookie, chewing it thoughtfully. "This is simply delectable," she announced when she'd finished it. Turning toward Mrs. Alcott, she waited until the other woman gave a slight nod. "If you agree, Charlotte, I'll speak to Mrs. Nelson today. She can be here tomorrow morning."

"I agree." Charlotte gave her guest a radiant smile. The Puddles problem had been resolved.

Ethan pulled out his watch and frowned for what seemed like the hundredth time. Class should have been over by now. Abigail had said she'd set a limit of an hour, not wanting to overwhelm the men and discourage them from returning, but it had been an hour and a quarter, and there was no sign of anyone leaving the schoolhouse. He snapped his watch closed. It was only fifteen minutes, no reason to be upset. The truth was, he felt like a schoolboy being forced to wait for a treat.

It had been a difficult day, and he'd looked forward to spending time with Abigail. As if the continued concern about the robberies weren't enough, his baseball team was becoming as blue as their name. Despite hours of practice and superior talent, they had yet to win a game. While Jeffrey crowed, the Laramie Blues grew increasingly despondent. Ethan knew of no way to encourage his men, especially when his own spirits had plummeted this afternoon when he'd received another letter from Mrs. Eberle. "Come home," his grandfather's housekeeper urged him. "He needs you."

Hah! Grandfather didn't need him. If he really was dying, all he needed was a manager for the railroad. There were dozens of men far better qualified than Ethan. As for home, the brownstone where Ethan had spent his childhood was no longer home. Home was wherever the Army sent him. Right now it was a single room that had felt oddly empty ever since he'd taken Puddles back to Abigail and Charlotte.

A round of applause rang through the night air, followed by the sound of men getting to their feet. Class was over. Ethan felt himself relax. Abigail would come out in a minute,

244

and though he had no intention of telling her about Mrs. Eberle's letter, just being with her would brighten the day. He took a step forward, then stopped, for when Abigail left the schoolroom, she was deep in conversation with Corporal Keller.

"I received a letter from Marta today," the corporal told Abigail. "She is unhappy with me. All her friends are married, and she feels—how do you say it?—left out." The corporal frowned. "I do not know vat to tell her. It vill take me three more months to save enough money to bring her here."

He wasn't eavesdropping, Ethan told himself. Anyone on this end of the parade ground could have overheard the conversation and Abigail's response. "If she loves you, she'll wait." Was she thinking of Woodrow, he wondered? It seemed to Ethan that Abigail had done more than her share of waiting for the man to propose. Had Ethan been in Woodrow's shoes, he would have made certain she was wearing his ring before she headed West, but of course he wasn't Woodrow, and it was silly to even think of sliding a ring onto Abigail's slender finger.

Corporal Keller appeared unconvinced. "I must get the money sooner. That vould be better." He nodded briskly. "I vill find a way."

Ethan felt like an insect whose antennae had suddenly begun to vibrate. How was Dietrich Keller going to raise more money? And how had he saved enough to send for his girl, anyway? It was no secret that enlisted men barely survived on their wages. Perhaps Keller was the soldier helping the outlaws.

Ethan left the shadows of the commissary storehouse and headed toward Abigail. As the corporal saluted him, he nodded. He'd speak to Keller later. Right now, he wanted to see Abigail. Correction: he needed to see Abigail. He needed to be reminded that something was right in the world.

"Your class went late tonight," Ethan said when the corporal had left. The smile Abigail gave him left no doubt that the delay had been good, and Ethan found himself smiling in response. This was what he had needed: a few minutes of normalcy.

"We were almost at the end of one of the readers, and they wanted to finish," Abigail explained. "I wasn't going to stop them, not when they seemed excited."

Ethan wrinkled his nose. "At least your students have a reason to be excited. The Laramie Blues certainly don't. Everyone's getting discouraged by our losing streak."

"That will end." Abigail spoke with confidence. "Jeffrey would never admit it, but your team is stronger than his. It's only been bad luck that you haven't won." Worry lines formed between Abigail's eyes. "You're not letting it bother you, are you? The scores have been so close that it's only a matter of time before the Blues win."

Ethan felt himself relax. This was why he'd wanted to be with Abigail, to have her put everything in perspective. "That's what I told the team, but thanks. It helps to have someone else confirm our strength."

As her forehead smoothed, Abigail nodded. "Any time. I told you once that I'm a good listener, and I mean it."

What would she say if he told her about the letter? Probably the same thing she had the last time—go home—and that was advice Ethan did not want.

"I need to take Puddles for a walk," Abigail said when they reached the Crowley residence. "Would you like to join us?"

Ethan nodded. Even though he didn't want to talk about Grandfather, he was far from ready to relinquish Abigail's company. "Believe it or not, my quarters feel lonely without your dog."

"He's not mine. He's Charlotte's," Abigail corrected him, "but I understand. The house seemed empty when he wasn't here."

It felt amazingly good to have Puddles greet him as if he were a long-lost friend. Perhaps this was what he needed. Perhaps he ought to adopt a dog of his own.

As they circled the parade ground, hoping to tire Puddles enough that he would sleep all night, Ethan and Abigail spoke of trivial matters, everything from speculating on how large Puddles would be when fully grown to whether or not there would be another hailstorm. And, as frequently as they spoke, they were silent, but while silence could be oppressive, this was comfortable. For the first time all day, Ethan felt at peace. The worries were still there, but they'd become muted. Though nothing had changed except his outlook, his world had shrunk to three inhabitants: a wonderful woman, a playful puppy, and himself, and so it was with reluctance that he bade Abigail good night.

Once in his quarters, the weight of the day returned. Pushing thoughts of his grandfather aside, Ethan focused on the robbery. Was it possible that Dietrich Keller was involved? The man appeared honest, but Ethan knew that appearances could be deceptive. He would learn more tomorrow morning when he questioned the corporal and his friends. In the meantime, he would sleep.

But sleep proved elusive, and Ethan found himself wandering aimlessly around his room. At least when Puddles had been here, he'd had someone to talk to. Ethan smiled, remembering how the puppy had strained at the leash when they'd approached the BOQ. It had taken all of Abigail's strength to keep him from climbing the stairs.

"See, he thinks he's yours," she had said with a laugh. "I won't tell Charlotte."

"Or Jeffrey," Ethan had added. "He'd probably welcome an excuse to give Puddles away permanently."

Ethan walked to the window, wondering if anyone other than the guards were out. Surely there were no runaway dogs. The night was calm, the parade ground empty. Ethan looked to the left, and as he did, he blinked in surprise. Why was Jeffrey returning from the stables? Tonight was one of his nights to play poker at the Officers' Club, and the game was still going on. Curious, Ethan hurried outside.

"You're getting back late," he said, deliberately infusing his words with a questioning tone as he matched his steps to Jeffrey's.

If his friend was surprised to see him, he gave no sign. Instead, Jeffrey said, "Charlotte's so busy with her sister that I feel like a fifth wheel around the house. I went for a ride to clear my head."

Ethan understood that need. "I wish I could clear mine. I keep thinking about the robberies." And Grandfather and Abigail, though he wouldn't admit that.

"The rifles or the stagecoach?"

"Both. I'm trying to figure out who else is involved."

Jeffrey kept his eyes fixed on the distance as he nodded shortly. "I haven't heard anything."

That was what Ethan had suspected. If Jeffrey had any clues, he'd tell him. But Jeffrey had not overheard Dietrich

Keller's conversation with Abigail. "How well do you know Corporal Keller?"

This time Jeffrey's response was a shrug. "As well as I know any of your men, I guess. Why?"

"Would you say he was intelligent?"

"I hadn't thought about it, but yes, I would."

"Smart enough to lead men?"

The question gave Jeffrey pause. "Probably," he said after a moment's deliberation. "Why?"

"I heard him talking about needing extra money. He claims he wants to bring his girl out here and marry her. Nothing wrong with that, but it sounded as if he has saved more than other men."

"And you think he might be getting that money illegally."

"Precisely."

"So, ask him."

"I am not a thief." Dietrich Keller's face flushed with anger as he glared at Ethan, seemingly forgetting that he was addressing an officer. The two men were standing in the small room next to the adjutant's office. Though Corporal Keller had appeared slightly apprehensive when he'd received Ethan's summons, the apprehension had turned to anger.

"If you didn't steal it, where did you get the extra money to bring your girl out here? And don't deny that you have it. I overheard you speaking with Miss Harding." Ethan kept his voice firm, knowing that men were more likely to break down and reveal the truth when pressured.

"I vill not deny it, sir. It is the truth, and everyone knows it. I vorked for that money. Some men pay me to shine their boots and buckles. I clean rifles for others. I save every penny I can, but I never stole anything. Never. You must believe me."

"The fact remains that someone took weapons from the storeroom. Do you know who it was?"

"*Nein.*"

Unfortunately, Ethan believed him, and that meant he was where he'd been the day before: no closer to discovering who was responsible.

Frances frowned when she realized that she'd turned right rather than left at the Y in the road. She never came this way, for the trail that was the Army's excuse for a road led to the river, and she had no desire to see that. The hog ranch, which was where she was headed, lay in the other direction, and yet Frances could not dismiss the feeling that there was a reason she'd come this way. It wasn't simply inattention. Something, some instinct, had led her toward the river. Intrigued, she flicked the reins and increased her pace. It might be nothing at all, a false alarm, but at least she'd know.

When she crested the last rise and looked down at the Laramie River, Frances whistled softly. She'd been right. There was a reason she was here, and it was to learn what Leah did when she left the ranch.

The fool! It was bad enough that Leah was with a woman from the fort, but of all the possible women, she had somehow gotten mixed up with Abigail Harding. That had to stop immediately, for Abigail was the one person who might be able to connect Mrs. Dunn with Peg. The lieutenant was a man and as unobservant as they came, but Abigail was different. Was that why she was with Leah?

Frances's frown deepened. Though Leah did not know what Frances was actually doing when she pretended to visit her fictitious ailing sister, she wasn't dumb. And neither was Abigail. Frances couldn't control Abigail, but she could ensure that Leah understood the consequences if she ever spoke to Miss Abigail Harding again.

16

"Jeffrey won't be happy." Charlotte sighed as the runner reached home. The Laramie Blues were at bat, and tonight it seemed as if nothing could stop them. While Crowley's Champs fumbled balls, dropped bats, and missed seemingly easy catches, the Blues were playing a virtually faultless game.

Abigail shifted the basket of baked goods from one hand to the other. Normally, she would have placed it on the ground during the game, but Charlotte had insisted on bringing Puddles with them tonight. At a minimum, the dog would have tried to stick his nose under the napkin. More likely, he would have devoured at least a couple of the cinnamon rolls she'd spent the afternoon baking.

When she'd returned from her morning ride without seeing Leah, Abigail had decided that kneading dough might ease some of the tension that had settled in her neck and shoulders. Today was the third consecutive day Leah had not come to the riverbank for her lesson, and that worried Abigail, making her fear that Leah was ill. There was only one thing to do. If Leah wasn't at the cottonwood tomorrow, Abigail would visit her at Peg's Place. In less than a month, Abigail would be on her way back to Vermont, and before she left, she wanted to see Leah finish another reader and begin lessons in basic arithmetic. Leah might still lack the confidence to leave the hog ranch and build a new life, but if she chose to go, those skills would help her find a position as a cook, even if she wasn't ready to work in a shop.

Abigail glanced at Charlotte, knowing her sister would not approve of a trip to the hog ranch. Nor would Ethan, but perhaps the trip wouldn't be necessary. Perhaps Leah would come for her lesson tomorrow. Abigail would worry about it then. Tonight was for baseball.

"It's about time the Blues won," she told her sister. "Ethan said they've been horribly discouraged." Who wouldn't be? No matter how hard they tried, Ethan's team had lost every game so far.

Another batter took his place, waiting patiently while the Champs' pitcher stretched his arms, then swung them in wide circles. It was a ploy familiar to everyone who'd watched the games this summer, an attempt to make the batter so anxious that he'd swing at anything.

"You always did champion the underdog." Charlotte's words were matter-of-fact.

Abigail would not deny the accusation. It was, she suspected, part of the reason she felt such a strong need to help those who were less fortunate or in times of trouble. "I know what it's like to be in second place. It wasn't easy being your sister. You had already mastered everything I tried."

As Puddles, apparently bored with being forced to remain stationary, began to dig a hole, Charlotte tugged on his leash before she looked at Abigail. "That was only because I was older. I knew how hard it was to do some things, so I tried to make them easier for you."

"And you did. I tried to do the same thing for Elizabeth." Abigail frowned at the pitcher and his seemingly endless warm-up exercise. "But, no matter what I did, I was always the second daughter. Sometimes I wondered what it would have been like if I'd been an only child. Did you ever think about that?"

Charlotte shook her head.

"Well, I did. On bad days, I'd wish I didn't have to share Mama and Papa's attention with anyone. Now, though, I look at Ethan and I'm glad I wasn't the only child. I can't imagine life without you and Elizabeth." Perhaps Ethan's childhood would have been easier if he'd had a sibling. At least then he would not have been the sole recipient of his grandfather's attention.

Crack! The batter hit the first pitch, sending the ball into right field as he began to circle the bases. When he reached home, breathless but clearly exultant over his run, Charlotte sighed again. "The Champs will never recover from this."

They did not. The Blues won by ten runs, their elation palpable as the last inning ended. While the Blues celebrated, Jeffrey stalked to the center of the parade ground and shook Ethan's hand. Abigail could not hear his words, but the firm line of his mouth told her that Charlotte had been right: he was not happy. Though it was only a game, the loss appeared to rankle more than it should have.

As her husband turned to leave, Charlotte handed Puddles's leash to Abigail. "I'd better go with Jeffrey."

With the basket in one hand, the dog's leash in the other, Abigail made her way to the triumphant team.

"Congratulations." Though she addressed the words to everyone, her smile was for Ethan, for she knew how much the win meant to him. His team's vindication was visible in the relaxed line of his neck and shoulders and in the smile that softened his face. "The Blues were great tonight." As if seconding Abigail's opinion, Puddles barked.

Ethan's smile widened into a grin. "Hear that, men? Even the dog agrees." He looked down at the basket. "Could it be that you have something for us?" Everyone on the post knew that Charlotte and Abigail brought baked goods to each game and presented them to the winning team. Ethan had groused about the tradition once, saying it made his team's defeat even more bitter. Tonight he was not grousing.

"Indeed, I do," Abigail said with another smile. "Tonight we have cinnamon rolls." A cry of approval met her words. In prior weeks, the treat had been simpler, normally pieces of cake left over from whatever Mrs. Channing had served for dessert, but there were no suitable leftovers from Mrs. Nelson's meals, because she served puddings and compotes rather than baked goods. "I made them myself," Abigail added.

Ethan raised an eyebrow. "You must have known we were going to win."

"I hoped that would be the case."

Lifting the napkin from the top of the basket, Ethan made a show of sniffing the contents. "C'mon, men. Let's enjoy Miss Harding's reward before Puddles takes a notion to help himself to the rolls." He sniffed again. "They smell mighty good."

As the men devoured the hearty combination of cinnamon and sweet dough, Ethan stood at Abigail's side. "This means a lot to the team and to me." He reached over and took her hand in his, squeezing it lightly. "Thank you, Abigail."

His hand was warm and firm, sending shivers of delight up her arm. Even through her gloves, Abigail could feel the differences between Ethan's hand and hers. His was larger. She'd known that. The flesh was firmer. That was no surprise. His grip was stronger. She had expected that. What she hadn't expected was that his touch would make her feel as if she were a precious object, worthy of being cherished. It was an unfamiliar sensation, but oh, so pleasant. Abigail looked down at their clasped hands, not wanting the moment to end. And then Puddles whined, putting his front paws on Ethan's legs.

"I think he's feeling left out," she said.

Ethan wrinkled his nose as he pretended to glare at the puppy. "Pesky dog!" As Puddles barked, Ethan released Abigail's hand, leaving her feeling somehow bereft.

"Abigail."

Her hand stopped in midair. She had been daydreaming, recalling how wonderful it had felt to have her hand clasped in Ethan's, and so she had been later than normal getting dressed this morning. On an ordinary morning, Abigail would have been downstairs, checking the porridge and making coffee. Today, she was about to pin her mother's brooch to her dress when she heard Charlotte's voice.

"Come here. Please."

Abigail's heart began to pound. Something was desperately wrong for Charlotte to sound so weak. She opened the connecting door and hurried into her sister's room.

256

"What's wrong?"

Charlotte's face was devoid of color. Not even when she'd been in the throes of morning sickness had Abigail seen her sister look so ill.

"I don't know." Charlotte's hand rose to her throat. "I feel worse than I have in weeks." She managed a weak smile. "Would you fetch Mrs. Grayson?"

"Shall I get Jeffrey too?"

If possible, Charlotte's face lost even more color. "No. I don't want to worry him needlessly."

Though Abigail was tempted to disagree, she did not. Instead, she hurried to the midwife's house, saying a silent prayer for her sister's health with each step.

"I don't understand." Mrs. Grayson had spent half an hour with Charlotte. Now she sat in the parlor, a cup of coffee in her hand. "None of the other women I've attended have had problems like this."

And that was what Abigail had feared. She'd asked a few discreet questions and had learned that, though Mrs. Grayson had no formal training as a midwife, she had a lot of common sense about childbirth and women's ailments, far more, according to the other women, than Dr. Pratt. Mrs. Grayson was well-regarded and hadn't lost a patient yet, but Abigail still worried that Charlotte's condition wasn't normal. "My sister was very ill as a child," she said, explaining what had happened then. "Do you think this might be related? The doctor warned that her lungs would always be weak."

Mrs. Grayson shook her head. "This isn't her lungs. If I

had to guess, I would say it's the result of high-strung nerves. Has Charlotte always been this easily disturbed?"

"No. Our mother claimed she was the strongest of us."

"She's not strong now. She'll need to spend three or four days in bed, and even then . . ." The midwife frowned. "To be honest, I'm worried about the rest of her pregnancy."

So was Abigail. She hated seeing her sister so ill, and even more she hated the thought that she would soon be thousands of miles away, unable to help Charlotte in any way. Perhaps she could postpone her return a week or so and still be there in time for classes to begin. She would check the schedule, but first she had to tell Jeffrey his wife was ill.

She found him in the post headquarters. "It's my fault." Jeffrey smacked his forehead with his fist when Abigail explained what had happened. "I should not have brought Charlotte here. Why couldn't I see that she's too fragile for this land? What will I do if she dies?"

"She won't." Abigail infused her voice with every bit of confidence she possessed. "Mrs. Grayson simply wants her to rest for a few days."

Jeffrey was silent for a few moments, his eyes staring vacantly into the distance. When he spoke, his words startled Abigail. "I was wrong. It's not my fault. It's yours. You should never have come here."

If the fort had had a church, Abigail would have gone there, seeking answers, begging for help. Poor Jeffrey. Her heart ached for him. Though he'd lashed out at her, and she had recoiled as if from a physical blow, Abigail had known that he acted out of hurt and fear. Jeffrey loved his wife, and the thought of being unable to help her was more than he could bear. That was why he was so angry. While she wished this were a problem she could solve, Abigail knew there was only one source of help.

Although she longed for the quiet solace of a church, Abigail reminded herself of what Papa had said so often, that God was everywhere and that prayer was effective wherever it was offered. She hurried home, then sank to her knees in the parlor and closed her eyes.

Dear Lord, I need your help. You know I love my sister and want only what is best for her. Is Jeffrey right? Did I misunderstand your will? Would Charlotte be happier if I weren't here? I'm lost now. Show me your way. Please, Lord. But there was no answer, nothing but the feeling that she had forgotten something important.

Somehow, Abigail muddled through the rest of the day. Though she wondered whether Leah had gone to the cottonwood, Abigail would not leave Charlotte, even for a brief ride. Perhaps she could go out tomorrow, but today she felt the need to remain close to her sister.

The train schedule confirmed what Abigail had thought, that she could not delay her departure and still return to Vermont in time for the first classes. She had to leave when she had planned. Her pupils were counting on her. Her fellow teachers were counting on her. As if that weren't enough, Jeffrey had made it clear that she was no longer welcome here, and so she would cherish each hour she had with Charlotte.

As they had the last time Charlotte was ill, Ethan and Jeffrey took their meals with the bachelor officers, leaving Abigail alone with her sister. Though she suspected Charlotte was not asleep, each time she peeked into the room, her sister's eyes were closed, and so Abigail did not intrude. Instead, she spent the day alternately worrying and reminding herself that there was no need to worry, that God was in charge. The one time she left was for her class, and, though she tried her best not to let her worry show, she knew that the men realized something was wrong, for they seemed more subdued than normal.

When class ended, Abigail felt her spirits rise. Perhaps Ethan would be waiting for her again. She had missed his company at meals today, and the thought of being able to talk to him had helped her get through the day. But he was not there. The parade ground was deserted, which meant that Ethan could be in his quarters or the Officers' Club, neither of which was suitable for her to visit. She would have to wait until tomorrow to speak with him.

"C'mon, Puddles," she said when she reached the house and untied him from the tree. Jumping and yipping, his ears flapping wildly, the black and tan dog was the picture of happiness. Someone ought to be happy, for Abigail most definitely was not. Though she knew she ought to return to Vermont, she could not dismiss her worries about Charlotte.

"What do you think, puppy?" she asked as they started their second circuit of the parade ground. If she had had any doubts that Puddles was growing, the fact that he wasn't tired after his normal walk would have quashed them. He acted as if he'd just awakened and seemed as full of energy as he had at the beginning of the walk. It was only Abigail who was tired.

And yet, though she tried, sleep eluded her. Perhaps that was why she heard Puddles whimpering. Descending the stairs, she found the dog sitting in his crate, a disgruntled look on his face.

"You don't like being alone, do you?" With Charlotte indisposed, Puddles had spent more time than usual alone today. If he'd slept then, it was no wonder he was awake now. Abigail stroked the puppy's head, then relented and lifted the lid from the crate. An instant later, Puddles was on the floor, gamboling at her feet, chasing his tail and yipping with pleasure.

Mama's cure for insomnia had always been warm milk. Though she doubted it would help tonight, Abigail reached into the icebox and withdrew the jar of milk. She might as well try Mama's remedy. She was heating the milk, watching the pan carefully so it did not boil over, when she heard heavy footsteps. Jeffrey had returned.

"Trouble sleeping?" he asked as he entered the kitchen.

Abigail nodded, uncertain what surprised her most, his amiable tone, the fact that he did not glare at the sight of Puddles, or his wet hair. Jeffrey looked as if he'd just bathed, but today was not bath day. She took a deep breath, then recoiled, her heart plummeting when she realized why Jeffrey was wet. He had attempted but failed to wash away the scent of perfume. Something about him, perhaps his clothing, still bore the fragrance she had smelled in the parlor the last time Charlotte had been so ill. He had been back to the hog ranch. *Why, Jeffrey, why?*

"I'm making warm milk," Abigail said, trying to keep her voice even. Nothing would be gained by questions or recriminations. "Would you like some milk?"

He shook his head. "Never could stand the stuff. But I'm glad you're awake. I wanted to talk to you, to apologize."

For what? The perfume? Though she longed to ask, Abigail said nothing, for she sensed that it was difficult for Jeffrey to even pronounce the word *apologize*.

He clenched his fists, releasing them slowly as he said, "I was out of line this morning. It's not your fault that Charlotte's ill. I know that. I think I knew it then, but I was so worried about her that I wasn't thinking straight. I'm sorry."

Abigail nodded. "It's all right, Jeffrey. I understand." And she did. What she didn't understand was why he smelled of another woman's perfume.

When Abigail climbed the stairs half an hour later, though the doors were closed, the thin walls did not block the sound of Jeffrey's snores or Charlotte's soft weeping. Wishing she could move her bed away from the common wall but knowing that would only reveal what she had heard, Abigail walked to the window and stared outside, hoping the sight of stars in the black Wyoming sky would comfort her. *Oh, Lord*, she prayed, *show me what to do.*

She closed her eyes, and as she did, images of Miss Drexel's Academy, her pupils, and Woodrow danced before her. It was early autumn, one of those perfect days when the sugar maples' autumnal finery shone against a deep blue sky. Abigail smiled at the memory of the brilliant orange leaves, recalling the girls' enthusiasm when she'd told them she and Woodrow would conduct classes outdoors that afternoon. Gradually the scene faded, like a daguerreotype left too long in the sun, leaving nothing but gray. Perhaps she should have felt a sense of loss, but instead Abigail was filled with anticipation as the scene began to change again. Just as gradually as the Vermont countryside had faded, a new picture began to form. When it was complete, she smiled. *Thank you, Lord.*

"I'm staying," Abigail told her sister the next morning. Though she wouldn't share the story of how the image of Charlotte's face had replaced her visions of Vermont, Abigail knew it was no coincidence. This was the answer she had sought. This was what she was meant to do.

Charlotte looked a bit better this morning, with color returning to her cheeks, and she managed a weak smile in response to Abigail's statement.

"I've decided to stay until the baby is born." Jeffrey might not be happy about her decision, but Charlotte needed her, and that was what mattered.

"Really, truly?" Charlotte's eyes sparkled with enthusiasm as she asked the question that had been a childhood refrain.

"Truly, really." Abigail responded, enjoying the way her sister's face brightened at the silly answer. Though tears glistened in Charlotte's eyes, Abigail knew they were tears of joy.

"Thank you." Charlotte reached out and grasped Abigail's hand, squeezing it between both of hers. "I wanted you with me, but I didn't dare ask. It would have been selfish of me to keep you away from the school and Woodrow."

Abigail shook her head. "It's not selfish. It's what sisters do. I'm staying."

"And I'm so very grateful. Thank you, little sister."

"Where are you going in such a rush?" Ethan sprinted the last few yards to join Abigail, then matched her pace.

"I need to send a telegram." Now that the decision had been made, she didn't want to delay in letting Mr. Barnett know. She looked up at Ethan, wondering how he'd react when he heard her news. "I've decided to stay until

Charlotte's baby arrives. I hope the school will give me a leave of absence."

It was absurd, the way her heart leapt at the sight of Ethan's smile. It wasn't as if he were anything more than a friend, and yet, Abigail could not deny that her pulse beat faster and that this friend's smile seemed to warm her face more than the summer sun.

"That seems to be good news for everyone. Puddles won't be lonely, Charlotte will have your help, and the Blues will welcome your cheering."

"Not to mention my cinnamon rolls."

"Not to mention that." Ethan's smile was replaced with an expression of concern. "What will you do if your leave isn't approved? It seems to me it's late for them to find a replacement."

"That's true, and Mr. Barnett might be angry enough not to take me back." Abigail had weighed that consideration. If she were delayed only a week or two, the other teachers could take over her class, but that could not continue for months, and it would be months before she returned to Vermont. No doubt about it: Mr. Barnett would be in a bind unless he accepted her suggestion and put Henrietta Walsh in charge of Abigail's classes. Though young and lacking experience, Henrietta was both enthusiastic and hard-working. She would be a fine substitute teacher.

"If they don't want me to return, I'll find another position. There are plenty of schools in Vermont." Admittedly, Miss Drexel's was one of the most prestigious, but even if she wasn't able to return there, Abigail knew her experience qualified her to teach almost anywhere.

"There are places other than Vermont." Ethan tipped his

head to one side, as if considering alternatives. "You could always stay here. I know Captain Westland would be glad to hire you for the whole year."

Placing her hand on her heart in feigned horror, Abigail pretended to shudder. "Stay here where hail is bigger than baseballs? Never!"

As she had hoped, Ethan laughed.

Corporal Keller was not laughing. Though the rest of the class cheered when Abigail told them she would remain until at least mid-November, he was silent. The normally jovial soldier was obviously disturbed, barely speaking in class, and when he did respond, his answers were wrong more often than not. Charlotte might tell her she couldn't solve everyone's problems, but that didn't stop Abigail from trying.

"Corporal Keller," she said as she dismissed class, "could you remain for a moment?" When the other students had filed out of the room, she turned to him. "Something seems to be bothering you. Can I help?"

"*Nein.*" It was a measure of his distress that he had resorted to German. "No one can help." His face crumpled as he said, "Marta married someone else. She vould not vait for me."

The corporal was right. This was a problem Abigail could not solve. "I'm so sorry," she said, wishing there were something she could do to bring a smile back to his face. But there was not.

She wasn't there. Abigail scanned the horizon, noticing how the once green prairie had turned golden brown, the legacy of summer's heat and dryness. Though the wind set the cottonwoods' leaves dancing, and a bluebird sang to his mate, there was no sign of Leah.

"There's only one thing to do," Abigail told Sally as she headed south. "We're going to pay a visit to Peg's Place." Not surprisingly, the mare did not respond.

The hog ranch was as dilapidated as Abigail remembered. The same chickens scratched in the dirt, while on the other side of the main building, a seemingly well-fed cat licked its paws. If, as Leah claimed, the cat's mission was to catch mice, it appeared that the ranch must have a substantial rodent population.

Perhaps it was the early hour, perhaps the heat. Whatever the reason, there were no signs of human life. Abigail dismounted, looped Sally's reins around the hitching post, then walked to the building. Uncertain of the protocol—did one knock or simply enter?—she hesitated. And as she did, the door swung open, revealing a woman whose imperious expression left no doubt that she was Peg, proprietor of the establishment that bore her name.

Of medium height and build, Peg had no distinctive features other than her mahogany hair and her perfume, which surrounded her in a cloud of the same fragrance that Abigail had smelled on Jeffrey.

"What do you want?" Peg demanded. Her voice was softer than Abigail had expected, with a faint Southern drawl.

Though a dozen questions popped into Abigail's mind, starting with this woman's relationship with Jeffrey, she pushed them aside. She had come here for only one reason: to see Leah.

"I'd like to speak with Leah."

Peg's eyes narrowed. "I'm afraid that won't be possible. None of my girls"—she emphasized the personal pronoun—"are allowed to associate with women from the fort. I'm sure you understand that it would not be good for business."

Though Abigail had not met Peg before, she was bothered by the feeling that something about her seemed familiar, but that concern paled compared to the fact that the older woman appeared to recognize her.

"How do you know that I live at the fort?" Abigail doubted Leah had said anything. Though she had claimed that Peg was mostly benevolent, Leah's unwillingness to accept a book even as a loan told Abigail she shared no confidences with her employer.

Peg's smile was arch. "Simple, really. I visit the fort occasionally to see whether the sutler has any goods my customers might enjoy."

That could explain why Peg seemed familiar. She might have been one of the women Abigail and Charlotte had seen near the parade ground.

"Then Leah is all right?"

"Indeed, she is. So you'd best be heading back to the fort, Miss . . ." Peg paused.

"Harding. Abigail Harding."

"And I'm Peg, but you already knew that, didn't you? Goodbye, Miss Harding. I trust I will not see you again."

Mrs. Eberle used to say that bad news came in threes. Perhaps good news did too. Ethan stirred the salt until it had dissolved in the vinegar, then began to polish his buttons. There had already been two pieces of good news. It had been good—excellent, in fact—that the Blues had finally won a game. Even Captain Westland, whom no one would call the most observant of men, had commented on the men's improved spirits. And then there had been the news that Abigail would be staying at least three months longer. That was definitely good. While Ethan regretted the reason, for Charlotte's ill health weighed heavily on both Abigail and Jeffrey, he was glad that Abigail had delayed her departure. There was no doubt about it. Fort Laramie was a happier place when she was here.

That made two. He would welcome a third piece of good news, especially if it provided a clue to the person responsible for the thefts.

"Have you seen her?" Oliver obviously saw no need for such social niceties as knocking on doors or delivering greetings. Instead, he barged into Ethan's room, a huge grin splitting his face.

"Have I seen whom?" Ethan tried not to smile, though it was difficult when Oliver was around. The man's enthusiasm was contagious.

"Melissa. Captain Westland's niece."

Ethan shook his head. While he had heard the captain say that his wife was returning from Kansas and was planning to bring their niece for a visit, he had not made the young woman's acquaintance.

"She arrived on today's coach," Oliver continued, the words tumbling like potatoes from an overturned cart. "Miss Melissa Westland is the most beautiful woman I've ever seen. Oh, Ethan, I'm in love."

"Again." Ethan chuckled. It was good to see Oliver looking happy, even if his infatuation would last no more than a week. At least for that week, he'd be cheerful, joking with the others, helping boost morale, and he'd have no reason to frequent the hog ranch.

Oliver clapped Ethan on the shoulder. "Love is grand. I know I keep telling you that, but don't just take my word for it. Find yourself a girl."

17

"Are you certain you don't mind?" Though Charlotte's face had regained its normal color, furrows appeared between her eyes, and she looked as if her bowl of porridge had suddenly lost its appeal. Surely she had no doubts that Abigail would agree to what was, after all, a simple request, and yet it appeared that she did. Perhaps this was further evidence of what Mrs. Grayson called delicate nerves.

"I don't mind," Abigail said firmly. "Not at all. You know I enjoy taking Puddles for walks. Besides, you need to save your energy." And trying to keep up with Puddles when he tugged at his leash was not the way to do that. Though Charlotte's recovery had been rapid, now that she was out of bed again, she had begun to remind Abigail of a whirling dervish, constantly in motion as she organized the women's sewing brigade. Anything Abigail could do to slow her down was good.

Her appetite apparently restored, Charlotte ate another spoonful of porridge before she smiled at her sister. "You can make it a long walk, if you want. Both Mrs. Alcott and Mrs. Montgomery are bringing food to the meeting."

"And you don't want Puddles to smell it."

"Exactly. You know the other ladies can't resist feeding him." As if Charlotte could. All Puddles had to do was look up at her with those soulful eyes, and she gave him a bit of whatever it was she was eating.

"Mission accepted." Abigail saluted.

As she had hoped, her sister laughed. "Not bad for a new recruit. Next thing I know, you'll wonder why you can't join the Army."

"Hah! That will happen when Puddles learns to fly." First he had to learn to walk sedately and to come when called.

"C'mon, Puddles," Abigail said after she'd tied her hat ribbons and buttoned her gloves. "It's time for you to learn how a well-behaved dog walks." She waited until they'd crossed the bridge before she began her first lesson, keeping the leash so short that Puddles had no choice but to walk next to her. Though the dog strained at the leash at first, when he realized that Abigail would not let him run and that he would receive a bite of the cake he enjoyed if he walked calmly, he seemed to resign himself to a slower pace than normal.

When they reached the huge cottonwood where she used to meet Leah, Abigail decided it was time for Puddles's second lesson. Letting out the leash, she allowed him to run to its limit. "Come," she called. At first, he ignored her, but she reeled in the rope, all the while repeating, "Come." When he reached her, she patted his head, praising him as if it had been his idea to return. "Good boy. Good Puddles."

After a few minutes, when he seemed to understand the command, Abigail removed the leash and let him run. "Come," she called. The puppy stopped, then tipped his head, as if considering the command. "Come." Abigail repeated the order, holding out a piece of cake. "Good dog." As he devoured the treat, she stroked his ears. "Good Puddles."

Seconds later, he raced away, clearly reveling in his new-found freedom. But each time Abigail called, he returned, and each time, Abigail smiled as she handed him the cake. Charlotte's puppy was a quick learner. She would let him run one more time before they headed back to the fort.

Puddles scampered away, going farther this time but remaining within sight. Abigail suspected that, while he clearly enjoyed his freedom, he wanted the security of knowing she was close. She watched him circling a large rock, his ears perked as if he saw something of interest. Remembering the time he had investigated a prickly pear cactus too closely and she'd had to pull thorns from his muzzle, Abigail called to him. For the first time, he ignored her command, not even looking in her direction.

"Come, Puddles." No reaction. "Puddles, come here. Now." He remained motionless, staring at whatever had fascinated him. "Come!" Abigail shouted the command, but the dog gave no sign of hearing her. Exasperated, she stalked toward him, realizing that he'd tired of the game and that they both needed to return to the fort.

"Come here, Puddles," she said when she was only a few yards away. The puppy whined but did not look at her. Something was wrong, for Puddles had never acted this way. It was almost as if he were mesmerized. And then she heard the rattle.

A minute ago, Ethan had been riding peacefully, looking for signs of deserters, hoping against hope that he'd find some trace of the kidnapped widow. The sun was out. If anything, the day seemed hotter than the past few, probably because there was no wind. Beads of sweat had dotted his forehead, though Samson had shown no signs of the heat bothering him. It had been an ordinary day, patrolling the countryside. But now Ethan was shivering as if he'd been caught in a blizzard. Even worse, he was filled with a sense of impending doom. The dread that clenched his heart had a name. Abigail. She needed him. Ethan knew that with every fiber of his being, and yet it made no sense. Abigail was the most self-sufficient woman he knew.

He shook his head, trying to dismiss the thought, but it was to no avail. His limbs still trembled, and his heart knew what his head tried to deny: Abigail was in danger. The feeling was irrational, the product of pure instinct. And yet . . . Never before had Ethan's instincts been so strong. They were practically shouting that he needed to return to the fort as quickly as he could.

"C'mon, Samson. Let's see how fast you can run."

As the gelding raced across the prairie, Ethan's eyes moved from side to side, looking for possible danger. There was no reason to believe that the Indians were on the warpath, nor was it likely that bandits were waiting to ambush a sole rider. The more common dangers were those native to the prairies themselves: varmint holes, yucca spines, and cactus thorns. A prudent man kept his mount safe from them. Ethan couldn't risk another injury, not when Abigail needed him.

He leaned forward, squinting to see more clearly. Was that a woman next to the boulder? Her dress and bonnet were gray, blending almost perfectly with the rock. If he hadn't been searching so intently, he might have missed her. Ethan's heartbeat accelerated as he urged Samson into a gallop. The object he had seen was indeed a woman.

"Abigail." He shouted her name, but she remained immobile, staring at the ground, every line of her body telegraphing fear. Though he would have given almost anything for it not to be true, Ethan's instincts had been accurate. Abigail needed him.

"Abigail! What's . . . ?" The words caught in his throat as he saw the answer to his question. There on the ground, its tail flailing with fury, lay one of the largest rattlesnakes Ethan had ever seen. Its tongue flickered; its eyes moved from side to side. Only Abigail kept it from striking, for she stood with one foot on the snake, directly behind its head. If she moved, if her weight shifted, the rattler would be free.

Oh, God, please. Unbidden the prayer reverberated through his mind. *Make my aim straight. Let me save her.* There was no room for error, and Ethan sensed that he would have no chance for a second shot, for Abigail appeared on the verge of collapse. He held his breath as he drew his pistol from the holster and aimed at the rattler. A second later, the snake was dead, and Abigail was screaming.

"No! No! No!" She crumpled to the ground, wrapping her arms around herself as she continued to scream. "Not again."

Ethan leapt from Samson and pulled her into his arms. "You're safe."

Her eyes wide with terror, Abigail began to beat on his chest. "Let me go! You killed him. You killed Luke."

Luke? What was she talking about?

"Let me go!"

When Ethan released her, Abigail slid to the ground. Though she had stopped shrieking, her body shook more violently than long grasses in a windstorm. It was the normal aftermath of danger. Ethan knew that, but he also knew that Abigail's reaction was extreme. Her eyes were glazed, and she stared into the distance, unseeing.

"You shouldn't be on the ground. There could be more snakes." She gave no sign of hearing him. "Abigail, please." Ethan reached down to lift her onto Samson. Whether she liked it or not, she had to leave. But before he could draw her into his arms, Puddles reached Abigail's side and began to lick her face. Where had the dog been? Ethan hadn't seen him near Abigail and the snake.

"Oh, Puddles, you naughty dog," Abigail murmured.

Ethan breathed a sigh of relief. This sounded like the Abigail he knew. Somehow the puppy had broken through her hysteria.

"Why wouldn't you come when I called you?" she asked.

As Abigail crooned softly, Ethan spoke. "We need to go."

She stared at him for a moment, her eyes reflecting confusion. Then a wash of color rose to her cheeks. "I'm sorry, Ethan. You must have thought I was a madwoman."

"What happened?" He stretched out his hand and helped her to her feet. Though the trembling had lessened, he doubted she could stand on her own.

"I was teaching Puddles to come when I called him, but he went too far and found the snake." She trembled at the memory. "When I got here, it looked as if it was going to strike. I couldn't let it kill Puddles, but I didn't know what to do other than step on it. That's when I realized that I couldn't move." Abigail took a deep breath, exhaling slowly, as if trying to calm herself.

"You're safe now." Ethan tried to reassure her. "But we need to get back to the fort." She couldn't walk, but Samson could easily carry the two of them. And Puddles. Ethan couldn't forget the dog, for the pup had moved to his side and was looking up with those mournful eyes.

"Hang on," Ethan said as he scooped Abigail into his arms. Her eyes widened for a second before she wrapped her arms around his neck. If she was surprised, so was he. Though he'd held her in his arms when they'd danced, this was different. Far different. Abigail was lighter than he'd expected, her arms softer than he'd remembered, her scent sweeter than anything he could recall. He would gladly have carried her the mile or so back to the fort, but that would only provoke questions for which he had no answers, and so he placed her on Samson's back, then handed Puddles to her. When he'd mounted behind her, determined that he would not let her out of his sight until she was safely home, Ethan flicked the reins. It was time to move.

"Who is Luke?" he asked when Abigail's breathing—and his own—had returned to normal.

He felt her stiffen, and she turned to look at him, her hazel eyes filled with sorrow. "How did you know about Luke?"

She was like a soldier after a battle, remembering only bits and pieces of what had happened. "You accused me of killing him."

Abigail shuddered. "I'm so sorry, Ethan. I must have lost my head for a moment. It's just that the gunshot and the blood brought it all back."

Ethan looked around. There was no sign of snakes here, and Abigail seemed stronger. He dismounted and helped her off Samson. This was one conversation he did not want to have on horseback. He needed to watch Abigail, to see her expression as well as hear her words.

"Tell me," he said simply.

She swallowed, and he saw pain reflected in her eyes. "Luke was one of my neighbors when I was nine years old. Most days he and his brother would play games like hopscotch and tag with me and my sisters, but one rainy day Charlotte was ill and the weather was so miserable that Elizabeth and I stayed indoors. Luke and Richard must have been bored, because they decided to play soldiers in their barn. They weren't supposed to, but they took their father's shotguns with them."

Abigail shuddered again. "I went to the outhouse, and as I was leaving, I heard the shot and the screams."

Even before she described the scene, Ethan knew what had happened.

"When I got there, blood was gushing out of Luke's chest and Richard was screaming as if he was the one who had been shot." Abigail clenched her fists, releasing them slowly. "I've hated guns ever since."

Memories of the attempted stagecoach robbery flickered through Ethan's brain. No wonder Abigail had been so alarmed when he'd pulled out his Colt. No wonder she cringed whenever a cannon was fired. She had even flinched at the Independence Day fireworks.

"It's true that guns can kill," he said, "but they can also save lives. Like today."

She nodded slowly. "I'm sorry for being so silly."

"Abigail, you're the least silly person I know. It's not silly to be afraid. Fear helps keep us alive. But you need to know how to protect yourself. We'll start your lessons tomorrow."

Abigail's eyes widened. "What kind of lessons?"

"Shooting. You need to learn how to handle a gun."

"I can't." Abigail began to tremble, and Ethan longed to draw her into his arms again.

"Yes, you can. You can do anything you set your mind to." He tried not to cringe at the image of her holding off that deadly serpent. "What if I hadn't come?"

She shook her head slightly. "But you did. God sent you at exactly the right time. I prayed for help, and he sent it."

Was it God's urging that had brought him to Abigail? Whatever the reason, Ethan was grateful he'd been there, for he couldn't bear the thought of losing this woman who had somehow found her way into his life and his heart.

Though he longed to hold her close, to tell her how much he cared, he could not, for the specter of Woodrow stood between them. Instead, Ethan forced a playful tone to his voice. "Perhaps you should pray for the strength to hold a gun."

He had meant it as a joke, but Abigail nodded solemnly. "I will."

There was no point in climbing the stairs, for she knew she would not sleep. To Abigail's surprise and Charlotte's delight, Jeffrey had returned from the baseball game with them, seemingly unconcerned that his team had lost again. Even more surprisingly, he had suggested he accompany Charlotte and Abigail when they took Puddles for his nightly walk. Abigail demurred, pleading fatigue after her long walk. She was not tired, but Charlotte deserved time alone with her husband, while Abigail needed time to think.

Fearing that the story would upset her sister's delicate nerves, she had not told Charlotte about the snake, but she could think of little else. Her fears, her prayers, the blood, Ethan's assertion that guns could save lives. They were all jumbled together, blended with the memory of Ethan's arms wrapped around her as they'd ridden back to the fort.

Abigail closed the back door behind her and walked toward the river, carefully latching the gate so that Puddles would not escape from the yard. Though Charlotte rarely ventured beyond the back gate, Abigail had taken frequent walks to this part of the river, enjoying the solitude. She wouldn't descend the bank, for it was steep here, but perhaps the sound of water flowing over rocks would soothe her. When she reached the edge of the bank, she sank to the ground. Surely she would be able to make sense of her thoughts here.

Closing her eyes, she focused on the soft murmuring of the river, the occasional squeaking of a ground squirrel, and the faint scent of wildflowers. Even with her eyes closed, she could picture the land, this harsh land that she had once despised but which had somehow captured her heart. It was a land of punishing wind, relentless sun, and poisonous snakes, but it was also a land of almost unimaginable beauty. Abigail knew that when she returned to Vermont, she would leave a part of her heart here. She would miss Wyoming, but even more, she would miss Ethan. Oh, how she would miss him!

She couldn't say how or when it had happened, but somehow he had become an important part of her life. When she chose her clothing for the day, she wondered whether he would find it attractive. When she took Puddles for a walk, she wondered whether she would encounter Ethan. When she helped Charlotte select menus, she chose foods she knew Ethan enjoyed. She looked forward to his company at meals and to watching him coach his baseball team. Those times were pleasant, but they were nothing compared to the way she had felt today when he'd held her in his arms.

Leaning back against him as they'd ridden, she had felt safe, she had felt cherished. Never, not even with Woodrow, had she felt as if she were the center of a man's universe, and yet that was how Ethan had made her feel. When they'd spoken of the snake and Luke, she had known that nothing was more important to Ethan than comforting her. Perhaps it was only because Ethan was a soldier, trained to protect others, that he had treated her that way. Whatever the reason, those few minutes had been truly unforgettable.

Ethan was unforgettable. But in a few months, he would be nothing more than a memory. Abigail covered her face with her hands, trying not to weep.

Ethan looked around the room, wondering if he should bother undressing and going to bed. He doubted he'd be able to sleep, for memories of the day's events continued to circle through his mind. Good and bad; fear and pleasure. They mingled as they swirled in his brain.

First had come the fear, sharper than the blade of a knife, spearing through him the moment he saw the rattler. He doubted he would ever forget the sheer terror of realizing that Abigail faced possible death. All of his senses had been heightened, leaving him intensely aware of his surroundings at the same time that he focused on the snake's head, knowing that he had only one chance to save Abigail.

And then, when the danger was ended, fear had been replaced by another, gentler yet equally powerful emotion. Perhaps the fear had sensitized him, increasing his awareness of Abigail as a woman. Perhaps. All Ethan knew was that when he had held her in his arms, he felt more than relief that she was safe. The cold fear that had led him to her had disappeared, replaced by an unfamiliar warmth. It had felt so good, so right, to have his arms around her that he had not wanted to let her go. Ever. And that was frightening in itself, for he had never before felt that way.

Ethan tugged off his boots and set them carefully beside the bed. They needed polishing, but he would do that in the morning. Tonight he wanted nothing to distract him as he tried to understand what had happened. It had been an extraordinary day, a day in which everything had been turned topsy-turvy, most of all, his heart. All because of Abigail.

No one had ever touched his heart the way she did. When he'd seen her in danger, Ethan had wanted to save her, but even more, he had wanted to be the one who would keep her safe, not just for today but forever. The feeling was so unfamiliar that he was unable to give it a name. It might be love—Oliver would probably claim it was—but Ethan wasn't certain. Nothing in his life had prepared him for love. For him love had been no more than a word, an abstract concept, and that left him no way to recognize it. All he knew was that whatever he felt for Abigail felt right, and at the same time, the enormity of it frightened him.

Though he had doubted it possible, eventually Ethan drifted to sleep, and when he did, he began to dream. At first the dreams were inchoate, mere fragments, but then he saw them. The man stood in the corner of the garden, his face partially hidden by the branches of the spreading oak tree. He was trying not to attract attention. Somehow Ethan knew that, just as he knew that the man was waiting for a woman. Hours passed, or perhaps it was simply a few minutes. Ethan didn't know, and, in the manner of dreams, it didn't matter.

At last the back door opened, and a dark-clad figure slipped from the house. Though the cloak hid her features, Ethan knew it was a woman who ran silently across the grass, her eagerness to reach the man evidenced by her speed. As she approached the tree, the man stepped forward, opening his arms in welcome, and the woman raced into them. For a moment, there was no sound, and then Ethan heard soft laughter. The couple smiled at each other, their happiness bubbling out like water from a spring.

As the cloud that had obscured the moon shifted, illuminating their faces, warmth filled Ethan's heart. These were not strangers. The man whose nose and chin so closely resembled his own must be his father, and there was no doubt of the woman's identity, for her face was that of the portrait he had found in the back of his grandfather's attic. These were Ethan's parents, and despite Grandfather's claims to the contrary, they were happy and in love.

In his sleep, Ethan turned to his side, and as he did, the dream continued. The couple remained sheltered under the tree, but their faces began to change, softening, blurring, then reforming. When the moon once again revealed them, Ethan gasped, for the couple who gazed at each other with such obvious devotion bore his face and Abigail's. It was right. Yes, it was right.

As he bent his head, intending to kiss her, she smiled sweetly and raised her lips to his. But before they could touch, the dream changed again. Ethan was alone in the garden, and the wind began to blow, the sound of tree branches rubbing against each other filling the air. His smile faded with the realization that he had lost Abigail. The house where they had been headed, the house he knew instinctively was their home, had vanished. All that was left was an empty yard and the sound of tree branches. And yet, how could that be, for the trees were gone?

Ethan woke with a start and reached for his pistol as he realized that what he had heard were claws scratching on wood. An animal had gotten into the BOQ. Alarm turned to relief as the scratching continued, accompanied by a familiar whimpering.

"What are you doing here?" Ethan demanded when he opened the door and Puddles raced in, running in circles around him, yipping with glee. The dog was supposed to sleep indoors, confined to a crate. How had he gotten out? A quick glance down the hallway explained how Puddles had been able to enter the BOQ. The wind had blown the door ajar, leaving enough space for an eager puppy to slide inside.

Though he couldn't help smiling at the dog's ingenuity, Ethan pasted a frown on his face as he said, "You don't belong here. C'mon. I'm going to take you home." But Puddles had other ideas, for he ran under the bed and refused to come out. As Ethan pulled on his uniform, he went from smiling to chuckling. Hadn't he warned Abigail that the tiny puppy she had thought so adorable would be a handful? "Sorry, boy," he said as he reached under the bed and grabbed the dog. "There are two lovely ladies who will worry if you're not home when they waken."

Suspecting that Puddles would not follow docilely, even if he found another leash for him, Ethan picked the dog up and carried him outside. When he reached the Crowley residence, he discovered the back door ajar and Puddles's crate overturned. Apparently the dog had grown too large for his bed and had been able to open it. Though there was no point in confining him to the crate again, Ethan was resolved that Puddles would not escape from the house a second time. Just before he closed the door firmly, he pointed his finger at the dog. "Stay," he said sternly. "Abigail's here."

Wonderful, unforgettable Abigail.

18

How could this be so difficult? Her arms ached, her neck was stiff, and her eyes felt as if someone had tossed a cup of dust into them. Abigail squinted, raised her arms again, and squeezed the trigger. Though her ears registered the noise and her arms jerked from the recoil, she didn't have to look to know that she had missed again, for there was none of the satisfying sound of wood splintering that had accompanied Ethan's shots. They'd been here for what felt like hours, and Abigail showed no signs of improvement. The only good thing she could say was that she had overcome her fear of firing a gun. When she had first picked up the revolver, images of Luke's lifeless body had flooded her mind, and it had taken all her willpower to replace them with memories of the snake's menacing fangs.

"I'm afraid I'm hopeless." Though she wanted to toss the gun aside in frustration, she laid it carefully on the stump that was serving as their table. No matter how inept she was, the Colt was still a valuable sidearm.

Ethan raised his eyebrows in an expression that could have been either surprise or disapproval. "I never thought you were a quitter," he said softly. To Abigail's relief, his voice held no note of disapproval.

"I'm not, normally, but this isn't normal. It seems like we've been here forever, and I still haven't hit the target." A target large enough that even a novice like Abigail should have been able to hit it. Instead of the small targets the soldiers used, which were positioned a substantial distance from the shooter, Ethan had appropriated the lid from Puddles's crate, and he'd placed it only a few yards away. If she couldn't hit something that big, how would she ever defend herself and Puddles against a snake? At least Ethan had set up the target far enough away from the fort that no one else would watch her ineptitude. Ethan was nothing if not considerate.

Abigail didn't know whether he had somehow realized how deeply she had been affected by their closeness yesterday, but if he had, he had been careful not to do or say anything that would embarrass her. Instead, he had told her of Puddles's nocturnal visit to the BOQ and had suggested checking the door each night. Then he'd handed her a Colt. Now he was trying to help her hit the target.

"This is only your first day." It must have been her imagination, but Abigail thought she detected a hint of amusement in Ethan's voice. He was wrong. There was nothing amusing about being such a miserable failure. Before she could form a response, he continued. "What would you tell your pupils if they were discouraged when they couldn't read one of Mr. Dickens's stories their first day of school?"

Abigail shrugged. The answer was obvious. "I'd tell them to be patient."

"Precisely. You need to be patient. Straight shooting is a skill that requires time. No one is perfect the first day."

"But you make it look easy." She glared at the pistol. "I would never have guessed that it was so heavy or that the bullets would go so far astray."

"You'll get used to it. I felt just as awkward my first time."

But that, Abigail suspected, had been a long time ago. "When did you learn to shoot?"

"My grandfather gave me a pistol on my tenth birthday. His housekeeper was appalled, but Grandfather informed me that every gentleman needed to know how to defend himself."

"And so he taught you to shoot."

Ethan shook his head. "No. He hired someone, just as he hired people to teach me everything from Latin to waltzing."

Though she knew Ethan had come from a wealthy family, his story underscored the differences in their backgrounds. "I never had a tutor. My parents couldn't afford one, even if they wanted to. We attended school, but they claimed they should be the ones who taught us the important lessons." And much of that teaching had been by example. It was from watching Papa do his best to right every injustice that Abigail had learned how important it was to help others.

The wind carried the sound of soldiers shouting, the incessant hammering at the administration building, and a crow's raucous cry, but Ethan appeared to hear none of them. His eyes filled with something that might have been sorrow, he nodded shortly. "Make no mistake. I learned a great deal from my grandfather. The problem is, I cannot think of a single good thing that he taught me. What I learned from him was to be suspicious of people's motives and not to trust anyone."

Abigail's heart plummeted at the bitterness she heard in Ethan's voice. "That is so sad." If his grandfather had been that cold, it was no wonder Ethan did not want to see him again. Still, Abigail could not shake the belief that Ethan would someday regret their estrangement. She sought a way to help him understand and possibly reconcile with his only living relative. "Your grandfather must be a very unhappy man."

Ethan was silent for a moment, his eyes fixed on the distance. When he spoke, his voice was flat, as if he were trying to control his emotions. "He wouldn't agree, but I suspect you're right. Now, let's talk of something more pleasant, or—even better—let's get back to your lesson."

With a sigh, Abigail picked up the pistol, trying to mimic the posture Ethan had shown her. She squinted, fixing her eyes on the target, and squeezed slowly. The recoil jerked her arms backward and her eyes stung from the smoke, but Abigail didn't care, for the sound of splintering wood filled her ears. "I did it!" she cried in exultation. While it was true that she'd clipped only the edge of the target, she had hit it. "Oh, Ethan, I hit it!"

Placing his hands at her waist, he lifted her off the ground and whirled her around. "I knew you could do it." As he set her back on her feet, Ethan grinned. "You're an amazing woman, Abigail Harding. I was right. You can do anything you set your mind to."

If only that were true. If only she could find a way to heal the emptiness she knew was deep inside him. *Please, God, show me the way.*

Once again, the days had fallen into a routine, and it was a good one. Abigail smiled as she walked toward the schoolhouse to conduct her class. There were many reasons to give thanks, the most important of which was that her sister was fully recovered from her physical ailments and seemed happier than ever. Charlotte didn't appear to mind that Jeffrey was gone every evening. For a while, he had returned home a few hours after the baseball games ended, but now he was out until close to midnight every night. Though Abigail would hear the heavy tread as he climbed the stairs, she gave silent thanks that she had detected no scent of perfume. Instead, his clothing frequently stank of cigar smoke. While the odor was detestable, it raised no unpleasant speculation, for her brother-in-law had announced that he was spending his evenings at the Officers' Club.

Her classes were going well too. Perhaps it was the knowledge that Abigail would not leave until mid-autumn that encouraged her pupils. Whatever the reason, the men were attentive and were making excellent progress. If only Abigail could find a way to help Ethan and Leah, her gratitude would be boundless.

Ethan tugged off a boot. He ought to be happy, or at least content. The men were in better spirits than they'd been all summer, and there hadn't been a single desertion in weeks.

Captain Westland believed the baseball games were responsible for the change in the men's attitudes, and he was giving Ethan credit for them.

"I can't expedite your promotion," the captain had told Ethan when he'd summoned him to his office this morning. "I wish I could, but you know that's not possible. What I can—and will—do is give you a citation. I want the men in Washington to know you're doing a fine job."

That was what Ethan wanted too—recognition of his abilities and accomplishments. That ought to be enough. Captain Westland's praise should have been what reverberated through his mind. Instead, he kept remembering Abigail's words. *"Your grandfather must be a very unhappy man."* It was as if she'd thrown rocks into a small pond, stirring up the mud, turning what had been clear water cloudy.

Was Grandfather unhappy? Ethan had never considered him in that light, but now that Abigail had churned up the waters, he had to admit it was possible. Grandfather had been widowed at an early age. His beloved daughter had married a man he despised, and then she had died, leaving him with the responsibility of raising a child. If that had caused unhappiness, was that the reason Grandfather had treated Ethan the way he had?

Again, Ethan conceded the possibility. All right. Say it was true. Just because he understood his grandfather a little better didn't mean he could change him. It wasn't as if Grandfather would suddenly turn into a benevolent man, a man who loved his grandson. Some people changed. Ethan believed that. But not Curtis Wilson. He would go to his deathbed the same curmudgeon he'd been when Ethan had lived with him. Ethan knew that, and yet he wished Abigail had not raised the subject, for he did not want to think about his grandfather.

Nor, for that matter, did he want to think about Abigail. Beautiful, sweet, caring, courageous Abigail. The woman who confronted her fears and surmounted them occupied far too many of his thoughts, and that was wrong. Abigail belonged to Woodrow, and while Ethan might not recall too many of the many Bible verses Mrs. Eberle had helped him memorize as a child, he did recall "thou shalt not covet." It was one of the commandments, the rules Mrs. Eberle had told him God expected everyone to obey. He would try—oh, how he would try—not to covet what was not his.

"There you are!" Oliver's voice boomed as he opened the door. "What are you doing indoors?"

He'd planned to polish his boots and brass, but instead he'd wound up staring sightlessly out the window. "Thinking."

"That's dangerous. A man should never think, unless it's about a woman." Oliver paused for a moment, then asked, "Is it?"

Ethan refused to answer. Though Oliver was quick to share his infatuations with the world, Ethan would tell no one of his feelings for Abigail. They were private and, more important, they were wrong.

"It is a woman!" Oliver fairly crowed. "That's the best news I've heard all day. Who is she?"

Ethan leaned forward, as if he were about to impart a secret. Lowering his voice to a conspiratorial level, he said, "My grandfather's housekeeper." It wasn't a lie. He had been thinking about Mrs. Eberle.

"The housekeeper!" Oliver stared at Ethan for a second before his lips twisted. "All right. You've made your point.

Whoever she is, you don't want me to know . . . yet." Oliver's smile said he was confident that the secret would soon be revealed. "You like to keep things close to your vest. Me? I don't mind folks knowing how I feel." Oliver's smile softened as his thoughts turned to his latest infatuation. "I tell you, Ethan, Miss Westland is the woman of my dreams."

Ethan tried not to smile at the number of times he'd heard Oliver utter those precise words. Only the woman's name changed, and that happened almost as often as the moon was full.

Oliver continued his litany of praises, his voice droning like a bumblebee. It was only when a clock chimed the hour that he stopped. "Let's go," Oliver said with a nod at the door. "We need you at the Officers' Club. We're one man short now that Jeffrey hasn't been coming."

This was the first time Ethan had heard Jeffrey had deserted his nightly card game. "Where's he been?"

Oliver shrugged as if the answer should be clear. "With his wife. Where else?"

"We've got a problem." Frances waited until the baron lit his cigar and took a few puffs before she broke the news. "Schiller is demanding a greater percentage of the take, and our friend at the fort is becoming difficult. I think he's developed scruples. Either that or he found Big Nose's stash." Frances doubted the latter. When she had asked the man point-blank, he'd looked as if he'd never heard of the outlaw. Though he might have been acting, Frances didn't think that was the case. He wasn't smart enough to lie convincingly.

The baron remained silent, only the slight lifting of his eyebrows revealing that he had heard her.

"So, what do we do?" At times like this, Frances wished she hadn't needed a partner. Life was so much easier when you didn't have to consult anyone else.

The baron narrowed his eyes, then blew out smoke rings, smiling at their perfect shape. With visible reluctance, he turned his attention to her. "That's twice you've said 'we.' You said we had a problem and asked what we should do. We don't have a problem." He emphasized the plural pronoun. "You do. So handle it. That's your job."

Frances inhaled sharply. While it was true that she preferred to work alone, she had learned that the baron was not easily pleased. The last time she had resolved a problem without consulting him, he had threatened to close down the hog ranch. "A few words to the fort's commander and you'll be out of business," he had said, the steeliness of his expression leaving no doubt that this was not an idle threat. But today he wanted no part in the discussion.

"If that's my job, what is yours?"

Laughter was his only response.

Abigail reached for her bonnet and gloves, all the while chiding herself for the worries that continued to chase through her mind. She had accepted the fact that she couldn't solve every problem, and yet she couldn't help wishing she could find a way to convince Corporal Keller that it was better that he'd discovered Marta did not love him now rather than after they were married. And then there was Leah. She deserved a better life than working at the hog ranch.

Abigail was still thinking of Leah when she entered the sutler's store. Standing motionless for a moment to let her eyes adjust to the relative darkness, she blinked when she heard a familiar voice. What was Leah doing here? Had she somehow known Abigail was worried about her? Abigail looked around, searching for the pretty blonde, but all she saw was a woman with hair so dark it was almost black.

"Leah?" she asked. When the woman turned, Abigail saw that it was indeed her friend. "I didn't recognize you."

Leah touched her hair. "It's a wig. Peg don't like . . ." She paused, correcting herself. "Peg doesn't like me to come here, but she needed some extra canned oysters. She's expecting visitors this week, and I reckon they're important folks, cuz she told us all to freshen up everything." Leah smoothed her skirts over her hips in a gesture Abigail had come to know meant she was uncomfortable. She cleared her throat before giving Abigail a weak smile. "I'm not supposed to talk to you. Peg told me she'd turn me out if'n I did."

"Then I'd better leave." Abigail did not want to get the girl in trouble. Working at the hog ranch was a terrible way to earn a living, but at least it kept Leah alive. If she was on her own with no money, she would not survive long.

"You don't need to do that. She'll never know, and I . . . I miss you."

Tears pricked Abigail's eyes. "I miss you too, Leah."

When Leah completed her purchases, Abigail accompanied her outside. "Would you like another reader?" They would pass by the schoolhouse on their way to the bridge, and Abigail could slip inside to get one.

Leah shook her head. "I don't dare rile Peg. She's been real cranky lately."

"I'm sorry. You were making such good progress."

Abigail and Leah were walking slowly along the perimeter of the parade ground when a soldier approached, his pace suggesting eagerness. A second later, he stopped abruptly and reversed course. A few seconds later, he turned again. This time he marched directly toward them, and as he did, Abigail recognized him.

"Good afternoon to you, Miss Harding." After only the slightest of pauses, Corporal Keller added, "And to you, Miss Anson."

Abigail blinked. She had not realized that Corporal Keller might be acquainted with Leah or, even if he were, that he would recognize her wearing the garish wig. "You know each other?"

"No." Leah practically shouted the word at the same time that he said, "Yes."

Abigail looked from one to the other. It was clear that they were both embarrassed, and yet the tender look Corporal Keller gave Leah made Abigail suspect his embarrassment was due to her presence, not Leah's.

"There is no reason to lie, Leah." Turning to Abigail, Corporal Keller added, "I do know Leah, but not in the vay you think. The night I learned Marta vas married, I did not care about anything except forgetting. I vent to Peg's Place and planned to drink until I could not remember anything. Leah vas there." The smile he gave her was warm, designed to comfort the young woman. "Ven she figured out vat I had in mind, she got me away from the bar." Corporal Keller paused for a second. "She took me to her room."

Leah kept her eyes fixed on the ground.

"There is no reason to be ashamed, Leah." The corporal

stretched out a hand, then withdrew it when he realized that Leah wouldn't take it. "Ve talked. Leah and I talked. And ven ve vere done, I did not care about whiskey. I did not even care about Marta." He looked at Abigail, his eyes shining with happiness. "Leah is the best thing that ever happened to me."

And, judging from the smile on her face, Corporal Keller was the best thing that had happened to Leah.

19

The sun beat down on the already parched parade ground, and the wind evaporated beads of perspiration almost before they could form. Only the occasional cloud brought relief from summer's heat, leaving the men groaning when the sun reappeared. It was no one's idea of a good day to drill soldiers, least of all Ethan's. He knew the men hated marching in the heat. Their dark blue woolen uniforms absorbed the sun's rays, leaving them even more uncomfortable than normal, and the boots whose warmth was so welcome when the thermometer remained well below zero during the long winters felt as if they were made of limestone on a hot day. It was a miserable time to be out on the parade ground marching in formation, and yet it was necessary. This was, after all, a military installation, and its soldiers needed to be in prime condition. Though the danger of an Indian uprising or skirmishes among the miners that would require the Army's intervention was low, his men had to be ready to fight on a moment's notice.

"Left, right. Left, right." The cadence continued, keeping everyone marching in time to the sergeant's commands. Ethan stood at attention, inspecting the company as it made its way around the parade ground. The men were doing well. Not even his instructors at West Point would have found fault with them.

This was what Ethan had been striving for: the best company in the garrison. There had been no desertions in the last month, and since the captain had agreed to add guards to the stagecoach, there had been no further robberies. Morale was higher than ever, in part, he suspected, because the men looked forward to their opportunity to guard the stage. Only Oliver had protested, claiming he did not want to leave Melissa Westland. It had been a direct order and one Oliver could not refuse, but he'd seemed mollified when Ethan pointed out that he would have the opportunity to buy Melissa a token of his affection while he was in Cheyenne. Indeed, life was better than Ethan could remember.

"Telegram, sir." Ethan turned, startled by the sight of a private slightly out of breath from double-timing across the parade ground. It was not unusual to receive a telegram. What was unusual was the apparent urgency of this one. "Mr. Peterson said it was important." The private held out the folded piece of paper.

Ethan nodded, dismissing the messenger. "Continue, men," he said as he unfolded the telegram. Had there been another stagecoach holdup? No. That message would have gone to Captain Westland. This telegram was addressed to Ethan.

"Regret to inform you . . ." Ethan scanned the rest of the brief message. Grandfather was dead. Ethan's eyes registered the words. The man who had been part of his life from his earliest memories, the man who had tried to shape Ethan into his own mold, had taken his final breath, and Ethan felt nothing. Nothing. He twisted the paper between his fingers, then straightened the crumpled sheet and read it again. Surely he should feel something. Sorrow, regret, even relief, not this total lack of emotion. This void was wrong. Ethan knew that, and yet he could not manufacture an emotion. His grandfather was dead, and the knowledge affected him less than today's weather.

"Company dismissed." Even the cheer that greeted Ethan's words evoked no feeling. It was as if something deep inside him had frozen. Or perhaps his feelings weren't frozen. Perhaps the telegram had sucked every bit of emotion from him, leaving a vacuum in its wake. What kind of man was he that he simply did not care?

As the men scattered, Ethan headed for the bridge. Normally he would have saddled a horse, hoping that a gallop would clear his head. But today there was nothing to clear. Perhaps a brisk walk would do what a ride could not.

It did not.

Ethan was not certain how long he'd walked. Somehow, even the simple action of pulling out his watch seemed like too much exertion. But the sun was lower now, and the air had begun to cool. He should return, and yet reluctance slowed his feet, for he had no answers. He still felt numb, and he didn't know why. Forcing his feet to move, Ethan crossed the bridge and reentered the fort, but rather than walk around the parade ground to reach his quarters, he turned left and followed the river's edge. There were fewer people this way, and that was good, for the last thing he wanted was to encounter another human being.

"Ethan! What happened?"

He turned at the sound of Abigail's voice. How could he have forgotten that this route took him along the back of the Crowleys' yard? Or perhaps he had not forgotten. The rapid beating of his heart suggested that he had come this way deliberately, hoping to see Abigail.

"I was worried when you didn't come for supper." She scrambled down the bank toward him, stopping when she was only a foot away, near enough that he could see the concern radiating from her eyes.

"Nothing's wrong." He wasn't about to confess that he'd spent hours wandering aimlessly, trying to fill the vacuum deep inside him. There were things a man would never admit, and that was one of them.

Abigail shook her head. "I don't believe that." She took another step toward him. "If you don't tell me, I'll continue to imagine all sorts of horrible things. You wouldn't wish that fate on me, would you?"

She cared about him. A flicker of warmth ignited deep inside him. This was what he needed: Abigail's . . . Ethan struggled for the word, settling for *friendship*. For the first time since he'd read the telegram, he felt alive. Still, he was reluctant to tell Abigail how he'd spent almost half the day.

"You're persistent, aren't you?"

She shrugged. "So I've been told. I suspect it's a better trait than being impulsive."

She was trying to make him smile. Ethan knew that, and he appreciated the effort, though it did not succeed. He might as well tell her about the telegram. Its contents would be public knowledge soon.

"My grandfather died." There. He'd said it.

Abigail closed the distance between them, placing her hand on his arm. "Oh, Ethan. I'm sorry."

"I'm not." The words came out unbidden, causing the blood to drain from Abigail's face. Now she knew him for what he was: a monster. "I can see I've shocked you. I shocked myself too. I knew he was ill, so this wasn't unexpected, but I thought I'd feel something when he actually died. I don't, and that's the worst part."

What was it about this woman that she breached his defenses? Ethan hadn't planned to tell her—or anyone—how he felt, and here he was, confiding the thoughts he had determined no one would ever know.

Abigail tightened her grip on his arm and looked up at him, her eyes filled with compassion and something else. If he didn't know it was impossible, he would have said it was understanding, but no one could understand.

"It's natural," she said firmly. "What you're feeling is natural."

"But I'm not feeling anything."

Abigail nodded. "Your body is protecting you from hurt. That's why you feel numb. And before you tell me that I'm not a doctor, let me remind you that I'm a minister's daughter. Papa told me he'd often see people whose loved ones had died walking around as if they were in a fog. He said sometimes it would take days before they could admit what had happened, and then they'd become angry. Papa claimed the numbness helped them deal with their sorrow."

It was an interesting theory. Unfortunately, it had one major flaw. "I didn't love Grandfather, and he didn't love me." As Abigail's eyes widened, Ethan continued. "Do you ever have nightmares, and when you waken, you tell yourself it was only a dream?"

Abigail nodded, confirming that she'd experienced the same feelings. But she hadn't, for her nightmares hadn't turned into reality. His had.

"My worst nightmare came true this afternoon." He could see the confusion in her eyes and knew he had to explain. "I'm just like my grandfather." That was truly the stuff of nightmares. "I realized today that I'm everything I hated about him. I'm a man who's incapable of caring about others."

When Abigail started to speak, Ethan shook his head. "All my life I hated Grandfather's coldness. I feared I was like him, but I hoped I wasn't. I tried so hard not to follow in his footsteps. That's why I joined the Army, because it was as different from running a railroad as anything I could imagine. But I can deny it no longer. I'm just like him, a miserable human being, unable to love and unworthy of being loved."

Abigail reached out to grip his other arm, as if to restrain him. "You're wrong." Her voice was low but fierce. It was an effort to comfort him, but, like her attempt to make him smile, it failed, for Ethan knew the truth.

"You never met my grandfather, so how can you say that?"

"Because I know you. You care about people. I've seen the way you treat your men. It's not just duty. You do everything you can to make their lives better."

He couldn't let her think he was some kind of hero when he wasn't. "That's hardly philanthropic. Whatever I do for the men is so they don't desert. That makes me look better. I may get a commendation for it, and it might increase my chances for promotion. It's all for me, just like everything Grandfather did was for himself."

Abigail shook her head. "You can tell yourself that if you want, but I won't believe it. As for the other side of the equation . . ." Her expression changed, becoming firmer. It appeared that the schoolteacher in Abigail had asserted herself. Ethan braced himself for a lecture. Instead, her lips softened and her voice was filled with fervor as she said, "Not only are you worthy of love, you *are* loved."

Ethan was mistaken. It wasn't Abigail the schoolteacher who spoke but Abigail the minister's daughter. She was preparing to give him a sermon, not a lesson. "I suppose you're going to tell me that God loves me."

"He does."

She didn't understand. She was trying, but she didn't understand. How could she? "That's easy for you to say. You're a preacher's daughter. You've lived your life according to the Good Book. Of course God loves you. My life hasn't been like that. I've done nothing to deserve anyone's love, especially God's. I'm not like you."

Abigail closed her eyes for a second, and Ethan wondered whether she was praying. When she opened them, they reflected an emotion he could not identify. "Oh, Ethan, you're wrong on so many counts. I'm just as much a sinner as you or anyone else, but I know that God loves me. He loves me so much that he sent his Son into the world to die so that I wouldn't have to pay the price for my sins. I didn't do anything to deserve that. There's nothing I could do that would make me worthy of a gift like that. Don't you see, Ethan? God offers love, forgiveness, and eternal life. Those are his gifts to me and to you. All you have to do is open your heart and welcome God into it."

The flicker of warmth that Abigail's caring had ignited

grew, and Ethan could feel the ice that encased his heart begin to melt. Was it true? Was love a gift, not something to be earned? Was it possible that all he had to do was accept that gift? "You make it sound easy. I know it's not."

A sweet smile crossed Abigail's face, and her eyes lightened. "It's the easiest and the most difficult thing you'll ever do. If you choose to accept God's gifts, your life will change in ways you never imagined possible. If you don't, life will continue the way it has. It's your choice, Ethan. No one can make it for you."

"You really believe this, don't you?"

"I do. But don't take my word for it. Read God's Word. The answers are there."

Ethan looked away, unwilling to face her penetrating gaze any longer. It was as if she could see inside him, and that was unnerving, for he didn't want anyone to know of the emptiness, least of all this woman. The vacuum deep inside was his private nightmare, something he did not want to reveal to anyone. He had believed it was a permanent part of him, but Abigail disagreed. She believed the void could be filled. Was she right? Was it God's love that Ethan lacked? Would God fill the empty spaces? He had to know.

"Where do I start?"

Abigail touched the windowsill before she pivoted on her heel and walked back to the door. Back and forth, back and forth. She'd been pacing the room for what felt like hours, hoping that the mindless exercise would exhaust her enough that she would be able to sleep. So far, it had not worked, for she kept remembering Ethan and the pain she had seen in his

eyes. There had been a flicker of hope when she had spoken of
God's love, but it had been quickly replaced by despair. *Oh,
Lord, only you can help him. Fill his heart with love.* Abigail
continued the silent prayer as she paced. Though she wanted
desperately to help Ethan, she knew there was nothing more
she could do. Ethan's future was between him and God, and
so, unable to do anything else, Abigail paced and prayed.

She was at the windowsill when she heard the soft knock
on the door.

"What's wrong?" Charlotte asked as she entered the chamber, her hand moving protectively to touch the baby she carried within her womb.

"I'm sorry I disturbed you," Abigail said. "I couldn't sleep."

Moonlight spilled into the room, revealing Charlotte's rueful smile. "It wasn't you. The baby woke me. I can't prove it,
but it seems that just when I get to sleep, he thinks it's time to
play." She touched her abdomen again, her smile broadening.

"Playing, huh?"

"That's better than believing he's deliberately kicking me."
Charlotte reached for Abigail's hand and pressed it to her
stomach. "Feel this."

As if on cue, the baby kicked. "He seems strong." Though
Abigail continued to remind Charlotte that the child might
be a girl, she had adopted her sister and Jeffrey's habit of
referring to it as "he."

"I can tell the difference week by week. He becomes more
active. Even though it interferes with my sleep, I'm thankful
that he's healthy." Charlotte let Abigail's hand drop. "You
haven't answered my question. What's keeping you awake?"

There was no reason to lie to her sister. "Ethan."

Charlotte nodded. "I thought something must be wrong

when he didn't come for supper. Obviously, you've learned what happened."

"His grandfather died." Abigail would not reveal the rest of their conversation or the fervent prayers she had offered on Ethan's behalf, but Charlotte deserved to know this much.

"I understand he was old and in ill health. It may have been a blessing."

Not to Ethan. His grandfather's death had triggered reactions Abigail could not have anticipated. Still, perhaps it was all part of God's plan. Perhaps he would use Curtis Wilson's death to bring Ethan to him.

Charlotte sank onto the chair next to Abigail's dressing table, clasping her hands over her stomach as she said, "This means Ethan is probably a very wealthy man now. Jeffrey said his grandfather was a millionaire several times over and that there are no other heirs. I wonder if he'll resign his commission to run the family's railroad."

Was that part of Ethan's dilemma? Though she thought it unlikely, Abigail was not certain. Ethan had claimed the reason he joined the Army was to have a different life from his grandfather's. Was he reconsidering now that his grandfather was dead? "He didn't say anything, but if I had to guess, I'd say that he wouldn't leave. The Army is Ethan's life."

Charlotte tipped her head to one side. "I believed the same thing about Jeffrey at one time, but he's started talking about resigning."

This was the first Abigail had heard that. "Would that please you?"

"Oh yes." The enthusiasm in Charlotte's voice left no doubt. "I try not to say anything to Jeffrey, but I long for a permanent home, especially with the baby coming." Charlotte frowned. "I'm sorry. I was digressing. Even if it was expected, news of his grandfather's death must have been a blow for Ethan."

"Yes." Although not in the way Charlotte believed. "His grandfather was his only living relative. Please pray for him. He needs to find peace."

Charlotte nodded. "Of course." Then she rose, moving to stand next to Abigail. For a long moment she said nothing, simply looked at Abigail. When she spoke, her voice was low, as if she did not want to be overheard. "I should have realized it before. You love him. That's why you care so much."

Abigail would not deny that she had strong feelings for Ethan. "I do care for him," she admitted. "But love? I don't know. Some days I'm not even sure I know what love is. What I do know is that I don't feel the same way about Ethan as I do about Woodrow."

When she thought of Woodrow, Abigail felt surrounded by comfort and predictability. There would be no surprises in a life with Woodrow, for he had everything planned. Ethan was different. Thoughts of him were accompanied by excitement and the challenge of the unknown. There would be nothing ordinary or predictable about a life with Ethan. Instead, it would be like the summers of her childhood, filled with promise. Abigail bit the inside of her mouth. It was foolish to even think of that, for Woodrow was waiting for her. He was a good man who cared for her, and yet . . .

"How do you know if you love someone?" she asked Charlotte.

Her sister shrugged. "You just do. In your deepest heart you know this is the man you want to share the rest of your life with."

Ethan stared out the window, watching the moon rise. Not for the first time he wished Oliver were here. The man's cheerful patter, even if it was about the beauteous Melissa Westland, would have distracted him, but Oliver was in Cheyenne, sicker than the proverbial dog, or so the telegram claimed. Though there were few details, one thing was clear: Oliver would not be taking the stagecoach back to the fort for at least two more days, and that left Ethan with little to do but think.

This was the third night since he'd learned of his grandfather's death and the third night that he'd been unable to sleep. Perhaps he'd been wrong, refusing Captain Westland's offer of compassionate leave to attend the funeral, but Ethan would not be a hypocrite, pretending a grief he did not feel. Undoubtedly the funeral would be well attended, with Grandfather's business associates filling the pews. The mourners had no need of Ethan.

There was no reason for him to be in New York, and indeed it was not thoughts of Grandfather that kept him from sleeping but rather Abigail's words. *"It's the easiest and the most difficult thing you'll ever do,"* she had said. Abigail hadn't exaggerated. Ethan had read the Bible verses she'd suggested. The promises she'd extolled were there in black and white for everyone to read. If a man believed them, they would provide comfort. Ethan did not doubt that. The problem was, he wasn't convinced they were anything more than words. Perhaps they meant nothing more than the Brothers Grimm stories he'd read as a child. Perhaps they were fiction, designed for entertainment, nothing more. It was true that they spoke of love, but love was a word that held no meaning for him.

And so he remained awake, letting the words circle through his mind, wishing he could believe as Abigail did, but knowing that was not possible. He was not a man of faith. Instead, he required proof, and there was no proof that God existed, any more than there was proof that God loved him.

Ethan sighed, wishing it were otherwise. He closed his eyes for a moment, seeking the peace he'd seen on Abigail's face, but all he found were more questions. How? Why? Why not? When he opened his eyes, he frowned at the sight of a man trudging into the fort, a bag slung over his shoulder, his stooped posture betraying exhaustion. Who was returning so late, and why hadn't the sentries seen him?

Thankful that he was still dressed, Ethan rushed outside, planning to confront the latecomer. Though it was possible the soldier was innocent, thoughts of the missing weapons and the stagecoach robberies were never far from Ethan's mind. "Halt!" Ethan ordered as he approached the man.

The soldier stopped, dropping his bag and saluting. "Yes, sir."

Ethan knew that accent. This was the man who needed extra money to bring his sweetheart to Wyoming. Once again his actions set Ethan's antennae to buzzing. "Corporal Keller, what are you doing outside, and what is in your sack?" Dietrich Keller looked down at the bag. "I vas hunting. I shot a grouse, but ven I vent to retrieve it, my horse ran away." He shook his head in disgust. "Such a *Dummkopf*. I must not have hobbled him properly. I hope he came back."

It appeared the corporal was innocent, for his story rang true, and the dead bird inside the bag seemed to corroborate it. There was one more thing to verify. "Let's go to the stable and see about the horse." When they arrived, the old gelding that the enlisted men rode when on day passes was there, chomping oats as if he'd done nothing wrong by abandoning his rider. Corporal Keller was guilty of nothing more than bad luck.

Ethan clapped him on the shoulder. "Next time, be more careful."

"I vill."

"Bowles, you need to hear this." The angry tone of Captain Westland's voice left no doubt that the news was not good. "There's been another stagecoach robbery. Yesterday evening," he announced when Ethan closed the door to his office. "The passengers are at the Rustic," he said, referring to the hotel that served as the local coach stop. "See what you can learn."

What Ethan learned was not encouraging. Although the passengers' descriptions confirmed that Privates Schiller and Forge had been involved, unlike the earlier holdups, there had been three bandits on horseback this time. That was not good news. Even worse was the fact that the gang appeared to consist of at least four, for the men on horseback had been assisted by a woman passenger, who'd held a gun on the others inside the coach, then escaped with them.

"I don't like it, sir," Ethan said as he reported to the captain. "The outlaws are changing their methods. This time the robbery was later in the day, and it was closer to Cheyenne than ever before. It will be harder to guess where they'll strike next."

The captain nodded. "What I want to know is how they knew Seton wasn't going to be on the coach. This is the one time in weeks that we haven't had a guard, and they picked it. That can't be a coincidence."

310

Ethan agreed. As much as he disliked the thought, once again the evidence pointed to someone from the fort being involved, for only people at the fort knew of Oliver's sudden illness.

"The road agents are smarter than I had hoped," Ethan admitted at dinner, when he'd finished telling Abigail and the Crowleys about the holdup. Charlotte blanched; Jeffrey's face reddened with anger; only Abigail seemed calm. She buttered a slice of bread and appeared to be considering his story.

"Do you suppose the woman who was kidnapped the last time was part of the gang?" she asked. "Maybe it was only a pretend kidnapping. Maybe she's the same woman who was on this coach."

It was an interesting thought and one that had not occurred to Ethan. "That would explain why we never found her." He took a bite of meat, chewing thoroughly as the possibilities whirled through his mind. Abigail's suggestion made sense. The only problem was that the gun-toting woman on yesterday's coach did not resemble the elderly woman who had been kidnapped.

Though the conversation turned to more pleasant topics, Ethan was unable to dismiss the thought of the robbery from his mind. When the meal was over and he and Jeffrey headed back to the parade ground, he turned to his fellow officer. "I still think someone from the fort is involved. I have no proof, of course, but my instincts tell me there's a connection."

"Just because Schiller and Forge were deserters doesn't mean anything."

"I know. The problem is, I caught a soldier coming in

311

after tattoo last night. His story sounded plausible, but now I wonder, especially since there were three men this time. What if he was the third?"

Jeffrey pursed his lips, as if considering the question. "Who was he?"

"Dietrich Keller."

Jeffrey's face darkened. "You'd better keep an eye on that one. I never did trust him."

❧ 20 ❧

Sally needed exercise, and Abigail needed a chance to think. This morning Charlotte was uncharacteristically out of sorts because Puddles had run away again, and even though Ethan had brought him back before breakfast, Jeffrey had grumbled about the puppy's behavior, declaring that if Charlotte could not control him, he would have to go. Predictably, Charlotte had burst into tears. Now she was in the backyard, attempting to train the dog and staunchly refusing Abigail's offers of assistance.

"Jeffrey's right. He's my dog, and I'm responsible." The look in Charlotte's eyes left no doubt that she was determined to do this alone, and so Abigail had donned her riding habit, as determined as her sister to be useful. At least there would be no disputing who should exercise Sally, for Charlotte could no longer mount a horse.

The dissention between Charlotte and Jeffrey was not the only thing concerning Abigail. The continuing stagecoach robberies haunted her. Perhaps it was because she had come so close to being a victim herself. Perhaps it was because she knew the puzzle plagued Ethan. Abigail wasn't certain of the cause. All she knew was that she wished she could help Ethan learn who was responsible.

Both of those concerns paled when compared to her worries about Ethan himself. Though he had said nothing, she knew that he still struggled with the idea that God loved him, for his eyes remained filled with pain. Each day Abigail gave him a folded piece of paper with a Bible verse she hoped would comfort him. Each day Ethan accepted it, but he never told her whether he read the verses or whether they helped.

"Going for a ride?" As Abigail passed the BOQ, Ethan called out to her. When she nodded, he descended the two steps from the porch and raised an eyebrow. "Do you have your pistol?"

"Even though we both know I couldn't hit anything I aimed at, yes, I do." Abigail touched her pocket. It still felt strange having the weight of the Colt there, but she did not doubt the wisdom of carrying it.

"May I join you?"

Abigail nodded, hoping Ethan didn't notice that a flush of pleasure colored her cheeks. Mama had insisted that a woman should never be the first to reveal her feelings. "I wasn't going anyplace special," she told Ethan. "I just want to exercise Sally."

"Samson will be glad to get out too."

When the horses were saddled, instead of heading east toward the bridge, Ethan turned Samson west. "It's probably silly," he said as they passed the Rustic, "but I thought that maybe if I retraced the stagecoach's route, I might learn something."

It was as Abigail had feared. Ethan was so consumed with thoughts of the robberies that he could think of little else, including the state of his soul.

"I keep thinking about the robberies too," she admitted. "I wish we knew who the woman was and where she lives."

Ethan's eyes scanned the horizon before returning to Abigail. "You sound as if you're convinced there's only one, but the passengers' descriptions are different. One woman had white hair and was elderly. The other was a blonde."

A month ago Abigail would not have given it a second thought, but that was before she had seen Leah in the dark wig. "It could be one woman with a wig," she said, telling Ethan about her encounter with Leah. "If I hadn't heard her voice, I wouldn't have recognized her."

"You might be right," Ethan admitted, "but that doesn't help us find her. She could be anywhere. Whoever she is, she's well hidden, just like the outlaws."

"At least you know who two of them are."

"And that's part of the problem." Ethan frowned. "Deserters usually try to get as far away from a fort as possible. Schiller and Forge seem to be staying close to our garrison. The only reason I can imagine is that their leader is here."

"At the fort?"

Nodding, Ethan outlined his reasons. "The way I see it, someone from the fort has to be involved, because only someone from the fort would know when guards were scheduled to be on the coaches. I don't think it was coincidence that the robbery attempts stopped when we put guards on all the stagecoaches."

Then why had the coach that Oliver was supposed to be guarding been attacked? Surely the person from the fort, if there was such a person, would have informed the outlaws that Oliver was scheduled to be on the coach. It was pure chance that he'd been taken ill. Or was it? Abigail did not like the direction her thoughts were headed. "Did Oliver tell anyone here that he was too ill to travel?"

Ethan nodded. "He sent a telegram that day."

The timing seemed somehow wrong. "Was it before the stage left Cheyenne?" The woman who had taken part in the robbery had boarded the coach in Cheyenne. It was doubtful she would have ridden it, had a soldier been one of the other passengers.

Though the sky was cloudless, Ethan's expression turned darker than a thunderhead. "The telegram came later. Oliver claimed he didn't wake up until afternoon, and when I asked him what had happened, he said he didn't remember much. According to him, the night before he helped some woman when she started to fall off the boardwalk in front of the hotel, and she was so grateful she insisted on paying for his dinner. She even ordered it for him, to make sure he had a good meal. The next thing he knew, he was so ill he couldn't stand."

Another woman, or was it the same one? There were too many coincidences for Abigail's comfort. "It sounds as if Oliver ate some spoiled food, but I thought it took longer for the symptoms to start." When Elizabeth had consumed a bad piece of meat, it had been hours before she'd been ill.

A gust of wind threatened to turn Abigail's hat into a tumbleweed. As she tightened the ribbons, Ethan smiled. "One thing you can be sure of in Wyoming is, if it's not windy today, it will be tomorrow." His smile faded. "Oliver's story could be true. He told me that if he eats mushrooms, he's violently ill almost immediately. There could have been mushrooms in something the hotel served."

"You don't sound convinced."

"I want to believe it, because Oliver is a friend, and yet . . ." Once again Ethan stared into the distance, as if the horizon held the answer. "It's possible that the woman he helped was the same one who held up the coach and that she deliberately ordered a dish containing mushrooms, but that assumes a lot of things, the most important of which is that she had to know Oliver can't tolerate mushrooms."

And that led back to someone at the fort's being involved. A stranger in Cheyenne would not have known that.

"I'd like to believe Oliver," Ethan continued, "because the alternative is that he pretended to be sick so that the bandits could attack the coach. I don't like that idea at all."

A man could only go so long without sleep. Eventually the need for rest caught up with him. Ethan yawned widely as he pulled off his boots. He knew he'd reached that stage. Though he was still disturbed by Oliver's possible complicity in the robberies, he would sleep tonight, even if thunder crashed and hail pounded the roof. Ethan yawned again as he folded his uniform before sliding under the sheets. Seconds later, he was asleep.

At first his slumber was dreamless, but then the sounds intruded, and he dreamt of an animal caught in a trap. A rabbit, a fox, perhaps a pronghorn. The trap was so far away that Ethan could not identify the creature. All he knew was that the creature was in pain. He turned, trying to block out the cries, but they continued, weaker now, yet just as insistent, piercing through the fog of Ethan's fatigue. It wasn't a dream! Sleep fled as Ethan bolted out of bed and opened the door. There was Puddles, lying on the threshold. The normally exuberant dog appeared to have collapsed.

"What's wrong, boy?" Alarm shot through Ethan. The puppy had never looked like this, his eyes dull with pain, his body virtually motionless, and he'd never sounded as if he were in agony. Ethan had heard the dog whimper when he wanted to come inside. He'd heard him yip with excitement and bark with alarm. Never before had he heard such piteous sounds.

"Puddles, what's wrong?"

As if in response, the dog staggered to his feet, then toppled over, his legs moving uncontrollably, his head tipped backward at an alarming angle. "Puddles!" Ethan knelt beside the puppy, his fear growing when he heard the dog's labored breathing. Though Ethan knew little about dogs, he knew this one's condition was serious. Each breath was more tortured than the one before, and with each one, Puddles seemed to weaken further.

"No!" Ethan scooped the convulsing puppy into his arms. He could not—he would not—let Abigail's dog die. Not caring about his own state of undress, he raced outside, and for the first time, he was thankful that the BOQ was next door to the post surgeon's quarters. By some miracle, the lights were still on in the doctor's office. "You've got to help me," he said when the fort's physician responded to his pounding on the door.

The heavyset man gave Ethan only a passing glance before focusing his attention on the dog in his arms. "I'm not a veterinarian," he said sternly. Though well regarded for his medical expertise, the doctor was not noted for his friendly manner. "If that's why you're here, you're in the wrong place. I don't know anything about dogs, and the only reason I'm still awake is that I have two men in the hospital who may not make it through the night. I was on my way to them."

"Please." Ethan hated to beg, but there was no alternative. Dr. Pratt was Puddles's only hope. "There has to be something you can do."

Though the doctor glared, Ethan thought he saw a hint of curiosity in his gray eyes. "All right. Bring him in." He ushered Ethan and Puddles into his office.

The doctor gestured toward the bare rectangular table in one corner of the room. While Ethan held Puddles, trying to keep the dog from sliding off the slippery surface during his seizures, Dr. Pratt examined him, peering into his eyes and mouth, running his hands and stethoscope over the puppy's body.

"It looks like some kind of poison to me," he said after what seemed like an eternity. "I would have expected him to expel it, but dogs aren't like humans. They don't spit out things that taste bad." He laid a hand on Puddles's right front leg, trying to still the thrashing. "Whatever it is, it's interfering with his heart. It's beating too fast. That might be what's causing the seizures. I'm not sure." The doctor took a step away from the table but kept his eyes on the puppy.

"Will anything stop the seizures?" Ethan could hear the difference in Puddles's breathing. Another few minutes, and he would have no strength left.

Dr. Pratt harrumphed. "I told you I don't know anything about dogs."

Puddles wasn't just a dog. He was Abigail and Charlotte's treasured pet. Knowing how much the two women doted on him and how devastated they would be if he died, Ethan resolved not to give up without a fight. "If it were a man, what would you do?"

An exasperated sigh greeted his question, but the doctor walked toward one of the tall cabinets and opened the door. Withdrawing a brown bottle, he said, "I'd give him this to slow down his heart rate."

"Can we try that?" Ethan didn't care what the medicine was, only that it might help Puddles.

Another harrumph was followed by a reluctant nod. "I suppose it can't hurt. The dog will die without it, so you might as well try." Dr. Pratt measured out a teaspoonful, mixing it with a cup of water. "Let's see if we can get him to drink this." As Ethan held Puddles's mouth open, the doctor poured the liquid down his throat. "Good," he said when the puppy swallowed. "If it's going to work, we'll know within a quarter hour."

But it took less than ten minutes to see the difference in the dog's condition. His legs stilled, and his breathing sounded more normal. Dr. Pratt pressed his stethoscope to Puddles's belly, then nodded. "It's working . . . so far."

"What do you mean, so far?"

"Just what I said. This was only the first treatment. He'll need three more before we know if he's going to recover. You need to give him a dose every two hours. If you wait too long, he'll die. If you give him too much, he'll also die. It's up to you, Lieutenant. I've done all I can." The surgeon reached for his coat and medical bag. "I've got two men who need me, so don't bother me again, no matter what happens."

Ethan nodded. "Thank you, doctor." At least now Puddles had a chance.

As he left the surgeon's office, Ethan debated telling Abigail and Charlotte what had occurred, then shook his head. There was no point in disturbing their sleep when he would do everything possible to save the puppy. Morning would be soon enough, for by then Puddles's recovery would be assured. Ethan refused to consider the alternative.

Even though it was only next door, by the time Ethan reached his quarters, the dog appeared to be asleep. The medicine had obviously taken effect, for Puddles's breathing was regular, and the whimpers had ceased. His own exhaustion returning in full force, Ethan placed a folded blanket on the floor, laid the puppy on it, then climbed into bed, knowing he'd waken in less than two hours. His West Point training had given him the ability to sleep deeply but waken when needed, almost as if he set an internal alarm clock. Seconds later, Ethan was asleep.

When he woke, he was disoriented for a moment, knowing only that it was the middle of the night and something was wrong. Then the sound of the dog's snuffling brought back the events of the night. It was time. Carefully, Ethan measured out the potent medicine, diluting it with water from his pitcher. Though Puddles still slept, he woke the dog and poured the liquid down his throat.

"Halfway there," he told Puddles. "By morning you'll be feeling much better." And so would he.

Though he couldn't explain what led him to do it, as he climbed back into bed, Ethan flicked open his watch. No! It couldn't be. Ethan gasped at the realization that his internal alarm clock had failed him. It had been only an hour since Puddles's last medication.

"If you give him too much, he'll die." Dr. Pratt's words echoed through Ethan's mind. He'd done it. He'd given Abigail's dog more medicine than he could tolerate, and now the puppy would pay the price. Puddles would die, and it would be Ethan's fault, his and his alone.

He knelt on the floor next to the dog, listening to his breathing. There was no question about it. Each breath grew more strained as the puppy's small body tried to overcome the effects of the medicine. Though Dr. Pratt had told him not to disturb him again, Ethan didn't care. He would take Puddles to the hospital and beg the surgeon to help. But as he reached to gather the dog into his arms, Ethan heard Puddles's breathing weaken again. It was too late. He wouldn't live long enough to get him up the hill to the hospital.

"Oh, Puddles!" Ethan's face contorted with agony as he realized there was no hope. There was nothing more he could do. His shoulders slumped, and he bowed his head, waiting for the inevitable. And as he did, a spark of hope ignited deep inside him. There was nothing he could do, but if Abigail was right, there was One who could save Puddles. She claimed he was a God of love. Surely that love extended to a desperately ill puppy.

"Dear Lord, show me what to do." Ethan spoke the words aloud, imploring Abigail's God to help him. "Puddles is innocent. He doesn't deserve to die. Show me how to heal him."

There was no answer, no message carved on tablets, no voice coming from the mountain. But as Ethan stared at the dog and listened to his uneven breathing, a memory surfaced. He'd been seven or eight, and though he could not recall what he had eaten, the pain in his stomach had been worse than anything he'd ever experienced, twisting his insides, making him cry out as the waves of agony increased. He remembered gripping the bedsheet so tightly he'd torn it and gritting his teeth when the pain became unbearable, but nothing helped. And then Grandfather had come into the room.

"You idiots!" he'd yelled at the servants who stood at Ethan's bedside. "Get me the ipecacuanha." Grandfather had forced Ethan to drink the foul-tasting liquid, then held his head as he vomited the contents of his stomach into the chamber pot. "I know you feel awful," he said, "but you can't let the poison remain."

Ethan blinked. That was it. He would force Puddles to vomit. It might not be enough, but purging was the only way he could slow the medicine's progress. How? That was the question. He had no ipecacuanha. Undoubtedly there was some in Dr. Pratt's office, but he would waste precious minutes carrying Puddles there and trying to find it. He couldn't wait that long. There was only one thing to do.

"Sorry, boy," he said as he forced the dog's mouth open and inserted his fingers. As he had hoped, the puppy gagged and regurgitated liquid. "Please, Lord, let it be soon enough." Puddles looked up at Ethan, his eyes dull and filled with pain.

"I know it hurt," Ethan said, "but it had to be done. Don't worry. I won't do that again." Unfolding the blanket, he wrapped the puppy in it and held him in his arms. There would be no more sleep tonight.

Ethan settled on the floor, his back against the bed. Though he dared not close his eyes for fear of sleeping, his mind wandered, returning to that horrible night of his childhood. After Ethan had emptied his stomach, Grandfather had put him back in the bed, smoothing the sheets over him, and he'd remained at his side until daybreak, holding Ethan's hand.

A warmth that owed nothing to the August heat began to spread through Ethan. He had forgotten that night, perhaps because Grandfather was gone when he wakened, and when he'd felt well enough to descend the stairs, he found that his grandfather had reverted to his normal demeanor, demanding perfection, dispensing criticism but never praise. And yet the night had happened. Ethan knew that, just as he knew that he had been wrong. His grandfather might not have been demonstrative. He might never have said the words. But he had loved him. His actions proved that.

By the time the sun rose, Puddles was sleeping peacefully. Though he appeared weak, and Ethan doubted he'd spend any time running today, there had been no more seizures, and his breathing was slow and even.

"Thank you, Lord." Ethan bowed his head as he knelt next to the bed. "Thank you for saving Abigail's dog. Thank you for showing me that Grandfather loved me. Most of all, thank you for loving me."

Abigail woke suddenly, aware that something was wrong. She lay for a moment, trying to determine what had alarmed her. There were no cries or groans from Charlotte's room. Nothing seemed amiss, but Abigail could not dismiss her fears. She dressed quickly, then descended the stairs. And as she did, she knew what bothered her. The house was too quiet. Normally by this time, Puddles was demanding to be let outdoors. But there was no sound of the dog, and his bed was empty.

"Puddles," Abigail called as she opened the back door. Somehow the puppy must have gotten out of the house again and was probably chasing ground squirrels through the yard. But the yard was empty. "Puddles!" Where could the little scamp be hiding?

Slowly, Abigail walked around the house, looking for the dog, dreading Jeffrey's reaction if Puddles had run away again. When she reached the front, she saw a soldier headed her way. She started to smile, for there was no mistaking Ethan's gait, but her heart plummeted at the realization that Puddles was not at his side. Wherever the dog had gone, it was not to the BOQ. Abigail's eyes narrowed. How odd. Ethan was carrying something in his arms, and it appeared that something was wrapped in a blanket. As he drew closer, she saw a dark head emerge. Puddles!

Abigail raced toward Ethan. "What's wrong?" For something was definitely wrong if he had the puppy wrapped like a baby.

Her gaze moved from the dog to Ethan. Though she'd expected to see concern etched on his face, Ethan was smiling. Not an ordinary smile but one so filled with joy that his face appeared almost radiant. Never before had Abigail seen Ethan look like this. The pain that had clouded his eyes was gone, replaced by the clear sparkle of happiness. And yet he was carrying the dog.

"What's wrong?" She repeated the question. The Puddles she knew would not tolerate being carried.

"Nothing's wrong, at least not anymore." Ethan looked down at the dog, and his smile faltered ever so slightly. "Puddles must have eaten something poisonous. I don't know how he got out or why he came to me, but he's all right now. He's a bit worn out from the ordeal, but he'll live."

Poison. Abigail's heart recoiled from the idea. Even

spoiled meat could kill an animal, and a puppy was especially vulnerable. "What did you do? How did you save him?" Abigail stroked Puddles's head and was rewarded with a soft whimper.

Ethan waited until she was looking at him again before he spoke. "It wasn't what I did. It was what God did. He saved your dog. Puddles would have died if it had been left to me." As he recounted what had happened, Abigail watched the play of emotions on Ethan's face—dismay, fear, relief, then joy.

"I don't know why Puddles came to me," Ethan said, "but I'm glad he did. Despite everything you told me and everything I read in the Bible, I was a doubting Thomas. I needed a sign before I'd believe it. Puddles was that sign. What happened last night showed me that love is more than a word. It's real."

Abigail watched as the man she loved nodded slowly. His voice was low and intense, filled with awe. "I knew that if God loved a puppy enough to save his life, what you said was true. God loves me too. He answered my prayers." Wonder shone from Ethan's eyes and colored his voice.

Abigail smiled as she laid her hand on top of his. "Mine too."

❧ 21 ❧

"Telegram, sir."

Though Ethan kept his expression impassive, his pulse raced as he accepted the folded piece of paper. "Thank you, private." This was what he'd been waiting for, the answer to his inquiries. Feeling like a traitor, he had telegraphed the hotel manager to ask whether anyone remembered Oliver Seton's illness. It seemed wrong to need corroboration of a fellow officer's story, and yet Ethan knew he had no choice. He had to discover the truth.

He took a deep breath before unfolding the telegram. A moment later he grinned, for the hotel staff confirmed Oliver's tale. The bellboy had heard him retching and had offered to call a physician. Even better, the maître d' remembered the blonde woman who had ordered Oliver's dinner, specifying that the green beans be cooked in mushroom broth.

Oliver had not lied. That was good news. Excellent news. Unfortunately, it did not bring Ethan any closer to finding the outlaws' leader.

Abigail smiled as she warmed the water for Puddles's bath. The pup wouldn't enjoy it. Much as he seemed to find delight in rolling in mud puddles, he protested each time she bathed him. Unfortunately for Puddles, if he was going to continue to live inside the house, he had to be cleaner. Even Charlotte, who rarely complained, had wrinkled her nose at the smell emanating from his fur. Part of the cause was undoubtedly the medicine he'd been given, but some of the stench was due to the dog's continued fascination with anything that smelled awful. If he lived in Wesley, Abigail had no doubt he would have joined the skunk family's nightly parade across the town square, with predictable consequences. As it was, his curiosity had almost killed him. The morning Ethan had brought Puddles back, he and Abigail had found a partially eaten dead squirrel in the backyard. It appeared the Puddles could not tolerate squirrel meat any more than Oliver could mushrooms.

"All right, boy. It's time." Abigail reached for the dog, who had attempted to hide under the bench, and hoisted him into the makeshift tub. As she soaped his back, she smiled again. The two weeks that had passed since the night of Puddles's ordeal had been the busiest she could recall, and the happiest.

Part of what kept her so busy was Puddles's training. When it became obvious that Charlotte was having no success, Abigail had assumed full responsibility for teaching the dog to obey simple commands. He now understood "fetch," as well as "come," "sit," and "lie down."

Puddles was making good progress. Abigail was thankful for that. She was even more thankful that he had recovered completely from his squirrel dinner, but the greatest cause of her happiness was Ethan's newfound faith. The change was remarkable. Ethan's walk was jauntier, as if he had cast off a tremendous weight. He laughed more often, and the faint lines between his eyes had disappeared, replaced by an expression of peace. Ethan was a new man. Though Abigail knew he was still troubled by his inability to prove who was behind the stagecoach robberies, he no longer seemed haunted by the lack of progress. Instead he was confident that he would capture the gang . . . in God's time.

"He's teaching me patience," Ethan confided one day before he began Abigail's shooting lessons.

Patience was a lesson she had yet to learn, for she chafed over her slow progress. It was true that she could now hit the target consistently, but it was a very large target. Still, Ethan seemed to think that was good enough. Even though she had never hit the bull's-eye, he had announced that next week they would use a smaller target. Abigail was not looking forward to that.

She did look forward to their nightly walks. Each evening they took Puddles out for exercise, and while the puppy gamboled beside them, she and Ethan would talk. Sometimes they spoke of significant things like Ethan's reading of the Bible. Other times they spoke of nothing more important than whether the dark clouds that filled the sky would bring hail along with thunderstorms. The subjects didn't matter. What did matter was that their conversations gave Abigail a new understanding of Ethan. Each day brought her closer to him, and though she had known him only a few months, she could deny it no longer. Ethan meant more to her than anyone else, even her sisters. She loved him.

"Yes, Puddles, it's true," Abigail said softly, admitting her love as she hauled the puppy out of the tub and began to towel him dry.

Charlotte had been right when she had said that Abigail would know when she met the man God intended for her. Unlike Charlotte's love for Jeffrey, which had happened practically at first sight, Abigail's had taken longer to blossom. At first she hadn't recognized the depth of her feelings, because they were so different from what she felt for Woodrow. Now she knew the truth. The love she had for Woodrow was sisterly love. She cared for him as she did for Charlotte and Elizabeth. Abigail's feelings for Ethan were far different. When she was with Ethan, she felt complete. Though she had not been aware that there was an empty spot deep inside her, when she was with Ethan, that spot was filled.

"All right, Puddles. We're done." Abigail drew the brush through Puddles's fur one last time before letting the dog go. As he raced in circles to chase his tail, she smiled.

A mere two weeks, but so much had changed. It wasn't only Ethan who had changed; Abigail had too. Ethan's faith had strengthened hers and made her realize that he was the man she wanted to marry, the man she wanted to spend the rest of her life with. Though they had never spoken of their feelings, there were times when Abigail believed Ethan shared her longings. There were times when she caught a wistful look, and other times when his smile seemed particularly warm. Was that love? Though she hoped it was, Abigail knew it was possible that Ethan regarded her as she did Woodrow, as a sibling or a friend.

Puddles whined and scratched the door, reminding Abigail that he was ready to go outside. She ran her fingers through his fur, smiling at the way the dog responded to a gentle touch. Woodrow had never wanted a dog, claiming they were too much work.

Woodrow. Abigail's smile faded at the thought of the man she had once planned to marry. She now knew that, no matter what happened with Ethan, she could not marry Woodrow. The orderly life he offered was no longer the one she wanted, for what had once seemed comfortable now appeared boring. Abigail bit her lip, thinking of how she had described Wyoming as boring. It wasn't. It was beautiful and alive, and being here had changed her in ways she had not dreamt possible. No matter what the future held, Abigail knew she would never forget this summer, for it had shown her what true love was. That was why she could not marry Woodrow. He deserved a wife who would love him the way she did Ethan.

The problem was how to tell him. Should she send him a letter or wait until she returned to Vermont to pack her belongings? Either way, Woodrow would be disappointed, possibly hurt, and knowing that wrenched Abigail's heart. Though Woodrow was a good man who deserved nothing but happiness, she was not the one to give him that happiness. Her hand on the doorknob, Abigail closed her eyes and bowed her head. "Dear Lord, you know what is in my heart. Show me the way. Give me the words I need."

When she'd tied Puddles to his favorite tree, Abigail frowned. The apron she'd worn hadn't protected her skirt from the dog's exuberant shaking, and it bore unmistakable water stains.

There was nothing to be done but change her skirt and hope that a good soaking would remove the stains.

As she climbed the stairs, the sound of soft sobbing came from Charlotte's room, setting Abigail's heart to pounding. Her sister was supposed to be having tea with the sewing committee this afternoon. Why hadn't she heard her return?

After a perfunctory knock, Abigail turned the knob and entered her sister's room. "What's wrong?" she asked. Charlotte lay face down on the bed, her shoulders shaking from the force of her sobs. "Is the baby all right?"

For a moment there was no sound save Charlotte's crying.

"Charlotte, please. You're scaring me." Never before had Abigail seen her sister like this. Even when their mother had died, Charlotte's grief had seemed muted compared to this.

Her sister turned, revealing a face blotched with tears. "Oh, Abigail, I don't know how much longer I can continue. I feel as if I'm living a lie."

Abigail crossed the room in a few swift strides and sank onto the bed next to Charlotte. Wrapping her arms around her shoulders, she drew Charlotte to a sitting position. "Sometimes it helps to talk," Abigail said as she handed her sister a folded handkerchief. "You know I'm a good listener."

Charlotte dabbed at her eyes. "I didn't want anyone to know. Today when Mrs. Montgomery was telling us how her husband dotes on her, I couldn't bear it. If I'd stayed, I would have cried like this, and I couldn't let anyone know."

"Know what?"

Charlotte's face crumpled again as she said, "My marriage was a mistake."

Abigail tried not to wince as she remembered the strange perfume. Though she had worried about her sister and Jeffrey for months, she had hoped she was mistaken in her fears, that there was an innocent reason for Jeffrey to smell of another woman's perfume.

"Why do you think that?" Abigail asked, tightening her grip on her sister's shoulders. "I know you love Jeffrey, and he loves you. I see it in his eyes when he's with you."

"He doesn't love me. Not anymore." Sobs wracked Charlotte's shoulders, and she covered her face with her hands. "I'm so ashamed. I thought I could be a good wife, but I've failed."

Poor Charlotte! If she truly believed that, it was no wonder her nerves were fragile. "You haven't failed. You're a good wife, and you will be a wonderful mother."

Charlotte looked up, her eyes filled with pain. "I know you love me and want me to feel good, but it won't work. I can't escape the truth. If Jeffrey was happy with me, he wouldn't be with another woman almost every night. I'm not as dumb as he thinks. I can smell the cheap perfume on his clothes."

"Perhaps there's a good explanation." Abigail was grasping at straws, but she had to do something to comfort her sister.

"What could it be? The only explanations I can find are that Jeffrey's either tired of me or he's upset because I've been ill so often. The result is the same: he's spending time with one of those women at Peg's Place."

As much as she wanted to disagree, Abigail could not. "I hope you're wrong."

Charlotte shook her head again. "I'm not. The only question is whether I can continue to live like this." She touched her abdomen. "My baby needs a father, but he needs a good one. I don't know if Jeffrey can be that kind of father."

"What would you do?" Surely Charlotte wasn't thinking

of leaving Jeffrey. Though she had more skills and money than Leah, living alone would be difficult. And there was the baby to consider.

Tears welling in her eyes, Charlotte shook her head. "I don't know. All I know is that I can't go on living like this. I need to know the truth, but . . ." The tears began to fall. "Oh, Abigail, I'm such a coward. I'm afraid to ask him. I don't want Jeffrey to know I don't trust him." Charlotte dabbed at her eyes. "Isn't that silly? I'm worried sick, but I don't want to do anything that might hurt him."

"You love him." And Charlotte was a peacemaker. She would never willingly confront anyone, much less someone she loved as much as she did Jeffrey.

"I do. I just wish I were as strong as you. Then I could ask him."

Abigail closed her eyes for a second, not liking the direction the conversation was heading. "Do you want me to ask him?" Though she did not want to interfere in her sister's marriage, if there was something she could do to ease Charlotte's pain, she would.

Charlotte shook her head vehemently. "No. That would be wrong, but could you . . ." She hesitated before completing the sentence. "Would you see where he goes?"

Slowly, Abigail nodded. "You know I'd do anything for you, sister of mine."

A weak smile was Charlotte's only response.

By suppertime, Charlotte's face bore no trace of tears, and if she was quieter than normal, neither Ethan nor Jeffrey seemed to notice. The men spoke of the upcoming baseball game, and when his team won, Jeffrey was in visibly good spirits. But when the game ended, he did not return home. He stayed on the parade ground long enough to enjoy the basket of cakes that Charlotte had brought, then left without an explanation. Though Charlotte said nothing, Abigail saw the anguish in her eyes and knew that she had no choice. She had to do what she had promised: learn where Jeffrey had gone.

When she and Ethan took Puddles for his walk, Abigail looked closely at the Officers' Club. That was where Jeffrey claimed he was spending most evenings. Fortunately, the night was unusually warm for mid-September and the door stood open, allowing her to see the occupants. The tables were filled with men playing cards and drinking spirits, but Jeffrey was not one of them. Abigail's heart plummeted at the realization that her sister's fears had been confirmed. In all likelihood, Jeffrey was at the hog ranch.

Abigail had no memory of what she and Ethan discussed as they continued their walk. She must have sounded coherent, and that was a small miracle in itself, for her mind kept shrieking, *No, Jeffrey, no!* When she returned to the house, Charlotte was already in bed, exhausted by the day's events. Locking Puddles in the back hallway, Abigail slipped out the front and headed for the stables. Though the soldier guarding the horses looked askance, he did not refuse to saddle Sally for her, seeming to accept Abigail's explanation that she was helping her sister. That much was true, even though the help she was providing was not simply exercising the mare.

She had emerged from the stables and was headed for the bridge when she heard the call. "Abigail! Where are you going?"

She frowned. Though ordinarily her heart would have beat faster at the sound of Ethan's voice, this was one time when she did not welcome his presence. He must have been visiting the cavalry barracks for some reason, and now he was coming toward her at double-time. "Where are you going?" he repeated.

"I'd rather not say. It's a family matter." Whether or not she and Charlotte were mistaken, it was better that no one—not even Ethan—knew of their suspicions.

Even in the dim moonlight, Abigail had no trouble seeing Ethan's frown. "I cannot believe your family knows you're out here." When she said nothing, he continued. "I won't ask why you think this is important, but you can't leave the fort alone at night. It's not safe. I'd worry every minute until you returned."

Abigail's heart warmed at the huskiness in his tone, for it told her that he cared for her . . . at least a little.

"Let me go with you," Ethan said, placing his hand on Sally's bridle. "I promise to keep whatever it is you're doing confidential. I won't even tell Jeffrey."

Abigail shook her head at the unintentional irony. "Jeffrey will know soon enough. The reason I'm out is that I'm looking for him. I have reason to believe he may be at Peg's Place."

"Jeffrey?" Astonishment colored Ethan's voice. "I know Oliver is a frequent visitor, but Jeffrey . . ."

"I'm afraid so. He's not at home, and he's not at the Officers' Club. I don't know where else he would be." She wouldn't mention the perfume. That detail was too damning.

Ethan hesitated for a moment before nodding. "All right. I'll get Samson, and we'll go to Peg's."

They rode in silence, and for the first time, the silence was not a companionable one. Abigail could not imagine what Ethan was thinking. For her part, she was praying her fears and Charlotte's would be unfounded, and that Jeffrey had not broken his marriage vows.

Though moonlight hid many flaws, the hog ranch still looked as seedy as it had the other times Abigail had seen it. Light spilled through the open windows, raucous laughter drifted onto the still air, and the smells of cheroot smoke and cheap perfume made her wrinkle her nose.

Ethan reined his horse in front of the main door and dismounted. "This is no place for a lady," he said, looking up at Abigail, "but I doubt I can dissuade you. Will you at least let me go in first?" When she shook her head, Ethan sighed. "You're a stubborn woman." But he helped her off the mare.

"Jeffrey's my family," Abigail said when her feet were on the ground. Though her legs were trembling at the thought of what she might find inside the smoky room, she knew she had no choice. "I need to find him."

Ethan opened the door and allowed her to precede him. While everything inside her shrank at the prospect of finding Jeffrey here, Abigail stood in the doorway and looked around, searching for her brother-in-law. A bar stretched the length of the far wall, the mirror hanging over it so covered with grime that it barely reflected her image and Ethan's. A few equally dirty glasses and bottles decorated two shelves. Four small tables were clustered in one corner, while a battered pianoforte occupied the opposite corner.

Though two men stood at the bar, apparently arguing with the barkeeper, and another was seated at one of the small tables, his attention on the scantily clad blonde who perched on his knee, none of them was Jeffrey. That left the large table in the center of the room, where eight men were so engrossed in their card game that they had not noticed Abigail's arrival.

Abigail took a step forward, grateful for Ethan's presence at her side. Papa would have called it a den of iniquity, no

337

place for his daughter. Mama would have swooned at the mere idea of Abigail setting foot inside. As the door closed behind her and Ethan, the saloon's occupants looked around.

The woman who'd been entertaining the cowboy in the corner jumped to her feet. "Miss Harding," Leah hissed as she covered the distance between them. "What are you doing here? This is no place for you."

It was no place for Leah, either, but Jeffrey was Abigail's primary worry now. "I'm looking for my brother-in-law," she said. "Is Lieutenant Crowley here?" When the card players had turned around, she had confirmed that none of them was Jeffrey. That did not mean that he wasn't on the premises, though, for he could be in any of the cabins. At least he was not with Leah. Somehow that thought comforted Abigail.

Leah bit her lip, her reluctance obvious. It was clear that she knew who Jeffrey was and that Abigail's question bothered her. "No." Leah shook her head, setting the golden curls to bouncing on her shoulders. She glanced at the man behind the bar, then turned slightly so he could not read her lips. "Yes, he is," she said, her voice so low that Abigail could barely hear her. "He's in the back room." When Abigail raised an eyebrow rather than ask the question, Leah said, "The entrance is 'round back. That keeps it private like."

Abigail nodded. "Thank you, Leah."

When she and Ethan were once more outdoors, Abigail drew a deep breath. "You don't have to come with me," she told him. Though Leah had said nothing, Abigail surmised that the back room was one where women entertained their clients. Perhaps its relative privacy meant it was Peg's special room. When Abigail opened the door, she would likely find Jeffrey in Peg's arms.

"I won't leave you alone." Ethan crooked his arm and placed Abigail's hand on it. If he noticed her trembling, he did not mention it, nor did he seem to notice that Abigail clung to him as if he were a lifeline. It was good, so very good, that he had insisted on accompanying her. Now that she was here and within moments of discovering how Jeffrey spent his evenings, Abigail wasn't certain she could have done it alone.

She and Ethan walked around the building, stepping carefully to avoid the piles of trash that the wind had blown in. When they reached the rear, Abigail took another deep breath, then regretted it. Whatever had been dumped here smelled worse than Puddles before his bath. Unlike the front of the building, the back had no windows. Only the light that shone around the frame identified the location of the door.

Abigail lifted her hand to knock, then let out a nervous laugh. Though etiquette demanded she announce her arrival, this situation was outside every rule of etiquette she had learned.

Ethan opened the door, pushing it inward, and Abigail stared as relief flooded through her. *Thank you, Lord.* As she had surmised, the room was Peg's, but it was not a bedroom. Instead, it held a round table where six men were playing cards, while Peg, dressed in a gaudy crimson gown that clashed with her mahogany-colored hair, watched.

"What do you want?" she demanded as Abigail and Ethan entered. "This room's off limits." The soft Southern accent was more pronounced now, perhaps because of her anger, for there was no doubt that Peg was angry.

"I'm looking for Lieutenant Crowley." Abigail's brother-in-law ought not to be here, and yet there he was, the only officer in a room devoted to gambling. Though his back was to her, there was no mistaking his hair or the set of his shoulders. He had to have recognized her voice, but he gave no sign.

Peg's lips curved in a scornful smile. "Jeffrey, your nurse-maid and her escort are here."

This time Jeffrey turned, his freckles prominent against the pallor of his face. "How'd you know?" The question appeared to be directed at Ethan.

Ethan placed his hand over Abigail's, as if to give her strength. "What we have to say is better said outside."

When Peg nodded, Jeffrey rose. Gathering the money piled in front of him, he stuffed it into his pocket. "Why are you here?" he demanded when they were outside and the door had closed behind them.

"A better question is, why are you here?" Ethan countered. "Aren't you the man who said he'd do anything for his wife?"

Even in the faint moonlight, it was obvious that Jeffrey's face had lost more color. "What does Charlotte have to do with this?"

Abigail took a step toward him and glared. "Charlotte's terribly worried about you. She keeps imagining all kinds of horrible things."

"You won't tell her I was here, will you?"

Though Abigail heard the desperation in Jeffrey's voice, there was only one possible answer. "I can't make that promise. Charlotte already suspects you come here. Either you tell her what you've been doing here, or I will. She needs to know the truth."

"The truth is I did this for her." Jeffrey looked at Ethan. "You know how little we get paid. I couldn't afford to give Charlotte everything she deserved. I had to find a way to get more money."

"And so you turned to gambling. The games at the Officers' Club weren't enough, so you came here where the stakes were higher." Though Ethan's voice was laced with scorn, Abigail knew that as heinous as gambling was, Charlotte would find it preferable to adultery.

"It's an easy way to make money when you're as good at it as I am."

The pride in Jeffrey's voice made Abigail want to slap his face. He was so concerned about winning at baseball and poker that he didn't seem to realize he was losing at something far more important: marriage. "It's also an easy way to make your wife cry."

"Charlotte's unhappy?" The man sounded surprised, almost shocked. Could he possibly have thought that Charlotte didn't miss him when he was absent almost every night? How deluded could he be?

"I suggest you ask her that yourself." Abigail said a silent prayer that her sister would have enough courage to tell Jeffrey exactly how she felt.

Ethan gave Jeffrey a shove, pushing him toward the front of the building. "Let's go. It looks like you've got some explaining to do."

When Abigail woke the next morning, it was to the sound of Charlotte singing. Her lovely soprano carried up the stairs, blending with the rattle of dishes and the clang of the teakettle.

"Oh, Abigail, you were right," Charlotte said as Abigail entered the kitchen. "It wasn't as bad as I feared." She poured boiling water into the teapot, placed it on a tray, and handed it to Abigail to take into the dining room.

"Jeffrey and I talked for hours last night," Charlotte continued. "I never realized he thought I wanted all these fancy things." She gestured toward the delicate china cups and the silver teapot. "They're nice, but not if it means he has to gamble to pay for them."

When they reached the dining room and had placed the dishes on the table, Charlotte turned to Abigail. "Jeffrey promised he'd never go back there. He's done with gambling." She put her arms around Abigail and hugged her. "Thank you. You're the best sister anyone ever had."

"You are looking at the happiest man on Earth." The grin that accompanied Oliver's declaration made his plain face glow. "The captain vouched for me. He telegraphed her father, and he gave his permission. I'm going to marry Melissa."

Ethan clapped his friend on the shoulder. "Congratulations, old man. You couldn't have picked a better wife." Unlike Abigail and the other women Oliver had pursued, Melissa Westland seemed well suited to both Oliver and military life. "When's the happy day?"

Oliver's smile dimmed. "That's the only bad part. We've got to wait almost two weeks for her parents to arrive, but by then the administration building should be finished. Melissa's looking forward to being the chapel's first bride."

Brides. Chapels. The words evoked painful images of Abigail walking down the aisle toward Woodrow. She hadn't said anything about him recently, but that didn't mean that she wasn't still planning to marry him. Rather than think about that, Ethan turned his attention back to Oliver. "It sounds as if big changes are coming."

Oliver grinned. "They've already begun. Now that I'm getting married, I won't be going back to the hog ranch. I said good-bye to Peg and her girls last night." A low chuckle accompanied Oliver's words. "Can you imagine? Peg asked if she would be invited to the wedding. She seemed sorry I was getting married."

More likely, she was sorry to be losing another regular customer. First Jeffrey, now Oliver. That couldn't be good for Peg's business.

"I'm not sorry," Ethan assured his friend. "I'm glad for you."

Oliver's grin widened. "Your time is coming. Just don't forget the pretty words. That's how you catch a wife."

But words, no matter how pretty, wouldn't help Ethan, for the woman he loved was going to marry Woodrow.

22

Abigail smiled as she buttered a piece of bread. Almost two weeks had passed since the night she and Ethan had brought Jeffrey home from the hog ranch, and they had been two of the happiest weeks she could recall. Though Jeffrey seemed quieter than normal and Charlotte did not speak of what had occurred, Abigail could not miss the tender looks they shared. Whatever had happened between them, it appeared that their marriage had taken a turn for the better, and for that Abigail was deeply grateful.

It wasn't only Charlotte and Jeffrey who were happier. Even though the bandits had not been caught, Ethan seemed more relaxed, perhaps because there had been no more robberies, perhaps because—like almost everyone on the post—he was caught up in the preparations for Oliver and Melissa's wedding tonight. He smiled more often, and with each smile, Abigail's heart soared. She had never, ever felt this way with Woodrow.

Woodrow. Abigail's smile faded as she reminded herself that she had to find a way to tell him that she could not marry him. Though she had started letters to him a dozen times, she had torn each one up in disgust.

"Oh, I almost forgot." Jeffrey nodded at Abigail as he helped himself to another serving of roast. "A letter came for you. I think it's from your beau." He reached into his pocket and handed her the envelope.

The handwriting was definitely Woodrow's. Feeling another stab of guilt that she had delayed so long in telling him the truth about her feelings, Abigail waited until she was alone to open the envelope. It was unlikely the letter would be filled with protestations of love, for that was not Woodrow's style, but her fingers still trembled as she withdrew the thin paper.

Dear Abigail, Woodrow had written. *This summer apart has given me time to reflect.* Abigail's eyes widened. Woodrow was not a reflective man. Once he made his plans, nothing would sway him. What had happened to change that? Had her prayers been answered? Was it possible that God had used the summer to reveal new sides of Woodrow at the same time that he had revealed facets of Abigail?

It pains me to say this, but I realize that I do not know you as well as I thought. I believed you wanted the same things I did—to live in Wesley, to teach at Miss Drexel's, perhaps one day to see a child of ours become the headmaster of the academy. Those had been her dreams. When she had set foot on the train headed for Cheyenne, Abigail had wanted nothing more than to live out those dreams. And then everything had changed.

Your letters paint a different picture. I see that you crave adventure and that you will never be fully satisfied with life in Wesley. Woodrow was right. Somehow, though she hadn't realized she was doing it, she must have communicated her change of heart. It seemed that Woodrow had recognized what was happening before Abigail had. Her old dreams had crumbled like the pages of the ancient book she'd found in the school's attic.

I know your sister is ill, but I also believe that if your heart were here, you would have returned for the fall semester. Tears welled in Abigail's eyes as she recognized the pain behind Woodrow's accusation. What she feared had occurred. She had hurt a man who deserved nothing but kindness from her. She had hoped to break the news to him gently, but now it was too late. There was no way to undo the damage.

Your actions have spoken loudly, and I've heard their message. Because you are not the woman I believed you to be, the plans I made for that woman no longer have any validity. A faint smile curved Abigail's lips. This was the Woodrow she knew, a bit pompous. She had always suspected that his occasionally bombastic prose was his way of compensating for his less than average stature, but perhaps it was simply a way to mask his pain.

I know I have no right to give you any advice, but I will offer it anyway. Stay in Wyoming. It is where you belong. Was he right? Abigail wasn't certain. The one thing she knew was that she did not belong in Vermont, teaching at the academy, planning to marry Woodrow.

Cordially, Woodrow Morgan. Cordially? Abigail raised an eyebrow. In the past, he had signed his letters "with much affection" or simply "your Woodrow." The formality combined with the use of his surname told Abigail this would be the last letter she received from him. Their friendship was ended.

Regret filled her heart at the same time that she realized this had been inevitable. Even if Abigail returned to Vermont, their relationship would have been strained, and it would have been difficult teaching at the same academy. Though she would always regret the fact that she had hurt Woodrow, Abigail felt a sense of relief that she had been unable to complete her letter to him. This way Woodrow could take comfort from the fact that he had ended their relationship, and perhaps one day he would find a woman who loved him as a wife should.

Abigail folded the closely written sheets and started to slip them back into the envelope when she noticed a few lines scrawled on the back of the last one. That was unlike Woodrow. He considered it a sign of an untidy mind to include a postscriptum, and he spent hours lecturing his students on the necessity for clear, carefully formed letters.

Curious, Abigail pulled the sheets out and read, *P.S.—By the time you receive this, Henrietta Walsh and I will be wed.*

When the import of the words registered, Abigail laughed at the realization that her prayers had been answered. Henrietta was the perfect wife for Woodrow. Although a bit young, she adored him, and—like Woodrow—her dreams were centered on life in Wesley. Henrietta was perfect. Absolutely perfect.

Men! Frances muttered a curse under her breath as she began the tedious process of unknotting her reticule strings. When she was annoyed with someone, she tied a knot, pretending it was a noose around the man's neck. Even if it was only make-believe, that helped. Unfortunately, she couldn't kill them all. She needed men, at least some of them. If only they weren't so difficult.

As annoying as he was, the baron provided a valuable service. He was the one who learned when wealthy folks were planning to travel, and when the jewelry they stole was too easily recognized, it was the baron who found buyers. Frances couldn't sever her ties to him. Not yet.

The others were different. There was Schiller, foolishly thinking he deserved a greater share of the loot just because he'd been wounded. That was bad enough. The other was worse. If Schiller was a fool, the man at the fort, as the baron called him, was simply stupid. He seemed to think he could walk away and no one would notice his absence. He claimed he owed it to the love of his life to not visit the hog ranch. Love! If anything proved the man had taken leave of his senses, it was that. Love was a fairy tale for fools.

As she untied the last knot, Frances chuckled. The fool and the stupid one both needed a lesson, and she knew just what that lesson would be. It was perfect. She would kill two birds with one stone. Even the baron would approve.

The evening was cool with a hint of frost, confirming Charlotte's observation that fall came early to the high plains. Abigail shivered as she accompanied her sister toward the site of tonight's festivities. Though it was only late September, the weather felt more like early November in Vermont. Warm days were followed by decidedly cool nights, some cold enough that Charlotte lit the stove in the parlor. There would, however, be no need for a stove in the administration building tonight. With everyone at the fort attending its inaugural event, the theater wing would be both crowded and warm.

Though it was still early when Abigail and Charlotte arrived, they discovered the room was rapidly filling with soldiers and their families, their enthusiastic greetings echoing off the limestone walls.

"You look especially lovely tonight."

Abigail smiled, not certain what pleased her more, Ethan's compliment or the fact that he'd singled her out for a moment of private conversation. She had not thought he'd see her, for her seat behind the pianoforte kept her hidden from the guests.

Rising and giving him a curtsey that showed off the skirt Charlotte had labored to complete, Abigail said, "It's the new gown. Charlotte insisted I needed something special for tonight." Abigail had been pleased when Melissa had asked her to play the piano for her wedding and even more pleased by Oliver's obvious happiness. Like Woodrow, Oliver had found the woman God intended for him. Now all that was left was Ethan, the man who stood so close that she could feel the warmth of his breath.

Knowing her cheeks were flushed, Abigail looked down at her gown. The lines of the rust-colored silk were deceptively simple. Somehow, Charlotte had draped the skirt without obvious tucks or pleats, making Abigail feel as if she were wearing a column of shimmering silk. It was a dress fit for a princess.

The expression in Ethan's eyes only deepened Abigail's flush. He tipped his head to one side, pretending to examine the gown. "The dress is pretty," he conceded, "but it's more than that. You look different. I can't put my finger on it."

With a self-deprecating shrug, he continued. "Mrs. Eberle always claimed I was the least observant child she'd ever seen, so I can't tell you what it is that seems different. All I know is that there's something."

Abigail laid the sheet music on top of the pianoforte and smiled again. Though the room was filled with people, their voices, the scraping of benches, and the click of boot heels forming a cacophony of sounds, this corner felt like an oasis, a pleasant respite from the noise. And while it was not the setting she would have chosen, Abigail wanted Ethan to know what had happened. She wouldn't tell him that she loved him. A lady could not do that. But she could tell him the truth about Woodrow.

"You're probably seeing relief."

"About your sister?"

"Partially." Ever since the night Abigail and Ethan had brought Jeffrey back from the hog ranch, Charlotte had been glowing with happiness. The reason wasn't hard to find, for Jeffrey was home every night. The evenings he played baseball, he returned with Charlotte as soon as the game ended. Other nights, he did not stir from the house unless he had duty. Charlotte was visibly pleased, and to her relief and Abigail's, her mysterious ailments had disappeared. Perhaps Mrs. Grayson was correct in believing that Charlotte's illness had been tied to tightly strung nerves.

"Charlotte is one reason. Woodrow is the other." When Ethan frowned, Abigail's heart skipped a beat. Was she right? Did he care for her? Was that why he didn't want to be reminded of Woodrow? "You know I received a letter from him." The frown disappeared. Though Ethan gave a short nod, he kept his face as expressionless as if she were discussing the color of thread for a piece of embroidery. Perhaps she had been mistaken in thinking he was bothered by thoughts of Woodrow. There was only one way to know.

"The letter told me of his marriage." It was the first time Abigail had spoken the words. Charlotte had been so preoccupied with plans for tonight's wedding that she hadn't asked what Woodrow had written, and Abigail had been relieved, for deep in her heart, she knew that Ethan should be the first to learn that she would not marry Woodrow.

As she watched, Ethan blinked and shook his head, as if he could not believe his ears. "His marriage?"

"To one of the pupils at the academy."

"I'm sorry."

Was he, or was he simply murmuring the expected words? Abigail hoped it was the latter. "I'm not. As I said before, I'm relieved." She took a deep breath, exhaling slowly in an attempt to control her emotions. So much depended on Ethan's reaction when he heard the rest of her story. "Even before I received the letter, I realized Woodrow was not the man God intended for me. I was worried about how to tell him without hurting him." Though she could barely keep her hands from trembling, Abigail managed a weak smile. "I should have trusted God. He had a better plan. Woodrow wasn't hurt—at least not much—and now he has the wife he deserves."

Though his face remained impassive, Abigail saw something—could it be relief?—in Ethan's eyes. "What about you?"

"I'm still waiting to learn God's plan for me." Abigail knew what she wanted. She wanted to marry Ethan. What she didn't know was whether that was part of God's plan for her.

Ethan's mouth started to quirk, as if he was going to smile or say something, but before he could do either, Charlotte

351

appeared at his side. "Oliver's looking for you, Ethan. It's almost time to begin."

As he nodded, Ethan grinned and mouthed the word "later," and a rush of happiness filled Abigail's heart.

Two hours later, Abigail was still smiling. The wedding had been beautiful, the perfect inauguration for the new building. Now, as the guests began to leave, she looked for Ethan.

As if he'd heard her thoughts, he appeared at her side. "I imagine Puddles is ready for a walk. May I accompany you?"

Though she welcomed the excuse to spend more time with him, Abigail had to shake her head. "Charlotte told me she and Jeffrey would do that tonight."

"Then, may I suggest we walk along the river?"

Happiness bubbled up inside her. This was the "later" Ethan had promised. "I'd enjoy that," she said as she reached for her cloak, smiling when Ethan took it from her and settled it over her shoulders. Perhaps it was only her imagination that his hands lingered a bit longer than necessary and that the warmth from his palms sent currents of excitement flowing through her blood. Perhaps, but not likely. All evening long, she had remembered his smile and the way he'd mouthed "later." Later had come, bringing with it an almost unbearable sense of anticipation.

They walked slowly, her hand on his arm, his placed on top of hers. It was a perfectly proper gesture, the act of a gentleman. It need not signify anything more than common courtesy, and yet Abigail could not ignore the waves of pleasure that swept through her, all because of Ethan's hand on hers. She had never felt this way with Woodrow, but then, she had never loved Woodrow the way she did Ethan.

Was it possible? Did she dare hope that he cared for her the same way? Could the reason Ethan sought time alone with her be because he wanted to speak of his feelings? A woman could not ask. She could not even hint at such matters, for that would be most unseemly. All she could do was wait.

They were within sight of the bridge when Ethan slowed his steps, stopping beneath one of the cottonwoods that had shed many of its leaves, allowing moonlight to spill through its branches. When Ethan removed his hand from hers, for a second Abigail felt bereft, but then he turned so he could face her, and as he gazed into her eyes, she saw the depth of his emotions.

"Abigail, I want—"

"Find the captain!" A hoarse shout rent the tranquil air. "A man's been killed!"

What a night! Thoughts raced through Ethan's brain faster than his feet raced toward the sentry. The evening had begun better than he'd dreamed possible. When he learned of Woodrow's marriage, it had been all Ethan could do to keep from shouting in exultation. Abigail wasn't promised or even almost promised to another man. He'd grinned like a foolish schoolboy at the realization that there was one less barrier between them. And then, just when he'd started to tell her how happy he was, Charlotte had interrupted. It was time for Oliver's wedding. Throughout the ceremony and the reception that followed, Ethan's heart had been filled with happiness, dreaming of the time when he would be alone with Abigail and could ask permission to court her.

The walk along the river had only heightened his anticipation. It would be the perfect place, the perfect time, and somehow he would find the perfect words to woo her. Everything was ready. Ethan was on the verge of speaking when he'd heard the guard's shouts.

What a horrible way to end the day. Ethan had sent Abigail home alone, promising to come to her as soon as he could, and then he'd headed toward the bridge. The sentry stood there, his post unnaturally stiff, the stance of a man horrified by what he had seen.

Ethan slid to a stop. "Thank you, private," he said, giving the soldier who was guarding the body a brisk salute. "Do you know who it is?" The dead man was dressed in an Army uniform but lay facedown. The brown hair protruding from his cap could have belonged to a hundred men.

"No, sir. I didn't want to move him."

Ethan understood the private's reluctance. Facing death was never easy, but now it was Ethan's job. He bent down and turned the body over, his lips tightening as he recognized the man. There was no mistaking those vivid green eyes, now staring sightlessly into the night sky. Johann Schiller, former Army private, deserter, and bandit, would never again menace a stagecoach. A single shot to his forehead had ended his life.

"No, sir," Ethan said half an hour later when he stood in Captain Westland's office. "I don't know why the body was brought here." When the men had lifted Private Schiller's body into a cart, the absence of blood on the ground and the chill of the corpse had told Ethan that the murder had taken place elsewhere. Where? When? And why had Schiller been brought back to the fort? Ethan didn't know.

"Perhaps it was a warning," he suggested. But that raised another question. A warning for whom?

"Have you learned anything?" Abigail handed the leash to Ethan. With the way Puddles was jumping on him, it was clear that the dog wanted to be next to Ethan. So did she. It had been almost a day since Johann Schiller's body had been found, a day when rumors had run rampant. Though Abigail had hoped the fort would return to normal by daylight, it had not. Everyone, it seemed, was disturbed by the news of the deserter's murder, and everyone had a theory about the killer, each less plausible than the previous.

Abigail had seen Private Schiller only once. That had been under decidedly unpleasant circumstances, but no matter how often she had wished that Private Schiller would be brought to justice and that the robberies would cease, she had never wanted his life to end. Charlotte, who'd had only a passing acquaintance with the private, since he'd deserted soon after she and Jeffrey reached the fort, had shuddered at the news. Even Jeffrey, who had once declared that Ethan should have killed Private Schiller rather than simply wounding him, had seemed upset. As for Ethan, Abigail had had no chance to discuss the murder with him, for he had remained closeted with Captain Westland until late last night. This morning he had assembled a search party that had left the garrison at daybreak. Now he was back, perhaps with news.

"We've learned nothing." Ethan shook his head as he bent down to ruffle Puddles's ears. "I'm not surprised. These people are clever, but I had hoped for something. My men and I spoke to the neighboring ranchers and everyone at

Peg's, but the answers were all the same. No one had seen or heard anything."

Though his tone was neutral, Ethan was unable to hide the tension in his hands. He might say nothing more, but Abigail knew that he was distressed. The stagecoach robberies had weighed heavily on him, and murder was much worse. No matter how she longed to recapture the magic of last night, that was impossible. Duty came first for Ethan, and right now his duty was to learn who had killed Private Schiller and why.

Ethan straightened and began to walk, letting Puddles run the entire length of the leash. "Wyoming is a big territory with very few people. It's not hard to hide something here." This time he sounded discouraged, and that wrenched Abigail's heart.

"I'm shocked!" To underscore her words, she clasped her hands, hoping her feigned surprise would cheer him. "Unless my ears deceived me, you just found something less than perfect about Wyoming."

As his eyes brightened, Abigail almost giggled. Her pretense was working. "You caught me red-handed," Ethan said with a short laugh, "but unless *my* ears deceived me, it sounded as if you did not share that opinion. Is it possible you've changed your mind?"

About Wyoming, perhaps, but not about the need to boost Ethan's spirits. Placing a cautionary finger over her lips in the universal sign for secrecy, Abigail nodded. "You must promise never to tell anyone." She imbued her words with melodrama. "It's true. You've discovered my secret. I no longer believe this is the most desolate place on earth."

Ethan tipped his head to one side, as if considering

something. "What about boring? I believe that was the word you used on the stagecoach."

His mood was definitely lighter, and though her heart soared, she tried to appear nonchalant. "It took me awhile—probably a lot longer than you—but I've grown to appreciate the open spaces. There are things about Wyoming I'll probably never consider beautiful—like yuccas . . ."

"And rattlesnakes."

Abigail gave an exaggerated shudder. "Especially rattlesnakes. But I've learned that the prairie has a subtle beauty. A person needs to search for it, but somehow that makes it more valuable."

Ethan's lips curved into a smile. "You could say that about many things in life, couldn't you?"

Abigail gazed into his eyes, and as she did, her heart began to pound. This was the Ethan she had seen last night, and yet that man had been a pale imitation of the one who now stood beside her. Never before had Abigail seen such warmth in a man's eyes. Never before had a smile seemed to promise so much. Never before had Ethan's voice sounded so enigmatic. What did he mean?

Ethan frowned as he laid his mail on the table. He'd had the perfect opportunity to tell Abigail how much he cared about her, but instead of declaring his intentions, he'd spoken of the search for Johann Schiller's killer. It was more than the fact that Captain Westland had put him in charge of the search. That was an order, and Ethan obeyed orders. But the compulsion was deeper than that. Perhaps it was an exaggeration to say he considered it his mission, but Ethan felt the need to see justice prevail. The fact that Private Schiller had committed many crimes did not exonerate his murderer.

It was true that the sight of Schiller's lifeless green eyes haunted Ethan, but that did not explain his reluctance to voice his feelings for Abigail. He could rationalize it and say that having a dog on a leash and being in full view of anyone leaving the Officers' Club was not the ideal situation for a declaration of love. Though accurate, that was only part of the reason. What had stopped him was the sense that the time wasn't right. There were too many things unfinished, and Schiller's death was only one of them. Ending the stagecoach robberies was another.

And then there was his grandfather. Ethan frowned again as he looked at his mail. A slim envelope and a medium-sized package. It was rare to receive one piece of mail. Two in one day was distinctly unusual. He glanced at the address on the envelope, shaking his head slightly when he realized that the letter was from Grandfather's attorney. It could wait. The contents of the package from Mrs. Eberle puzzled him. Ethan had left nothing of value when he'd fled the brownstone mansion. What could be inside? There was only one way to learn.

Carefully, he untied the string and unwrapped the box, then lifted the lid, revealing another envelope on top of two wrapped packages. "You should have these," Mrs. Eberle had written in her unschooled script. "Mr. Wilson said you were to have the Bible." That explained the larger of the packages. "I found the other when I cleaned his desk."

Ethan removed the brown paper wrapping from the Bible Grandfather had kept in his room. More than once he had told Ethan how the book bound in black leather with a simple cross embossed on its cover had been in the Wilson family for generations. "This is the story of my family," Grandfather had declared when he forbade Ethan to open it. "The records of generations and generations of Wilsons are listed here. Those who were not worthy of the Wilson name have no place." And that, Ethan knew without asking, included him and his parents.

He traced the outline of the cross, remembering how as a child he had longed to open the Bible and read the names inscribed within. Today there was no one to stop him. Though he cringed at the thought of what he would find, there was no point in delaying. Grandfather was dead, and the Bible was Ethan's. When he read the final entries in the family pages, he would know the truth.

Ethan flipped through the first pages, not caring about the early generations of Wilsons whose births, marriages, and deaths had been recorded there. It was the last one that would reveal Grandfather's true feelings about him and his parents. Was his mother's name blotted out, as he feared?

Ethan turned the page and stared. Instead of the solid black line he had expected, the record of his mother's birth remained. And, to Ethan's astonishment, Grandfather had recorded not simply Mother's death, but also her marriage, the dates of Father's birth and death, and Ethan's own birth. The handwriting was shaky, telling Ethan his grandfather had waited many years before inscribing the family history, but the records were there.

Tears welled in Ethan's eyes as he looked at the evidence that his grandfather had indeed cared, that he had not chosen to obliterate all memories of his daughter and her family. And, even though Ethan had run away, distancing himself both physically and emotionally, Curtis Wilson had not disowned him. It had been Ethan who had created the estrangement.

Would things have been different if he had visited Grandfather when he graduated from West Point? Would they have been able to establish a close relationship as adults? Would they have understood each other better? It was too late to know, too late to undo the years of silence. As Ethan closed his eyes, trying to keep the tears from falling, he knew that for the rest of his life he would regret his failure to try.

He reached for his pen. Perhaps one day he would record his own marriage and the dates of his children's births, but for now there was only one entry to be made. With great care, he inscribed the date of his grandfather's death.

Closing the Bible, Ethan looked at the other package. Unlike the Bible, which had been protected by brown paper, this one was wrapped in what appeared to be a woman's linen handkerchief and was tied with a faded pink ribbon. Ethan's heart stopped for a second, then raced as if trying to make up for the skipped beat when he saw the monogram on one corner of the handkerchief. VEW. Veronica Elaine Wilson. His mother. Ethan took a deep breath, trying to control his emotions. He had believed that Grandfather had destroyed his daughter's possessions, but it appeared that he had not, any more than he had expunged her from the family Bible.

His heart filled with anticipation, Ethan tugged on the end of the bow to unfasten the ribbon, then removed the handkerchief, revealing a small packet of letters yellowed with age. He stared at the first one. Though he recognized his mother's name and address, the handwriting was unfamiliar. All he knew was that a man had penned these letters. Should he open the envelope? Ethan hesitated, wondering who the author was, and then he smiled. The letter was addressed to Veronica Bowles. Bowles, not Wilson. The letters were from his father.

Ethan ran his finger over the carefully formed letters. His father had written this. His fingers had touched this envelope, perhaps lingering over the address as Ethan now did. His mother had read the letter, cherishing the words her husband had written. Perhaps she kept the letters as mementos for herself. Perhaps she had somehow known they would be the only legacy Ethan would receive from his father. Perhaps it didn't matter. What mattered was that the letters were Ethan's sole link to his parents.

He shook his head as he debated whether or not to read them. It was enough to know that they existed. Slowly, Ethan rewrapped the letters in the handkerchief.

He looked different. Abigail darted another glance at Ethan, seated across the dinner table from her. His eyes were darker, filled with something she could not quite identify. It looked like regret, and yet she saw peace there too.

"I heard you had a big mail call today." Jeffrey inclined his head toward Ethan as he spoke.

"My grandfather's housekeeper sent me the family Bible and some letters my father had written."

Abigail nodded slowly. The letters must be the cause of the regret she had seen in Ethan's eyes. "You hadn't read them before?"

"I hadn't known they existed." Ethan laid down his fork and looked directly at Abigail. "It's difficult to explain, but I felt as if I'd been given a treasure."

"You have, haven't you?" Jeffrey's voice held a note of annoyance. "With your grandfather gone, you're heir to his fortune."

Ethan flinched as if he'd been struck, but he said only, "If I accept it."

"What do you mean 'if'?"

Ethan turned to face Jeffrey. "I received a letter from my grandfather's lawyer, explaining that I could refuse the bequest. I suspect my grandfather half believed I would. That's why he named some distant cousin as the contingent beneficiary." When Jeffrey raised an eyebrow, Ethan continued. "It's the first I heard that term, but then I had no reason to know about beneficiaries, contingent or otherwise. I've never been in this situation before."

"What are you going to do?" Charlotte, who had remained silent, posed the question.

Ethan shrugged. "I haven't decided." He returned his gaze to Abigail, smiling when his eyes met hers. "It depends."

23

Had she been mistaken? Three times now Abigail had believed that Ethan was on the verge of admitting he cared for her, perhaps even that he loved her, and yet each time that he had seemed close to a declaration, he had gone no further. First had been the night Private Schiller's body was found, then the next evening when they had walked with Puddles, and lastly the day Ethan had received word of his inheritance. Abigail understood what had stopped him the first night, but the second puzzled her. That evening Ethan's mood had shifted from discouragement to apparent tenderness and then back to a stoic discussion of the murder. Why? Was he afraid of her reaction, or had she simply misunderstood? Though it was true that she hadn't expected Ethan to say anything more at the dinner table the day he mentioned his

363

father's letters because Charlotte and Jeffrey had been there, Abigail had thought the look he'd given her when he'd said "it depends" meant that he wanted to discuss his grandfather's legacy with her. She did not understand why he had not.

"I don't think it will be much longer."

Abigail stared at her sister. Had Charlotte somehow read her mind? No. Charlotte was speaking of her baby, for she laid her hand on her stomach. The two women were in the parlor, putting the finishing touches on the baby's layette, while Jeffrey, at Charlotte's insistence, was at the Officers' Club.

"I know that sitting here watching me sew isn't very exciting," Charlotte explained. "That's why I told Jeffrey I didn't mind if he went to the Officers' Club a few nights a week. I don't want him to be bored like you."

"I'm not bored."

Charlotte's expression said she didn't believe her. "Then why do I catch you staring into the distance so often?"

Abigail flushed. She hadn't realized her distraction was obvious. "I'm thinking."

"About Ethan?"

"Yes." There was no reason to deny it. Charlotte had already guessed that Abigail harbored more than friendly feelings for him. "I've never felt like this about anyone. I think about him all the time." It seemed as if everything reminded her of Ethan. Yesterday, when the story her class had been reading featured a brother and sister, she'd found herself pondering how different Ethan's life might have been if he'd had a sibling. And today, when she'd gone to the sutler's store to buy another spool of thread for Charlotte, she'd seen a warm scarf and had wondered if Ethan would like it.

Charlotte's eyes sparkled. "That's normal when you're in love. You love Ethan, and that makes him the center of your life. It's only natural."

"I do love him." Abigail wondered if she'd ever tire of saying those words. "But what if he doesn't love me? What will I do then?"

Charlotte reached over to pat Abigail's hand. "Don't worry. Ethan loves you. I can see it in his eyes."

Oh, how Abigail wanted to believe that. Charlotte was a married woman. She knew more about men than Abigail, and yet . . . "If he loves me, why hasn't he said anything?"

"I don't know."

Ethan turned down the wick to extinguish the flame, throwing the room into darkness. It was no use trying to read, just as it was probably futile to climb into bed. If tonight was like the last few, he wouldn't be able to sleep, for thoughts continued to whirl through his brain. Private Schiller's murder, his grandfather's death, his father's letters, Abigail. Always Abigail. No matter what he was doing, he couldn't get her out of his mind. The truth was, he didn't want to.

He chuckled as he threw back the blankets and slid into bed. It appeared he'd inherited at least one thing from his father, and that was his fascination with a woman. Ethan had read the first letter from the packet, smiling when Father told Veronica—his Veronica, as he referred to her—that he thought of her every hour of every day. The words confirmed what Ethan had come to believe, that Stephen Bowles had been as deeply in love with Veronica as Ethan was with Abigail.

Abigail. Ethan laced his fingers beneath his neck and smiled. He had it all planned. Tomorrow he would ask Jeffrey to take Charlotte on a walk, leaving Ethan and Abigail alone. Even if the night was cold, they'd sit on the porch for propriety's sake, but it would be late enough that they wouldn't be interrupted by others. When they were alone, he would take her hand in his and tell her how much he cared. And then . . . That was where Ethan's planning stopped. He didn't know what would happen next, for everything depended on Abigail. He could only hope she cared for him.

Ethan swung his legs off the side of the bed, realizing there was no point in pretending to sleep, just as there was no point in pretending that all he wanted from Abigail was caring. Caring was fine. Caring was what friends or siblings felt for each other. Ethan wanted more. Much more. He wanted Abigail to love him as much as he loved her.

He made his way to the window and glanced out, his eyes widening when he saw a man leaving the barracks. His furtive movements, the way he kept his head lowered and looked back over his shoulder, as if afraid of being seen, told Ethan there was nothing innocent about this. He threw on his clothes and raced outside, but he was too late. The man was gone.

"Lieutenant, you gotta see 'em." The sergeant's words came in spurts, as if he'd run across the parade ground. "I left 'em right where they were."

Ethan looked up from the report he'd been writing. "What is it, Sergeant?"

"I reckon you oughta see 'em. Over in the barracks."

"See what?"

The sergeant only shook his head. "Best you see for yourself."

When they reached the barracks, Ethan stared at the gleam of gold and red only partially hidden behind a soldier's footlocker. No wonder everyone was alarmed. Men did not leave belongings outside their lockers, and they most definitely did not leave precious jewelry on the floor. There was no doubt that what the sergeant had found was a pair of women's ruby and gold earrings.

"These look like the ones reported stolen in the last stagecoach robbery," Ethan said, as much to himself as the sergeant.

The sergeant nodded. "That's what I figured. I reckon Dietrich's got some answering to do."

Ethan frowned as he read the name on the footlocker. Every time something suspicious happened, Dietrich Keller seemed to be in the middle of it. Though he had had plausible explanations in the past, there was no ignoring the presence of stolen goods. How could the man have been so careless or so stupid as to leave them where anyone could find them? The earrings were small enough to tuck in a watch pocket where no one would have seen them.

Ethan turned to the sergeant. "Tell Corporal Keller to report to me."

When the man arrived, Ethan wasted no words, simply held out the earrings. "Explain to me how these happened to be next to your locker, Corporal."

"Vat are they?" Though Dietrich looked genuinely puzzled, Ethan knew that a man who was willing to steal could also be good at masking his emotions. Hadn't he and Jeffrey both commented that Dietrich Keller was smarter than many of the men? This might be part of his act.

The sergeant snorted. "I don't reckon Lieutenant Bowles

will buy that innocent bit. We know you stole them. Likely you're involved with them stagecoach robbers. Might be you're the one who killed Schiller."

The blood drained from Dietrich's face, and when he spoke, it was in rapid German.

"English, Corporal."

Despite Ethan's admonishment, the man continued to babble in German. Though it could have been pretense, Ethan suspected the man was so disturbed that he reverted to his native language.

"Fetch Miss Harding for me," he ordered the sergeant. "Perhaps she can translate."

When Abigail arrived, the fact that her hat was crooked spoke of her concern. Still, even with her bonnet askew, she was the most beautiful woman Ethan had ever seen. It was irrational. He knew that, and yet his spirits soared at the sight of her. Alone he'd been frustrated; perhaps together they would be able to get to the bottom of this mess.

"What's wrong?" Abigail looked from Ethan to Corporal Keller, something about her expression reminding him that the corporal was one of her students. He doubted she had faced situations like this at that fancy girls' school in Vermont.

Ethan explained what the sergeant had found and that Dietrich appeared incapable of speaking English. "I'm afraid I need an interpreter. Would you ask the corporal where he got these earrings and why he was leaving the barracks around 10:30 last night?"

As Abigail posed the questions, Dietrich gesticulated wildly, shaking his head while his words came out in a torrent. Abigail listened carefully before turning back to Ethan. "He says he never saw the earrings until you showed them to him. As for the other question, he was reluctant to say anything, but he finally admitted that he wasn't in the barracks at 10:30. He left around 9:00 and didn't come back until after midnight."

Ethan turned to the sergeant who'd been guarding the door as if he expected Corporal Keller to flee. "If he's telling the truth, someone must have seen him." While most of the men would have been asleep by 10:30 when Ethan saw the man leaving the barracks, at least a few would have been awake at 9:00. "See what you can learn." When the sergeant left, Ethan turned back to Abigail. "Where did Corporal Keller go last night?"

"To Peg's. He says he spent the evening with Leah and didn't return until after midnight."

"Is this true?" Ethan addressed Dietrich directly.

"*Ja.*"

A few minutes later, the sergeant returned. "Private Harrison confirms Keller's story. He said he heard him leave around 9:00, but he can't say when he came back."

Though it sounded as if the corporal was telling the truth, at least about where he had been, Ethan could take no chances. It was possible Dietrich had done more than visit Leah. He might also have picked up a share of the stolen goods. Unfortunately, that theory did not explain the man who had left the barracks so stealthily.

Ethan nodded at the sergeant. "Take Corporal Keller to the guardhouse and keep him there until I return." When the two men left, Ethan turned to Abigail. "Would you be willing to go with me? Leah's more likely to speak to you than to me."

"Don't you believe Corporal Keller?"

Ethan did not answer directly. "I need to be certain."

Abigail saw doubt in his eyes, as if he were as puzzled as she that a seemingly intelligent man would leave such incriminating evidence out in the open.

Ethan nodded shortly. "I wouldn't be doing my job if I didn't try to corroborate the man's alibi. Will you help?"

Of course she would. Abigail would do anything she could to help him. And Corporal Keller. Though Ethan might not be convinced, she was certain her pupil was innocent of anything more serious than having left the fort without permission.

When they reached the hog ranch, the yard was empty, but the sound of hoofbeats brought a woman out of the main door. Though she no longer wore the flamboyant crimson dress and her hair was more simply styled, Peg's face was as angry as it had been the night Abigail and Ethan had found Jeffrey here.

"You again?" Peg tossed her head in apparent disgust, setting loose a wave of cloying perfume. "Jeffrey ain't here."

"We know that." It was Ethan who replied as he dismounted and helped Abigail off Sally. "We'd like to speak with Leah."

Peg's lips curved into a mocking smile. "When men come here, it ain't to talk to my girls."

Though Abigail could not explain it, the hairs on the back of her head rose. Something about Peg bothered her, tickling the edges of her memory. How Abigail hated when that happened. The thought hovered on the fringes of her brain but refused to come close enough for her to capture it. She narrowed her eyes, trying to focus on the woman who stood only a yard away. "We'll pay for her time, if that's what you're worried about."

Peg snorted. "I ain't worried about the money. I just don't like having you around. Folks like you are bad for business." She tipped her head to one side, as if calculating the damage they could inflict simply with their presence. At last she nodded, her reluctance evident. "Leah's in the third cabin. Make it quick."

"Thank you." Before Peg could change her mind, Abigail started toward Leah's cabin. "Peg reminds me of someone," Abigail said as they walked. "I wish I knew who. I feel as if it's important, but I can't explain why."

Ethan shrugged. "I'm the wrong man to ask. Didn't I tell you that I'm the least observant male ever born? You're probably just remembering the night we saw her with Jeffrey."

That was possible, but Abigail doubted it. Her instincts had not been aroused that night or the day she had first met Peg, but they were shrieking at her now. "One thing that bothers me is Peg's speech. It was different that night, more cultivated, and I remember a Southern drawl."

Ethan shrugged again. "I don't recall anything being different. To be honest, all I cared about was getting Jeffrey out of there."

They had reached the third cabin. Ethan started to knock on the door, but Abigail held up a restraining hand. "Leah," she said as she knocked more softly than Ethan would have, "it's Abigail Harding. I'm here with Lieutenant Bowles. We'd like to ask you a few questions."

The scraping of a chair and some rustling preceded the opening of the door. When Leah emerged, she was clutching a shawl around her shoulders, her disheveled hair telling Abigail they had wakened her.

"What's this about?" Leah asked. Devoid of its usual paint, her face looked young, almost innocent, though her eyes revealed the toll that years at Peg's had taken. She regarded both Abigail and Ethan with suspicion.

Ethan took a step forward before he said, "We're here about Corporal Keller. When did you see him last?"

The way Leah's lips thinned and her fingers gripped the shawl left no doubt that she was unwilling to speak.

"Tell us the truth," Abigail urged the young woman. "It's all right. You won't hurt the corporal."

Leah's eyes darted from Abigail to Ethan and back again, her reluctance almost palpable. It was only when Abigail gave her another reassuring smile that she said, "Dietrich was here last night. I know he wasn't supposed to leave the fort, but he did."

When Ethan said nothing, Abigail continued the questioning. "Do you remember when Dietrich arrived and how long he stayed?" If Leah was to be his alibi, the times had to be consistent.

Leah nodded. "He came before 9:30, and he didn't leave until after midnight."

"You're sure?" Ethan's voice was harsher than Abigail would have liked, and she saw Leah flinch.

"I'm sure. He isn't in trouble, is he?" Worry lines formed between Leah's eyes, and her voice cracked. "He only came to protect me. I knew one of the ranchers was expected last night. A bad one. He's mighty rough on a girl when he's been drinking, and most nights he's been drinking."

Abigail kept her expression impassive, although her heart bled for Leah and all the others who had been subjected to the rancher's cruelty.

"I told Dietrich about him," Leah continued, "and he said he'd come. He paid for my time so I didn't have to entertain the rancher. You won't put him in the guardhouse for that, will you?"

Ethan shook his head. "It's not for me to decide."

Leah took a step forward and laid her hand on Abigail's arm. "Dietrich's a good man, and I ain't . . ." She flushed, then corrected herself. "I'm not saying that just because he wants to marry me." She looked up at Ethan. "Dietrich said the captain had to give his permission. Do you reckon he'll do that?"

For a second Abigail thought Ethan would shake his head. Instead he said, "I'll talk to him."

Her smile one of pure happiness, Leah nodded. "Thank you, Lieutenant."

"I believe her," Abigail said as she and Ethan rode away from the hog ranch.

"So do I. Someone tried to frame Dietrich."

"Obviously, but why him?"

A gust of wind blew a tumbleweed in front of their horses, causing Sally to skitter sideways. Ethan waited until Abigail was once more riding next to him before he said, "It's probably because he's an immigrant. Everyone knows that Johann Schiller was involved in the robberies. Someone wants me to think that Dietrich was too."

"Who would do that?"

Ethan was silent for a moment. When he spoke, all he said was, "I wish I knew," but something in his expression told Abigail he had his suspicions.

Someone had been in his room. Ethan knew it the moment he opened the door. He had expected some sort of reaction to what he had done today, but not this. While he doubted that anyone would be angered by his asking Captain Westland to approve Corporal Keller's marriage to Leah and to sentence him to only ten days in the guardhouse rather than a full month, Ethan had known his belief that one of the officers was involved in the robberies and the attempt to implicate Corporal Keller would trigger a response, especially since it had resulted in Captain Westland's conducting what was tantamount to an interrogation of each officer. Ethan had expected a reaction, but he hadn't thought it would be so personal. Still, there was no denying that he had had an uninvited visitor. The room held an unfamiliar smell, and the intruder hadn't completely closed one of the chest drawers.

Ethan's heart began to pound as he realized what he'd placed in that particular drawer, and the suspicions he'd entertained turned to certainty. It was no coincidence that he'd had a visitor within hours of Captain Westland's beginning his questioning, just as it was no coincidence that the visitor had searched Ethan's chest of drawers.

Ethan tugged the drawer fully open, his heart thudding as his fears were realized. The packet of letters was gone, replaced by a single sheet of paper. "If you want your treasure, come to the back room at Peg's." Though the writer had tried to disguise his penmanship, he had given himself away with his wording. Only one man knew that Ethan considered those letters his treasure. Jeffrey. The man he thought shared his sense of duty and honor was involved in the robberies. It had to have been Jeffrey who had notified the outlaws when a coach would be unguarded and Jeffrey who had planted the stolen earrings by Dietrich Keller's footlocker.

Ethan saddled Samson and headed for Peg's, wishing he

were wrong but knowing he was not. The letters were the lure. Ethan had no doubt Jeffrey intended to demand a ransom for them, but why had he chosen Peg's for the rendezvous? Perhaps he wanted more than money. Perhaps he was simply unwilling to work alone. That must be it. For some reason, Jeffrey wanted an accomplice with him, probably Peg.

They were waiting for him. Ethan knew they would be, which was why he drew his weapon before he pushed the door open. The room was as he remembered it, with a large round table in the center and a small bar on the right wall. Today, though, the chairs were empty. Today there were no half-filled glasses, no cards and chips on the table. Instead, Jeffrey stood behind the table where he'd once played poker, while Peg leaned against the bar. And though Peg appeared to be unarmed, Jeffrey had his pistol pointed at Ethan.

"Drop your weapon."

Ethan stared at the man he'd once considered his friend. The man who had insisted Ethan share his dinner table stared back at him, his eyes filled with hatred.

"Drop it," Jeffrey repeated.

"I don't think so."

Behind him Ethan heard the door close. There had been a stiff breeze. Perhaps it had blown the door shut. He didn't dare take his eyes off Jeffrey to see what had happened.

"Don't be a fool." The voice came from behind Ethan and was accompanied by the unmistakable pressure of a pistol against the back of his head. It had not been wind closing the door, but another man entering the room. "No letter is worth dying over." The man's voice was cultured and bore a faint accent that reminded Ethan of his grandfather's business associates.

Ethan remained motionless, considering his alternatives. They were decidedly limited. While he might be able to shoot the gun from Jeffrey's hand, the stranger would kill him. The steel in his voice told Ethan that. Reluctantly, he let the pistol slip from his hand.

"He's all yours, Jeffrey." The man shoved Ethan forward, then moved into the shadowed corner of the room. Though Ethan could see his outline and the gun he kept pointed at him, he could make out no features.

Jeffrey's smile held no mirth, only gloating. "Sit down, Ethan," he said, gesturing toward the table. "You might as well be comfortable."

Ethan remained standing. There would be no comfort here, and sitting would put him at an even greater disadvantage than he already was. "Where are the letters?"

It was Peg who answered. "They're right here," she said, patting the side of her reticule. "You can have them when we're done."

"How much do you want?" As he'd ridden to the hog ranch, Ethan had tried to guess the amount Jeffrey would demand. A thousand dollars? Two? Either would be a fortune to a man accustomed to living on military pay.

Jeffrey's smile widened, but there was no friendliness in it, merely the stretching of his lips. "Not much. Just your signature on one piece of paper." He shoved a sheet of cheap paper across the table.

"What . . . ?" Ethan picked it up and began to read. "This is a will."

"Exactly." The gloating Ethan had seen on Jeffrey's face was echoed in his words. "You're going to leave everything to me. I deserve it more than that contingent beneficiary."

The way he spat the words told Ethan that Jeffrey had gone beyond reasoning. He was clearly obsessed with money. But why, and why did he think he deserved Ethan's inheritance?

"Why should I give you so much as a penny?"

"Because you messed up everything else." It was Peg who spoke. When Ethan darted a glance at her and saw her twisting her reticule strings, a memory resurfaced. There was something familiar about that. Abigail had said that Peg reminded her of someone, but who?

"We had a good scheme." Peg glared at Ethan. "Made plenty of money from those stagecoach robberies, but you couldn't let us continue. No, you had to get the captain to assign guards to every stagecoach. What were we supposed to do? We can't poison 'em all the way we did your friend Seton. You were putting us out of business, Ethan Bowles. Left us no choice but to find another way." Peg exchanged a glance with the man in the shadows. "Now your grandfather's timely demise—and your own, of course—will make up for all that you took away."

The man in the shadows chuckled. "Best of all, it'll look legal."

Ethan's gaze moved from the man to Peg and then to Jeffrey. What a fool he'd been. He had been so confident of himself that he had underestimated his opponent. He should have brought others with him. Then he wouldn't be in this predicament, but his pride—his foolish, foolish pride—had blinded him to the possibility that Jeffrey and his accomplices might intend to kill him. Now he was alone.

As a warmth flowed through him, Ethan's tension ebbed. He was not alone. He was never alone. Keeping his eyes fixed on Jeffrey and his gun, he breathed a silent prayer. *Dear Lord, is this your plan for me?* He wasn't afraid of death. The Bible promised that death was the beginning of something far better than life on Earth. Ethan knew that the promise was real, just as he knew that death would unite him with his parents. He wanted that someday, but not yet. Not when a life of love and happiness stretched in front of him. Not when the images of his children chasing a puppy that bore a striking resemblance to Puddles danced in front of him. Not before he told Abigail that he loved her.

It was too late. He had been too late to build a loving relationship with his grandfather, and now he was too late again.

Ethan took a deep breath. *If this is your will, Lord, give me strength, and somehow, some way let Abigail know how much I love her.* He didn't expect an answer, but deep inside him, Ethan heard a voice say, *Delay.* Though it seemed like an odd command, Ethan knew better than to ignore it.

He looked directly at Jeffrey. "Since you plan to kill me no matter what I do, you might as well answer a few questions, starting with how you got involved in all this."

Though Jeffrey's shoulders straightened, as if the story would increase his stature, he looked at Peg. When she nodded her approval, he said, "I needed money, and gambling wasn't enough. As good as I was, there were still nights when I lost." Though Peg snorted, as if disputing Jeffrey's claims of gambling prowess, he continued. "Peg offered me the chance to make money by stealing. I never lost that way." Jeffrey glanced at the pistol in his hand. "I took rifles at first. It was so easy. No one questions an officer. All you have to do is look like you know what you're doing, and they walk away."

No wonder no one had discovered who was responsible for

the rifle thefts. Jeffrey had been conducting the investigations until Ethan arrived. How he must have laughed at the irony of being chosen for that particular duty.

"You're right," he said, as if he had read Ethan's thoughts. "Captain Westland had no idea he was setting the fox to guard the chickens."

Peg laughed. "Tell him the rest, Jeffrey. Let the man go to his grave knowing he solved the mystery, even if it won't do him any good."

Jeffrey nodded. "Rifles were good, but Peg had a better idea: stagecoaches."

"All you had to do was tell her which coaches had no one from the fort on them." Ethan finished the sentence.

"That's right. It worked perfectly until you decided to come back from Cheyenne a day early and foil a robbery. That was your first mistake, Ethan."

Perhaps that was how Jeffrey saw it, but Ethan couldn't regret that day. Not only had he kept innocent civilians safe, but that day brought Abigail into his life. "Was the hog ranch just a front?" Ethan addressed the question to Peg.

She laughed as she put another knot in her reticule strings. "Oh no. It was a good source of money on its own, plus it gave me a chance to meet men who—with a little persuasion—could help."

The last piece of the puzzle fell into place. "So you encouraged Johann Schiller and Robert Forge to desert."

Peg nodded. "Among others. It's a shame Schiller became greedy. When he demanded more than his share, I had no choice but to end the problem."

"Just like we're going to end this problem." Jeffrey's laugh left no doubt of his meaning.

"Enough talking." The man spoke from the shadows. "Sign the paper, Bowles."

Delay. The word reverberated through Ethan's mind. "Why should I, when you're going to kill me anyway? I'm not anxious to die, but I'm even less anxious to give you my inheritance."

"You'll give it to me." Jeffrey's voice rang with confidence. "That's the only way you can prevent Abigail from having an unfortunate accident." The light in Jeffrey's eyes told Ethan he was not bluffing. "I'd be better off without her meddling."

He was mad. It was the only explanation, and yet knowing that did nothing to reassure Ethan. If Jeffrey was willing to kill him, he'd have no compunction about killing again.

"How do I know Abigail will be safe if I do sign it? It's not as if I'll be here to watch you."

Jeffrey chuckled. "You'll have to trust me."

Not likely. "You'll have to do better than that. I want a guarantee that nothing will happen to Abigail. Without that, I won't sign anything."

"Bring me the paper, Peg." The man in the shadows' voice betrayed his annoyance. "I'll add a codicil to it. If this Abigail should happen to die from anything other than natural causes within two years of Lieutenant Bowles's death, Jeffrey will forfeit the money."

"But . . ."

"Shut up, Crowley." Though the words were crude, the man's voice was not. It wasn't only his accent that reminded Ethan of his grandfather's associates, now it was his vocabulary. The man in the shadows sounded like one of Curtis Wilson's attorneys.

Before Ethan had a chance to reflect further on the identity

of Jeffrey's partners, Peg handed him the will. A quick pe-
rusal told Ethan the man had done what he'd promised. If
Jeffrey wanted the money—and Ethan had no doubt that he
did—Abigail would be safe.

"It's time," the man said. "Sign the paper, Bowles."

24

bigail cringed. Even though Mrs. Grayson insisted it was simply a matter of time, and Charlotte herself had advised Abigail to take Puddles for a walk, Abigail hated feeling helpless. Charlotte's groans and the occasional anguished cry had been going on for hours, leaving Puddles so distressed by the sound of his mistress's pain that Abigail had banished him to the yard, where he'd set up a mournful howling. There were times when she felt like howling herself. Even prayer, which had always been an unfailing comfort, did not bring her the peace she sought. Her sister was in pain, and there was nothing she could do.

Abigail blamed herself for not having recognized the signs earlier. Though Charlotte had been uncharacteristically quiet at dinner, Abigail had thought nothing of it, attributing her sister's silence to the fact that she and Ethan had dominated the conversation with stories of the attempt to implicate Dietrich in the stagecoach robberies. It was only after the men had left that Abigail had noticed the furrows between Charlotte's eyes.

When she'd asked, Charlotte had admitted that she was experiencing some discomfort but had insisted it was too soon to bother anyone. Babies, Charlotte claimed, took hours—sometimes days—to make their appearance. Besides, this was probably a false alarm. But by midafternoon, Abigail could wait no longer. Charlotte hadn't been able to hide the fact that the pains were increasing in intensity and frequency, and so, even though her sister protested, Abigail had fetched Mrs. Grayson.

"You're further along than I would have expected, especially for a first child," the midwife said when she examined Charlotte.

A sheepish expression on her face, Charlotte admitted that she'd been having pains since the middle of the night. "They were twinges at first," she told Mrs. Grayson. "I thought they'd stop, and even if they didn't, there was no reason to tell anyone."

Abigail nodded as another memory resurfaced. Those had been signs of strain she had seen on Charlotte's face when the sergeant had summoned her to Ethan's office. At the time, Abigail had been too concerned about Ethan to recognize that her sister needed help too. "You should have told me."

Just as she should have told Jeffrey. But once again Charlotte had been adamant. "There's nothing he can do. It would only worry him to know I was in pain."

That had been hours ago. Though she hadn't agreed with Charlotte, Abigail knew that the problem would be resolved at suppertime. When he returned for the meal, Jeffrey would learn that his child was about to be born. But he did not come, and neither did Ethan, and that worried Abigail. While it was possible that one of the other soldiers had seen her escorting Mrs. Grayson to the house and had told Jeffrey, Abigail would have expected him to come home, if only briefly. Surely he would want to know how his wife's labor was progressing.

"What's the matter, boy?" Abigail looked down at Puddles's food dish. Though he normally devoured food as soon as it was served, today he'd sniffed the bowl, then turned away. "You're worried too, aren't you?" She sat on the porch step and reached out to stroke the puppy's head. "She'll be all right." *Soon*, Abigail prayed. *Bring this baby soon.*

But when she opened the door to Charlotte's room, the midwife shook her head and mouthed the words "No change."

Mrs. Grayson was wrong. There had been a change. The baby might not be any closer to being born, but Charlotte was noticeably weaker. All color had leached from her face, leaving her looking decades older than her twenty-five years and reminding Abigail that some women died in childbirth. *Please, Lord, save my sister.*

Her heart pounding with alarm, Abigail reached for Charlotte's hand. "Hold on to me," she said. Mama had always claimed that the two most important elements of healing were prayer and human touch. Abigail had been praying for her sister, and whenever she was in the room, she extended her hand to Charlotte, letting Charlotte squeeze as hard as she needed when the pains began.

This time Charlotte shook her head. "Find Jeffrey. I need to see him."

The trembling in Charlotte's voice distressed Abigail even more than her request. Her sister sounded as weak as she looked, and the distant expression in her eyes made Abigail fear the situation was more serious than she had believed.

"Hold on, Charlotte. It's just a little while longer." Though Abigail had no way of knowing whether that was true, she wanted to encourage her sister.

Charlotte gave an almost imperceptible shake of her head. "I need Jeffrey," she repeated.

Mrs. Grayson nodded. Turning away so that Charlotte could not hear her, she said, "Perhaps it will help. This agitation is not good for the baby."

Abigail forced a smile onto her face. "Don't worry, Charlotte. I'll find Jeffrey. By the time he gets here, you'll have your son in your arms, and Jeffrey will be the proudest papa Fort Laramie has ever seen." *Please, Lord, make it so.* Abigail squeezed Charlotte's hand and pressed a kiss onto her forehead. "I love you, big sister," she said softly.

Charlotte's eyes lit. "I love you too." And then another pain gripped her.

Abigail grabbed her hat and gloves and threw a cloak over her shoulders. Though the days were still warm, October evenings were decidedly cold, reminding everyone that winter was not far away. Instead of following the road, Abigail took a shortcut across the parade ground, praying all the while that Charlotte and the baby would be safe and that she would find Jeffrey at the Officers' Club. Since women were not allowed inside, she pounded on the door.

Seconds later, Oliver opened it, his eyes widening in surprise. "Miss Harding, what are you doing here?"

"I'm looking for Jeffrey. Is he here?"

Oliver shook his head. "Not today. I saw him leaving the fort in the middle of the afternoon. Sorry, Miss Harding, but I don't know where he was heading."

Abigail did. There was only one place her brother-in-law would have gone that would have kept him away from home at suppertime. *Oh, Jeffrey, why did you go there today of all days?*

"Was Lieutenant Bowles with him?" That would explain why neither man had come for supper.

Oliver shook his head again. "I haven't seen him all afternoon." He turned to face his fellow officers. "Anyone seen Crowley or Bowles?"

The replies were negative, leaving Abigail no alternative but to continue her search. She headed for the stables, stopping abruptly when she realized she did not have her pistol. If Ethan had been with her, she would not have worried, but she had promised him that she not leave the fort without it. Heedless of decorum, Abigail picked up her skirts and ran back to the house. Minutes later, she was mounted on Sally, the pistol secured in her pocket, heading for the hog ranch for the second time that day.

The sun was just setting when she arrived, but the evening festivities were in full swing. A man was singing along with the out-of-tune piano, accompanied by bursts of laughter when he forgot the words to the bawdy song. Outside, half a dozen horses stood next to the hitching rail, nickering among themselves. Abigail slid off Sally, looping the reins over the rail, then hurried to the rear of the long building. If Jeffrey was here, and she was certain he was, he would be in that back room with the other high-stakes gamblers, playing poker while his wife labored to birth their child.

Abigail clenched her fists, wishing she could knock some sense into her brother-in-law. Papa had claimed that gambling and drink were diseases, that once people were infected, they had trouble resisting the lure. Jeffrey, it appeared, was one of those unfortunate souls. Abigail couldn't stop him; she could only hope that Charlotte would forgive him again.

Taking a deep breath in an attempt to calm her thoughts, Abigail rounded the corner of the building. As she approached the rear entrance, she saw that the wind had blown the door ajar. Though light spilled onto the ground, telling her the room was occupied, the sound of men's voices did not drift onto the air. Instead, there was an ominous silence. While it was possible that Jeffrey had been here, and he'd already left, if no one was inside, the lamp should not be burning.

"Sign the paper, Bowles." A strange man's voice barked the command.

Abigail flinched. She hadn't seen Samson at the hitching post, but there was only one Bowles in the area. Why was Ethan here, and what was the paper he was being ordered to sign? And, if Ethan was in this room, where was Jeffrey? The questions whirled through her mind.

Though she had made no attempt to soften her footsteps as she came around the building, now Abigail's instincts urged stealth. She crept toward the door, hoping the opening would be wide enough that she could see what was happening. Trying to make no sound, she peered inside, then bit back a gasp. It couldn't be. This had to be a nightmare, but it wasn't. The wind that blew her skirts and the hard-packed earth beneath her feet were real, no figment of her imagination.

Abigail's heart stopped for an instant before beginning to pound as her brain registered what her eyes had seen. Ethan was here, and so was Jeffrey, but neither man was playing poker. Ethan stood with his back to her, while Jeffrey . . . Abigail's heart sank as she stared at her brother-in-law. There was no doubt about it. Her eyes had not deceived her. Jeffrey had his gun aimed directly at Ethan.

Abigail forced herself to breathe evenly as she tried to understand what she was seeing, and for a second, she was back in the barn, watching Luke's lifeblood seep away while Richard screamed. It wasn't the same. That had been an accident. This was not. Jeffrey was threatening Ethan.

Something was horribly, horribly wrong. There were no cards or glasses on the table, no sign that anyone had been gambling, so it couldn't be that Ethan had interrupted a card game. From her perspective, Abigail could see only the table and the two men who stood on opposite sides, but somewhere in this room was the other man, the one who had ordered Ethan to sign a piece of paper. He must be the reason Jeffrey held the gun.

On his own, Jeffrey wouldn't harm Ethan. He wasn't a killer. And yet the Jeffrey in this room was not the Jeffrey Abigail knew. This Jeffrey's eyes were cold, and his expression could only be described as murderous. Though she wanted to deny it, Jeffrey appeared prepared to shoot a fellow officer. Not just a fellow officer but another West Point graduate. A man he had shared meals with all summer. His friend, or so Abigail had believed.

She clasped her hands together, trying to still their shaking as she remembered Ethan's enigmatic expression when they'd returned from the hog ranch this morning. At the time, she had thought he had strong suspicions of who had tried to implicate Corporal Keller. Was it Jeffrey? Was he the man who had been assisting the outlaws? As distressing as the thought was, it mattered little right now. What was important was helping Ethan.

He had no gun. A quick glance confirmed that his gun belt was empty. Even worse, the odds were stacked against him, for somewhere in that room was the man who'd ordered him to sign a piece of paper. That man would be armed. Perhaps even now he had a pistol aimed at Ethan. Two with weapons against one unarmed man. Ethan had no chance.

Dear Lord, show me what to do. Abigail fingered the pistol in her pocket, then shook her head, knowing her aim was still so poor that she might hurt Ethan when all she wanted to do was disarm Jeffrey. There had to be another way. Ethan could defend himself, if she could get the gun to him. The question was how to do that. Abigail took a deep breath and exhaled slowly. Distraction. It was Ethan's only hope.

Throwing open the door, she burst into the room as if she'd just arrived. "Hurry, Jeffrey!" she shouted. "Charlotte's time has come. She needs you." As she raced across the room, Abigail darted glances around her. The odds were worse than she'd thought. In addition to Jeffrey and the stranger who clung to the shadows, Peg stood next to the counter, her reticule dangling from one hand. Ethan had moved ever so slightly as Abigail shouted, but he appeared to be keeping his attention focused on Jeffrey, regarding him the way she had the rattlesnake that had threatened Puddles.

Ethan dared not move, but she could. "Quickly, Jeffrey! Charlotte and the baby need you." Abigail continued toward him, hoping he would not view her as an adversary. She had to distract him enough that she could knock the gun from his hand, then give Ethan her pistol.

As Abigail's words registered, blood drained from Jeffrey's face, leaving his freckles in sharp relief against the pale skin. He took a step toward her, but the hand holding his gun never wavered. The first part of her plan wouldn't work. She didn't dare try to disarm Jeffrey, for his gun might go off and hit Ethan. All she could do now was try to get a weapon to Ethan.

"Not so fast, Crowley." The words came from the shadows, the same voice that had demanded Ethan's signature. "Your work isn't done."

She wouldn't look at the stranger. She wouldn't let anyone distract her. Abigail kept moving. Another two steps, and she'd be close enough to Ethan to hand him her pistol.

Ethan turned, as if he'd read her thoughts. "Go home, Abigail," he said firmly. "You shouldn't be here."

She couldn't leave, not when he was in danger. Abigail reached into her pocket.

"Abigail." The man in the shadows chuckled. "I think we just found the way to persuade Lieutenant Bowles. Tie her up, Peg." As Abigail started to pull the pistol out, the man's voice deepened. "I wouldn't make any sudden moves, young lady. My gun is pointed at you, and I never miss."

He wasn't bluffing. Abigail knew that. She stopped. Peg might try to tie her, but she wouldn't make it easy. As the woman came toward her, she lurched. It was, Abigail realized, the first time she had seen Peg move. The other times they had met, Peg had remained stationary, but now, though her limp was pronounced, Peg was closing the distance between them more quickly than Abigail had thought possible, her fingers gripping the strings of her reticule.

A limp. A reticule. Abigail's eyes widened when she saw

the knots. The last piece of the puzzle fell into place. No wonder Peg had seemed familiar.

"Mrs. Dunn!" As memories flitted through Abigail's brain, she realized that Mrs. Dunn—or Peg or whatever her real name was—had planned to help rob the coach she and Ethan had been on. That was why she had struggled to retrieve her reticule. It wasn't smelling salts she had wanted. In all likelihood, the reticule had contained a gun.

Peg must have been the woman on all the coaches. It made sense, for she had a supply of wigs to disguise herself, and Leah had said she left the hog ranch to visit her sister occasionally. Abigail was willing to bet there was no sister and that each "visit" coincided with a stagecoach robbery.

Peg's grin held little mirth. "So you recognized me, did you? Fat lot of good that'll do you now."

"Maybe it will." She couldn't—she simply could not—let Ethan die. Abigail yanked the gun from her pocket, aiming it at Peg at the same time that she swung her foot toward the woman's injured leg. With her attention focused on the gun, Peg didn't see the kick coming.

"You—" Peg let out a string of epithets and doubled over in pain. It was the break Abigail needed. She swung around, hoping to move so quickly that the man in the shadows would not realize what was happening. "Ethan, catch," Abigail shouted as she tossed the pistol toward him.

From the corner of her eyes, she saw Jeffrey move toward Ethan, as if in slow motion. "Dodge!" she shouted, but Ethan did not. Gun in hand, he leapt forward, tackling Jeffrey and dragging him to the ground. Abigail heard grunts and groans as the two men rolled on the floor, punching and kicking.

"You're useless, Crowley." The man from the shadows was closer now. "Kill him," he urged. "We'll copy his signature."

There was no response, only the groans of two men, each trying his best to beat the other senseless, and Peg's continuing chorus of curses. As the tone changed, Abigail looked down. Peg was struggling to her feet, pure rage distorting her features.

"I'm not finished with you," she muttered. But she was, for Abigail reached behind her, grabbed a chair, and smashed it over Peg's head, trying not to wince at the sound of wood splintering. She had never before inflicted injury on another human being, but never before had the man she loved been in danger.

It all happened so quickly that afterward Abigail could not say which occurred first. Peg slumped to the floor, a shot rang out, and a man screamed, his voice so distorted with agony that Abigail could not identify it. Even worse, the grunts and groans stopped, replaced by a low moan.

Abigail closed her eyes as the moans reverberated through her, transporting her back to the day Luke had been shot. *Not again!* She couldn't lose another friend. *Please, God, save Ethan. Save them both.*

Her hands clammy with fear, Abigail crossed the short distance to the men. She would help them. It couldn't be too late. But the sight was even more alarming than the sound of anguished moaning. Though Jeffrey's body was sprawled on top and blood pooled beneath Ethan, neither one was moving. Whose blood was it? There had only been one shot. Surely they were not both injured . . . or worse. *Please, God, no.* Behind her, Abigail heard footsteps and the slamming of a door. The man from the shadows was gone, leaving disaster behind him.

As Abigail knelt, she could hear rasping breathing and another groan. "Ethan, Jeffrey, speak to me."

She looked down. Jeffrey must be crushing Ethan, but though she tried to move him, Jeffrey was too heavy to budge.

"I'm all right."

The sound of Ethan's voice made Abigail light-headed with relief. *Thank you, Lord.* One of her prayers had been answered, yet blood still streamed onto the floor.

"What can I do?"

"I don't know." Ethan placed an arm on the ground as he spoke, then levered himself upward, pushing Jeffrey aside. "The bullet hit him." He turned Jeffrey over, revealing a face that was far too pale. As Ethan opened Jeffrey's jacket, searching for the wound site, blood continued to spurt from Jeffrey's chest. Just like Luke.

Abigail shuddered. Though she sent a fervent prayer heavenward, she knew the truth. No one could survive losing that much blood. While Ethan pressed his handkerchief on the wound, trying to staunch the flow, Abigail knelt next to her brother-in-law and gripped his hand as she'd gripped Charlotte's only an hour before.

"Live, Jeffrey. You've got to live."

But he could not. Jeffrey's face was gray, and his eyes had begun to glaze. Though her face was directly over his, Abigail wasn't certain whether he recognized her, whether he knew anything more than that his life was ebbing away. It seemed like an eternity, but it was probably only a few seconds before Jeffrey opened his mouth as if to speak. Abigail bent nearer, but no words came out, only a hoarse croaking.

"Charlotte," Jeffrey said at last. "Love . . ." An ominous

rattling accompanied his final word, and as Abigail watched, the light faded from his eyes.

"Oh, Jeffrey." Abigail released his hand as her tears began to flow. Though the Jeffrey she had seen tonight had been a stranger, memories of the man who had loved her sister crowded her mind. That Jeffrey had not deserved to die.

Gently, Ethan touched her shoulder. "There's nothing more we can do for him." Behind them, Peg began to stir. "Let's get her to justice." He reached for Peg's reticule, pulling out the strings she'd knotted and using them to tie her hands behind her back. "That'll hold her until we get to the horses. I've got rope there."

"I won't go." Peg spat the words at him. "You've got no proof." As she began to shout obscenities, Ethan withdrew her handkerchief from the discarded reticule and formed it into a gag.

"Come, Abigail." He urged her to rise. "It's time to go."

Reluctantly, Abigail stood, then looked down at the now still body. "We can't just leave Jeffrey."

Ethan nodded. "I'll come back for him," he promised, "once we get Peg onto the horse." He looked around. "Her partner's gone. Unless Peg identifies him, he'll go scot-free." The thought obviously rankled.

What worried Abigail more was the prospect of facing Charlotte. Somehow she would have to find the words to tell her sister what had happened, that she was a widow and that the baby she and Jeffrey had longed for would grow up without a father.

"Poor Charlotte."

Ethan nodded again. "At least she has you."

Her whole body trembling at the thought of Charlotte's

future, Abigail recalled her journey west. Though she had come to Wyoming Territory to help her sister, she had not dreamt that Charlotte would need her the way she did now.

Ethan marched Peg in front of him, keeping a tight grip on her shoulders. When they reached the front of the building, he whistled, and Samson emerged from behind the second cabin. No wonder Abigail had not seen him. While the horse stood motionless, Ethan slung Peg over Samson's back, then looped ropes around her arms and legs. Though she struggled, it was clear that the restraints would hold, at least until they reached the fort.

"I've got one more thing to do." Ethan entered the saloon, emerging a moment later with two soldiers.

"They'll take Jeffrey to the fort," he explained as he helped Abigail mount Sally. "The only good thing I can say about today is that the stagecoach robberies will end. Peg arranged everything with Jeffrey's help. Now that Jeffrey's gone and Peg will be behind bars, there's no one left to plan a holdup."

"What about the man who shot Jeffrey?" Though she had not seen his features, Abigail pictured him as the face of evil.

"I don't know what his role was," Ethan admitted. "Maybe Peg will tell us."

The way their prisoner thrashed against the ropes suggested she would not cooperate. "Even if she doesn't," Ethan continued, "with guards on all the coaches, the outlaws won't be successful. Whoever he was, the man will have to find another way to make a living."

Abigail thought about Peg and the discovery that she had pretended to be Mrs. Dunn. "Peg must have been the woman on each of the coaches that was robbed."

Ethan nodded. "It appears she was the mastermind. We

knew the bandits were clever, but it was brilliant to get someone at the fort involved." His voice betraying no emotion, Ethan outlined Jeffrey's role in the robberies.

While Ethan spoke, Abigail's hands grew clammy inside her gloves. "Poor Charlotte." She would be devastated by the news that her husband had been a criminal.

As the lights of the fort drew near, Abigail asked the question that was foremost on her mind. "Why was Jeffrey threatening to kill you?"

When Ethan described the ransom note, Abigail's spirits plummeted again. Was there no limit to Jeffrey's sins? "I knew money was important to him," she said softly. "Charlotte told me Jeffrey's family was very poor, and he couldn't forget that, but . . ." Abigail shuddered at the memory of Jeffrey's gun pointed at Ethan and the hatred she had seen in his eyes. "I would never have thought Jeffrey would go to such lengths for money." The gambling had been bad enough, but stealing and murder . . . The thought made Abigail cringe.

Though night obscured Ethan's expression, his voice was solemn. "No matter how well you think you know someone, you never really know what's inside another person's heart." He opened his mouth as if he were going to say something else but did not. Instead, when they crossed the bridge and reentered the fort, Ethan guided the horses toward Abigail's house.

"Once Peg's locked up, I'll take Sally back to the stable. Then I'll bring Jeffrey here," Ethan said as he helped Abigail dismount.

She shook her head. "Please wait." They would have to prepare Jeffrey's body for burial, but Abigail did not want to think about that now. Though the events at the hog ranch had obliterated everything else from her mind, as she had approached the fort, memories of her sister's ordeal came rushing back. She had to learn what had happened to the baby and to Charlotte.

Taking a deep breath to quell her trembling, Abigail climbed the front steps and opened the door. There was a moment of silence, and then she heard the cries. Nothing had changed. Charlotte was still enduring the pain of childbirth. But as the wail continued, Abigail knew she was mistaken. It wasn't Charlotte who cried; it was her child. Abigail raced up the stairs, all the while praying that her sister was safe. As she stood in the doorway, Abigail looked at the bed that had been the scene of so much pain and her heart leapt with joy. Charlotte lay there, propped up against a mound of pillows, a tiny infant in her arms, a smile of pure happiness on her face. Though still a bit pale, her cheeks had regained most of their color, and her eyes sparkled. Charlotte's baby had been safely delivered, and judging from the absence of Mrs. Grayson, Abigail's sister was no longer in any danger. *Thank you, thank you, thank you.*

"Oh, Charlotte!" The tears that welled in Abigail's eyes were a combination of happiness, relief, and sorrow.

"Jeffrey?" Charlotte's smile of greeting faded at the realization that her sister was alone.

The time had come. Abigail crossed the room in three swift strides and reached for Charlotte's hand. With it clasped between both of hers, she said simply, "I'm sorry, but he's . . ."

"Gone." Charlotte pronounced the word, her voice as lifeless as her husband. "Jeffrey's dead. I feared it was so."

Sinking onto the chair next to the bed, Abigail stared at her sister. She had expected tears, anger, and cries of denial, but not this. "How did you know?"

Charlotte's eyes filled with tears as she looked down at the child sleeping in her arms. "When the baby was born, I experienced the most wonderful sense of fulfillment. It was unlike anything I've ever known, but it was followed almost immediately by a sense of deep loss." Charlotte looked up at Abigail, not seeming to care that tears streamed down her cheeks. "I couldn't imagine why I felt like that. All I knew was that something important was gone from my life. I thought it might have been the aftermath of giving birth, but when I saw you there alone, I knew it had to be Jeffrey." Charlotte tightened her grip on Abigail's hand. "What happened?"

Abigail decided to start at the end. There would be time enough to explain the rest later. "He was shot by a strange man. I don't know who the man was. I never even saw his face, because he kept to the shadows."

For a second Abigail thought Charlotte was satisfied, but her eyes narrowed. "Was Jeffrey at Peg's? Tell me the truth."

Abigail nodded.

Charlotte closed her eyes, and Abigail watched her take a deep breath, as if to calm turbulent thoughts. "Was he gambling again?" She opened her eyes to watch Abigail's response.

"No, but . . ."

"Something worse." It was a statement, not a question.

Oh, how Abigail wished Charlotte hadn't insisted on the truth. It was too soon for her to hear everything, but now there was no choice. Abigail would not lie. "He was involved in the stagecoach robberies."

As Charlotte shuddered, the sleeping infant stirred. "I should have guessed. I knew something was wrong, because Jeffrey always acted a bit differently whenever anyone spoke of the robberies. At the time, I thought it was that he was disturbed by the stealing, but it wasn't that at all. He didn't want anyone to realize he was responsible." Charlotte pressed a kiss on her child's head. "I never thought Jeffrey loved money so much that he would die for it."

Abigail heard the pain in her sister's voice. More than anything, she wished she could take away that pain, but she could not. All she could do was offer a bit of consolation. "Jeffrey loved you most of all. His last words were your name and 'love'."

As her lower lip trembled, Charlotte bit it, then looked up at Abigail. "I loved him too." She tugged her hand from Abigail's and wrapped both arms around her baby. "It'll be all right, little one. I'll give you all the love you need."

When Abigail descended the steps an hour later, relieved that Charlotte was finally sleeping, she found Ethan sitting in the parlor. He'd taken the time to change his uniform and wash his face and hair, so he was no longer stained by Jeffrey's blood. Though his forehead was furrowed with worry, his eyes shone with an emotion Abigail could not identify. It looked like hope and apprehension blended with something else, something she dared not name for fear of being wrong.

"How is your sister?" Though filled with concern, Ethan's voice held no hint of the tenderness Abigail had imagined she saw in his eyes. This was Ethan her friend, nothing more.

She kept her own voice even as she said, "Right now, she's pretending nothing happened. She did that when our mother died, almost as if she could bring Mama back if she didn't admit that she was gone." It hadn't lasted long, and when the numbness had worn off, Charlotte had been overcome with grief. Abigail knew that would happen this time, and she suspected the grief would be deeper and more intense than before, for Charlotte's life had changed almost beyond recognition in the space of a few hours.

When her initial spate of crying ended, Charlotte had taken a deep breath, shuddering only slightly as she introduced Abigail to her nephew. "Jeffrey and I hadn't decided on a name, but I'm considering David. I'm afraid this little one may have to slay some giants in his life." Charlotte's lips trembled, and Abigail knew she was close to tears again. But then she had straightened her shoulders and begun her pretense of normalcy.

Abigail took the chair opposite Ethan's, waiting until he was seated again before she spoke. "Before she finally drifted off to sleep, Charlotte was talking about moving to Cheyenne. She claimed there was no place for her here."

Ethan nodded. "What your sister said is literally true. Army dependents have no legal status at a fort. If the soldier dies, they face immediate eviction."

Charlotte must have known that, and—being Charlotte—she had begun to deal with her changed circumstances. "That hardly seems fair." Abigail looked at the parlor with its elegant furnishings and wondered whether Charlotte would take them with her or whether she would try to start anew.

"It isn't fair," Ethan agreed, "but those are the regulations." He paused for a second, and once again concern deepened the lines between his eyes. "I had to report everything to Captain Westland. Since we're not overcrowded, I convinced him to let Charlotte stay for another month."

It appeared Ethan had been busier than she had realized, for in addition to his official duties, he had found time to help Charlotte. No wonder Abigail loved him. He was kind and caring, and though he might not use the word, he was loving.

She swallowed deeply, trying to control her overflowing emotions. "Thank you," she said as calmly as she could. Dare she hope that Ethan loved her? He did. She was certain of that. It was only the nature of that love that she did not know, that and whether he would admit it.

"A month will give Charlotte and me a chance to make plans." It would also give Abigail another month to store up memories in case at the end of that time she and Ethan parted forever.

Her words seemed to disturb him, for Ethan's lips tightened, and he looked away, as if suddenly uncomfortable with the direction the conversation had taken. Abigail tried but failed to tamp down the hope that he dreaded the possibility of their parting as much as she did.

"About your plans . . ." His voice sounded strained, and the worry lines that formed between his eyes reminded Abigail that, as horrible as her day had been, Ethan's had been worse. He was the one who had faced death.

Still staring at the wall, he said, "The time never seems to be right." Abruptly he turned to face Abigail, and when his gaze met hers, she saw hesitation in his eyes. Whatever Ethan was going to say, he wasn't sure how she would receive it.

He swallowed again, and as he did, his expression changed. Worry turned to hope. "Oliver told me ladies expect pretty settings and special words," Ethan said, his voice deep with emotion. "I wanted to give you that. I even had it all planned, but then . . ." He paused, and the furrows between his eyes told Abigail his thoughts were troubled. "This evening changed everything. I can't wait any longer. Facing death made me realize there is no time to waste. Tomorrow might not come, and there may be no second chances." His lips tightened as he said, "I've done a lot of things wrong in my life, but in the moment when I knew I was about to die, I had only one regret. I didn't want to leave you without telling you how I feel."

Abigail felt elation rush through her veins. Though Jeffrey's death cast a horrible pall on the day, one good thing had happened: the barriers that encased Ethan's heart were gone, freeing him to express his feelings. Her heart so filled with emotion that she was unable to speak, Abigail smiled at Ethan, hoping he would see the love shining from her eyes.

He extended his hands, his brow smoothing and his lips curving into a smile when Abigail placed her hands in his. His hands were warm and comforting, his smile the one she had dreamt of so often. If dreams came true, soon he would say the words she longed to hear: *I love you.*

Ethan's smile faded slightly as he said, "I know you dislike the West and Army life, but there's no way around it. I owe the Army another year. Will you wait for me?"

Those weren't the words she had expected. "Wait for what?" Abigail wouldn't make the mistake of assuming she knew what Ethan meant. Though the look in his eyes, a look that mirrored her own, spoke of love, she needed the words. Why wouldn't he say them?

Ethan rolled his eyes. "There I go again, putting the cart before the horse. It's your fault, you know. I was never this way before I met you." He tightened his grip on her hands. "I love you, Abigail. I love your smile, your kind heart, your impulsive nature. I love everything about you." Ethan paused, and she sensed that the man who had faced death without flinching was afraid of her reaction. "Is it possible that you love me?"

Her dream had come true. Her heart overflowing with happiness, Abigail smiled at the man she loved so dearly. She had longed for three special words, and Ethan had given them to her. Not once but three times. And if that weren't enough, the momentary fear she'd seen had shown her the depth of his love. Ethan loved her. He loved her, and now she could tell him of her own love.

"Of course I love you." Abigail infused her words with every ounce of sincerity she possessed. Ethan must never, ever doubt how much she loved him. "I think I've loved you from the first time I saw you, although I didn't recognize it at the time. I thought God brought me to Wyoming to help Charlotte, but as the weeks passed, it seemed that he had more in store for me. Now I know what it was. He brought me to you."

"And used you to show me what love is." Ethan rose, tugging Abigail to her feet. "Will you make my life complete? Will you marry me when my time with the Army is ended?"

There was only one possible answer. "No."

As Ethan's eyes widened, Abigail saw disbelief on his face. "You won't? I don't understand. If you love me, why won't you marry me? Don't you want to?"

Again, there was only one answer. "I do want to marry you, Ethan. More than anything else."

His confusion was endearing, and Abigail knew they'd speak of this moment for years to come. "Then why did you refuse me?"

"It wasn't your proposal I refused; it was the timing. Why should we wait a year?"

"Because you hate Army life. I don't want to start our marriage knowing you're miserable."

"Oh, you silly man." Abigail smiled to take the sting from her words. "How could I be miserable if I'm with you? The only thing that would make me miserable is being apart. I love you, Ethan. I want to spend the rest of my life as your wife . . . starting now."

Ethan's smile threatened to split his face. "That's the Abigail I love: headstrong and impulsive, with a heart that's bigger than all of Wyoming. I wouldn't have you any other way."

Dear Reader,

One of the questions I'm often asked is how I get the ideas for my books. The answer is that oh-so-frustrating "It depends." And it does. Each book is different from every other.

Those of you who've read my bio know that I'm an avid traveler, and so you probably won't be surprised to learn that *Summer of Promise* was inspired by a trip. I've always been fascinated by the pioneers who traveled West in covered wagons, so what better place to visit than Fort Laramie, where all the wagon trains stopped to rest and stock up on supplies before crossing the Rockies?

At the time that I planned the trip, I had no intention of setting a book there. It was simply a chance to escape the seemingly unending work associated with moving into a new house. But inspiration strikes when you least expect it.

When we arrived at the fort, I was struck by several things. First of all, it didn't look like my image of a Western fort. There's no stockade surrounding the garrison. Instead, it's open and seemingly unprotected. The second surprise was that the buildings didn't fit my picture of Army construction. The barracks and the officers' housing were constructed of a variety of materials and, combined with the central parade ground, made the fort look like a New England village. The third surprise was that, although this was once a military installation, it felt peaceful. In other words, it wasn't what I had expected.

Prior to that day, if someone had asked me to write a book set at Fort Laramie, I would have assumed that it would take place during the great migration and that the heroine would be part of a wagon train. But as I walked around the fort and learned more about its history, I became fascinated with its final days. During its last decade of existence (the 1880s), Fort Laramie saw no wars, and not even much in the way of conflict. Instead, it was a place where officers lived in relative luxury, where their wives held teas and balls, and where the parade ground boasted gaslights and birdbaths.

I was hooked. And so, in the space of an afternoon, when all I had expected was a little recreation, I had the beginning of a book. As it turned out, not just one but three. I realized that Abigail was one of three sisters and that each of them deserved her own book.

Charlotte's comes next. I don't want to spoil the story by giving away all her reasons, but I can tell you that Charlotte moves to Cheyenne to build a life for herself and her son, never dreaming that she'll find both love and danger in the territory's capital.

Did you wonder what happened to the baron? The answer is coming in the next book, and it just might surprise you. Book 2 in the Westward Winds series will be available in the spring of 2013.

And, for those of you who've said that a year is too long between books, I'm delighted to tell you that Revell will be publishing my Christmas novella this fall. It's also set in Wyoming but brings you a whole new cast of characters. I'm excited about it and hope you will be too.

As always, I look forward to hearing from you. It's true: you are the reason I write.

Blessings,
Amanda Cabot

Acknowledgments

Writing any book requires a lot of research, and this one was no exception. Three visits to Fort Laramie, dozens of books, and hours of internet browsing provided the foundation, but there were still gaps in my knowledge. Fortunately, three women generously gave of their time and expertise to fill in those gaps.

I owe much gratitude to:

Kayce Lassiter, who took time from her own writing schedule to answer my seemingly endless questions about horses. Kayce has been an immense help, not just for this book but also for the Texas Dreams trilogy. Thanks to her, I know now what ailing horses should be fed and how to deal with an injury, not to mention hundreds of other details of equine life.

Peggy Griffin, who answered my online plea for information about snakes. I appreciate Peggy's not laughing at

409

my total ignorance about reptilian behavior, at least not when I could hear her. Not only did she tell me what a snake might have done, but she suggested a plausible reaction for my heroine.

Sandra Lowry, librarian at Fort Laramie National Historic Site, who provided myriad details of life at the fort in 1885 and whose meticulous research kept me from putting my hero in the wrong uniform.

Kayce, Peggy, and Sandra, you have my heartfelt thanks.

Dreams have always been an important part of **Amanda Cabot**'s life. For almost as long as she can remember, she dreamt of being an author. Fortunately for the world, her grade-school attempts as a playwright were not successful, and she turned her attention to writing novels. Her dream of selling a book before her thirtieth birthday came true, and she's been spinning tales ever since. She now has more than twenty-five novels to her credit under a variety of pseudonyms.

Amanda is a member of ACFW, a charter member of Romance Writers of America, and an avid traveler. She married her high school sweetheart, who shares her love of travel and who's driven thousands of miles to help her research her books. A few years ago they fulfilled a longtime dream and are now living in the American West.

Don't miss any of the

His letters captured her heart—
would the Hill Country heal her soul?

 Revell
a division of Baker Publishing Group
www.RevellBooks.com

TEXAS DREAMS series!

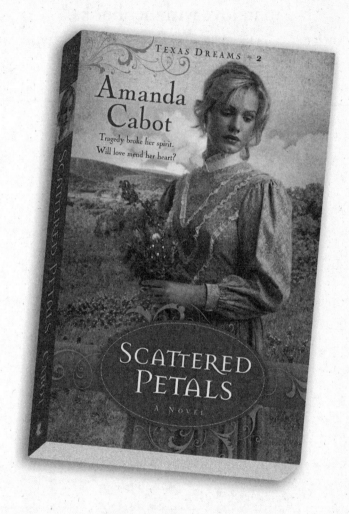

Tragedy broke her spirit.
Will love mend her heart?

"Amanda Cabot's characters and storytelling create the extraordinary out of this Texas tale. I'm in love with her books."

—Laurie Alice Eakes, author, *Lady in the Mist*

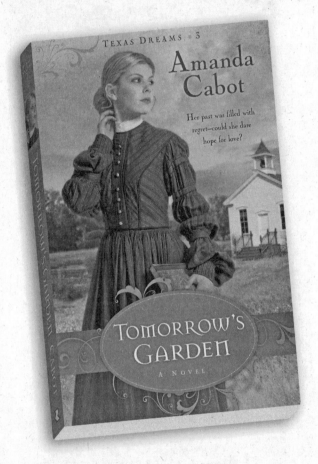

Readers will love this story of overcoming powerful odds and grabbing hold of happiness.

MEET AMANDA CABOT AT

www.AmandaCabot.com

Sign up for her newsletter and learn fun
facts about Amanda and her books!

f Amanda Cabot